HEIST FOR A LIFE

TWELVE TERRITORIES
BOOK ONE

CHINA ANDIE

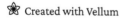 Created with Vellum

To those who are lost:
You're exactly where you're supposed
to be, at this very moment.

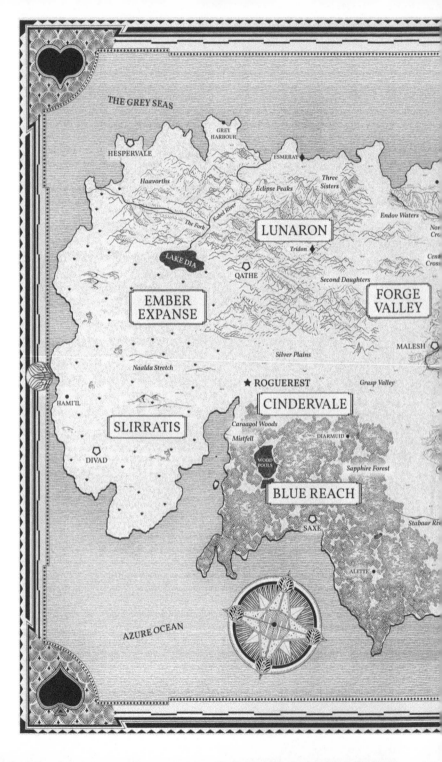

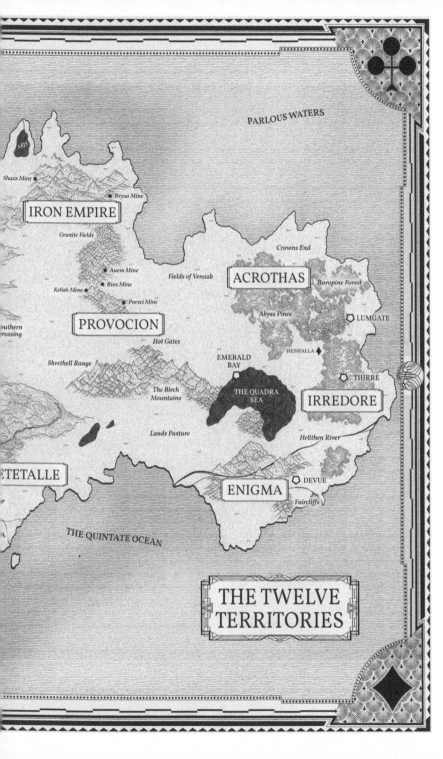

THE TWELVE
TERRITORIES

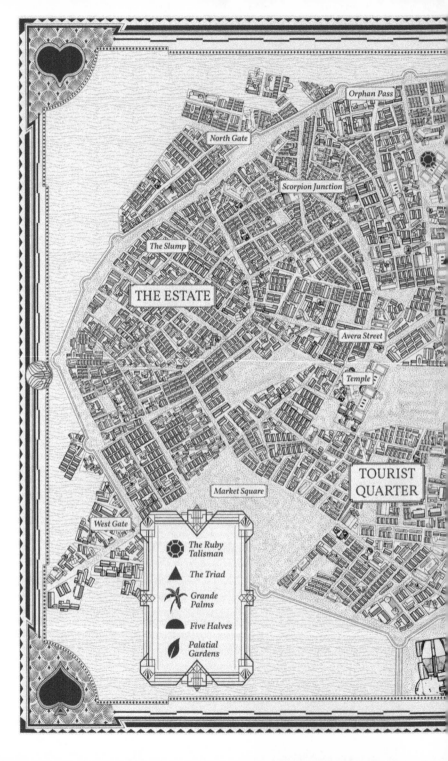

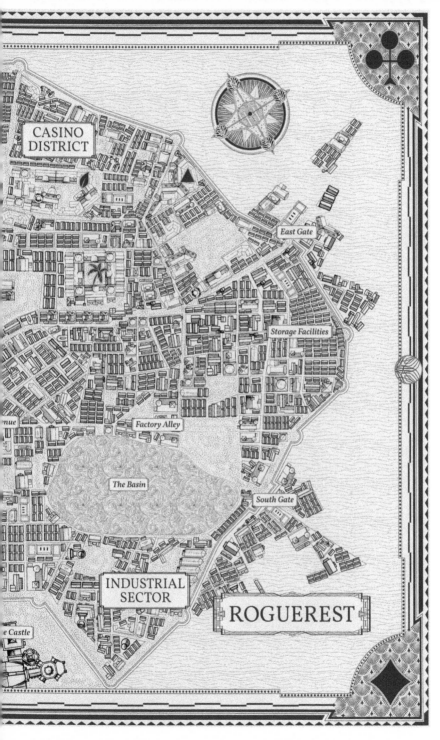

Dear Reader,

This book contains themes that may be distressing to some, including depictions of anxiety and panic attacks, physical and psychological abuse, and overwhelming loneliness.

Look after yourselves out there.

TEN YEARS

As she stood behind the defendant's table of the Roguerest City Courtroom with no legal representation, Rosie could only think one thing:

She'd cocked up.

"It is with overwhelming evidence presented by the prosecution that Rosie Wren is found guilty on one count of premeditated and attempted theft of artwork from The Ruby Talisman Hotel and Casino," the judge droned, tweaking his wiry moustache as if he'd rather be anywhere else.

"As agreed with Mr Lawrence Haart, owner of The Ruby Talisman and of the artwork in question, you will be sentenced to ten years of unpaid service under Mr Haart's employ, to work in his organisation where he sees fit. You will also have two curses bestowed upon you: a *supresis,* in order to stop you from attempting theft again, and a *captipheus,* so that you are confined to the bounds of your workplace."

The crack of the judge's gavel coming down sealed Rosie's fate.

Ten years. Two curses. Unpaid service. She'd *royally* cocked up.

PLAYGROUND OF MANY, PRISON OF FEW

R osie held a pair of designer stilettos in one hand and a clump of human hair in the other.

An ordinary morning at The Ruby Talisman.

Far from her most bizarre find, she wondered who the hair once belonged to and whether they were still in the hotel. Perhaps they were gorging on the bottomless breakfast buffet downstairs, in awe of the diverse spread of local Roguerest delicacies. Or maybe they were facedown in the grimy cobblestones of the market square, sluggishly regaining consciousness with no comprehension of the night before, yet another victim of The Ruby's seductive nightlife.

Realising she still held a stranger's hair in her hand, Rosie shuddered and tossed it into the rubbish bag on her cart, furiously wiping her palm on her itchy red work smock whilst being careful not to tug the crisp white apron loose from around her waist.

The Ruby prides itself on staff uniformity and discretion, she'd been lectured on her first day. *Be available, be observant, be invisible.*

It had become her mantra from the first day, both an anchor and a purpose to keep her going.

Be available, be observant, be invisible.

She considered the stilettos hooked on two fingers of her other hand. Despite the scuffs and mud they'd likely earned during the events of the night before, the slick black shoes were undoubtedly upscale, fashioned from smooth leather with crystals embedded down the sharp point of the towering heel. Rosie had dreamt of purchasing shoes like these.

She envisioned herself sauntering into one of the many exclusive boutiques in the Tourist Quarter, the ones guarded by a doorman who vetted the customers by their appearance. Upon entrance, she'd be welcomed with a fizzing, fruity cocktail and a tray of exotic canapés, doted on as if nothing were more important than her impending purchase. The shop assistants would laugh politely at everything she said, praise every style choice she made, and above all, ensure that she enjoyed spending her money as much as they enjoyed relieving her of it.

She eyed the shoes in her hand and figured that they were roughly her size. Scanning the hotel room as if expecting someone to be secretly watching her, she toed off her black, standard-issue loafers and placed the stilettos on the garish red carpet.

Could she?

"I'm not stealing them." Her voice was barely above a whisper. "I'm trying them on. *I'm not stealing them.* I'll put them back."

Bracing for potentially agonising pain, courtesy of her *supresis* curse, she slipped her first foot in, then the other. Miraculously, she remained unharmed. It encouraged a laugh to bubble up from her chest, filling the room with a joyous sound otherwise foreign to her.

She ambled towards the floor-to-ceiling mirror and stumbled, floundering in the unfamiliar footwear. Barely managing to stay upright, she shuffled over to the mirror like a newborn fawn, each step a revelation. As she took in the sight of her taller, more elegant reflection, the hotel room around her faded away into insignificance.

She was no longer a lowly maid confined to a ruby prison, but a businesswoman, a roaring success who turned heads wherever she strode and demanded respect from those who dared to approach her.

She was no longer in the city of Roguerest, not even in the wider territory of Cindervale. No, she was much further afield than that. She could travel wherever she desired, without qualms or doubts. She flitted across the Twelve Territories according to her own whims, seeking out the most formidable artefacts to pilfer and pawn, casing out the seemingly impregnable homes of exclusive treasures just ripe for the picking.

She was no longer subservient. She was no longer dancing to the beat of someone else's drum. She was twirling and swirling and dipping to her very own snare, master of one and captive of none. The world around her blurred and swam, a stream of lights and wonders to explore.

"Songbird?"

A knock at the door made her trip, rolling her ankle and crashing down to the floor. Disorientated and fearing discipline, she shucked the dreamy shoes from her feet and scrambled up as the knocking continued.

"Rosie, I know you're in there."

It was Jakob.

Perfect.

She placed the shoes neatly by the mahogany dresser and straightened her uniform, slipping her loafers back on whilst she regarded her appearance in the mirror.

Gone was the illusion of grandeur, and with it, the blinding lights and splendour of a life unknown. In its place was the cold, stark reality of The Ruby Talisman; playground of many, prison of few.

Rosie gathered her cleaning supplies back onto her cart with haste and fixed the room to a standard that the management team would be proud of.

Be available, be observant, be invisible.

She repeated the mantra in her head to ground herself as she approached the door to the hotel room and reluctantly swung it open. Leaning against the frame with his arms crossed, as if there were no issues more pressing than her whereabouts, was Jakob Haart.

His pristinely tailored burgundy suit fit him like a glove, only serving to elevate his tall, lean figure. The black silk shirt beneath his jacket clung tight to his chest due to his posturing, and Rosie had to remind herself that despite the pretty package, the contents inside were toxic to the marrow.

Jakob was *not* her ally anymore.

He raised a manicured eyebrow and asked, "Not stealing anything, are we?"

His malicious grin conveyed what they both already knew; she couldn't steal anything even if she wanted to. Not without encountering brain-numbing, nerve-frying, white-hot agony. One of two curses placed upon her as punishment, the *supresis* ensured that if she were to consider stealing something as meaningless as a toothpick, she would endure a pain so crippling that she'd collapse to the floor, no use to man nor beast.

She'd foolishly tried it once. Never again.

"Jakob," she drawled, suddenly hyper-aware of every inch of her appearance. "To what do I owe the...*pleasure?*"

He cocked his head, looking her up and down. It was a withering perusal that said he didn't consider her worth the time it took to greet her with respect.

"That's no way to greet your employer, now is it?"

Rosie grimaced. "You're *not* my employer."

His venomous smile grew impossibly bigger as he stepped directly into her personal space. She knew all too well that stepping back was akin to cowering, so she had no choice but to endure his close proximity. She'd lost not only her dignity because of Jakob Haart, but also her freedom. She'd be damned if he considered her fainthearted on top of that.

"I suppose you're right." He chuckled as if they were old friends, which she supposed they were. "That honour belongs to my father. I am, however, the ring leader at The Ruby, so the daily responsibility of your servitude falls to me—a responsibility that I take *very* seriously."

Rosie bit her tongue to stop herself from lashing out, barely holding on to her limited self-control. Instead, she composed a list of the many things that she desperately hated about the young man standing in front of her.

His arrogant, privileged attitude. Before the failed heist, when they were both just teens roaming the streets of the city, she'd found it strangely charming. She saw it now for the truly loathsome trait that it was.

His intense gaze. Once upon a time, it had been solely focussed on her and she'd been flattered—in love, even. These days, she knew the secrets hidden behind those burnt umber eyes, and detested the way they narrowed whenever he deceived her.

His complete lack of morality. This particular trait had served her well when they'd plotted their heist together, because it meant he'd operated in a grey area of right and wrong. However, it hadn't served her so well when he'd betrayed her to his father and ensnared her within The Ruby Talisman.

Rosie straightened her spine and rolled her shoulders, lifting her chin as she said, "What do you need?"

Jakob placed his hands on either side of the dark wood door frame, leaning in so that Rosie could feel his minty breath tickling her nose. He licked his lips, gaze darting over her features, and she inwardly cringed at how her heart picked up a little.

"Come to my office."

She narrowed her eyes. "Why?"

"I don't think you're in a position to question my authority."

Rosie tried to think of a sarcastic quip, but nothing came to mind quick enough, so she gritted her teeth and maintained her stance, waiting for him to step away first. She had to hold on to the little wins with both hands, which meant standing her ground every time they interacted.

With no sense of urgency, Jakob slunk back out of her personal space and slipped his hands into his trouser pockets, nodding towards the service lift in a silent gesture for her to follow. She lugged her cart out of the hotel room and began pushing it down the corridor, shadowing the lazy gait of the guy who controlled her every waking moment.

She didn't study his lithe form from behind. *She didn't.*

"Leave the cart by the lift," he instructed without sparing her a glance.

They made their way through a staff-only door, and Rosie followed his order, allowing him to board the service lift first. She leaned against the back wall as he pushed the button for the ground floor, not looking at her once.

They rode down in silence, the groaning and grinding of the lift mechanism providing a break from the palpable tension between the two of them. Gone were the days when they'd never run out of topics to talk about. They shuddered to a halt, and Jakob slid the rusty door open, striding down the back corridor that employees used to navigate the ground floor out of sight from guests.

Rosie was almost at a run, trying to remain a few paces

behind Jakob as he stalked towards one of the many doors into the grand foyer. She tried to predict what Jakob might want, but the list of possibilities was quite literally endless, and she couldn't afford to say no to him these days. If she showed too much attitude, he wouldn't hesitate to contact his father and have Rosie's sentence doubled—something she couldn't bear to comprehend.

Jakob pushed open a door into the foyer and didn't stop to hold it open for her. Rosie caught the door as it swung back towards her, only inches from slamming into her nose. Her knuckles were white as she grasped the glossy red door, taking some much-needed calming breaths before she stepped out into the chaos.

"Nine more years," she said through gritted teeth. "Just nine more."

Rosie walked into the foyer. Jakob's office was opposite the entrance, its door tucked behind the reception desk. In an effort to draw in naive tourists and weary travellers with its taste and luxurious comfort, the foyer was perhaps the most elaborately decorated room in the entire hotel. No one could resist the allure of The Ruby's stellar hospitality.

The room was vast, with a double-height ceiling seemingly held up by the palatial columns placed at equal intervals. The floor was made of a marble so white and glossy that it reflected the sprawling mural on the ceiling. Red storm clouds shrouded Aakla, the pure God, in beauty and innocence; while opposite her, veiled in darkness, Venaak, the God of Sin, sneered. Between the two of them, in pastures green, was Midina, the mediator God, who maintained peace amongst the turbulence. The mural was The Ruby's ultimate boast, as the painter who'd been commissioned for the piece was renowned across the territories, believed to be touched by Midina herself.

Two sweeping staircases framed the archway into the

casino. Even at this time of day, the soundtrack of raucous laughter and triumphant cheers could be heard.

A marble counter running half the length of the room served as a reception desk. No guest at The Ruby had to wait more than a minute for service—it was blasphemous to even consider the notion.

On one side of the main entrance—a gold-plated revolving door with a trio of gargoyles atop it—was the concierge desk, and opposite it was a twenty-four hour bar that served complimentary drinks to any guest or visitor. Rosie never touched anything from it; every drink was laced with bruise root, a natural substance that made the consumer more amenable to persuasion.

The remainder of the foyer was filled with plush red velvet sofas and chairs that were almost always filled with people caught in the irresistible trap of The Ruby. They'd most likely leave broke, in handcuffs, or dead.

Rosie cringed, watching naive guests wander from one of the many restaurants straight into the casino for another day of gambling. Once they were inside, the poor souls couldn't help themselves. It was all part of the allure.

Realising that Jakob had disappeared and she was yet to follow, Rosie quickly marched to his office. As much as she wanted to study the room and the crowds like she used to do on the streets, there wasn't any time.

The red door to Jakob's office was adorned with a gold nameplate at eye-level, stating in an ostentatious script that Jakob was the manager of The Ruby Talisman. In reality, he was far too young to effectively manage anything, let alone the most popular hotel in all of Roguerest. But a growing team of deputy managers ensured that the hotel remained afloat and in profit despite being figure-headed by an eighteen-year-old with no formative life experience or formal education in hospitality.

Rosie knocked without further preamble, knowing that she couldn't put off the inevitable forever. Jakob made her wait for a few beats before allowing her entrance, another subtle reminder that his position was more important than hers.

Upon entrance into the office, Rosie kept her eager eyes from scanning the room as she truly wanted to. She couldn't afford to give him the satisfaction of knowing that she loved the room. She didn't love it because it was his, but because the walls were lined with bookcases that reached the ceiling. The hand-carved mahogany was polished every morning by one of the numerous maids in the hotel so that it shone from every angle. The hundreds, if not thousands, of books that lined the shelves ranged from ancient copies of religious texts to the latest best-seller from three territories over.

Rosie had dreamt multiple times of losing herself in the office, with only the crinkled leather spines and the smell of generations-old literature as company. Instead, she had to settle for sneaking in through the ventilation shafts at night and stealing books with the hope that Jakob wouldn't notice a missing spine here and there.

She kept her gaze straight as she strode in, finding Jakob in the wingback leather chair behind his oversized desk. His flaw-less olive skin appeared to glow in the radiant lighting of the office, the wall sconces highlighting his angular jaw and cheek-bones. The large bay window behind him lit every strand of his perfectly quaffed dark hair, granting him a pseudo-halo as if touched by the hands of Aakla.

Though there were two comfy chairs in front of the desk, he declined to offer her a seat. The chairs were for guests only. She stood, diligently waiting for further instruction.

Be available, be observant, be invisible.

"As you well know," he began, leaning back in his chair and

propping his feet up on his desk, "it's the final of the Twelve Territories' Kaarmiach Tournament this weekend."

She did know. It was all anyone had been able to talk about in the hotel for weeks. The Ruby had won the bid to host the final this year, and it was a privilege most revered.

Kaarmiach was the favoured card game across all of the Twelve Territories, though Rosie had never played it and certainly wasn't interested in starting. The tournament was open to anyone who wished to enter, but by the time the final rolled around each year, the very same five people were in the running for the colossal monetary prize. They'd garnered so much attention across the territories that they were known as the Kaarmiach Five, adored and doted on as if they were royalty.

"Two more of our VIPs will be arriving today," Jakob continued. "Which leaves the final guest, Kitty Khalar, whose car will roll up tomorrow morning at eleven o'clock. *Sharp.*"

His emphasis on the time raised red flags for Rosie. She was a mere maid at the hotel, she had no reason to interact with the celebrities in residence for the long weekend. In fact, she'd rather not, if possible. But it didn't surprise her that Kitty Khalar had her own motorcar. The engineering feat was still relatively new and only the most wealthy could afford one.

Rosie cleared her throat. "Why do I feel like you're about to ask me to do something out of the bounds of my regular duties?"

Jakob's answering smirk told her all she needed to know.

This weekend was going to be anything but regular.

"I have a special assignment for you over the next four days, and I trust that you'll carry it out with the utmost discretion. Miss Khalar contacted us recently with a very specific request. She's been suffering at the hands of pesky thieves on her travels, and she still needs a personal liaison throughout her stay with us; someone to act as a middleman between her and us. One who can be trusted not to let their wandering, pilfering hands be led astray but also knows the ins and outs of the hotel and the city."

Rosie blinked a couple of times, translating what he'd said from his politically correct, diplomatic spiel into something more tangible and honest.

"You'd like me to be her servant because I can't possibly steal anything from her," she deducted, crossing her arms over her chest.

"I believe her exact words were *personal liaison*."

"And what are your words?"

His eyes sparkled in macabre delight. "Servant, butler, lackey—whichever makes you feel as if you have some semblance of self-respect left."

Knuckles white and jaw clenched, Rosie bit back a retort for the sake of her own hide. She took a slow, deep breath in until she felt as if her chest would burst, then quietly released it.

Be available, be observant, be invisible.

"She will be staying in Suite Rouge, as will you. There's a butler's cupboard in there that I'm sure you'll find up to standard. We'll even provide you with blankets and a pillow, so count yourself lucky. It'll be like a short getaway for you."

The smugness exuding from Jakob was aggravating.

How had she ever found it attractive?

Rosie replied, "A getaway and yet I'm still being paid. How lucky am I?" She paused before adding, "Oh, wait. I'm not paid in the first place, so I suppose that negates the luck involved. I'll stay in unpaid service, simply in a different location. I'm positively glowing at the thought of it."

Surprisingly, Jakob didn't morph into his angry, defensive self. He stood up, straightened his jacket, and rounded the desk, leaning against the front of it with his legs crossed at the ankle. Rosie could've sworn the edge of his lips was twitching slightly.

"I'll take your sarcasm because my father's not here." He sighed. "Though please don't take my placidity for acceptance. That's the only back-chat I'll allow on the matter." He folded his arms across his chest again, then pushed off the desk and began to pace in a circle around Rosie. She decided not to give him the satisfaction of turning around to keep an eye on him, remaining rooted in place.

"You're to be on your best behaviour this weekend," he lectured. "The whole of the Twelve Territories will be looking at The Ruby, so we have to remain the epitome of elegance and wealth. Above all, everyone must have a roaring good time. You will not leave Miss Khalar's side during her stay unless she instructs you to do so. You will work, sleep, and breathe at her discretion alone. If I hear so much as a squeak of disobedience from you, I won't hesitate to tell my father and have your sentence doubled."

The threat of twenty years at The Ruby instead of ten was almost becoming idle and repetitive by this point. She couldn't bear it if she were to have her punishment doubled in length, but she also couldn't stand the fact that Jakob held it above her head like a knife on twine. Only he could sever the string and bring the knife down—a fact that he not only used to his advantage, but revelled in.

Having complete control over Rosie was what made him tick. And now that she thought about it, he'd always been that way. She'd just been too in love to realise that his generous provisions for her were simply another form of control.

"You need to be waiting in the foyer ahead of her arrival in the morning, not a hair out of place." His voice was much closer this time, his breath tickling the hairs on the back of Rosie's neck. "You are to stop at nothing to get her what she wants, however ludicrous or lavish the request. If she needs you in the middle of the night, you'll be there. If she needs you when you're exhausted or hungry, you'll be there. If she needs you because she wants something to entertain her, you'll be there."

He leaned over her shoulder so that his lips pressed gently against her ear, the stubble on his jaw tickling her wherever it touched. She shivered and cursed her body's reaction to him.

This was not the Jakob she fell in love with.

She *had* to remember that.

"Am I clear?" He spoke quietly, completely crowded into Rosie's personal space. She despised him and missed him and couldn't escape him.

"I think"—she paused for effect and to gather her words—"that I understood you correctly. Though you'll have to excuse my stupidity if something got lost in translation. I'm just a lowly servant girl, you see."

For a brief moment, she felt like the old Rosie again. Like the Rosie who'd been confident and strong and daring. The Rosie from before her imprisonment. From before the daily berating, humiliation, and disrespect.

Jakob's jaw clenched as if he too noticed the flash of her previous self, but he didn't stop to acknowledge it. He pulled away from her and sauntered behind his desk once again, resting his hands against it as he bore holes through her with his gaze.

"In the morning, you're to report to Suite Rouge instead of your usual duties. You will ensure the suite is clean enough to eat from the floor, and then you'll wait in the foyer for Kitty's arrival. Now, get out of my office and get back to work."

Rosie didn't need to be told twice.

CHAPTER 2

KINSHIP

Rosie's room in the hotel was perhaps more aptly described as a cupboard.

Hidden in the depths of the underground service corridor between the kitchens and the laundry, there was a rather inconspicuous door. The dirty brass nameplate read *storage,* and Rosie had always thought it an accurate term for her imprisonment. She was being stored for a decade to keep her out of trouble.

If you were to venture inside said storage cupboard, you'd find a room just longer than a single bed and only twice as wide. There was a single bed pushed up against the right-hand wall, which the door would bang against every time it opened, and a small bedside table next to it, upon which the only lamp in the room sat. Beneath the bed was the only real storage that Rosie had for her clothes and other belongings, though these were kept to a minimum.

She had fashioned a large net attached to hooks in each corner of the room that hung close to the ceiling and provided extra storage for larger items, like the red ball gown she donned every Friday night when she was required to perform in the main bar of the casino. It was voluptuous and layered and everything that Rosie hated in a dress, but like most things in her life, it was out of her control.

As Rosie closed the door behind her and fumbled in the momentary darkness for the lamp, she took comfort in the familiar smells of laundry powder and savoury food that combined to make something entirely unique to her little cupboard. Her *home*.

She slumped onto her creaky bed and sat for a moment, digesting the events of the day so far and her new responsibility.

"Sounds like an Imperial's term for *bitch* to me," she muttered to herself, untying her apron and folding it neatly.

Imperials were at the top of the divine food chain. Everyone within the Twelve Territories was born with a single divine ability, and every ability could be sorted into one of three categories: Imperial, Elemental, or Artist.

Imperials possessed an ability that could control other people, be that manipulating emotions, restricting movement, or even possessing someone. The real number of different Imperial abilities was unknown as many were kept secret. Imperials were more often than not in positions of power, which was what made the government of Roguerest so corrupt. The city was ruled by Imperials with agendas of their own, yet they were also the people allowed to pass laws, dole out punishments, and control the population. Both Jakob and his father, Lawrence, were Imperials, though Jakob had never revealed the nature of his divine ability to Rosie.

Elementals could control a particular aspect of an element. Though not as highly regarded as Imperials, they were still an important part of society and often earned a very good living because of their abilities.

Those with an Artist ability, like Rosie, were seen as the

lowest ranking and were therefore often the poorest citizens. Unless struck lucky with the opportunity to perform and tour the Twelve Territories, an Artist would likely end up in jobs serving those with more wealth, opportunity, and divine heritage. Artist abilities ranged from dancing to acting to drawing and singing. Many Artists were street performers or entertainers for wealthier families.

Rosie regularly imagined what it would be like to leave the city of Roguerest and tour Cindervale as a singer. The concept of leaving Cindervale altogether to visit the other eleven territories was her long-term goal, all of which she was planning meticulously in her travel journal. City by city, territory by territory.

But the only goal she was focussed on right now was getting out of The Ruby.

Just hold on for nine more years, she told herself.

It was as she reached for her travel journal on her bedside table that she noticed something stuck to the shade on the lamp. Frowning, a shiver ran through her as she realised what she'd discovered.

A note.

Though the prospect of someone being inside her private space without her permission was quite violating, it wasn't the first time this had happened. She suspected that it wouldn't be the last, either.

A month or so into her time at The Ruby, she'd received her first anonymous note. It told her in not so many words that she'd be given the opportunity to exact her revenge on the people who'd wronged her. That she just had to hold on for a little while longer for the puzzle pieces to fall into place.

At first, she'd disregarded the note as a taunting joke from Jakob—and she still hadn't completely ruled that theory out. However, as the months went on and she received several more notes, she began to realise that they weren't taunting at all. In fact, they were quite hopeful. The writer knew the truth of the failed heist that Rosie and Jakob partook in, and they wanted to assist Rosie in taking back what she so rightly deserved. Though she'd vaguely attempted to figure out who might've been leaving the notes for her, they arrived of their own free will and with no particular schedule.

She looked now to the note on the lampshade and plucked it up, hungrily drinking in the familiar elegant scrawl on the paper.

This weekend is your only chance. If you desire revenge on those who've wronged you, follow my instructions and the painting will be yours come Sunday evening—along with your freedom.

Rosie thought someone had clamped her throat shut as she tried to swallow.

This weekend?

It would be impossible to find more than a smattering of moments alone over the following four days, let alone enough time to steal a painting that was housed under twenty-four-hour surveillance. If she were to be seen within the general vicinity of the painting in the gallery, she'd be severely punished. After failing to steal the artwork once already, it was hardly surprising.

How did her secret penpal think she'd manage a heist with no prior planning and no viable access to the painting?

It had to be a hoax.

She felt now more than ever that Jakob could potentially be the puppet-master behind the notes. It was surely a trick to land her in more trouble with Lawrence. She knew that Jakob was his lap dog, but stooping low enough to actively try and trip her up? That was certainly new.

Attempting to steal the painting—on the busiest weekend in the entirety of Roguerest for several decades, no less—was most certainly a suicide mission.

Just the thought of stealing it managed to trigger her *supresis* curse, crippling her with full-body agony. She crumpled to the floor and convulsed as wave after wave of bone-jarring pain started at her head and radiated through every joint and muscle until she lay motionless, gasping on screams. The spasms were not dissimilar to sailing a treacherous ocean, swelling and retreating with torturous highs and blessed lows. She tried in vain to soothe the burning and crushing sensations that wracked her from top to toe.

When she triggered her curses, all she could do was wait for the pain to peter off. It could've been seconds or minutes before the world around her came back into focus, the dark spots in her vision giving way to blurred surroundings. Sweat dripped from her forehead onto the concrete floor where she'd collapsed, and her breath came in ragged pants that ached inside her chest. Though she'd grown more familiar with the consequences of her curses, they were in no way painless or easier to face.

Foolish, she scolded herself. If she was going to think about the subject of the notes without repeatedly causing herself pain, she'd have to be smarter about it. She'd have to find a loophole, a way to think *around* the parameters of the *supresis*.

Fumbling to a seated position on the floor, the questions in her head mounted quicker than she could comprehend. Refusing to trigger the curse again, she scrunched the note up in her palm and threw it into one of the drawers under her bed, hoping to forget about it.

It's not as if she could realistically do as the note asked. Even if she was given the perfect opportunity, she still had her *supresis* to contend with. Furthermore, she couldn't leave The Ruby for love nor money. Once the deed was done, she wouldn't be able to escape the hotel.

That was her second curse. A *captipheus* curse placed on her meant that she couldn't leave the walls of The Ruby Talisman, not even a step outside the front door, without suffering the same debilitating agony that she experienced when trying to pilfer something. The Ruby was to be her gilded birdcage for a decade—quite possibly the most important decade of her life.

She considered the contents of the note again.

If the writer were sincere in their intentions, they would need to lift both of her curses. The only person who had that ability was the one person Rosie would never trust.

Lawrence Haart.

Jakob's father not only owned The Ruby Talisman and numerous other casinos, hotels, and high-end businesses in Roguerest, he also had a seat in the government as an advisor. Anyone with sense knew full well that he had the government in his pocket.

When Rosie had been tried in court for the attempted theft of Lawrence's painting, from his own hotel, he'd played the *pity-on-the-poor-street-girl* card and offered to give her the opportunity to work off her punishment at The Ruby. The court had been eager to agree with this idea, as it saved them having to deal with her in the city's overly full prison. Lawrence's influence over Roguerest knew no bounds. There wasn't a great deal that you could pursue in the city without him knowing.

Deciding to overlook the note and the potential deceit involved for the time being, Rosie swiftly changed from her gaudy work smock into some cotton trousers and a loose-fitting blouse. She left her uniform loafers on as they were the only pair of practical shoes she owned. She didn't like to think about the towering, velvet stilettos that she was required to wear with her ghastly ball gown. They were covered in marks from wear and had been rescued from the hotel's lost and found when she'd first arrived.

She grabbed her travel journal and locked her door as she left, sauntering down the dingy corridor towards the vast kitchens. The tiled floor was chipped and cracked every other step, and the grime seemed to have seeped into the bones of the corridor, not shifting despite being cleaned daily. The smell of whatever had been on the lunch menu still lingered, making Rosie's stomach gurgle in protest.

When she first started her service in the hotel, she'd learned that not only would she be unpaid, but she also wouldn't be fed. The hunger she'd felt during her first week at The Ruby was like nothing else she'd experienced. At least on the streets, she was able to swipe odds and ends from the local market or beg the old baker on the corner of Hellie Hove and Saak Street to give her the stale bread he usually fed to the birds.

But trapped inside The Ruby with two curses bestowed upon her, Rosie had thought she'd perish before the first week was over.

For her first week, all she'd consumed was room-service leftovers she'd scrounged by asking the guests politely as she cleaned their rooms. It was humiliating and dehumanising, but she'd had no other choice. The only time she'd tried to ask for some food from the kitchens, she'd been chased out by the head chef who'd been wielding a meat cleaver and shouting profanities. To make matters worse, she hadn't yet been given any tips, so couldn't even attempt to buy something from the gift shop or at the bar. She would have given anything to chow down on one of the overpriced chocolate bars with "The Ruby Talisman" printed in gold lettering.

She didn't have a penny to her name and she hadn't eaten in two days—not a great start to a decade-long sentence.

It was as she lay on her bed that night, in tears at the pain and emptiness in her stomach, that she'd truly thought the next ten years would last forever. She figured that she'd starve to death before her sentence was up, which would save everyone a great deal of hassle.

In her frustration, she decided that she'd march down to the kitchens and plead the chef for something to eat in exchange for work. She would wash dishes or mop floors or peel vegetables. She just desperately needed something to eat.

Surprisingly, upon entering the kitchen, she'd found it empty. She'd grinned and darted into the large pantry. It was much more spacious than her own room, with concrete shelves lining the walls stocked with every food imaginable. She'd delighted in what she found; pickled vegetables, stewed fruit, meats, eggs, pastries, and much more. She couldn't decide what she'd eat first.

She'd lifted a hand to swipe a slice of a particularly scrumptious-looking apple pie, perfectly golden brown with a delicate lattice on the top, when she felt as if she'd been clubbed by something catastrophic from behind. Collapsing to the floor like a sack of potatoes, she'd imagined this was what dying was like.

All she could hear was high-pitched ringing. All she could feel was a crushing and burning sensation inside and outside of her skull. There had been nothing in that moment but the sheer agony radiating from her head to her toes. Her skin had been on fire. Her veins had pulsed with acid. Her teeth clenched so hard that her jaw had clicked in protest.

She'd begun to convulse under the pressure of it all, her

body wracking with tremors, her only salvation being the cool concrete floor of the pantry. She couldn't see. Her vision had been a mass of darkness interjected with flashing streaks on the backs of her eyelids as the waves of poison streaked through her.

Over and over, this went.

Pulse. Pulse. Pulse.

Tremor. Tremor. Tremor.

After what must have been forever, as the pressure inside her skull mercifully but gradually began to subside, she'd realised that the high-pitched ringing she could hear was her own scream. It had petered off as she came back to reality. Her entire body had been covered in a sheen of sweat, and she'd realised with embarrassing horror that she'd even drooled during the awful episode, creating a small puddle on the floor.

Her convulsions had dwindled until she was left a shivering mess, covered in sweat and curled into a foetal position as she began to sob in pure, unadulterated sorrow.

She couldn't even take a slice of pie. She was surrounded by the most wondrous food in Roguerest, all within a torturous distance. As she lay there, she could smell the yeast and rich spices.

She could almost taste it.

"...can you hear me, songbird?"

The voice that had entered her consciousness was warm and unfamiliar. A hand had begun stroking her hair, and a stranger entered her blurry vision. All she could make out had been his brown skin and neat buzzcut—everything else remained out of her reach, like a faraway dream.

"Take it easy." His voice had been clearer then. "Just take a few deep breaths for me. In and out—that's it. There we go."

His soothing baritone had been the only thing that

anchored her to the present, and it brought everything crashing back into sharp, painful focus.

She'd grasped onto anything that would keep her grounded, choosing to focus on his eyes; a bright, beautiful grey colour that reminded her fondly of a wool scarf she'd once swindled from a market stall. "I've lost you again, haven't I?"

The stranger had brought her back from her reverie, still stroking her sweaty hair back from her forehead in a mollifying gesture.

"Your eyes are like my old scarf."

The eyes in question had crinkled in the corners as he'd smiled down at her. "I'll take that as a compliment, shall I?"

"It was a very nice scarf."

"I should think it was. How about we get you sat up?"

Rosie had nodded enthusiastically and allowed herself to be dragged into a seated position and propped against one of the concrete shelves, her legs out long in front of her.

"Who are you?" she'd croaked, her throat sore from screaming.

"My name is Khristann."

"Why did you call me 'songbird?'"

"I saw you performing in the casino bar last night. You're quite talented."

She'd processed the information, everything trickling back to her at an infuriatingly slow pace. Khristann had crouched next to her, dressed in chef's whites.

"Uh...I was just—I was getting some... some food. That's all."

He'd raised an eyebrow, but didn't move.

"That much is apparent," he'd mused. "Can I ask why you feel the need to steal from my pantry rather than simply asking? Especially if it causes you such pain."

Confused, Rosie had blushed. "I thought—the head chef, he

told me that I couldn't...I shouldn't eat from the kitchens, but I don't have anything else. I tried to eat the scraps from room service but there haven't been any in two days now. I'm just so hungry and I'm sorry but I couldn't—"

"Whoa." He'd raised his hands in a calming gesture. "Take a breath. You're not in trouble."

"I'm—I'm not?"

He'd given her an easy smile. "Not at all. Why don't you tell me your name?"

"If you saw me perform last night, then you already know that information. And by the sounds of it, you know about my curses too."

"That doesn't mean I wouldn't like you to introduce yourself. I don't want you to feel as if we're on uneven footing, but I'll admit that when I started working here a couple of days ago, I was briefed on you and your situation."

Rosie had flushed and looked away. As if she'd needed any more embarrassing, new employees were being warned about her like she was a caged animal, just waiting to pounce on her next unsuspecting victim.

"Rosie." She'd given him a nod but didn't otherwise move. "I'm Rosie."

"Well, Rosie, why don't you gently stand yourself up? I'll cook you something decent whilst you explain your side of the story."

She'd done exactly as he'd instructed, even following his tapping gesture that had insinuated she should sit on the stainless-steel work surface.

He'd prepared her possibly the best meal she'd ever consumed, and she'd explained everything—her sentence, her new role, her lack of income and food, as well as delving a little into her past as a street child.

He, in turn, had explained that the previous head chef had

quit unexpectedly and with no notice, so he'd been drafted in to take over the position from another luxury hotel in the area.

"Thank you for listening," she'd eventually said as she'd wiped up the remaining gravy on her plate with some more bread.

"That's quite all right. I promise I'll never chase you out of my kitchen like my predecessor. You're welcome here whenever you need something to eat."

She'd given him a genuine smile. "I can't tell you how much I appreciate that."

"We're all just trying to survive, right?"

She'd felt an immediate kinship with Khristann and decided in that moment that perhaps her sentence wouldn't be so bad after all.

"Right," she'd replied.

CHAPTER 3
MADE AND DESTROYED

A year later, Rosie was still visiting the kitchens multiple times a day to sneak food from Khristann. None of the kitchen staff ever spoke about her visits, and she assumed they'd been instructed by Khristann to keep it quiet.

"What's on the menu today, boss?" she asked as she found her friend cleaning one of the surfaces. The lunch period was over, and soon the preparation would begin for the evening rush, which was why Rosie chose this time to visit. The two of them would share a meal and catch up.

"You're in for a treat today, songbird." Khristann let his cloth rest over his shoulder as he pulled a tray from one of the many roaring ovens, sliding it over to Rosie.

The aroma of vegetables and rich spices filled the air, eliciting a groan and a broad smile from her. She grabbed some tarnished, old cutlery for the both of them—a far cry from the ostentatious gold cutlery that guests used—and began to dig into the dish without a second thought. The hit of salt and rich tarragon made her want to groan.

"Slow down there, save some for me," Khristann joked, scooping some up for himself. "How has your day been so far?"

Rosie contemplated telling him about the note, but for a split second, she considered that he could've been the mystery author, the one to keep her hooked and wriggling on her escapist pipe dream like a trout on a line. He was seemingly the only human in all of the Twelve Territories who showed genuine interest in her existence. She doubted she'd have found it within herself to persevere and survive this long if it weren't for him and his boundless generosity.

He was her only family, so how far would he go to protect her? *To free her?*

"Pretty normal," she responded, wiping some sauce as it dribbled down the sharp point of her chin. "I found some incredible shoes in one of the rooms."

Khristann smirked as he speared a chunk of potato. "You tried them on, didn't you?"

"Of course I did."

He laughed between mouthfuls. "I wouldn't expect any less."

"I, uh—I bumped into Jakob as well."

"Bumped into?" Khristann didn't look convinced. "Or did he seek you out and harass you again?"

"The latter," she relented. "He informed me of a special task that I need to carry out over the tournament weekend."

"Do I even want to know what dangerous dance he has you doing now? The quicker we sever the puppet strings he relies so heavily on, the sooner you can be treated like a human being again."

Rosie faltered as she lifted her fork to her mouth, filing the strange statement away for later. Could it really be Khristann leaving her notes?

"It's nothing like that—I hope. I have to act as a *personal liaison* for one of the finalists in the tournament."

He scoffed. "That's Jakob-talk for *bitch*."

"That's exactly what I thought."

"On the plus side, you'll get up-close and personal with one of the Kaarmiach Five. Not many people can say they've done that."

She scrunched her nose in disgust and scraped up some more vegetables. "Is that supposed to be a plus side? I think it's quite the opposite. In fact, I couldn't think of much worse than having to deal with the whims of a spoiled, pretentious celebrity. I imagine I'll be coming down here at all hours of the night to fetch exotic foods that we most likely won't have in stock."

Khristann laughed and shook his head. "Don't write them off so quickly. You could be surprised."

Rosie shot him a sceptical glance and finished eating, letting out a sigh as she leaned against the counter, her belly full but her mind racing.

"That's an awfully big sigh for such a little songbird," he commented as he took the dish and began to wash it up.

"I'm just unsure of how this weekend is going to go," she replied, alluding to more than just her new role. She wasn't sure what would happen in the next two days or if she'd still be at The Ruby come Monday morning.

"You and me both," Khristann replied, placing the dish on the drying rack and turning back to her. He pointed at her travel journal. "What exciting places have you found recently? Any that have made it onto the list?"

Rosie felt excitement fill her, and a beaming smile spread across her face as she thumbed open the tattered and almost-full journal. Every page was covered in maps, photographs, drawings, and handwritten notes; it was so thick that it didn't close anymore. She collected postcards and stamps and train timetables too, anything that would help her when she was finally free. She wouldn't look back at Roguerest for a second.

She would walk out of the city gates and never return to the place that had both made and destroyed her.

"When I was in Jakob's office the other night, I found a book about a temple on the northern coast of Lunaron, in a city called Esmeray."

She flipped through the pages of her journal until she found the new black and white photographs that she'd torn from the book and stuck in.

"The temple is gorgeous, but look at the white-sand beaches that surround it," she explained, pointing to the pictures and seeing Khristann nod. "Apparently, Esmeray is thought to be the home of their God, Nuray, so there's a lot of tourism. But I just want to run my hands through the sand and run into the ocean. I suppose a trip to a holy temple wouldn't be *so* bad whilst I'm there."

Khristann chuckled and flipped through a couple of pages, looking over maps with annotations and highlighted routes.

"There's a city I found in Irredore too," she continued. "It used to be the Artist hub of the territory before the civil war. I know Irredore is the furthest away of all the territories and that it's been completely decimated, but I'm still curious to go there and see what's left. I think there's lots of stories to be told from the remains."

Khristann gave her a gentle smile, one that she couldn't tell if it was understanding or resigned. His next question was phrased like a statement.

"You've got it all planned out, haven't you?"

She nodded. "I've definitely got an idea of where I want to go."

"Even though it's nine years away?"

Rosie grimaced at the reminder and looked down at the journal.

"This journal, the research, the planning...it's all that's

keeping me sane in here. I need a focus point or I'll crumble. I have to have a northern star to work towards. Knowing that there's life for me after this prison sentence is vital. I have to remind myself every day that there's a light at the end of the tunnel."

Khristann wrapped his arm around her shoulders and pressed a kiss to the top of her head.

"I know you do, songbird. Just be careful when you're sneaking into the library and Jakob's office. I don't want you getting into more trouble than you already are."

Rosie relaxed into their embrace and closed her eyes, breathing in Khristann's familiar scent: herbs, laundry detergent, and something smokey that always lingered.

"I'd rather get in trouble for having hope than be praised for complacency."

CHAPTER 4
GENEROUS MASTER

During her first year at The Ruby Talisman, Rosie had explored every room, service corridor, ventilation tunnel, nook, and cupboard. Being confined to the same four red walls had provided a wealth of time in which to traverse the hotel, much like the wayfarer she frequently dreamt of being. There wasn't a single scratch in the hotel that she didn't know about.

Her incessant need to know every entrance, exit, and secret hiding spot was fuelled by her unnatural talent for infiltrating places she wasn't welcome. Part of what made her such a splendid thief was this talent; she wasn't able to execute anything worthwhile unless she knew an environment as well as the map of fine lines on her palm.

This was the main argument that she used to punish herself for the failed heist that had landed her in the hotel in the first place. Never before that wretched day had she scrimped on reconnaissance before a job. Then again, never before that wretched day had she been in love with the biggest distraction of all: Jakob Haart.

There had been plenty of warning flags leading up to the

execution of the biggest theft she'd ever attempted, but Jakob's arrogance had seeped into her much like red wine on a pristine, white tablecloth. He'd assured her that he knew the hotel well, that he knew the rotations of security guards. He'd grown up around the hotel, so who could possibly know it better than him?

Rosie had put blind faith in someone that she'd known a meagre few months, something that she swore over and over again that she'd never be foolish enough to do once more.

She'd been duped by the widely acknowledged Prince of Roguerest and subsequently strung out to dry in the most shameful, overt way. Every citizen within the boundary walls of the city knew her name and her face. They knew what she was capable of, what she'd done, and what she'd failed in doing. Her face had been plastered across newspapers and bulletin boards throughout her trial in a smear campaign she knew had been carefully orchestrated by Lawrence.

As soon as she made it out of Roguerest, she'd travel to places where she was a nobody, a passing ghost with delicate, wandering hands.

Her unrivalled knowledge of the hotel's geography was how she knew that if she were to climb the service stairs in the west corner to the third floor, wait for the stairwell to empty, and nimbly jump up onto the bannister rail, she could push open the vent cover in the ceiling and haul herself up into the narrow, hot shaft behind it. Once she'd done this, she could soundlessly crawl past four vents until she came upon one of the grates that ventilated the library.

Open to guests and employees alike, Rosie was alone in being denied access to the library by the guards stationed at its entrance. Knowing her love of literature and learning more about the territories, Lawrence found macabre satisfaction in depriving her of yet another necessity—access to knowledge and education. Jakob, the loyal watchdog that he was, had no problem following his father's orders.

Hence her reason for clambering through sticky, dusty ventilation tunnels to enter the library unbeknownst to the guards at the door, closer to ornamental nutcrackers than any real sense of security.

Laid atop one of the towering oak bookshelves, her nose mere inches from the ceiling, Rosie was devouring a travelogue about a sprawling city in Forge Valley. It was the second largest territory after Lunaron, and apparently, all of the galleries and museums were free to enter there. A scheme from the government had been implemented several years prior to try and even out the class differences between the Artists who created the work and the Imperials who could afford to consume it.

A city with free-to-enter galleries would definitely be added to Rosie's travel to-do list. Her love of borrowing expensive things and not returning them had stemmed from her passion for beautiful art that she wasn't allowed access to. She'd been a stubborn child, determined to take the things that others decided she wasn't allowed because of her social status.

Her love of reading had begun at a young age, when escapism was her only form of solace as an orphan raised by the streets of Roguerest. She'd grown up reading novels that she could steal from tourists or from other street children who weren't careful enough with their few possessions—though they would often swap books with each other or leave them to younger kids when they were finished with them.

Just as Rosie turned to a full-colour sketch of a mosaic-tiled square in front of a towering cathedral, she was dragged from the suspension of a city unknown back into the grim reality of The Ruby.

"I suppose you think you're smart, don't you?"

Rosie startled so much that she tumbled off the bookcase,

managing to save herself from a complete knock-out by grasping onto the top shelf at the very last moment, leaving her hanging for everyone to see. Heaving out a frustrated sigh, she let herself drop the few feet to the floor, landing in a crouch, ready to pounce at whomever had disturbed her.

She reluctantly glanced up through her eyelashes to find Jakob, arms crossed and eyebrow cocked up. Taking a moment to orientate herself back into the real world and away from the city in Forge Valley, she rose to a standing position with her shoulders rolled back and her chin jutted out.

"Jakob."

"Rosie."

"To what do I owe the—"

"Shelve the book and come along. We'll discuss your blatant lack of rule following at a later date. There's no time for it now."

Curiosity piqued, Rosie fumbled to place the book on the nearest shelf, not caring to look for its original home in alphabetical order, before trailing behind an already-pacing Jakob. She would return to the book and tear out some of the photographs on her next secret trip to the library.

"Where are we going?"

No response.

They passed through the library with ease and ventured out into the social space beside it, filled with drunken guests in a haze of euphoria, hooked on the drinks laced with bruise root. The warm afternoon was rapidly fading into depthless twilight outside, a signal to inebriated patrons that their behaviour could morph into something much more outrageous without the same restrictions of daylight.

Rosie lithely dodged a stumbling woman tripping over her own feet as she struggled to keep up with Jakob's strides towards the lifts. The attendant for the floor scrambled to call the nearest one upon seeing Jakob's formidable figure heading in his direction.

By the time they reached the jittering attendant, a set of doors slid open to reveal the plush, red satin-lined lift with another attendant inside. Rosie didn't dare to enter first, waiting for Jakob to waltz forward before she trailed after him.

"Foyer," he grunted to the young employee, who hurried to push the large gold button for the ground floor. The silence that ensconced them was unpleasant and served to reinforce Jakob's dominance.

Rosie despised it.

"What's the rush for?" She defiantly broke the silence.

With an exasperated sigh, Jakob replied, "Two more of our tournament VIPs have arrived."

Rosie tried to connect the dots. Her VIP for the weekend, Kitty Khalar, wasn't supposed to arrive until the following day.

"I'm afraid I'm going to need another clue."

Jakob heaved out another sigh, pinching the bridge of his nose.

"Please be quiet." The request was strangely tender, though still frustrating.

"I was right in the middle of reading about this city in Forge Valley—"

Jakob looked up at her. His transformation from resigned to aggressive was instantaneous.

"You just don't know when to shut that smart mouth, do you?" Jakob pounced like a panther would on its prey—without warning and with brute force.

Rosie was slammed against the wall of the lift, producing an ominous groan from the mechanics in the shaft and a whimper from the poor attendant on the other side. Jakob's slightly trembling hand pressed against the centre of her chest, pinning her to the gold handrail that circled the lift at waist-height and dug into her lower back painfully. He crouched slightly so that his face was a breath away from her own, his gaze rapidly searching her features for any sign of remorse.

"Why do you do this?" His voice was an angry whisper. "All I ask is that you respect me. Why must you fight me at every turn?"

Floored by his show of genuine emotion, Rosie squared her shoulders and kept her gaze stark. "Respect is earned, not demanded or conquered."

The resounding *ting* of the lift's bell signalled that they'd arrived in the lobby, and the attendant pulled the internal gate open with shaking hands.

"Get your act together." Jakob all but spat on her as he pushed away and strode into the lobby. Rosie took a second to catch her breath and gave the petrified attendant a short, sharp nod as she set off to catch up with her demented keeper.

Jakob's act may have convinced the lift attendant that he was in control, but Rosie knew better. She knew the tremble of his hand against her chest and the almost imperceptible waver in his voice. Jakob was afraid, and he was lashing out to try and regain some control.

The foyer was filled to the brim with excited tourists and bustling employees, lapdogs to momentary masters. Luggage carts rattled, shameless people draped in gaudy fabrics laughed loud enough to draw everyone's attention, and Rosie realised that as much as the circus was overwhelming and almost too bright to look at, it was rapidly becoming a circus that she was part of—that she considered home.

She quick-stepped around a stray suitcase that had jumped ship from a cart and followed Jakob behind the imposing reception desk towards the end where his office was situated. Agitated and wary, Rosie reminded herself of the mantra that served to ground her.

Be available, be observant, be invisible.

She realised with horror that as Jakob reached his office door, he didn't enter and allow the door to slam in Rosie's face but instead straightened his clothes, ran a hand through his dark hair, and rolled his shoulders. When his knuckles rapped against the wood, Rosie knew exactly what it meant.

Lawrence Haart had paid them a visit. No wonder he was afraid.

"Enter," came the gruff voice from inside.

Given no time to prepare herself as she usually did for an ordeal with the one man she loathed more than his son, she reluctantly followed Jakob into the office and kept her gaze on the plush red carpet, finding a single piece of lint particularly interesting. She tried to covertly straighten her smock and hoped to Aakla that she didn't have a hair out of place. Lawrence would use any excuse to taunt or punish her.

The damning sound of the door clicking shut was followed immediately by a somewhat calming sense of quiet as the soundtrack of the zoo in the foyer was mercifully muted.

Rosie still hadn't dared to peer up to her true jailer, but saw in her peripheral as Jakob sat in one of the two seats that faced the imposing desk. The quiet of the room only served to remind each person present who was the dictator and who was the jailbird. Rosie wouldn't speak until spoken to, as it would likely result in punishment later on.

"Rosie, my dear." Lawrence's smooth tone haunted her nightmares. "Do have a seat. You're in no trouble, and as you know, we pride ourselves in ensuring our employees are well cared for."

Rosie followed his instruction without retort. Sitting ramrod straight in the chair, she didn't allow herself to renege her guard or crumble under the intense gaze that she could feel burning away at her skin.

"*Look at me.*" His timbre transitioned from polite to malicious. With reluctance, Rosie lifted her head until she came upon the man himself, the tyrant who dictated her every move, every breath.

Lawrence Haart was undeniably attractive, a trait he used to his utmost advantage as a wolf in sheep's clothing. Though his thick, dark hair was streaked with grey, it was perfectly styled, without a strand out of place. Everything about the man's posture spoke of accomplishment, arrogance, and a thoroughbred upbringing. He was the mirror image of Jakob, down to the olive tone of their skin and the narrowing of their dark eyes.

Lawrence was the kind of man who knew exactly how to draw the best out of a person, to help them achieve their greatest potential. However, his fondest talent was transforming that person into a commodity. He could take an innocent and find their passion, elevate them and provide for them until they were revered for their attributes, then flip a switch and use them until they were drained dry. He would suck every ounce of passion from their bones until the one thing that person once considered a gift became the thing that they hated most about themselves. And when they were a husk of their former selves, ashes barely strung together, he would let them blow away in the wind as if they'd never existed.

Then he'd move to his next unsuspecting victim.

And so the cycle continued, over and over again.

Rosie had watched him over the past year, and he'd done it with countless people, leaving them lost, broken, and outcast, swept under the rug of upper-class Roguerest society.

He'd done it to her too. She no longer sang for the joy of it like she used to. She sang because it was her duty as a puppet in The Ruby Talisman show. One of the few things she'd found joy and pride in had been snatched away and used against her.

"How are you, my dear?" Lawrence had effortlessly transitioned back to the polite employer, his penetrating gaze locked onto Rosie.

"Very well, thank you."

He was famous around Roguerest as a charming, respected, and charitable man, who for all intents and purposes was in charge of the city despite the formal government that was in place. He helped to feed the poor, regularly visited The Estate and shook the hands of street children, helped to *rehabilitate* criminals, and gave employment to those who desperately needed it. He was the knight in shining armour that Roguerest relied upon. To just have spoken to him, touched him, or been in his presence was known as a local blessing.

But underneath the pomp and glamour of his celebrity status, he was conniving, evil, and toxic—a fact that very few people were privy to. Behind closed doors, in the presence of Jakob and Rosie, he sheathed the sword that he slay metaphorical demons with, shucked off his shiny armour, and revealed the monster beneath.

"I trust that my Jakob has informed you of your special task for the tournament weekend ahead. It's quite the honour that we've bestowed upon you. I hope you take it as a token of our appreciation for all your hard work."

The Rosie from before her imprisonment wanted to snap back with, "A temporary change of master and duties is not an honour. It's an exercise of control for the sake of stroking your own ego."

However, the Rosie she was now mumbled, "I do. Thank you very much for your generosity."

Though she hated herself for it and never felt as insignificant as when in Lawrence's presence, he had every ounce of her being under his thumb. She had no choice but to buckle to his control and do exactly as he said. She couldn't risk further imprisonment on top of her lengthy decade. She wouldn't survive it.

"Now to the matter at hand. Miss Khalar will be arriving tomorrow, as you know, and has sent forward a specific request for a generous stock of *shenakk*. As it's a specialty of Irredore, it's not particularly popular in these parts, and we only have a couple of bottles on hand."

Rosie had heard of *shenakk* but never tried it herself. She'd been told that the potent alcohol could floor even the most seasoned drinker between the second and third shot.

"I have a special task for you this evening." Lawrence's face contorted into demonic joy. "I'm going to allow you out of the hotel."

Rosie was almost entirely positive that she'd hallucinated.

"Excuse me?"

"I'm going to alter your curse to allow you out of the hotel and the Casino District, across to a friend of mine in the Tourist Quarter. He owns an apothecary there which serves as a front for his distillery. You're to travel there and there alone, pick up what I've ordered, and return here immediately."

Rosie's head was spinning. *She was being allowed to leave the hotel?*

"I, uh—I don't understand, sir."

"That's all right, Rosie. I know that Artists aren't so intelligent, you poor souls. Let me explain myself better." The pity that dripped from his words was for her ridicule alone.

Rosie clenched her fists but fought to reign her expression into numbness, allowing the demon in front of her to assume whatever he liked about her intelligence. Penance for his sins would come crashing down soon enough. She could feel it in her bones.

Be available, be observant, be invisible.

"As with my ability to endow curses upon you, I can also

alter them at my will. You've been such a good girl for us this past year, so I figured that we could give you this...*favour*. You can feel the fresh air of our great city on your face again, even if only for a couple of hours. You can wander amongst the delirious masses, revel in the sprightly atmosphere of the Roguerest nightlife, and then return here refreshed and full of gratitude for your generous master."

His act was so polished that had anyone else been witness to their conversation, they'd be entirely convinced that Rosie was the luckiest employee in the world. How fortuitous to have such an understanding, kind boss. But Rosie knew better. She saw beneath the armour and fraudulent smile.

A favour from Lawrence Haart was not a favour at all. It was a binding contract to exist at his will until further notice, waiting to be called upon for some horrific assignment that would likely end up in arrest or death.

It had to be a trick, but she couldn't possibly decline. Declining his trap was far worse than walking straight into it.

"I—thank you. You're very kind."

His devilish grin remained firmly in place. "I know I am."

"Father." Jakob finally spoke up. "Are you sure this is a good idea?"

"You dare to doubt me?"

"No, I just—"

"You may take your leave. You're not needed any longer."

For a moment, Jakob didn't move, clearly contemplating defying his father but inevitably crumbling under his scrutiny. Rosie risked a glance at the only person in the room who could potentially protect her from the monster lurking behind the mahogany safety barrier. She wanted to plead with him not to leave, not to surrender her to the whims of a demon, but when their eyes met, his were blank as if he truly couldn't care less.

She'd hoped, as the lesser of two evils, that he would

perhaps give her an out or pretend to care for her wellbeing. Alas, he was predictably passive and cowardly in the face of his father.

"I'll be waiting for you in the foyer, Rosie."

If his words were supposed to provide some form of comfort, he'd fallen incredibly short.

The resounding click of the door mechanism falling back into place was all that signalled his exit, leaving Rosie in the claws of her tormentor. She peered back up at him and regretted it instantaneously.

His smile was innocent but his eyes...his eyes promised a world of pain.

"Why don't we change that curse?"

His predatory gaze followed her as she stood calmly and rounded the desk, standing in front of him with her jaw clenched. Just the thought of him touching her made her want to run to the communal staff showers and scrub herself in searing water. He might be polished on the surface, but his touch left stains that couldn't be removed with soap.

Although he was still seated and she stood taller than him, the way he leaned back in his chair to look at her spoke volumes.

He finally stood, towering a foot above her. She could feel his minty breath tickling her upper lip and the rise and fall of his chest on her own. She shuddered, trying to take soothing breaths as quietly as possible. She could feel the sweat trickling between her shoulder blades. Her hands trembled lightly. The back of her throat ached, and her eyes burned. She couldn't let him see her cry.

"Let's see what we can do about that pesky curse of yours, hm?"

He lifted his hand to tuck a stray piece of her red hair behind her ear in what would otherwise be considered a tender gesture, then placed his palm on her forehead.

Rosie couldn't bear to maintain his vulturous gaze any longer, so she let her eyes fall closed as the warmth from his hand grew to a scalding temperature. The unwelcome memory of the first time this had been done just a year ago came flooding back, along with the anxiety and despair of her sheer hopelessness in the situation.

Be available, be observant, be invisible.

Lawrence's ability didn't need words or actions. He was formidable because he used only his mind to inflict pain on others.

The searing heat pulsed mercilessly until, without warning, it dissipated as quickly as it had come, leaving sweat dripping down Rosie's cheeks. She revelled in the small victory that was sweat dripping onto Lawrence's pristine leather shoes that likely cost more than any of his employees earned in an entire year.

He didn't seem fazed by it, though, once again looking at Rosie as if he'd devour her at a moment's notice, leaving nothing but bones behind. He ever so carefully wiped a droplet of sweat from her brow with his thumb before it fell into her eye.

Be available, be observant, be invisible.

"All done," he murmured with a soft smile. "Now, that wasn't so bad, was it?"

All she wanted to do was dart out of the office and wash the vile man's touch from her skin; but knowing that it would land her in hot water, she merely nodded her faux agreement.

"What do you say?" His incessant patronising tone was enough to encourage rising bile in Rosie's throat.

"Thank you."

"Thank you, *what?*"

"Thank you, sir."

"That's better." He mercifully freed her from his grip, and she stumbled away from him as if drunk, immediately rounding the desk and putting as much distance between them as possible.

She could still feel his touch. She could still smell his breath. She needed to get it *off*.

"Jakob will give you the address of the apothecary," Lawrence lazily explained, acting as if his touch hadn't just assaulted her inside and out. "You are to go there and come straight back. Your curse hasn't been removed, but the parameters have been altered. You can't outsmart me, so don't insult me by trying."

He spoke to her as if talking about the sticky heat outside and not the control he held over her body. Rosie stayed silent, the air of the office suffocating her. She needed to get out. She needed to get him off her.

"Thank you, as always, for being such a delight to have around." His smile made a return. "Such a good girl."

"May I"—she swallowed down her dizzying nausea—"may I go?"

He dragged out a suspended silence just to taunt her, his brow quirking slightly. His warm expression haunted her. His innocent smile could destroy cities. It destroyed *her*.

His power was not in physical strength or aggression. His power was in psychological torture; the knowledge that there was no escape from him was a more potent affliction than any punch or kick.

"Of course, you can, dear. Why didn't you just ask?"

Rosie didn't wait for further conversation as she threw the office door open and vaulted out. Khristann's lunch churned in her stomach. She wiped the persistent sweat from her face and scrambled down the length of the reception counter. Upon reaching the end, she found Jakob speaking with one of the concierges. He turned to her with concern.

"Rosie, what happened?"

"Please don't embarrass me further by pretending to care," she snapped, humiliated and exhausted from her run-in with Lawrence. She needed a shower. She so desperately needed a shower.

"Wait." Jakob grabbed her wrist to stop her from walking away. "I'm sorry I couldn't do anything for you, I just—"

"You just nothing," she snarled, squaring up to him without any energy left to fear reprimand. "I am so tired...so sick and tired of being treated like an animal—of being manhandled as if I have no rights and no feelings. I'm a *human being,* Jakob."

She was surprised to see regret cross his features.

Had he abruptly developed compassion and empathy?

"Come downstairs with me, and we'll talk about this." He kept his voice lowered in order to stave off any unwanted attention.

"I-I don't need to talk about anything with you." Rosie yanked her wrist from his grip as her emotions began to get the better of her. "Leave me alone. Both of you. I can't get away. I-I'm not just..."

She huffed out a curse when she couldn't string together a sentence. Her mind crumbled from facing her tormentor again without any warning or chance to prepare.

"Songbird," Jakob whispered, still holding on to her wrist. "Let me take you somewhere quiet. Let me help you."

Rosie finally snatched her wrist from his grip. "I'm not going anywhere with you," she hissed, taking a deep breath so that she could find the right words. So that she could try to express the hatred and helplessness she felt when it came to the Haarts.

"One day"—she swallowed the rising lump in her throat—

"one day, I'm going to save myself in spite of everything you and your father have put me through."

Knowing that he wouldn't chase her and make a scene in the bustling foyer, she marched away with her head held high. But, deep inside, her heart was in shreds beneath the expensive leather shoes of one Lawrence Haart.

CHAPTER 5

THE DEPTHS OF A DEMENTED METROPOLIS

Despite Rosie's revulsion where Lawrence was concerned, she couldn't bring herself to spend longer than absolutely necessary in the mangy employee shower block. Using a nail brush, she'd scrubbed her ashen skin beneath the scalding water until it came up the hue of her red hair.

She'd dressed in a clean cotton shirt and a pair of tapered trousers that she'd shamefully accepted as a hand-out from a guest a couple of months back. They were a perfect fit, and the dozy woman who'd given them to her had owned several other pairs like it, citing that she'd worn this pair once already so had no further use for them.

Resigned to wearing her work shoes, Rosie paced back to the main entrance, anxious to take in a deep breath of the Roguerest air outside. She'd never go as far as to call it fresh— that was a direct contradiction of the truth thanks to the Industrial Sector within the city's walls, which left an inescapable layer of muck on every surface outside.

When she found herself perched by the concierge desk, a shadow amongst the animated riffraff that surrounded her, she realised the difficulty she faced in plucking up the courage to walk through the polished revolving door.

What if Lawrence had tricked her? What if this was just another harsh game for his own sick entertainment?

"You're nervous," a familiar voice spoke from beside her.

She chose not to respond, cursing herself for not hearing his approach.

He continued, "I promise you, this is no trick."

She whirled around to face Jakob, a scowl across her features. He held out a piece of paper presumably containing the address needed. She snatched it from him and tucked it away in her pocket.

"Please, just stop," she hissed in a low tone. "Stop acting as if you care all of a sudden. I won't fall for any more of your mind games—or your father's."

She had to give it to him, his downtrodden face was perfect. His hurt expression had been whittled to faultlessness. She found herself wanting to believe him, wanting to see the old Jakob in his mannerisms.

"I understand you have no compulsion whatsoever to trust me, and I honestly don't blame you, but I still care for you, Rosie."

"*Please,*" she scoffed. "Do us both a favour and give up the act. Where was this care in the last year? Where was it when you humiliated me on a daily basis? When you made me feel less than a dog brought in off the streets?"

He had the good graces to appear contrite.

"There's progress being made behind the scenes," he murmured without making eye contact. "There are things going on that you couldn't comprehend, and, believe it or not, all I've ever tried to do is protect you from my father. I failed today, and I'm truly sorry."

Rosie trembled, abhorred by his audacity. She would stride

through the door momentarily without fear; the potential pain of her *captipheus* curse was less than the agony of the current conversation.

Why was he so set on making her life miserable?

She considered what he'd said and was once again struck with the thought that perhaps Jakob could be the mystery author of the notes she'd been left.

...progress being made behind the scenes...

...protect you from my father...

"Something that you've always failed to realise," Rosie began, her voice soft but determined, "is that you have a *power*. You have a birthright and a divine heritage and an empire. You have a...a privilege." She paused as she gathered her thoughts. "And although you don't choose to actively abuse this privilege like your father does, you choose to stand by and let the abuse happen." Her throat felt tight and her voice cracked as she added, "You choose complacency."

Jakob blinked several times, his expression becoming crestfallen.

"And I think"—Rosie really stared into his eyes this time—"that complacency makes you just as bad, if not worse, than the abuser. You have the power to stop it and yet you just...stand by and watch instead."

He ducked his head and cleared his throat, scratching the back of his neck before looking back up into her eyes.

"Rosie...I'm trying, I—"

"I loved you once," she rasped, her fists clenched. "I loved and trusted you, but you used me for a quick sense of adventure, for bragging rights to your clueless friends who spend their days sneering at people like me. You were complicit then and you're just as complicit now." She shook her head as she turned away and began walking towards the door. She couldn't bear to keep looking at the old Jakob shining through. She couldn't be reminded anymore of what they once were.

"Rosie, please just—"

He didn't finish his sentence, and Rosie knew it was to save his pride in the busy foyer. She expected no less from him. His cowardice would always shine through in the moments that truly mattered, which was how she knew without a doubt that despite his words, he would never genuinely protect her from anything—not if it meant risking embarrassment or seclusion from his father's wealth.

Jakob liked the idea of being the hero until it meant sacrificing too much.

Taking a shaky breath, Rosie entered the revolving door. Everything blurred into a slow pace in time with her heartbeat. She felt as if she were trying to walk on pulp, her slowed steps sinking into sponge. Her pulse was a drum. Perspiration beaded on her top lip.

Would the torture of her captipheus *curse come when she got outside?*

She pushed the bar in front of her anyway, soon reaching the opening where she'd either have to brace herself and tumble out or concede to the same mousiness that ruled Jakob and walk back into the safety of the entrance hall.

"I am *nothing*"—she grunted and pushed forward—"*nothing* like him."

A gust of humid city air washed over her as she gasped and threw herself out of the door and into a pile on the marble steps. She felt her chest constricting as she gazed up at the roof of the covered entrance above her, breath laboured and unsteady.

She was outside of The Ruby.

"Miss, are you all right?" The doorman on duty bent over her, and she recognised him as Hector, a meek boy a year younger than her with a babyface. Much like the majority of employees in the hotel, he owed a debt to Lawrence.

"Wait. Rosie?"

He fumbled her into a sitting position, and she gathered that she'd drawn the attention of a small crowd in the entryway but failed to care.

She was outside.

"How are you outside?" Hector continued, "Are you escaping? Someone could see you, don't you need to—"

"Hush," she mumbled, feeling as if she were having an out-of-body experience. She managed to stand and couldn't help whipping her head back and forth as she took in the sight of the infamous street that The Ruby opened onto.

She drew in deep lungfuls of air, the faint stench of the Industrial Sector hitting her nose, signifying a slight breeze coming from the south. Despite the darkness, the street appeared as if it were still daylight, flashing lights adorning each of the buildings and street performers playing with fire to create flashes and sputters of gorgeous, ember illuminations.

The noise was deafening as hundreds of stumbling, raucous tourists made their way into the numerous casinos in the aptly named Casino District. Visitors came to Roguerest for one thing alone, so it only made sense to dedicate an entire quarter of the city to those wishing to gamble their riches away. Roguerest was nothing if not accommodating.

"Rosie?" Hector urged again.

"I've been allowed out for the night," Rosie replied dreamily, her attention drawn to the lights of the city as if she'd never seen them before.

She was peering at Roguerest through fresh eyes. *Free eyes.*

"You have?" Hector spluttered. "What are you doing talking to me, then? Go and do something outrageous, be merry and con a tourist into buying you expensive drinks. Live like there's no tomorrow."

"There isn't for me out here."

"Exactly. *Go,* Rosie."

She didn't need to be further encouraged. She ignored the stares of pompous guests still lingering and bounded down the marble steps, her heart pumping viciously in her chest.

She was outside.

The marvel of the jolly tune spilling from a nearby bar was not lost on her, neither was the symphony of street vendors hoping for a late-night sale as the roads and alleyways rapidly filled. She heard the roar of a motorcar somewhere in the distance and the even *clip-clop* of hooves on cobbles.

Roguerest in the daytime was a swarming circus of excited families and exuberant marketeers, but at night, the city transformed into a festival of colour and delight. It became a spectacle that could scarcely be described to its fullest unless witnessed in the flesh. The music was louder, the thrills deeper, and the darkest sins became revered virtues. The criminal underbelly of Roguerest came alive, throngs of opportunists sliding from the darkness to make a profit from the misfortunes of others. The call of danger was irresistible to those with both money and time to burn.

The combination of mystery and pleasure was like nothing else Rosie had experienced. It was addictive even to a native.

A year ago, before she'd been imprisoned in her gilded cage, she'd known every alley and building in the city. She'd traversed every rooftop and knew at least three ways to exit any given place. She may not have been royalty, but Roguerest had been her kingdom.

Remembering that she hadn't been granted all night to carry out her task, she paused and pulled the paper from her pocket, reading Jakob's elegant penmanship.

M. L. Jack's Apothecary. Scythe Street, Tourist Quarter
   Please behave - J.

Rosie had spent much of her childhood on Scythe Street, a notorious haven for the sly pickpockets of the city. She'd learned every trick in the book on sleight of hand by the time she was ten years old, most of which she'd practised on Scythe Street. It was unique for the fact that there were so many small alleyways between the buildings, which allowed for quick escapes when particular lifts didn't go to plan.

Her greatest finds and biggest risks had occurred there. She had fond memories of the dirty cobblestones and the echo of her own pounding footsteps as she made a getaway. The street joined onto the large market square that housed hundreds of stalls and thousands of people at any given moment, providing an ideal place to disappear at the drop of a hat.

Had Lawrence sent her there on purpose?

Putting her stray thoughts to one side, she began the trek through the city, ducking and weaving to avoid the blissfully unaware hoards of revellers. She melted back into old habits as if she'd not been away, hugging the shadows and pausing in discreet alcoves to check if she had any nosy followers. The thrill of being back in her element was unrivalled. She couldn't restrain the beaming smile on her face.

She was home. She was outside and she was *home*.

Street performers ensured there was never a moment of silence throughout her walk, and the overflowing noise from bars, casinos, and restaurants wrapped her in a cosy blanket of familiarity. She could smell the spilled liquor on the cobblestones beneath her and taste the designer herbal cigarettes of the upper class as they passed.

As she wandered past Five Halves, another of Lawrence's casinos, she identified plain-clothed employees standing outside the entrance, singing enticing tunes and praising the odds of winning if only you were to take a step inside.

Lights flashed and women laughed. Winners cheered and drinkers stumbled. There was nothing like a night on the streets of Roguerest.

Rosie savoured every second of her journey to the Tourist Quarter. She would remember it each night as she slept in her hot, cramped cupboard until Lawrence deemed her worthy enough of leaving again. Or until he had another *favour* for her.

As she crossed Frontier Lane, the threshold of the Casino District and the Tourist Quarter, she came across The Heckler, an alehouse that claimed to encompass all that Roguerest represented in a polished, tourist-friendly atmosphere. Only locals knew that the truest representation of the city was housed deep in The Estate—the quarter of the city where the majority of them lived. Most of it was poverty-stricken and filthy, though there were more decorous areas where middle-class citizens took residence.

A local woman dressed in a brown, fringed flapper dress stood on a pedestal beneath the bowing entrance of The Heckler, hollering about the impending tournament that weekend.

"The Kaarmiach Five are upon us!" she wailed, a mischievous grin accompanying her exaggerated arm movements. "The Heckler is a favourite haunt of the one and only, Phoenix Mikelle! Come and join us for the weekend, and you might just encounter him in his home-away-from-home!"

The small swaying crowd that had gathered around her *ooh'd* and *aah'd* in all the right places, many of them bumbling in through the double doors moments later. The smell of burning sage wafted out from inside.

The woman stepped down from her elevated position and took a swig from a tankard on the squalid pavement beneath her. Upon rising up to begin her jeering again, she made eye contact with Rosie, who'd unknowingly paused to watch the performance.

The woman's lips quirked up on one side. "What they don't know won't hurt 'em, eh?"

Of course, the woman could detect that Rosie was no traveller. Rosie couldn't help but smile at the camaraderie between them.

"Has Phoenix Mikelle ever stepped foot inside The Heckler?"

"He walked past us once. What's the difference? Ya know what it's like 'round here."

"I certainly do." Rosie looked to her feet.

"Do I know ya from somewhere? Ya face is real familiar."

Taking that as her cue to move on, Rosie shook her head without making eye contact and began traipsing towards her destination once again.

She couldn't have a moment—a *conversation*—without her tumultuous past rearing its head.

Pushing deeper into the roaring streets of the Tourist Quarter, Rosie passed all sorts of emporiums, night markets, and well-known courtesan houses with men and women bowing out of balconied windows, calling for a companion for the evening. By the awed gazes of passers-by, they would have company in no time.

Rosie avoided unnecessary interaction, keeping her figure hunched and in the shadows wherever possible—just another phantom in the depths of a demented metropolis.

As she pressed on, the streets filled to suffocating levels. The city flooded with visitors for the tournament weekend, and Rosie soon found herself far too close to the strangers for her own comfort. The final straw, however, was watching as the beginnings of a fight broke out in the middle of the crowded street.

A man in his mid-twenties with a bottle of ale in each hand

had clearly over-indulged and stumbled over a cobblestone, flying into a group of women dressed to the nines and knocking several of them to the ground. Before anyone could intervene, one of the women shot to her feet; her hand wrapped around the man's neck in an instant, his eyes instantly bulging out of his head.

"You got ale on my gown, you heathen," she hissed. "And all over the cobblestones. I think you should clean it up. *With your tongue.*"

It was that moment that Rosie realised the woman was an Imperial. The man's eyes widened slightly as he tried to fight the compulsion, but it was a pointless effort. A second later, he crouched on the grimy cobblestones, licking ale whilst the rest of the women stood up again.

No one dared to intervene as the Imperial straightened her black floor-length dress and swept her hair over her shoulder as if nothing had happened.

She addressed her friends, "Shall we go to The Ruby Talisman next? Less of the riff-raff in there."

"Hey!"

Everyone turned to see a group of young men approaching —friends of the poor man on the ground if their age range and similar cheap suits were any indication.

"What've you done to my friend, Imperial scum?"

Rosie knew it was her moment to make a swift exit.

Spying an alleyway between the city library and a clothing boutique, she slithered into the darkness again before potentially colliding with a gaggle of middle-aged women singing a tone-deaf rendition of a sea shanty as they blundered across the pavement, oblivious to the beginnings of a fight starting.

Gasping, Rosie hugged the grimy stone wall of the library and rested her head against it. She'd seen Roguerest in many states throughout her life, but this level of debauchery was something entirely new. The thoroughfares had never been like this, even during the high season.

Deciding at once that she wouldn't hazard the streets any longer, she knew her only option was to seek refuge upwards. She pulled herself from the wall and sauntered further into the alleyway, knowing full well that if she were to go further than the dumpsters halfway down, she'd be putting herself in a perilous situation. She knew the kind that operated down this alley and wasn't in a position to cross them.

She took a moment to familiarise herself with the side of the clothing boutique, soon locating the path that she'd taken numerous times in the past to scale the same building.

It started with the ventilation unit, then a quick hop to grab the lightly protruding ledge, a swing of her legs to propel her over to the sawn-off iron bar, and a foot into the indentation she'd made herself many years prior. After a leap, a few near misses, and a pitch between two crumbling balconies later, she hauled herself up onto the flat roof of the boutique, laughing like a child as she lay on her back. The stars weren't visible in Roguerest even on a clear night because of the lights adorning every building, but growing up, Rosie would pretend that she could see them sparkling back at her, winking and seeing her as no one else had.

Victorious and slightly out of breath, she stood and viewed the city from roof height, feeling all at once in her element. If the streets of Roguerest were special, the rooftops were something else. Though the noise from below permeated the limited peace of higher up, it had a distant quality as if it were an afterthought.

The memories of traversing the very same rooftops throughout her entire childhood came rushing back, assaulting her with memories of exciting and perilous times. There wasn't a building that Rosie hadn't scaled.

This—*here*—was her domain.

Before her imprisonment, the legions of other petty criminals in the city had started to take notice of her. The failed heist had been meant to cement her reputation, to crown her as a hellion and a rogue.

Rosie considered her prior budding reputation as she began to run, vaulting across buildings and chasing away lingering shadows of others just like her. Perhaps they would talk, perhaps they would think that she'd broken free of her curses. They could think whatever they wished of her because nowadays, she was no rogue. She was a mere servant to the gentry.

Oh, how the mighty fall.

As the roofs gave her a much more direct route, she arrived on top of the apothecary swiftly, skidding to a halt and peering over the ledge onto Scythe Street. It was just as busy as every other road in the Tourist Quarter.

Adrenaline pumped through her veins. Her blood sang. She was free. Even if just for a couple of hours, she was once again an anchorless entity, the city her oyster.

She turned to face the doorway on the roof that led down into the top floors of the apothecary building. The swollen, wooden entryway was predictably locked, giving Rosie a chance to test her prowess in lock-picking once more.

Searching the rooftop for anything that could help her, she uncovered a small, rusty coil spring in the gutter. Now, she just needed—

"Ah." She laughed, striding over to a pile of what looked like discarded rags. Upon further inspection, she saw that they were clothes still attached to a line with pegs.

She cracked the wood of a peg away from its centre spring and then held the two pieces of metal in her palm, marvelling at the thrill of it all. She was certain that the electric pleasure of finding her way into places that she shouldn't would never wane.

Minutes later, she'd picked the lock of the door and pushed it open, descending the rotting staircase with the utmost care. She ignored the three floors that she passed on the way down, not needing to waste time exploring the darkness that laid in wait. Her business was on the ground floor.

As she reached the bottom of the staircase, she noticed the unfinished, peeling plaster of the walls transforming into a velvety, green wallpaper. Glossy skirting boards appeared, and the floorboards became varnished.

All at once, the wear and tear of life in Roguerest was covered over with faux glamour, much like those who resided inside the city's walls.

Rosie peered down the darkened corridor beside her, assuming that it led back towards the distillery that Lawrence had mentioned. Shuddering at the thought of the wretched man, she approached the dark door directly in front of her, pressing her ear to it.

The sounds of the shop front were muffled behind the wood, a series of disjointed murmurs. Rosie crouched and peered through the large keyhole, assessing the situation inside. She saw two teenage girls speaking with an older man, who she presumed was Mr Jack.

Taking the opportunity of a turned back, she opened the door just enough to sneak through the gap and close it behind her. Spying the counter where purchases were rung up, she snuck behind it and settled onto the rickety three-legged stool usually reserved for Mr Jack.

She witnessed as the two girls decided against their purchase and were shown out by the apothecarist. He heaved out an exasperated sigh as he locked the door and leaned his head against it.

Rosie took that as her opportunity to pipe up, still riding on the confidence that being back in her domain had given her. Out here, she wasn't a servant to the Haarts. She was Rosie Wren, a thief and a wraith.

"Mr Jack, I presume?"

"What?" He twisted around in shock, his eyes wide. "How did you—where did you come from?"

"I believe you have some *shenakk* for me."

She watched the mental calculations in real time.

"Mr Haart sent you?"

Instead of replying, Rosie quirked an eyebrow and crossed her arms over her chest.

"Right. Of course. I'm so grateful for his custom. Please do tell him that if he needs anything else in the future, I am more than happy to—"

Rosie fazed out his incessant rambling as she remembered what Lawrence had said. He'd referred to the man as a friend, and yet clearly, this man was nothing more than a commodity.

Of course. She mentally slapped herself.

Lawrence didn't have friends.

"—and I said to my wife, this is the good fortune we've been looking for. The opportunity to collaborate with such a generous man as Mr Haart is not to be missed."

Mr Jack stood in front of her on the other side of the counter with a naive look of glee on his weathered face, making the lines around his eyes and mouth even deeper. His leathery skin was tan, and his gleaming green eyes showed such simple ignorance.

"I know we're strangers, but can I give you some advice?" she mused.

He frowned. "I—yes, I suppose."

"Working for Mr Haart is not good fortune. Take the cash for this job and forget it ever happened."

His expression sobered.

"What do you mean?"

"That's my advice, Mr Jack. Take it or leave it."

He frowned, and his moment of pause gave Rosie the moment she needed for a flash of inspiration to strike and a grin to spread across her face. She might as well take advantage of her limited freedom in the city and acting as Lawrence's lackey.

"Mr Haart also asked for a couple more things," she announced.

"Anything. Anything at all. What can I help him with?"

She slid off the stool and leant against the counter.

"Have you got a chisel and a hammer?"

CHAPTER 6
KEEPING SECRETS

S uite Rouge was the penthouse complex at The Ruby, comprised of two suites that were adjoined by a door in the middle. The suites were mirror images of each other, both boasting an open-plan living and kitchen space, two ensuite bedrooms, a large rooftop terrace, and several balconies.

The sort of guests that usually stayed in the suites left a lot of mess and made a lot of noise—something Rosie wasn't looking forward to accommodating over the weekend.

As she stood in the doorway of one of the suites the following morning, she silently thanked the other house-keeping staff who had prepared the rooms so well. All she had to do was add the finishing touches whilst doing her own recon. She'd woken half an hour earlier than needed in order to take her time sussing out every inch of the suite.

She placed the large vase of red roses that she'd been carrying on the long dining table and made sure they were centred before turning back to the quiet space. There were several stages to efficiently surveying a room for someone like Rosie; the first was noting every potential entrance and exit.

She breezed through each room, mentally logging every

door, window, ventilation grate, and concealed cupboard. She'd been in the suites before but knew from experience that getting lazy on recon was a one-way ticket to disaster. It never hurt to double-check for any changes.

"That's how you ended up here, after all," she mused to herself as she tested the locks on the balcony doors. She looked through the glass doors at the balconies, counting any potential escape routes in the form of drain pipes, trellises, and railings.

Once the exits and entrances had all been noted, she moved on to the next stage: hazards. In theory, anything could prove to become a hazard, but the main things she looked for were creaking floorboards and doors, mirrors, and precarious or noisy decor.

She began her slow but thorough walkthrough of the entire complex, memorising every single creak of floorboards or squeaking hinge on a door. She noted that the large rugs in both sitting areas weren't fixed to the floor and could prove to be a slip or trip hazard. She also turned on all the taps to listen for how the pipes sounded in the walls and if the drainage was noisy or not.

The final stage of the process was any item—or person, in some situations—that could help her in a time of need. She opened each cupboard and drawer in the kitchen to note what cutlery was available. Though she didn't foresee needing a weapon, she wouldn't be caught dead in an unexpected situation without a way to defend herself. She also checked every storage cupboard and wardrobe in both suites for any other form of makeshift weapon or tool.

Some of the garish sculptures littered throughout the penthouse had sharp edges, which could prove useful. Rosie eyed a particularly grotesque bronze rendition of the male form and shuddered at several parts of the sculpture that would make a useful weapon.

When she was satisfied with her recon, she blew out a deep breath and collapsed onto one of the sofas in a dramatic fashion worthy of a theatre actress. The room was mercifully silent, and white noise rang in her ears as she closed her eyes to take in the calm before the storm.

Anxiety began to bubble in her chest at the mere thought of the weekend ahead, a warm sensation that, if allowed to grow, would bloom into a full-blown panic. She resorted to grounding herself in the moment to stem the anxiety, running through all of her senses.

She could smell the fresh-cut roses on the dining table. She could feel the smooth velvet sofa beneath her. She opened her eyes to see the ostentatious crystal chandelier above her. She could taste her excessive, metallic saliva. She could hear...nothing.

There were no sounds.

Absolute silence.

No knocks or bangs or laughs or distant chatter. There were no noises. Nothing. It was too quiet. Why was it so quiet? Her heart began to pound in her chest. She couldn't hear anything. It was so quiet. It was *too quiet*—

A key clattered in the lock of the front door, and she shot up in an instant, straightening her work smock and running a hand through her hair. If it was either of the Haart men, she couldn't have a hair out of place. She couldn't afford to give them any more ammunition to torment her. She eyed the sofa and realised that it was clear she'd been sitting on it, but she didn't have time to straighten it.

Shit. Shit. Sh—

The door swung open to reveal the familiar figure of Khristann in his chef's whites, bright against his brown skin. Rosie sagged in relief. She'd never been so pleased to see his shaved head and broad shoulders filling a door frame. Khristann caught her eye and began to wheel in a gold trolley stacked with fresh food and dishes under shiny domes.

"I knew you'd be up here," he said, allowing the door to swing closed behind him.

He pushed the hospitality cart into the kitchen, and Rosie tentatively followed him, curious about the sweet aroma that had filled the room. She swiped her sweaty palms on the itchy fabric of her uniform and worked to compose her expression into something a little less panicked.

"Are you all right, songbird?"

She looked up to find Khristann studying her with slightly narrowed eyes.

"Yeah," she breathed, the panic in her chest finally settling. She focussed on the smell of the food. "I'm okay."

"Well, I'm glad to hear it. I brought fresh waffles for you."

Rosie broke into a grin. "With berries and syrup?"

"Would I dare to bring you anything else?"

They settled into companionable silence whilst Rosie ate and Khristann unloaded fresh tarts, breads, and pastries into the suite's pantry.

The waffles were perfect, as always; crispy and golden on the outside, fluffy and pale on the inside. The sweet fried treat was her favourite breakfast, and Khristann made sure to prepare it for her whenever he had the chance.

As she ate, her thoughts drifted to the night before and the victorious sensation she'd experienced wandering back through the streets of her city, a suitcase brimming with *shenakk* trailing behind her.

She'd taken the opportunity to revel with strangers and dance in the street along the way, her looming imprisonment approaching with each step, twirl, and skip that she took. The music was so much louder, the streets busier and the lights brighter, and she memorised each detail with the utmost care and deliberation. Roguerest was meant to be experienced in the flesh, not through prison bars.

Upon her return to The Ruby, she'd waited on the marble steps for as long as she could, seated beside the revolving door with the suitcase at her side, refusing to renege her freedom until absolutely necessary. She'd noticed Jakob waiting inside, watching her with pity through the floor-to-ceiling windows, but she'd pretended not to notice. She'd watched in silent fascination as hundreds of people entered and exited the hotel, varying stages of inebriation and debt discernible on each face she saw.

It wasn't until the clock tower in the market square, loud enough to be heard throughout the entire city, struck ten resounding rings that Rosie began to feel a gnawing sensation inside her head. Opting for the least amount of pain possible, she'd stood and brushed herself off, keeping her head held high as she picked up the suitcase and took one final look at the rowdy street in front of her, blazing in all of its devilish glory.

Giving it a weak smile, she'd proceeded to accept her fate by striding into the foyer of The Ruby and dropping the suitcase at Jakob's feet, an ominous *clink* from inside punctuating her arrival. She'd ignored his attempt at conversation and strode into the bowels of the hotel with her newly acquired tools tucked into the back of her trousers.

She'd spent several hours rereading every mysterious note she'd received in the year she'd been at The Ruby and meticulously *not* thinking about heists of any kind. Instead, she'd thought about *wine tastings*. In particular, the very important *wine tasting* she needed to plan before the end of the tournament weekend. The one where she'd need all sorts of tools to open crates and barrels of wine. Wine that was being stored in the gallery upstairs.

Wine.

Realising that she could think her way around her *supresis* curse had been a game changer.

A clang of dishes brought her back to the present.

Once she'd finished her plate and rubbed her bloated belly, Rosie asked, "Why didn't you get one of your lackeys to bring up the food?"

The sound of jars and cans being shuffled around came from the pantry as Khristann organised it.

"Because I knew you'd be up here making sure everything was in ship-shape until the last possible moment. And I knew you hadn't stopped by the kitchens for breakfast this morning because of that."

Rosie's cheeks warmed a little, but all she felt was a deep sense of gratitude towards the man who had become an older brother and father figure to her.

"You're too good to me." She tried to pass it off with a chuckle as if the gesture didn't mean everything to her, but she should've known that he would see straight through it.

"Rosie," he sighed, coming out from the pantry. "You know I'd do anything for you, right?"

She met his steely gaze and found no humour there. When he said anything, did he mean...*anything?* Did he mean he'd plan a heist? Did he mean he'd risk it all to try and free her?

"Songbird?"

She cleared her throat. "Yeah. Yes. I know that."

He nodded and straightened some pans hanging on hooks above the stove, no longer looking at her but still tensed as if he wanted to speak.

"Khristann," Rosie broached carefully, "is everything all right?"

"Of course." He turned back around with his warm smile firmly seated back on his lips. "I'm just a little nervous about how much pressure has been put on me this weekend. The Haarts only accept perfection, as you know."

She wasn't sure if she believed the change in topic, but she let it slide for the time being. There wasn't enough evidence to suggest the mysterious notes were from Khristann, and he'd done nothing in the past year to make her doubt him.

"You and I both know that perfection is the only option around here," Rosie said with a quiet laugh, breaking the tension that had somehow built up between them in a way that it never had before.

Perhaps they were both keeping secrets.

CHAPTER 7
A GAMBLER WITH GOOD FORTUNE

As Rosie waited in the buzzing foyer—full of tourists and employees alike excited for the imminent arrival of the most popular member of the Kaarmiach Five—she listened to the incessant babbling of the excited concierge beside her. His name was Oscar, and he was only fifteen, but his family, much like the majority in Roguerest, could barely afford the cost of living in such an affluent city. He'd begun working at The Ruby before Rosie had arrived and could always be seen with a smile on his tan face that brought out his dimples.

As she stood beside the concierge desk like a loyal dog, awaiting the arrival of the ominous Kitty Khalar, she repeatedly counted the foyer's entrances, exits, hazards, and helps to pass the time.

"Oh shit, she's actually here," Oscar swore from beside her. He pointed to the carriage stop outside the front of the hotel, where a sleek black motorcar had stopped, and a footman was opening the door.

"She's just a woman," Rosie huffed. "I don't understand what the big deal is."

He turned to her with a bewildered look. "*Just* a woman?

She's Kitty Khalar, reigning *kaarmiach* champion. She couldn't be *just a woman* if she tried."

"It's a good thing I was asked to look after her this weekend, otherwise she'd have to deal with your fumbling and bumbling." Rosie resisted the urge to roll her eyes. "She may be famous across all the territories and richer than either of us can even imagine, but she's still just a woman. One who was blessed with the divine ability of card play. She's just a gambler with good fortune."

Before Oscar could try to further convince her of the virtues of the card player, the woman of the hour ascended from her gleaming vehicle with more flourish than the gussied-up show-girls performing at Five Halves with all of their bells and tassels. The pictures that routinely circulated of Kitty Khalar in newspapers and on posters had not done her justice. Rosie was immediately sucked in by her mere presence despite the fact that she hadn't even stepped foot inside the hotel yet.

The young woman drifted forward from her car with a natural grace and was immediately surrounded by her entourage, draped in a cumbersome cloak of oil-slick feathers and groomed by multiple hands to fix her hair and outfit. Her glossy, onyx hair was cropped just above her jaw and the strip above her left ear was shaved to a stubble, revealing the tattooed symbols that originated from her homeland of Irredore. Her expression was schooled into immaculate composure as she waited for her posse to stop preening over her.

A small crowd had gathered at her arrival, screaming her name; they were audible even in the hotel foyer. She really was a spectacle.

She lazily held up a hand, and her team immediately backed away from her, leaving her to glance over the growing crowd and gently wave as she began striding up the steps of The Ruby. Her aura was that of royalty, and she was clearly aware of it. Her loyal employees followed behind her, carrying luggage that was swiftly taken from them by the hotel's porters and placed onto gold luggage carts.

Be available, be observant, be invisible.

"What a waste of space," Rosie muttered to herself, envisaging the lousy weekend ahead and the preposterous tasks she'd have to endure. She had much more interesting things to consider. Things that involved *wine.*

"Are you kidding me?" Oscar gasped. "Just look at her. She should be *royalty.*"

"No, she should stop acting mightier than everyone else. *Gods,* just look at her waltzing in as if she owns the place."

"That's the waltz of a winner. I've already placed my bets on her for this weekend, so she'd better live up to her reputation."

Kitty pushed through the revolving door and arrived in the foyer with pure arrogance, her feathered cloak trailing just behind her and her entourage of four behind that. The group consisted of three women and a young boy, perhaps only ten or so. They stood stationary, taking in the sight of the gaudy foyer in awe, but Kitty appeared bored.

Rosie had to swallow the bitter taste in her mouth and hold back the eye roll begging to come out. Instead, she took the moment to step forward.

"Hello there, I'm—"

"Miss Khalar, what an absolute honour it is to have you. My name is Jakob, and I'm the manager here at The Ruby Talisman Casino and Hotel, the finest hotel in all of Roguerest." Jakob's slimy hospitality voice preceded him as he seemed to appear from nowhere, approaching Kitty with his right hand over his heart in an Irredorian gesture of greeting and respect. "We've been anticipating your arrival since the moment it was announced we'd be hosting the *kaarmiach* final, and I can't tell you how pleased we are to accommodate you here for the tournament. We have stopped at absolutely nothing to ensure your stay here with us is luxurious, enjoyable, and, of course, comfortable."

Kitty's expression remained solemn and unamused.

Jakob fumbled to fill the silence. "We've assigned you a personal liaison from The Ruby Talisman as you requested prior to your arrival. She will assist and advise you throughout the duration of your stay with us. Whatever you need, you can ask her at all hours of the day, and she'll do her best to indulge your every whim. I can assure you that she'll prove more efficient and trustworthy than your previous personal liaisons. This is Rosie Wren."

Kitty's face remained unchanged, save for a slight raise of her eyebrow. Rosie itched to wipe the ego away with her nimble hands.

How would she like to be duped? To have her precious fortune snatched away by a lowly personal liaison?

"*Rosie*," Jakob hissed, clicking his fingers and pointing to the space next to him.

She wanted nothing more than to throttle him for treating her like some sort of dog, but instead gritted her teeth and took a deep breath, moving forward to greet the spectacle of a woman in front of them with her hand over her heart. The gesture was not common outside of Irredore, especially since the civil war there, but Rosie knew there'd be consequences if she didn't fawn over the woman in whatever way possible.

Be available, be observant, be invisible.

"Miss Khalar, it's a pleasure to meet you. My name is Rosie, and I'll be your personal liaison during your stay here at The Ruby Talisman."

She felt like a broken record, repeating all the information that Jakob had already provided, but she had to do it out of courtesy for their VIP guest. Her cheeks flamed at the level she'd been reduced to whilst working at The Ruby, but she feared that Lawrence had cronies covertly watching the exchange. Though she knew she could push her luck with Jakob, another run-in so soon after the previous day with the *people's hero of Roguerest* was not high on her to-do list.

Kitty belatedly flicked her eyes over Rosie but showed no hints as to whether she approved of her new servant or not—something that only proved to further infuriate Rosie.

Who did she think she was?

The entire foyer had hushed to listen to the exchange, every person waiting with baited breath to finally hear Kitty speak.

When she did, it was rather anticlimactic.

"I see," was all she said, nonchalantly gesturing to one of her entourage to come forward so that she could murmur something in their ear.

Jakob took the opportunity to bend down slightly and warn Rosie. "If I hear that you have behaved anything but obedient, I will ensure that my father extends your servitude from ten years to twenty."

Apparently, the developing compassion from the day before had vanished as soon as duty called. Jakob was nothing if not predictable. Perhaps Lawrence did have cronies watching after all.

"I would never—"

"Don't try me, Rosie." He stood straight again and fixed his phoney smile back onto his face.

Nine more years, Rosie told herself. *Just nine more years of this and then I'm free again. Unless...*

"Miss Khalar is rather tired from the long journey," one of her employees said. "Could we please be escorted to our rooms?"

"Of course. Of course." Jakob gave Rosie a solitary slap on

the back, and she jolted forward, turning to lead the way to the lifts through an archway next to the reception desk.

Rosie felt as if a thousand eyes were upon them as they traversed the foyer, multiple sets of footsteps echoing her own. The base of her neck tingled under watchful gazes as she covertly straightened her uniform without breaking pace. She sincerely hoped she was doing nothing worthy of later punishment.

She signalled the attendant as they approached the lifts, and he scrambled to hail multiple for the large group. When the first car slid its doors open, Rosie stood aside and gestured for Kitty to enter first. A smug-looking Jakob followed her. Content to allow the lift to fill with Kitty's entourage and then take the next car, she remained to one side as the first of the group stepped forward.

However, the enigmatic VIP had other plans. She wordlessly held a hand up to her assistant, who immediately stopped and took a step back. Kitty then made eye contact with Rosie and indicated with a leisurely come-hither gesture that she was to join them.

Gods, Rosie inwardly cursed but boarded the car anyway, watching as the attendant, Vanya, closed the inner gate and pressed the button for the penthouse floor with the utmost delicacy.

As the outer doors closed, a heady silence fell upon the four of them.

Rosie waited. Gears ground. Cables scraped.

Still, she waited.

She cleared her throat. Vanya sniffed. Jakob adjusted his tie.

They waited.

Rosie shifted her weight to the other foot. Kitty remained still as a statue.

"The penthouse suites," Vanya mercifully announced a

moment later. She pulled the inner gate aside just as the doors opened, revealing the plush interior of the penthouse corridor.

Kitty strode forward without needing encouragement. A stray feather from her cloak on the floor of the lift was the only clue that she'd stepped foot there. Jakob ignored the task of picking it up—of course, it was beneath him. Rosie resisted the urge to growl in annoyance and plucked the feather up, handing it to Vanya. Giving her a friendly smile and a salute, she followed the top dogs into the corridor. Though she'd been at The Ruby a year, Rosie still cringed in second-hand embarrassment at the splashy decor, her cheeks glowing almost the same colour as the wallpaper.

The wood trimming throughout the corridor had been painted a garish gold, matching the lustrous furniture and oversized chandeliers. The hand-painted wallpaper varied in shades of red, detailing a seemingly never-ending forest with woodland animals and gold flowers to accent it. There were only two doors in the corridor, both painted gold and leading to the two exorbitant suites making up the penthouse complex.

On the floor below them were the eight State Suites where the other VIPs and their teams were staying for the tournament. Rosie wondered if they acknowledged the clear favouritism that followed them wherever they went and if it rankled them or not.

Though the penthouse suites were connected by an adjoining door inside, Rosie doubted that it would be unlocked for the duration of this stay. She assumed that Kitty would have an entire suite to herself and her posse would have to bunk up and divvy the remaining suite between them. She envisaged having to fetch numerous sets of extra bedding as well as folding beds.

Perfect.

"You'll be staying in Suite Rouge for the weekend, Miss

Khalar," Jakob fawned as he pulled a large key from the inside pocket of his perfectly pressed suit. As he unlocked the door, the sounds of another lift arriving on their floor with the gaggle of Kitty's associates onboard could be heard.

Jakob pushed open the large door and then pinned Rosie with an icy glare.

"Go and show Miss Khalar's employees to their suite," he instructed without preamble. "I'll ensure that Miss Khalar is settled and understands *exactly* what your job is."

Be available, be observant, be invisible.

He held out a matching key to the one still in the door of Suite Rouge for her to take, but it never made it into her hand.

"That won't be necessary," a conceited voice spoke from just inside of the suite. Both Jakob and Rosie turned to look at Kitty, surprised to have heard her voice once again.

"Miss Khalar, I—"

"You may go, Jakal."

"I—" Jakob flushed and clenched his jaw. "Of course, Miss Khalar. If you need anything at all, please don't hesitate to call the foyer and ask for *Jakob.* They will direct you straight to me."

Though she showed no outward emotion, Rosie could've sworn that she saw Kitty's eyes crinkle ever so slightly in the corners. She didn't respond to Jakob's comment.

Rosie gave him a smug grin as she pointed to the waiting guests at the other side of the corridor.

"Behave," he grunted.

"As if my leash will allow me to do anything else," she replied lowly enough that Kitty wouldn't hear.

They parted ways, and the tightness in her chest abated just enough that she could enter the suite and close the door behind her. She prepared to further introduce herself and detail the itinerary for the weekend.

Be available, be observant, be—

"Rosie."

She twisted to face her temporary overseer.

"Yes, Miss Khalar?"

"Are you to stay in this suite with me?"

"Yes. There's a butler's cupboard that I'll be staying in in case you need me throughout the night. However, if it makes you uncomfortable to have someone else—"

"Where is this cupboard?"

Feeling bowled over by the mere presence of the young woman in front of her, Rosie opened and closed her mouth a couple of times before coming to the conclusion that nothing else would come out. Rosie escorted Kitty to an inconspicuous door, disguised as one of the mahogany wall panels, and pressed a segment of the dado rail that was a hidden door handle. The panel swung silently inwards, and Rosie clicked the lamp on as she strode in.

Embarrassment rolled off her in waves as she lowered her head at the sight of her room for the weekend. It was slightly bigger than the one she usually stayed in next to the kitchens, but this one had no bed. A pile of blankets and pillows on the floor between two shelving units signalled where she'd be attempting to rest for the forthcoming nights.

She waited for Kitty to say something but was once again left in silence. Humiliated and unable to bear it for a second longer, she glanced up to see that the woman of the hour was staring at her with profound interest.

In the dim lamp light, her eyes glowed a magnificent emerald hue against her brown skin. It immobilised Rosie, her breath caught in her throat. From the side, she could see that Kitty's nose was slightly hooked and her chin protruded beneath her full lips. Every one of her features had somehow been accentuated with shaded powders applied to the contours of her face. She was quite possibly the most beautiful young woman Rosie had ever met.

Kitty's husky voice broke the silence. "Your complete submission is rather astounding."

Of all the things Rosie had imagined her saying in that moment, from jeering and mocking to pitiful apologies, the detached but factual statement that rolled so effortlessly off her tongue was not one of them.

Rosie spluttered, "Excuse me?"

Kitty blinked a couple of times as if checking herself and cleared her throat. "I meant to say that you're to stay here. I don't want you out of my sight."

What a bizarre woman, Rosie thought.

"Of course, Miss Khalar," she replied without hesitation.

Kitty began to walk away but thought better of it at the last moment.

"And, Rosie?"

"Yes, Miss Khalar?"

"Call me Kit."

CHAPTER 8
BAND OF MOTLEY INDIVIDUALS

After allowing several porters in to deposit numerous green leather trunks, Rosie busied herself in the kitchen as Kit explored the rest of the suite. There was a thick layer of tension that Rosie desperately wanted to cut through, but she had no idea how; so she busied herself with other jobs that she assumed Kit would want her personal liaison to do. She began boiling a kettle full of water on the stove in case Kit required a hot drink and double-checked the walk-in pantry to ensure that everything she'd filled it with that morning was still there.

Upon leaving the pantry, Rosie was surprised to see the woman of the hour propped against the kitchen island, waiting for her. She'd removed her ostentatious feathered cloak to reveal a more modest outfit underneath; a simple black blouse with matching tailored trousers. She looked oddly normal in the kitchen, and Rosie found herself slightly taken aback by it.

"Is everything all right, Miss—ah, Kit? Would you like some tea or maybe something to eat? The water should almost be boiled."

"Tea sounds wonderful." Kit's stoic expression warmed. "Enough for six, if you could."

"Of course."

Kit watched with vague interest as Rosie sought a bone china teapot with matching floral teacups from one of the cupboards. She painstakingly placed each teacup onto a saucer and adorned every one with a strainer and a small tea biscuit that had been baked fresh that morning. Turning to the shelf that held several glass jars filled with tea leaves, she paused and looked back to Kit.

"Which tea would you prefer?"

Kit tilted her head slightly. "Which would you recommend?"

Surprised at her question as opposed to a demand, Rosie paused before suggesting vosofras; a sweet, floral blend local to Roguerest. As she prepared the pot and reached for the kettle, a knock on the internal door sounded throughout the suite. Rosie paused making the tea and shifted towards the door when Kit held up a hand.

"You finish the tea." She appeared amused. "I can manage answering the door by myself."

Rosie frowned and could feel frustration brewing as she tried to pin Kit down. Despite the aloof, conceited character that had not long ago swaggered through the hotel's foyer, the young woman appeared to be more talkative and amiable behind closed doors. Rosie didn't let herself overthink the contradiction as she heard several people entering the suite. The fragrant vosofras filled the air as footsteps came closer.

"—will start unpacking the trunks."

"We'll need to press your outfit for this evening, assuming that you'll be making an appearance in one of the restaurants."

"I need the trunk with my herbs and ingredients in it. The

porters must have brought it in here by mistake because it's not in our suite."

Rosie didn't look up as she finished pouring the boiling water into the tea pot and placed the dainty lid on with a quiet *clink*.

She hoped the entourage liked her. She hoped they weren't too aggravating over the weekend. She even hoped that perhaps one of them would treat her with respect, though she wasn't counting on it. They never did. She supposed, however, that Kit was already proving to be different to her initial expectations, so maybe the entourage wouldn't be so bad either.

"That's all well and good, but I think some introductions should be made first." Kit's voice stuck out amongst the other unfamiliar ones.

Rosie made sure to keep her gaze trained on the pot of tea as the group approached, her foot tapping quietly.

She felt anxiety bubbling in the centre of her chest and a tightness in her lungs.

Be available, be observant, be—

"Rosie."

She lifted her head to see Kit standing with the three women who'd accompanied her into the hotel. The four of them were looking at her expectantly, and she lurched forward to begin pouring the tea.

"Apologies," she muttered.

"That can wait," Kit interrupted. "It won't be properly brewed yet."

"Can I fetch you all something to eat?" Rosie tried instead. "Fresh pastry? There's a loaf of bread that was baked just this morning. If you'd prefer that I make you some—"

Kit held up her hand again, a gesture that Rosie began to realise she did often when she wanted quiet.

Was it charming or rude? Rosie couldn't tell.

"Let me introduce you to the band of motley individuals that I keep around." Kit gestured to the three women with flourish. "First of all, we have Florelle. She ensures that we all stay healthy throughout our travels. She keeps a stock of medicinal ingredients and has a keen interest in plants and wildlife. Feel free to share any knowledge you have of local fauna with her; I'm sure she'd be more than thrilled to add to her vast catalogue."

Florelle was a short and curvy young woman, perhaps five or so years older than Rosie, with a mass of long, mossy green braids arranged in a swirl on top of her head. A handful of the braids hung down to her hips, adorned with gold thread and burnished beads that caught the light when she moved. She didn't maintain eye contact for long before she looked away, twisting one of the many rings on her fingers.

"Then we have Jal," Kit continued, gesturing to the taller woman in the middle. "Her tasks include outfitting me on a daily basis and providing me with any alterations."

Jal was a willowy natural beauty and the tallest of the group. She wore a white lace smock that cinched in to accentuate a tiny waist. Rosie tried not to stare as she took in the uneven scarring on the bronzed skin of her face.

"Nice to meet you." Jal's voice was warm and welcoming.

Rosie nodded but didn't reply as Kit pointed to the last of the women.

"And this here is Mae. Jack of all trades, she is essential to our travels and is very good at...*adapting* to our multitude of needs." The two women shot each other a look of amusement as if there was an inside joke that Rosie didn't understand.

Mae's lazy posture and crossed arms spoke of confidence that Rosie wished she possessed. She wore a white, collared shirt that appeared to be tailored for men; it gave her frame a more androgynous appearance. Rosie spied the waistband of some black leather trousers and wondered how she could survive in the heat wearing the tight garment.

"It's a pleasure to meet you all," she greeted, still uncomfortable and feeling awkward. "Would you like some tea?"

"That'd be great." Mae winked at her and leaned on the marble counter on her forearms. "Whatever tea you've chosen smells incredible. Are they shortbreads?"

Rosie paused as she went to slide a cup across to her, pleasantly surprised at Mae's warmth and how it made the anxiety in her chest fizzle out. Perhaps they wouldn't be so bad to deal with after all.

"Yes," she replied. "They were freshly made this morning for you."

Mae grabbed several from the plate in the centre of the kitchen island whilst also taking the one from her saucer.

"I'm going to see if my trunk is in here," Florelle said quietly to Kit, then looked at Rosie with a timid smile. "I'll come back for some tea. Thank you."

Rosie began pouring tea into the six cups, meticulously wiping away any stray drips. Only once the three remaining women had taken some tea did Kit signal to one of the remaining cups.

"You can have some too."

Rosie looked up to meet her gaze and frowned.

The sixth cup was for her?

"Oh." She swallowed and licked her suddenly dry lips. "I mean, thank you."

Who *was* Kitty Khalar? Was she the imposing enigma or the relaxed employer offering tea?

Before Rosie could give it much more consideration, rapid footsteps could be heard coming through the adjoining door into the suite. The young boy who'd accompanied the women into the foyer came bounding through, tendrils of his shoulder-length hair escaping from the restraint at the base of his neck as he ran.

"Kit!" He reached them with some sort of palm-sized contraption in his hand, made up of nuts and bolts and random pieces of metal. He whined, "It got broken in the move, now what am I going to do?"

Kit raised an eyebrow, and her expression took on a childish amusement that almost made Rosie take a step back. The expression was a direct contradiction of every poster and newspaper article she'd ever seen with Kit's face on it. The sharp angles were infinitely softer.

"I'm sure you'll fix it up as you always do, Hud. Where are your manners? Put the device down and introduce yourself to our personal liaison for the weekend."

He groaned and slid the mass of metal onto the kitchen island before turning around to Rosie, making sure to drag his feet a little.

"I'm Hud." He held out a hand, which Rosie shook. "I'm the next biggest inventor in all of the Twelve Territories. You can have my autograph now if you'd like."

Rosie couldn't help but smile at the young boy's audacious attitude.

"It's a pleasure, Hud. I'm Rosie. If there's anything you need over this weekend, don't hesitate to find me and I'll see if I can fix something up. There's a cup of tea for you here."

Hud scrunched his nose and shook his head. "Tea is gross."

"Drink the tea, little one." Jal's eyes crinkled in the corners as she spoke like an older sister might. "It might give you the growth spurt you've been so patiently waiting on."

"*Fine.*" He noisily slurped one of the teas down despite the heat and haphazardly tossed the cup back onto the saucer with a rattle. Rosie gritted her teeth but relaxed when the cup was mercifully still in one piece. He scooped his contraption back up and dashed out of the room once again, a whirlwind of gangly, pale limbs.

"So that's Hud," Mae said with barely restrained laughter. "He's our little apprentice."

"He seems...lively," Rosie responded, to which all three women broke out into similar smiles.

Jal rolled her eyes. "'Lively' is certainly one descriptor." She finished her tea and pushed the cup and saucer across the island. "I really should get on with the unpacking and ironing of all our clothes. We decided that I'd take the spare room in this suite so all of your clothes are in here with the two of us," she addressed Kit. "Is that all right?"

"Of course. Do you need help?"

"No, I'll be okay. I can put Hud to work. He should do something to help every now and again."

Kit was allowing her employees to stay in her suite *and* offering to help unpack?

Rosie couldn't help but be surprised—yet again—at the strange woman in charge. She couldn't decide if she should reprimand herself for making such broad initial judgements or stay guarded in case it was all an elaborate ruse to gain her trust only to humiliate her later on.

She wouldn't put it past Lawrence to plan something like that. In fact, she'd grown to expect it of him.

"I'm gonna to get on with unpacking too," Mae decided as she straightened. "Thanks for the tea, Rosie."

Instead of replying, Rosie began quietly clearing away the tea cups, save for Kit's that remained grasped in her hand. She piled them next to the deep kitchen sink and began filling it with hot, soapy water. The otherwise static silence of the room had her hackles raised, and she once again felt the sensation of being watched from behind.

Her chest tightened.

Be available, be observant—

"Rosie."

Kit was much closer when she turned around, holding her teacup out between two long fingers.

"Thank you," Rosie murmured, taking the cup. "I'll wash these, and then I can help with unpacking if you'd—"

"All of that can wait. Let's go over my itinerary for the weekend so that we're both singing from the same song sheet, as it were."

"Oh. Of course." Rosie hastily dried her hands and followed Kit to the sofas.

Kit draped herself across one of the red velvet sofas with the arrogance of the celebrity she'd been in the foyer. Her legs were gently crossed at the ankles and resting to one side as she propped herself up on her elbow and lazily gestured for Rosie to come closer. She was the epitome of poise and grace once more, her expression carefully curated into vague interest.

She'd somehow transitioned from relaxed employer to imposing enigma again. The scariest part was how effortless the shift was, as if practised over and over again until it became natural to remain in a constant state of transformation. Rosie vaguely considered what the real Kit might act like when she was alone with no one to cast judgement. Was she an empty husk, unsure of her true identity? Or was she more alive than ever, a free soul no longer trapped by the bounds of societal expectation?

"You can sit, Rosie."

She gingerly did as was told and found her fingers drumming lightly against her knee. She had the strange urge to burst out into song or dance just to break the seal of tension that had settled on them.

"There are several compulsory functions over the weekend

for me to attend," Kit stated. "Can you remind me what they are?"

"Yes." Rosie wrung her fingers in her lap as she was put on the spot. "There's a formal dinner for you and the other finalists tomorrow night before the first game, which will begin after a short break. The following day, you'll have a luncheon, again with the other finalists and various other VIP guests, before proceeding with the final round of the tournament that evening."

Kit didn't appear excited or fazed by the information.

"And what about tonight?"

Rosie paused. "Tonight?"

"You didn't specify any activities tonight."

"I can certainly try to organise something for you. There's plenty to see throughout the city that I'm sure would interest you. I won't be able to join you because I have to sing in the hotel tonight, but I can arrange an escort to—"

"You sing?"

Rosie scrambled to keep up with her rapidly changing attention.

"Yes, I'm—I sing in the hotel every Friday night as part of my employment contract." Kit didn't acknowledge the information in any way, so Rosie rambled on. "You're welcome to explore the hotel and casino this evening. It has an eclectic mix of restaurants, bars, and other social spaces that I'm sure you'll love. I'm more than happy to give you a tour of the building before I go to perform later."

"That won't be necessary."

It felt like one step forward and two back every time Kit spoke. Rosie frowned a little as she tried to figure out what the young woman wanted.

"How about I—"

"I think I'll watch you sing this evening," Kit continued,

thoroughly surprising Rosie and adding a new dimension of pressure to the performance.

"You will?"

Kit gave an almost imperceptible nod.

"I start at eight," Rosie explained. "I can organise a VIP booth for you so you're not swarmed by the riff-raff."

Kit pursed her lips. "Yes, that will be necessary."

"Is there anything else you wanted to do whilst in Roguerest? I can organise any excursions or meetings for you."

Kit's gaze drifted to one of the large windows in the suite, showcasing the surrounding roofs and buildings below. She was quiet for a few moments before turning back to Rosie.

"I'd like a tour of the city tomorrow by a local—by *you*, in fact. I don't want any glamour or celebrity treatment. I want a simple tour of the most precious and real parts of the city by someone who knows it well. Am I to assume that you're the best person for the job?"

Rosie's brain spluttered to a stop as she tried to process how she might pull off such a feat. If Kit wanted a local's tour of the city, then Rosie was most definitely the person for the job, but it would mean another run-in with Lawrence. The thought of his slimy touch made her shiver and bile bubble in her throat.

Was the possibility of Lawrence touching her again—exercising his control over her body again—worth the opportunity to leave The Ruby?

One glance out of the window and then back to the world-famous card player in front of her told her everything she needed to know.

Absolutely.

She couldn't give up any opportunity this weekend, no matter how uncomfortable it made her. This was a once-in-a-lifetime occasion.

"I'll have to...I need to get permission first," she explained, unsure of how much Kit knew about her sentence. "I'll check with my boss that my duties to you can include a tour of the city."

Kit smirked and leaned forward so that her elbows rested lazily on her knees.

"Surely, your duties to me are whatever I deem them to be?"

Rosie swallowed a lump in her throat. "Yes. I suppose you're right. But I still need to get permission from Lawrence—*ah,* Mr Haart."

Kit studied her for long enough that Rosie noticed, leaving her feeling flayed open and wanting to retreat into herself. Her skin prickled, and she blinked several times, hoping it would break Kit out of the moment.

What did Kitty Khalar see when she looked at her? A mere maid? A naive teenager?

"Very well," Kit dismissed and let her gaze fall back to the large window again. Rosie took it as a hint to leave and stood, making her way into the kitchen to clean up the remnants of their tea.

Florelle wandered back into the living space from the bedroom with a slightly scrunched brow, fiddling with one of her braids.

"I can't find my trunk in here either," she explained to Kit. "It's not here."

"You've checked outside in the corridor?"

Florelle nodded. "It's definitely not here."

Kit looked over at Rosie and she flushed as she averted her gaze to the washing up, embarrassed that she'd been caught watching their exchange instead of pretending not to exist like she was supposed to.

"Don't fuss with that," Kit called from the sofa and beckoned her over with a wave. "I need you to help Florelle track down her missing trunk. I'm sure it hasn't gone far."

"Of course," Rosie replied with a nod, smiling at Florelle, who looked at her feet when their eyes met.

"Whilst you're at it, go and organise whatever you need to do for a tour tomorrow," Kit added. "And could you ask that scheming manager of yours to join me for breakfast here in the morning? We have business to discuss."

Rosie hid her surprise at the request.

What business did Kit have with Jakob?

Pushing her questions away, she replied, "Right away."

CHAPTER 9

LOST LUGGAGE

I t wasn't until they were in the lift halfway down to the foyer that Rosie realised that if she didn't broach a conversation first, the timid Florelle wouldn't talk at all.

"So..." Rosie broke the awkward silence, flicking her gaze to Vanya, who stared straight ahead, pretending not to listen. "How was...your journey?"

She cringed immediately at the cliché question and had to stop herself from smacking her forehead.

Seriously? That's what she was going with?

"Uh, it was long. I guess."

Rosie nodded, then realised that Florelle wasn't saying anything else.

"Where did you come from?"

She looked over to the young woman and saw her staring intently at her feet, wringing her hands in front of her.

"Shretha."

Rosie blew out a deep breath as she realised that attempting conversation was more painful than Jakob's attempts to act sympathetic.

Nevertheless, Rosie pushed, "Where's that?"

Vanya cleared her throat in the silence that followed, and Rosie felt like crawling out her own skin to avoid the awkwardness. She was really trying, but Florelle was potentially the most introverted person she'd ever come in contact with.

"It's on the...the southern coast of Etetalle." Florelle finally looked up to meet her gaze, but immediately looked away again. "Near the border with Blue Reach."

Rosie nodded, trying to encourage her, only to remember she wasn't looking.

"So that must be a four or five day drive from here?"

Florelle nodded.

"At least you have those fancy motorcars, though," Rosie pressed. "Are they as comfortable as they look?"

Florelle nodded.

Just as Rosie was about to heave out a sigh of frustration, the lift pinged for the ground floor.

"Foyer," Vanya announced, giving Rosie a sympathetic smile as the doors slid open.

"Thanks, Vanya," she mumbled, running a hand through her hair as she and Florelle walked off the lift and into the zoo that was the main foyer.

"We'll start at the concierge," she explained without looking back. "I'm not sure how a trunk could've disappeared between your arrival and our journey upstairs, but stranger things have happened—"

She turned to look at Florelle and realised she wasn't behind her, leaving her talking to herself. Rosie frowned and craned her neck to try and see where she could've gone, but wherever it was, she'd been swallowed up by the excitement of the masses and the wailing saxophone coming from one of the bars where a band was playing.

She half-heartedly called out, "Florelle?"

She was shoved forward by someone passing behind her

and grunted in frustration, blowing out a calming breath as the hoards continued to shout and laugh and sing and be sickeningly *joyful*.

The saxophone transitioned into a dramatic but upbeat piano solo that had people around her up on their feet dancing. She still couldn't see Florelle as everyone moved around her, and it only annoyed her more.

She decided to head back the way she'd come, unceremoniously pushing through guests and employees alike until she reached the bank of lifts again. Rosie wanted to let out a shout of frustration, but instead held onto the little patience she had left and made her way out to the concierge desk instead.

She'd have to find Florelle later once she'd tracked down her luggage. She could already tell that the weekend was going to be a long one.

"Oscar," she greeted the young concierge who was writing an appointment in the diary on his desk. He looked up at her, and his signature dimples came out as he smiled.

"Shouldn't you be brushing shoulders with the big wigs?"

She huffed. "They're already proving more trouble than they're worth. Has the entirety of the Twelve Territories descended on the hotel?"

She gestured to the madness surrounding them. Hundreds of people had piled into the foyer and were spilling into the casino and bars.

"As soon as Miss Khalar was out of sight, they let every man and their dog into the hotel. Everyone is desperate to catch a glimpse of Kitty or one of the other Kaarmiach Five. I bet Jakob is rubbing his hands together in glee at the amount of money piling in already."

They rolled their eyes in unison, then laughed.

"Anyway." Oscar clapped his hands together. "What can I do for you?"

"One of Kitty's guests is missing some of her luggage," Rosie explained, eliciting a frown from Oscar. "My thoughts exactly. Her name is Florelle, and I'm assuming it's a green trunk like the rest of them. It's full of herbs, and I've been tasked with tracking it down."

Oscar drummed his fingers on his desk as he thought. "The only suggestion I have is to check the motorcars in case it was left behind. I suppose if it wasn't labelled and then passed through a few people, it could've gotten lost in translation, in which case, it'll have been taken to the lost luggage room. It's right by the garage anyway, so you might as well check both."

Rosie groaned out her frustration and rested her head on the concierge desk. Oscar chuckled.

"Come on, songbird. The weekend's only just beginning."

She scoffed. "You mean the nightmare's only just beginning."

The garage was easily accessed from the employee corridor in the basement of the hotel. It contained a vast array of carriages and even some motorcycles. This weekend, however, there were several sleek motorcars parked in neat lines, all belonging to the Kaarmiach Five. The glossy paint and smooth curves of the bodywork were illuminated by the lights overhead, and Rosie took a moment in the otherwise quiet garage to ogle the marvels in front of her.

She reached out to touch one of them, almost afraid it would bite as her fingers made contact with the cold metal of the large, round headlights, akin to eyes in a face.

She was touching a real-life *motorcar*. What was her life?

She laughed, and it reverberated through the garage as she began peeking into all of the vehicles, pressing her nose against the glass of the windows and trying to guess which car belonged to which member of the Five.

Purpose entirely forgotten, she tried one of the doors to a particularly outrageous two-seater and found it open. She wasted no time climbing inside, restraining a cackle as she felt the smooth leather seats beneath her and reached out for the steering wheel. Pretending to drive was even more fun than she'd imagined, and she took a rare moment of unadulterated enjoyment in imagining herself speeding across the territories, the wind blowing through her hair and laughter howling from her chest.

In her daydream, she had a stolen painting on the passenger seat and a bag full of pilfered cash in the floor well. She was flying down a dirt road away from the demons of Roguerest and towards the freedom that called to her on a daily basis. She was on her way to—

The creaking of the door into the garage gave her pause. She ducked down in her seat and looked across the garage to see an unfamiliar man entering from the employee corridor. The first thing that caught her attention was his impeccably tailored suit and sharp haircut. His glossy black shoes reflected the lights, and his numerous rings glinted as he lit up a cigarette. His skin was a golden brown colour, and his dark hair was styled similarly to how Jakob wore his, giving the man a youthful appearance.

Rosie watched him for a minute or so as he smoked and leaned against the concrete wall of the garage. She couldn't place him no matter how hard she tried, which made her increasingly frustrated. He'd used the employee corridor and was clearly familiar with the hotel, so how had she never come across him before?

She was sure she'd remember his roguish beauty and sharp jawline.

Just as she was about to get out of the car and introduce herself, the door to the corridor creaked open again, and she held her breath as she watched Khristann walk through in his chef's whites.

Rosie ducked down in her seat further. She could barely see above the dashboard of the motorcar, only just able to see Khristann's head as he saw the mystery man and a smile broke out across his face. Rosie was glad that she'd left the door to the vehicle ajar as she heard the beginnings of their conversation.

"Rupee, my man." Khristann laughed, and they pulled each other into a familiar embrace, holding on tight for a few moments.

Rupee? Who was this man?

The two of them began shoving each other playfully like brothers before Rupee offered Khristann a cigarette. He surprised Rosie entirely by accepting the offer.

She frowned as her heart beat a little faster in her chest.

What was she witnessing?

Khristann asked, "Since when did you have a beard?"

Rupee chuckled and scrubbed a hand over his short, neat beard.

"Since travelling around the territories on a wild goose chase became my main occupation," he replied, crushing the stub of his cigarette beneath his shoe. "How've you been?"

"You know how it goes," Khristann replied vaguely, giving a quick glance around them to confirm the garage was empty. Seemingly happy with his findings, he continued, "Jakob has been breathing down my neck all week."

"Why does that not surprise me?" Rupee huffed, shaking his head.

Rosie sucked in a breath.

Did Rupee know Jakob?

"I'll be glad when this weekend is over and we can get back to normal. It's been a long year," Khristann said.

"That's an understatement. I'm just excited to have your culinary prowess back in my life again. I've missed your falafel flatbreads."

Khristann chuckled as he blew smoke above their heads.

"I'll get you one sorted as soon as I have a minute to breathe."

"Monday morning, then?"

They both laughed and nudged each other like old friends, leaving Rosie baffled as to who Rupee was and how they knew each other. They were clearly friends from before Khristann's time at The Ruby.

Rosie was growing uncomfortable with how much she actually knew about Khristann. She'd always thought of him as a chef first and foremost, but she hadn't considered that he had a life outside of The Ruby. She didn't have a life outside of it, so it was hard to imagine that all of the other employees got to go home each day and see family or friends.

There was a whole side to Khristann that she had no clue about, that he'd never shared with her. But his mysterious meeting with an unknown man was definitely suspicious. Combined with the fact that they both knew Jakob and that Khristann apparently smoked in his spare time, did Rosie really know him at all?

"I should probably get back before someone starts whining," Khristann said, stubbing out his own cigarette on the floor. "It was good to see you again, Ru. I've missed you."

"You mean you've missed my hand-rolled herbals," he teased, holding up a tin of what Rosie assumed were cigarettes.

"That too," Khristann replied, pulling him back into a hug. "Come down to the kitchens whenever you want some good grub. Even if I'm busy, I'll find some time to fix you up with something."

"Sounds good."

They parted with some playful back slaps, and Khristann disappeared into the employee corridor again, leaving the garage in peaceful silence once more with only the lingering smell of basil and lemongrass from the cigarettes.

Rosie watched as Rupee tucked the small tin into his jacket pocket and straightened his tie. He was as tall as Khristann, perhaps six and a half feet, but his skin was a much warmer and slightly lighter shade of brown. Plus, his face was a slimmer shape, and his cheekbones were higher. They definitely weren't related, but were obviously very close friends.

Rosie watched him whistle a jolly tune as he waited long enough to not arouse suspicion, then made his way into the corridor as well. Finally on her own again, Rosie sat up in the car and heaved out a breath, not sure where to start with gathering her thoughts.

The emotion overriding everything else seemed to be confusion. She thought that out of everyone in the hotel—everyone in Roguerest—that Khristann was her family and could be trusted. Was that still true?

She rested her head on the steering wheel for a second or two as she gathered her thoughts, the joy from before completely lost under the heavy dread settling on her shoulders.

She had no idea who to trust, no idea who she could turn to for advice. Normally, she would've confided in Khristann, but now he was the problem. She was utterly alone in this. Alone and overwhelmed.

Realising that she'd been away from Florelle and distracted from her task for too long, she hopped out of the car and straightened her uniform reflexively.

Luggage. She needed to find the lost luggage.

Checks inside all of the motorcars revealed no joy as far as belongings, so she crossed the garage and pushed through a rusting metal door that groaned open to reveal an elderly woman behind a desk, her half-moon glasses perched precariously on the end of her crooked nose. She looked up at Rosie's entrance. There were no windows and only a single bulb overhead to provide light. One wall was covered in shelving that held varying items and boxes that spilled over onto the floor.

The woman croaked, "What have you lost?"

So much, Rosie thought.

The woman closed the novel she was reading and heaved herself to a standing position, looking as if she might blow over at any moment from the slightest breeze. Her white hair was perfectly permed, and her Ruby uniform was pressed to perfection.

"Luggage," Rosie replied. "A green trunk that would've come in within the last half an hour."

The woman sighed and practically creaked as she fell back into her chair.

"Can't help you there. Nothing has come in yet this morning. No trunk. No bags. No people. You're my first visitor today, kid."

Rosie huffed out a frustrated breath but nodded with a tight smile anyway.

"Thank you"—she checked her name tag—"Dorothea."

Dorothea simply waved her away and cracked open her book again, dismissing Rosie without another look.

Now what would she do?

On her way back up to Suite Rouge, she tried to come up with an explanation that wouldn't frustrate Kit or Florelle. The trunk had mysteriously disappeared without a trace. How did she begin to explain that?

As she thanked Vanya on the way out of the lift on the penthouse floor, she began practising what she would say.

"I looked everywhere," she whispered. "I'll keep looking until I find it."

She looked up from her hands and stumbled to a stop. Her jaw clenched reflexively, and she closed her eyes whilst taking a deep breath.

"Typical," she muttered, opening her eyes again and looking down at the single green trunk waiting in front of the door to Suite Rouge.

CHAPTER 10

PINNED DOWN BY A GHOUL

Rosie learned from one of the receptionists in the foyer that Jakob was attending a meeting in the Gold Gates bar, one of many within the hotel. The bar was decorated as if it were the gates into Nirvana, the home of the righteous God, Aakla. White fabric had been draped on the ceiling to look like clouds, and Rosie imagined what it would be like to climb up and touch them. As she entered, the sounds of ice in cocktail shakers punctuated laughter and excited chatter. The smell of fried food wafted over her as a waitress breezed past with a tray of what looked like chicken wings and various dips. She counted every entrance and exit in the same way she breathed—without thought.

Rosie waved at the guard posted just inside the bar and approached the maître d'. Her face wasn't familiar to Rosie; though there were hundreds of employees, so it was impossible to know everyone.

"Hello"—she checked the woman's name tag and put on her friendliest smile—"Clarisa. I was told that Mr Haart was having a lunch meeting here, and I need to speak with him."

Clarisa pasted on an exaggerated smile.

"Unfortunately, Mr Haart asked not to be disturbed through his meeting."

"He says that frequently, but this is urgent. I know where his regular table is, so I'll just—"

"Rosie, please," she urged, her smile gone. "If you go over there, then my job is on the line."

"Jakob would never fire you for letting me through. He knows that I'm looking after a VIP right now. I need to speak with him." Rosie didn't explain herself further, darting past the maître d' station and up the few steps into the main bar.

"Rosie!"

She ignored the frustrated huffs behind her and pushed through the busy bar towards the back. Hanging fabric provided privacy to the several round booths. Rosie strode through gaps in the mass of people and soon found herself walking behind the circular bar and into the far corner.

The drapes around the booth were drawn closed; the two silhouettes behind the fabric were the only clue that it was occupied. Instead of ripping the drapes open like she wanted to, Rosie straightened her uniform and rolled her shoulders. She ran a hand through her hair and worked to unclench her jaw. It was only Jakob in there, but she had no idea who he was meeting with, so if she didn't look perfect, she could cause herself more trouble.

Deep breath in, deep breath out.

"Excuse me, Mr Haart?" she called out in her sweetest voice, knowing that humiliating Jakob in front of a client or business peer would only land her in hot water later on. Interrupting his meeting was bad enough.

"Yes?"

Rosie faltered. Two voices had called out in unison, which could only mean one thing. She panicked and backed away.

Unfortunately, a scowling Jakob pulled open the curtain before she could escape. Behind him in the booth sat Lawrence in all his tailored glory.

Just the sight of him made her body go rigid. Her tight chest sparked into a rumbling panic, just waiting to erupt.

"Rosie?" Jakob's eyebrows shot up. "Is everything all right?"

"I'm sorry—I didn't know you were with—I'll find you later."

Lawrence's unmistakable chuckle sent shudders through her body.

"Why don't you join us? It would be such a waste for you to have come all this way with no resolution to your problem."

"It's all right, sir. It's not urgent—"

"Sit," Lawrence demanded.

Jakob silently pleaded her with his gaze, and she relented, pushing down the dread rising from deep in her gut. She slid into the booth and ended up in the middle of the father-son duo, which meant that she was trapped until one of them let her leave.

As the drape around them fell closed again, the vague hope of a passerby protecting her diminished. She kept her gaze trained on the gold plating of the table, so shiny that she could almost see her reflection in it.

"To what do we owe the pleasure, dear Rosie?" Lawrence asked, swirling amber liquid in his glass. "I trust that you didn't interrupt our meeting for something menial?"

"No, I just—"

"Should you not be looking after Miss Khalar? Are you faltering on your duties already?"

"Not at all, I actually—"

"I trusted you, Rosie. I sincerely hope you're not embarrassing me or my business by dallying around the hotel. We've given you a privilege and an opportunity here. You're so lucky to be in this position."

She floundered and tried to control her quickening breathing. Should she interrupt Lawrence to try and save her hide or let him finish berating her for something she hadn't done? Luckily, Jakob made the decision for her.

"Father, let her speak. She clearly came here for a reason."

Rosie didn't dare move as she waited for Lawrence's response. Her hands closed into tight fists on her lap.

"Fair enough," he agreed. "Speak."

She tried to swallow back the nausea rising inside her, but somehow had no saliva left in her mouth.

"M-Miss Khalar is getting settled in Suite Rouge," she began, plucking up the courage to turn and look Lawrence in the eye. She immediately regretted it. "She's made a request that needs your approval."

Lawrence's expression was passive as he asked, "Which is?"

Rosie sucked in a deep breath, but it didn't help the suffocating sensation gripping her ribs.

"She'd like a tour of the city tomorrow. By a local." She paused and licked her dry lips. "By me."

"Is that right?" Lawrence's mouth quirked up, and he shook his head lightly as he took a sip of his drink.

"I told her that I'd have to ask for permission and that if I wasn't able to do it, I'd find someone else instead; but she insisted that I be the one to do it."

"I'm sure she did."

"Father," Jakob sighed. "We have to do everything we can to accommodate the woman. Our reputation is at stake here."

Lawrence closed his eyes for a second before piercing Rosie with a stare.

"Isn't it funny?" he asked, though Rosie knew from his tone that whatever *it* was, it certainly wasn't funny. "I give you one taste of the outside world, I grant you a true gift out of the goodness of my heart, and the following day, you come back to me demanding more. It appears Rosie Wren is greedy, isn't she?"

Rosie cringed as she plotted out the remainder of the conversation in her head. No matter what she said next, it wouldn't end in her favour. So she chose not to say anything at all. It would only get worse from here. She'd angered him. The panic brewing in her chest began to grow.

Be available, be observant, be invisible.

She dropped her gaze to the table and waited.

"Don't you think that I can see through you by now?" Lawrence lowered his voice to a murmur. "Do you suppose I'm a fool?"

Only the outside noise of the bar filled the silence that followed, though it seemed miles away from their secluded booth. Rosie's heart pounded. She'd never make it out of the binds that Lawrence held her in. She'd be underneath his thumb for the rest of her life. She had been naïve to think that she'd ever escape the treacherous monster that held a blade above her head. It was only a matter of time before he let it fall on her.

"Father, I can easily check whether this is a genuine request." Jakob's voice somehow sounded like a saviour. "I'll pay Miss Khalar a visit this afternoon to ensure she's settled in and happy with her accommodation."

Lawrence waited a beat before making a noise of agreement.

Jakob continued, "Was there anything else, Rosie?"

Strangely, she felt grateful for him trying to ease her discomfort. It was nothing close to standing up to his father for the cruelty and injustice done to her, but it was a damn sight better than nothing at all.

"Miss Khalar..." Rosie's voice cracked, and she cleared her throat, trying again as heat crept up the back of her neck. "Miss Khalar requested that you join her for breakfast in the morning. She mentioned that she had some business to discuss with you."

She looked up into Jakob's eyes and prayed that he wouldn't ask further questions. That he'd let her out of the stifling grip of his father.

He asked, "Just me?"

"Just you."

"Very well." He stood and fastened the button of his suit jacket. He moved out of the booth and held the drape open, gesturing for her to leave.

Thank the Gods.

She couldn't scramble up quickly enough as she scooted across the black leather of the booth and stood. Just as she stepped forward, the cool air of the bar gracing her skin and promising to tame her anxiety, a firm grip encircled her wrist from behind.

"Not so fast, Rosie."

So close. So *damn* close.

She was tugged back until she faced Lawrence once again, a wolfish grin adorning his features. He tightened his grip on her, his thumb rubbing circles on the back of her hand whilst Rosie tried to swallow down her revulsion.

It didn't work. It sat like a suffocating lump in her throat. If she tried to speak, she knew that nothing but a croak would escape. She looked away from his consuming stare and focused on his empty glass.

It was getting harder to breathe. She couldn't get air into her lungs. She couldn't focus on anything but the roiling, twisting, consuming sensation in her chest.

"If your request is genuine, then I expect to see you in the morning at eight o'clock in Jakob's office," Lawrence instructed. "I will alter your curse for the day, but please rest assured that you won't find an escape this time either."

His hand clamped down until she felt as if the bones in her hand would shatter.

"Look at me," he hissed. She reluctantly did, and his vicious stare imprinted itself on her brain. "If you dare to embarrass me, I promise you this: I will find you no matter where you try to hide, and I will rain down agony on you. You'll wish you'd spent your meagre freedom drowning yourself in the Industrial Sector basin."

Rosie flinched.

"Am I understood?"

"Yes." Her voice trembled. "Yes, sir."

"Wonderful." He beamed as if he'd just offered her the trip of a lifetime rather than a death sentence. "Run along now, dear. Jakob and I have further business to discuss."

She didn't remember leaving. She didn't remember running through the hotel. She didn't remember any of the faces that she passed. She didn't know how long it took or how she got there, but she somehow ended up on her creaky bed in the basement, panting in tight breaths and clutching her ribs.

The room around her swirled and darkened as she gasped, tears streaming down the sides of her face and into her hair. Heat bloomed from the centre of her chest, and a tingling sensation spread across her tongue.

She could still feel his touch. She could still smell his cologne. She could still hear his voice. She couldn't escape. She would never escape. Forever. She'd be here forever. His slimy touch. His eyes. Those eyes. Forever.

Be available, be observant, be invisible.

Be available, be observant, be invisible.

Be available, be observant—

"Rosie!"

Hands grabbed her arms and held her down. She kicked out and tried to scream, but nothing would come out. She tried to gasp for air, but all she could see was those eyes. His eyes.

She scratched the hands that pinned her to the bed. She screamed. She couldn't have anyone touching her again. They needed to let go. It was *him* again; his clammy hands were gripping her like a vice.

Why wouldn't he let go?

"Rosie—*ow!* Rosie, it's me!"

Khristann's face filled her blurry vision, and she felt his warm palms settle either side of her sweating face.

"Don't touch me," she gasped. "Let go. Please, let go!"

His hands shot back, and he gingerly stepped away with his palms up in the air and a distraught look on his face.

Khristann. Not Lawrence. It was Khristann.

"Just breathe, songbird. I'm here now."

"Don't—don't touch me."

"I'm here; you're all right."

"He won't let go."

"You're okay now—"

"Nothing about this is okay!"

Rosie managed to grab onto some sense of reality. Sweat fell from her chin in a steady *drip, drip, drip* on her chest. Her lungs continued to heave as she realised just how ragged and strained her breathing was. Her throat ached, and her eyes burned.

"I'm sorry," she croaked and began to cry.

Khristann sat on the bed next to her, careful not to touch her but perched close enough to show his support. He murmured words of affection and comfort till she calmed. Though Rosie wasn't paying attention to what he said, their eyes remained locked on each other.

Her scarf—his eyes were the colour of her old scarf.

"Can I touch you?"

She hesitated but eventually nodded.

"Yes." Her throat was raw, and her voice was raspy.

He tenderly wiped the stray tears from her cheeks. "What happened to you?"

He held onto both of her hands, his touch nothing like the monster upstairs. His hands were warm and calloused, scarred from multiple cheffing accidents. His touch was grounding.

This was *Khristann*.

"I don't know," she mumbled.

"You're lucky I had to fetch some spare whites from the laundry, otherwise I wouldn't have been walking through here. I wouldn't have heard you."

Rosie flushed. "Was I *that* loud?"

"I thought you were being attacked." He furrowed his brow and shook his head. "I didn't know what I'd find when I came in. You looked as if you were pinned down by a ghoul. You weren't breathing properly, songbird. I thought for a second that I'd lose you."

Rosie didn't know what to say.

"Talk to me. Let me help you."

"I don't know what happened," she rasped. "One second I was in Gold Gates and Lawrence had his hand around my wrist. The next, I'm in here and I can't breathe. I couldn't *breathe*. That's when you came in."

"That bastard," he growled. "Did he hurt you?"

Rosie focussed on his pinched brow and enraged gaze. No matter what was going on behind-the-scenes, he really did want to protect her.

"Not really," she whispered. "It's just that whenever he touches me, my brain seems to nosedive, and I start to sweat and shake. I just want to get out of there. I *had* to get out of there." Her voice broke as she added, "Why does he do this to me?"

Khristann looked truly crestfallen as he leant forward to kiss her forehead, then rested against her and held her in his arms.

"I'm so sorry, songbird. I truly am."

CHAPTER II

FORMIDABLE AND WONDROUS

Rosie spent the remainder of the afternoon in and out of fitful sleep. She half expected to wake to Jakob standing above her, demanding to know why she'd abandoned her post as VIP liaison. Though it seemed luck had been in her favour when she rolled over to see that it was an hour until she was due to sing.

She sat up and rolled her neck, joints creaking and clicking. She needed to get gussied up in her evening attire and check in on Kit before her show started.

Rosie braced to stand on achy legs but halted. There was another note attached to her bedside lamp.

"No," she whined, letting her head fall back. "Not now. I have too much to worry about already."

Against her better judgement, she snatched the note up.

Sunday evening during the final of the tournament is your only chance. Please take it. There will be nothing in your way during the interlude; you only have to worry about yourself.

The author's pleading meant one of two things: they were

either keen on Rosie's freedom or desperately trying to salvage a selfish plan to incriminate her. She hadn't even begun to consider how she might make it into the gallery—she was forbidden to access it and was under constant surveillance. She would have to spend some time tomorrow thinking through a plan for the *wine tasting*. At least she had her pilfered chisel and hammer from Mr Jack to get her started.

The issues were piling up as she contemplated who might have left the note. The caring tone of it spoke volumes, but when paired with Jakob's perplexing comment from the night before...

"There's progress being made behind the scenes... There are things going on that you couldn't even comprehend, and believe it or not, all I've ever tried to do is protect you from my father."

More than ever, the signs were pointing to Jakob, but Khristann was also becoming more suspicious as time went on. Questions swirled as Rosie tried to pinpoint any singular reason for Jakob to free her. She'd loved him once, and he remained adamant that he'd loved her too, but was that enough? Enough to risk his inheritance, his job, and his entire life?

The idea was reminiscent of the young, boyish Jakob she'd known before, when they were content to wander the streets of the city for hours on end. Not a homeless thief and an heir to a dynasty. Just Rosie and Jakob.

Which Jakob was the authentic one? The past or present?

She looked at the clock on her nightstand again and realised she'd wasted precious time. She needed to get dressed and return to Suite Rouge.

Rosie knocked on the suite door and realised she hadn't organised a VIP booth for Kit in the bar.

"Shit," she swore, slapping her forehead and turning to leave when the door opened behind her.

"Hi, Rosie."

She turned to see Hud waiting in the doorway, barefoot and dressed in a shirt covered in black streaks with a pair of shorts. He clearly wasn't joining them for the evening.

"Hi," she replied. "Is Kit all right? Does she need anything from me before I go down to the bar?"

Hud frowned and pulled open the door.

"I've got no clue. Why don't you ask her yourself?"

He darted away from her, obviously busy with something much more interesting, leaving her to wander into Kit's side of the penthouse complex. She allowed the door to close quietly behind her and listened for sounds of life in the rooms.

Kit and Florelle could be heard fussing over something in one of the bedrooms, whilst Hud sat on one of the sofas with a contraption in his hands, the tinny notes of a jazz song coming from the gramophone on the sideboard. He was entirely engrossed in the thing in his hands, so he didn't see as Rosie wandered to the adjoining suite door and peered through the gap. There was no one in the living space of the attached suite, but she could hear some voices coming from one of the bedrooms.

"It's only for this weekend, baby."

"I know, but the whole setup makes me nervous. As if we don't have enough going on with the tournament and all eyes on us in this city, we've also got—"

"Everything is set; stop worrying so much."

"And what if a certain someone decides not to take part?"

"We'll cross that bridge when we get to it. If you continue to frown like that, everyone will know that you're nervous. *Kit* will know."

Rosie pressed closer to the gap in the door as she placed the voices; it was Jal and Mae.

"I'm allowed to be nervous; this whole feat is nothing to do with the money—it's personal. We don't deal with personal issues."

"Why don't you tell that to Kit? I'm sure she'll be happy to point out exactly why rules have to be broken sometimes."

One of them sighed.

"I know you're right; it's just hard when so much relies on the unknown."

"We can do this, just as we've done everything before."

"I know."

"It's you and me, remember? I'll never let anyone hurt you again."

"I know." Another sigh. "I love you."

"I'm glad to hear that hasn't changed. Now let's go. Kit will be waiting for us."

Rosie sucked in a sharp breath and quietly backed away from the door, avoiding the creaking floorboard on the left and rounding the small corner of the living space. Hud was still engrossed in his invention, and Kit was only just emerging from the bedroom, fussing with her outfit.

"Rosie," she greeted. "I was concerned you'd disappeared on me."

"I'm sorry." She fiddled with the billowy tulle of her dress tangling around her legs. "I spoke with my boss, and he's letting me join you in the city tomorrow morning—"

"I'm well aware. Mr Haart paid me a visit this afternoon."

Rosie's eyes flared.

"Which Mr Haart?"

Kit raised a single eyebrow. "Junior. Jakob, I believe?"

Rosie sighed and composed herself.

"My performance begins in fifteen minutes. Would you like me to take you downstairs?"

"I certainly would. I'm not likely to traverse this maze on my own. Though I must admit, I feel underdressed now that I've seen your outfit."

Kit was in *no* way underdressed. She was wearing a floor-length black gown made from netting that hinted at her body beneath. The dress stuck to her like a second skin, sequins sewn into swirling floral patterns that hid enough to be demure but revealed enough to be daring. She was gorgeous.

"No, you're—you look—it's perfect. You look great."

Rosie wanted to bury her head in the sand.

"I'll take any compliment I can get." Kit sauntered to the door and pulled it open. "The others will be down shortly to keep me company."

She turned back to look at Hud, who hadn't paid any attention to the exchange.

"Behave, little one."

He grunted but didn't look up. "I'm not little."

"You are until I say you aren't."

She left the suite, and Rosie followed as quickly as she could without tripping in the layers of her dress. She stumbled once but regained momentum as she trailed closely behind, scrambling to press the call button before Kit would have to. The journey to the foyer passed in delicate silence, neither of the young women or the lift attendant broaching conversation.

Rosie couldn't believe how the afternoon had run away from her. She'd achieved nothing and would be berated should Jakob or Lawrence find out. She hadn't even had a chance to plan the *wine tasting,* let alone carry out her duties as a personal liaison.

Had Kit needed anything? Had Jakob noticed her absence when he'd visited Suite Rouge?

The lift attendant announced, "The foyer."

"This way," Rosie said as they arrived in the grand entrance hall, audible gasps following every guest they passed. She didn't need to venture a glimpse behind her to imagine what Kit looked like. Her expression would convey disinterest at the fawning people surrounding her. She would be equal parts formidable and wondrous, yet she wouldn't make eye contact with a single person.

Her footsteps clicked through the room, claiming each patron's attention. Rosie kept her eyes focussed on the large arch that signalled the entrance to the casino so that she wouldn't wither beneath the collective gaze on them.

The casino was all lights and noise, a cacophony of joyful cheers and drunken laughter. She was immune to the awe of it nowadays, though once she'd been like everyone else, entranced by the soundtrack of elation that filled every inch of the space. The ringing of winner's bells and the clinking of glasses would always haunt her dreams no matter how far she travelled from Roguerest.

The casino was situated in the centre of the building, spanning as far as the eye could see, with a bar conveniently placed in the middle. Save for the surrounding four red walls, there were no visible barriers in the space, which only served to make it more immense. The chandeliers were high enough that the ceiling appeared miles away, and yet the casino was warm and inviting. Even the smells in the room were enticing: a mixture of savoury food and expensive perfume, topped off by the fresh-cut flowers adorning every available archway and column.

Rosie led the way to the bar, covertly catching the attention of the manager who supervised the seating arrangements. He narrowed his eyes at her but softened considerably when he noticed the VIP guest following behind.

"I need a booth for Miss Khalar. A *private* booth."

"You, uh...you should've notified us ahead of time, Rosie." He clambered for his seating plan.

"I'm well aware of that." She gritted her teeth. "But we're here now."

"Right this way, Miss Khalar." The manager pasted on a brittle smile. "We have a booth waiting for you."

Be available, be observant, be invisible.

The mantra served everyone, not just Rosie. Guests didn't need to know of mishaps or oversights; it was all part of the seamless Ruby Talisman experience. Rosie knew full well that at least one booth remained reserved each night in the bar in case Lawrence or Jakob dropped in for a drink. If there were no remaining booths for Kit to occupy, they would use the one for the bosses and pray that neither of the Haarts paid a visit.

"Here we are." The manager gestured to a circular booth on a pedestal with a *reserved* placard in the centre. He removed it and used his handkerchief to dab at the perspiration on his brow.

"I suppose this will do," Kit confirmed, her expression flat.

"My name is Lenox, and I'm the manager this evening. If there's anything you need at all, please don't hesitate to ask. May I get you a drink?"

Kit drifted into the booth, removing a single hair from her face and gracefully placing it back amongst the sleek up-do that Jal had likely styled for her.

"*Shenakk* on the rocks," she purred.

"Right away."

Rosie grabbed Lenox by the arm as he turned, leaning close to his ear.

"No bruise root in any of her drinks."

He sneered. "You think you're in charge here?"

"I think I'm in charge of keeping Miss Khalar happy this weekend, under the orders of Lawrence and Jakob. If you drug her, they'll have you on your backside in The Estate tomorrow with a sore ego and no job."

He sighed but gave her a sharp nod and walked away.

Rosie faced Kit again, momentarily dazed by her. She was dazzling when she was in public, dressed up and assessing people with a hooded stare. Rosie could understand why people fawned over her. She was untouchable, which only made everyone more curious about who she was beneath the glitz and glamour.

Rosie cleared her throat and averted her gaze when she realised she'd been staring.

"Is there anything else I can get you?"

Kit pursed her lips and shook her head. "That'll be all, thank you."

Effectively dismissed, Rosie tried to walk away with her dignity intact despite almost tripping multiple times in the impractical dress. She told herself that no one was looking at her, they were too distracted by Kit to notice the bumbling employee in the ridiculous tulle ball-gown.

As she approached the small stage to one side of the bar, she was thankful that her setlist remained the same each week. If there was one thing she could rely on in the madness of her job, it was that her gig in the casino was a constant. The pianist, Kian, was already performing an endless slew of background music. He gave her a warm smile as she settled in place behind the microphone, straightening her gown and hair as she gave a brief glance around the room for either of the Haarts. She luckily came up empty.

"Good evening, everyone," she tentatively said into the microphone. She closed her eyes for a second and allowed her performer's persona to settle in, her eyes hooding just a little and a lazy smile stretching across her lips.

The patrons of the bar and surrounding casino turned to

assess who was speaking, but she never had to worry about catching anyone's attention. As soon as she began to sing, no one would be able to look away—of that, she could guarantee.

"My name is Rosie, and I'll be your entertainment this evening," she purred.

Once she began singing, every soul within listening distance was enraptured. It was always the same. She didn't have to think about lyrics or melodies. The music flowed from her as if it were the most natural thing in the world. She supposed it was the most natural thing in the world to her.

It was Rosie's divine ability.

She was a songbird. She could hold a person's attention simply by singing, and they wouldn't be able to look away. She used to love singing and grew up doing it whenever she could, but Lawrence had sucked that joy from her life too, forcing her to perform like a monkey in his sick circus.

Though she usually lost herself in the music and didn't watch the audience, this time was different. She couldn't stop her need to impress Kit. She would scan the crowds, content with their utter admiration of her vocals, then find herself settling upon Kit again. She remained stony-faced and unaffected by Rosie's ability.

Impossible.

Try as she might throughout the entire set, Rosie's vocal prowess did nothing to affect her new boss, though the rest of the audience hung from her every word. When she drew the set to a close with a bow, the casino erupted in applause and pleas for more. She politely waved off their requests and stepped down from the stage, smiling her thanks to Kian, who resumed playing an unobtrusive lullaby to maintain the atmosphere.

Rosie courteously declined numerous invitations from passersby who offered her company for the night. Her cheeks flushed as she found her way back to Kit's booth, which now also held Jal and Mae, both of them decked out in cocktail attire.

"Did Florelle not fancy an evening in the casino?" She queried the notable absence.

"Someone has to shepherd Hud into some form of obedience," Mae explained, patting the empty spot in the booth beside her. "Join us for a drink?"

Rosie's gaze flitted to Kit for permission. She received an almost imperceptible nod and sat down.

"What's your tipple of choice?" Jal was unrecognisable with sleek, straight locks replacing the wild curls that Rosie had witnessed earlier. Her tanned skin was flushed and had a natural glow.

"I shouldn't drink whilst I'm working. Water will be absolutely fine, thank you."

"Nonsense." Mae waved off her refusal. "How about a glass of local wine? I've heard it's pretty outstanding—"

"She will remain sober," Kit ordered.

Heat crept up Rosie's neck as she looked down at her hands. Jal and Mae dismissed the stunted exchange and fell into an easy conversation of their own, leaning close to each other and laughing.

Taking the opportunity to retreat into her own thoughts, Rosie went over the note she'd received earlier. She considered how she might steal the painting this time. If she remembered correctly, the gallery had twenty-four hour guards at the entrance and rotating shifts of two guards within—

A searing pain erupted in her temple and spread to her sinuses. She barely stifled a gasp as the blazing agony flowed through her jaw and white noise filled her ears. Liquid fire blazed through her veins and numbed her other senses. She couldn't see or smell or hear. She broke out in a sweat as she tried to covertly breathe through the pain. It was burning through every muscle and tissue in her body, rendering her rigid and motionless.

How could she be so stupid? Her *supresis* curse.

Her jaw clenched, and her teeth ground so hard that she thought they might crack. It was all-encompassing, but she had to focus on keeping it contained. Triggering one of her curses in mixed company gave a new meaning to embarrassment. It showed everyone around her that she was controlled by someone else—that she'd forfeited the rights to her own body.

Unfortunately, a quiet wheeze escaped her when the pain pulsed and became unbearable, which must have caught the attention of the three women at the table. Her fingernails dug into her palms so viciously that she felt the skin break.

"Rosie and I will take our leave now."

Kit offered no further explanation.

Did she know how much pain Rosie was in?

No one spoke as her wishes were adhered to. Rosie's vision began to return, and she stumbled as she stood. She tried to breathe normally through the waning pain and allowed Kit to take hold of her upper arm, steering her away from the table. It wasn't until they'd left the bar and were almost out of the casino that the burning sensation relented enough to concentrate. She focussed on the warm hand on her arm and soon found herself back in the lift, blanketed in a numb silence once the doors closed.

The raucous nightlife in the hotel had been mercifully shut off, giving Rosie a chance to catch her breath. She sagged against the hand rail, not bothered that both Kit and the attendant were watching her. Sweat beaded on her forehead, and the pain of her *supresis* curse kindly disappeared completely, leaving her well aware of the state her body was in.

She must look like a wreck.

Clearing her throat, she straightened and dabbed at her

forehead. She rolled her shoulders and faced the lift doors, not making eye contact with the other two. She would hold onto her last semblance of dignity even if it killed her.

She was in control. She had to be in control of *something*.

"The penthouse suites." The attendant's voice made her jump.

Rosie waited for Kit to exit the lift first, following behind and taking the opportunity to glance in the large gilded mirror on the wall between the two suites.

Her white skin was ghostly pale and her cheeks flushed, the curse taking its toll on her. Her hair was mussed and frizzy, and she had a couple of scratch marks on her arms that she couldn't even remember giving herself. It served as a reminder of her place in the world, of her status as a servant to those more powerful than her. She was a songbird and nothing else. Her destiny was to entertain Imperials.

Be available, be observant, be—

"Rosie." Kit had opened the door to Suite Rouge already. "I won't wait all day."

"Sorry, Miss Khalar."

Floundering in the mass of skirts, Rosie reached the door just before it closed in her face and shouldered it back open.

"Follow me." Kit didn't wait for a response.

Rosie trailed after her into the second bedroom of the suite. She was momentarily stunned by the sheer volume of material and beauty products strewn across the room, various trunks used as tables to display an array of jewellery and droves of footwear. The room had been transformed into a dressing room, and Rosie couldn't comprehend the cost of its contents.

Kit scanned a rail of garments, flicking through them until she found an emerald silk pyjama set comprised of shorts and a cami top.

"Go and change." She held out the hanger.

Rosie tilted her head and opened her mouth to say something but nothing came out. Settling on a shy smile, she took the clothing and ran her fingers over the luxurious material. It was unlike anything she'd had the pleasure of wearing. Infinitely soft and lightweight—

"Rosie."

Their eyes connected for a few seconds, and time seemed to stretch between them.

"*Go.*"

"Yes, Miss Khalar."

"I've told you before. Call me Kit."

Rosie nodded sheepishly as she walked away.

"You can use one of the bathrooms to wash," Kit continued. "I'll see you early in the morning because we have a lot to discuss. Starting with your divine ability."

CHAPTER 12

PRISONER IN A CRIMSON CAGE

R osie never usually struggled tumbling into a deep slumber, dreaming of places she'd never been and people she'd never met. This night, however, was an outlier.

She'd changed and gone to bed in the cramped butler's cupboard of Suite Rouge hours ago. She'd tossed and turned and fumbled, growing more frustrated, until she threw her blankets off with a huff and stood up. Her back ached from lying on the floor. The silk pyjamas she wore were creased and damp. The air was hot and dry due to the heating pipes running along the walls and beneath the floorboards.

As her tongue stuck to the roof of her mouth, she realised she desperately needed a glass of water.

Stretching her creaking joints, she turned the tarnished door knob as quietly as she could and pulled the door open, slinking into the darkness of the suite. She crossed to the kitchen silently, glad for having scoped out the creaky floorboards the day before.

Recon always paid off.

The only light to give her a sense of direction came from the moon, a beam of pure white light that she crossed for a second before becoming invisible again. The only noise to be heard came from the grandfather clock in the living room.

Tick. Tick. Tick.

As soon as her eyes had adjusted to the darkness, she fixed herself a glass of water and sighed at the cooling sensation. She leaned against the kitchen island and let her eyes fall closed, appreciating the fragile quiet of nightfall. Despite the flashing lights far below on the streets of the city, the penthouse complex was high enough above the ground that the darkness wasn't touched by such a distraction. It was a crisp black witching hour in Suite Rouge.

Rosie took a deep breath and settled into the rare peace.

A strange sense of stillness blanketed her. In that moment, even if it was fleeting, she was safe. Her guard was down. Her head fell back and she blew out the breath she'd been holding.

How had she ended up here?

An imposter in a lavish palace. A thief in a playground of potential marks. A prisoner in a crimson cage. She'd come far from her days on the streets, but she'd also not come far at all. She'd gained a roof over her head, clothing, food, and safety from the darkest corners of Roguerest. But what had she lost as a forfeit? Freedom, bodily autonomy, and her entire sense of self.

Quite the trade.

"What have we here?"

Rosie flinched at the familiar voice. She lifted her head and opened her eyes, still surrounded by darkness. She'd been so lost in thought that she hadn't heard Kit approach.

"Is there a midnight explorer in my suite?"

"It appears so." Rosie cleared her throat and furrowed her brow as she considered how to approach their conversation.

Remembering her place, she stood straighter as she added, "I apologise. I needed a glass of water. Can I get you anything?"

"There's no need to be formal when it's only the two of us." The smile was evident in Kit's voice. "Do the employees never sleep?"

A grin spread across Rosie's face.

"What can I say? It turns out that blankets on the hardwood floor are not conducive to good rest."

Kit laughed. "You're not so shy in the dark. Is this the real you?"

Rosie considered her answer for a second. She decided to take a leap. "The only time I can be myself these days is when people can't see me."

"Hmm. Well, you're safe with me—darkness or not."

Tick. Tick. Tick.

As much as she loved the dark, Rosie was unsettled by not seeing Kit's facial expressions in their conversation. She couldn't read someone if she couldn't see them.

She felt along the kitchen cabinets until she found the fourth cupboard, the one that held the candles and candelabras used to set the large dining table. Grasping a taper candle and a polished gold holder, she swiped the box of matches from the stove and assembled then lit the candle.

A moment passed before she dared to venture a glance upwards from the flame. Her eyes adjusted slowly to the minimal light cast by the flickering candle, but she saw the outline of Kit immediately.

As she came into better focus, Rosie barely recognised her. Her face was naked, a stark contrast to the dark streaks of makeup that had adorned her eyes and cheeks throughout the day before. She looked younger—timid and exposed. Her skin was still flawless and glowed in the low light, her high cheekbones accentuated by shadows. Her normally sleek hair was mussed and pushed back from her face, revealing her true self instead of serving as armour for the illusion of Kitty Khalar.

Of all the versions of this young woman that Rosie had met within the past day, she knew with startling clarity that the stripped back slip of a thing, dressed in what she could now identify as a silk robe, was the real Kitty Khalar.

This was *Kit,* exposed and alarmingly human. She wasn't a famous card player like this, nor was she an enigma or a boss. She was just a young woman, only a year or two older than Rosie.

"It's nice to finally meet you," Rosie murmured.

"I find that the small hours encourage authenticity."

"I think I prefer you like this."

Kit's lips twitched. "Hmm."

She rounded the kitchen island and walked into the pantry, managing to find her way with the minimal light. A moment later, she reemerged with a fruit pie adorned with golden lattice pastry and snagged two dessert forks from one of the drawers.

She placed the pie on the surface next to Rosie and dug in without preamble, leaving the spare fork on the marble. Though Rosie wanted to pick the fork up and dig in too, she hadn't been offered any and knew that her *supresis* curse would kick in. The tendrils of control it held over her life were suffocating. She couldn't enjoy pie in the moonlight with an interesting companion. She couldn't function like a regular human being. It was a noose around her neck.

Be available, be—

"Rosie?"

She glanced up.

"What's mine is yours."

She didn't need further instruction as she scooped up the

fork and lifted a piece of pie to her mouth. The delicate, flaky pastry was a paradise of sweet and tangy fruit. Her eyes fell closed at the simple pleasure.

She hadn't eaten a proper meal since Khristann had brought her breakfast the previous morning, though she'd gone much longer before without substantial nourishment.

"Tell me about your curses." Kit's voice was barely above a whisper.

Rosie didn't rush her next mouthful of pie. She didn't make eye contact either. Of course, Kit knew about her afflictions. Jakob had likely mocked her when he'd visited Suite Rouge the afternoon before, telling Kit all the ways she could taunt her if she wanted to.

"I should've figured that you knew." Rosie evaded the question, taking another forkful. "You don't need to worry; they restrict me from doing any unsavoury behaviour. I won't be stealing from you any time soon."

Kit tutted. "I'm not worried in the slightest."

When Rosie focussed on the pie rather than the conversation, her companion prodded further.

"For now, in the dark, you're not you and I'm not me. We're just two girls having an honest conversation. Talk to me." She waited a beat before adding, "I would never judge you."

Rosie hadn't thought of herself as a girl in...well, *ever*. Though she was only seventeen, she'd been an adult for as long as she could recall. The streets showed no mercy to children. Innocence was weakness. Cunning was valuable currency.

"I suppose I am just a girl," she relented, humming around a mouthful of pie and relishing the taste. "And I suppose you are too, despite your daytime pomp and peacocking."

Kit smirked. "The ruse is up. You've caught me." She took another mouthful of pie. "Now that we're on a level playing field, will you indulge me? Tell me about your curses."

Rosie met her gaze and restrained a smile. She liked this version of Kit. Did anyone else know her in this capacity? Did her entourage get to see this side of her?

"I'm not sure how much you know about my past from other people," Rosie began, "or about the reason that I'm here. But I can give you the *honest* version of events if you'd like."

"Take it away."

They both took several more chunks of pie. The flame between them crackled ever so softly. Long shadows blended into the surrounding darkness.

"I don't remember being anything other than a street child. Necessity bred nimble fingers, and I grew up stealing food to eat, clothes to survive... I wouldn't take cash unless it was absolutely necessary. The local vendors were all aware of my social status. They knew I didn't have money of my own. A lot of them refused to serve me because they knew the cash was pickpocketed from clueless tourists." Rosie fiddled with the fork in her hand whilst she decided how much to share. "But despite my lack of family—lack of everything, really—I enjoyed my simple little life. Sure, I lived hand-to-mouth, but all I cared about was surviving. I envy my old self. I envy the simplicity of it all. Find food, eat, avoid danger, repeat."

Kit pushed a piece of pie around the dish, listening intently.

"I was only fifteen when I met him." Rosie felt the memories rushing back. "I remember every detail of that afternoon—the heat, the rancid smell of raw meat, the jeers of tour groups. It's a lifetime ago now, a world away from all of this. In the midst of the market in the Tourist Quarter, I picked the wrong pocket." She smiled at the memory. "He informed me later on that he'd been watching me, waiting for me to approach him, which is why he'd seemed the perfect mark—he did it entirely on purpose. I'd thought I'd executed the manoeuvre perfectly; a purposeful *bump* into each other, my left hand on his shoulder in apology, my right hand in his pocket, lifting the bulging wallet in there.

"He caught me red-handed with that charming grin plastered all over his face. He was familiar to me because I'd seen his picture in the newspaper, so I knew that he had money. For a moment, I thought that I'd blown it—that a boy from a wealthy family would cry for a market guard and I'd be thrown into jail. It's sad to think back on, but I felt relief for a second or two; even though I'd be in a disgusting jail cell, at least I'd have a permanent roof over my head with three meals a day."

Rosie scoffed and picked at the edge of the pie with her fork.

"I was so naïve," she whispered, shaking her head. "But he didn't call for help or try to restrain me. Instead, he told me that he'd use the money I'd almost stolen to buy me a hot meal and a night in a hotel. He told me that...that I was better than a petty thief. That's how it all began—a charming smile and a few compliments. I was hooked. This boy, only a year older than me and from riches that I didn't dare to imagine, had taken an interest in me. In *me.* I remember lying in bed that night on a luxurious mattress—a *real* mattress—and thinking, *how did I get so lucky?*"

Kit pushed off from the island, and for a moment Rosie thought she'd grown bored. Instead, she fetched a glass from one of the kitchen cupboards and filled it with water, returning to the island and taking a sip.

"I suppose"—Kit's voice was low and raspy—"that you weren't lucky at all?"

Rosie scoffed. "No. Not in the slightest."

"Otherwise, you wouldn't be here with me and with two curses pestering you."

Rosie set the fork down next to the pie dish and leaned on her forearms with her head bowed. Thinking about her old self and the old Jakob always brought a strong sense of melancholy. It was like mourning something that could've been. Mourning something that was so close at one point she could almost taste it.

"So what happened next?" Kit pressed.

Rosie blew out a heavy sigh but continued the story.

"Jakob paid for me to stay at an inn—nothing fancy, just a family-run place in The Estate that most tourists wouldn't dare venture to. But to me, it was everything. I had a bed, one that was mine, and I didn't have to worry about leaving at a moment's notice should the real owner come home."

Kit cleared her throat. "You squatted in the beds of strangers?"

It wasn't pity or horror in Kit's voice, more along the lines of admiration.

"I would watch particular houses—the ones with travelling businessmen or those working nights—and I'd wait for them to leave. I was chased from bedrooms more times than I can count, leaping from windows and climbing up walls. I know every inch of Roguerest, every alleyway and rooftop, every escape route. But after I met Jakob, I didn't have to concern myself with any of that anymore. I had a bed and hot food, I had security for the first time in my life. He was my protector. It's no wonder I fell head over heels in love with him. He visited me every day, sometimes dressed in the finest suits I'd ever seen and sometimes dressed as if he were just a boy on the streets too. But no matter what he wore, he was always the same Jakob.

"He asked me to teach him sleight-of-hand tricks, told me that he had no interest in his family's wealth, and that he wanted to earn his own way in the world. He wanted to leave all the glamour behind and start a normal life. I ate it all up like a lovesick fool."

Kit sighed. "You were just a child."

"I've never been a child. I wasn't allowed a childhood. Though compared to now, I suppose I was just a child. I'm not the same person I was two years ago, not even close. Before I knew it, months had passed with Jakob, and we spent more time together than we did apart. That's when he..."

Rosie's throat closed. She blew out a deep breath.

"That's when he came up with *the idea*. The heist that would provide us with the funds to travel all of the Twelve Territories. He said he'd got it all figured out. It was a flawless plan. The painting, a famous landscape housed within the gallery of The Ruby Talisman, was ripe for the picking. He'd grown up around the hotel, so he knew it well, or so he told me. I'd pulled off small thefts here and there within the city as I grew older and no longer cared about what I stole. I'd pawn my take and use the money to buy whatever I needed to survive that week from vendors who would sell to me. I grew bolder as time went on, but I never would've planned something as outlandish as Jakob proposed. I knew in my gut that the plan was too good to be true, but I was blinded by him. I didn't research the hotel adequately. I relied on his word and his hand-drawn diagrams of the hotel's layout. It was destined to go wrong."

Rosie scrubbed a hand over her eyes as she relived her own downfall. It didn't hurt any less now than it had a year ago.

"And when the chips were down, he bailed. I stood in the gallery with a rope hanging from the air vent above, a painting rolled up in my hand and a shattered frame on the floor. As soon as the voices came, he disappeared. I was all alone in that room. I learned the sanctity of intuition that day. I learned that I can't trust anything or anyone but myself."

Rosie straightened and picked her fork up again, eating more pie.

"Your curses were your punishment," Kit surmised.

Rosie thought about her answer as she chewed.

"Lawrence, he...he isn't what everyone thinks. It's all an act. The charity, the generosity, the camaraderie... He's a fake and a con-artist—I should know. He controls most of the government here, has them all in his pockets, so it was all too easy for him to gain control of me too. He said that working off my punishment in The Ruby was much more fitting than spending a decade in a jail cell. He's an Imperial. He can put curses on others and remove them at his will, which is exactly what he did to me. I have a *supresis* and a *captipheus,* one to stop me from stealing or even contemplating it, and the other to confine me to the four walls of the hotel."

Rosie had to push through her next sentence, her skin flushing and her hands balled into fists. "I work as a maid, but I'm a general dogsbody; I'm whatever Jakob or Lawrence dictates on a daily basis."

There was a beat of quiet.

"Which, this weekend, is my personal liaison," Kit filled in without judgement, simply as an observation.

"Exactly."

Silence blanketed them again.

Tick. Tick. Tick.

"If you could leave Roguerest, where would you go?"

Rosie welcomed the change in topic. Her lips curled up as she thought about her dream of travelling. "Where wouldn't I go? The possibilities are endless. I have a journal that I've been using to collect research and plot out the route I'll take when I get out of here. I'll travel all over the Twelve Territories, right to the very edge of Irredore."

Kit smiled at that, picking at the pie once again.

"Irredore is beautiful, I'm sure you'd love it."

Rosie thought Kit was going to describe her homeland

further, but she remained quiet. Maybe she would open up if Rosie gave her a little more information.

"My divine ability, as you witnessed earlier, is singing." She pivoted the conversation. "When I was younger, I would dream of performing on big stages in front of vast crowds that I couldn't see the back of. Now I want nothing less. I hate performing in the casino."

"Because you don't do it for enjoyment anymore," Kit stated. "You do it as part of your punishment, which is sure to bleed any enjoyment from it. But I have a feeling that you don't know your full potential."

Rosie frowned, making eye contact with her for the first time in several minutes.

"What do you mean by that?"

Kit's smirk was only slightly infuriating. "I've come across a few like you, though none as powerful. Do you realise that you're much more capable than just singing for an audience? Your power runs deeper than that."

Rosie's heart skipped a beat.

"But I'm just an Artist. I just sing."

"For starters, you are not *just* anything, Rosie. You had the audience captivated tonight. You had every single patron under your spell, and you didn't even realise."

"And what about you?"

Kit cleared her throat and smiled as she looked at her hands.

"I was also entranced, though I was sober enough to realise what you were doing."

"What was I doing?" Rosie was almost scared to hear the answer.

"You were hypnotising them. You could've instructed them to fight to the death, to tear limb from limb until only one remained standing, and they'd have done it. They'd have clambered to annihilate their friends for the opportunity to be the last one standing for you."

Rosie didn't breathe. Didn't blink.

Tick. Tick. Tick.

"You're not just a songbird, Rosie. You're a siren."

CHAPTER 13

SHRINK BACK INTO THE SHADOWS

A *siren?* Surely not.

"I think you're wrong," Rosie croaked. "I would know if I could hypnotise people. I've known my ability my whole life, and you've known it for less than twenty-four hours."

"Would you know? What if you'd never been taught that it was possible? You grew up without any education in divine abilities, without any guidance about nurturing your gift. How would you know your potential?"

"I..." Rosie couldn't string a sentence together as she rapidly flicked through every memory she possessed of singing to people. She couldn't pinpoint a single moment that indicated any greater power. She'd never thought about pushing the boundaries of her ability because she'd never deemed it possible.

She was just an Artist.

"Someone would've told me by now," she attempted, clasping her hands together and taking a step back. "Khristann or Jakob or someone. Lawrence must know; he knows everything. There's no way he could've missed this."

"What if," Kit broached carefully, "they were entranced enough by the minimal energy you were expelling to simply assume you had a wonderful voice? Between you not putting any effort into hypnotising anyone—because you had no concept of your true power—and them still being affected by your minimal input, everyone has remained gloriously clueless."

Rosie put more space between them, running a hand through her hair as she approached the sofas and collapsed onto one.

This couldn't be right.

The flickering light in the room moved, the shadows creeping across the walls and slinking into new positions as Kit brought the candle to the coffee table. Elegant as ever, she relaxed into the other end of the sofa and watched Rosie for a few moments.

"I know this must be hard for you to comprehend, having lived your whole life without knowing your true ability, but—"

"How did you know?"

Kit tilted her head and considered the question.

"How did you know?" Rosie snapped, turning to face her fully. "If everyone else, sober or not, has been *gloriously clueless* to my ability—including myself—then how have you swooped in and come to this conclusion immediately? Why were you not hypnotised too?"

Kit seemed affronted by her rapid change in tone and looked away.

"I will admit that I knew you were a songbird before I arrived. In my communications with the hotel about needing a personal liaison, Jakob mentioned that you were a singer. He apologised in advance for your need to perform in the casino and any duties to me that it would distract you from."

"That doesn't explain how you knew that I would be a siren."

"I didn't." Their eyes connected again. "But in my past experiences with songbirds, I've come across varying levels of power. I wasn't expecting you to be a siren, but I was prepared for it in advance. Doing what I do, being in the public eye and having strangers clamber for things from me at any given moment, I'm constantly on guard. I have to protect myself from the divine abilities of others, or I'll fall prey to someone greedy for what I've earned."

The explanation was sobering.

Rosie shrunk back, averting her gaze and collecting her thoughts. Perhaps she'd jumped to conclusions. She certainly felt guilty for pushing the matter and forcing Kit to confront the realities of being Kitty Khalar.

"I'm sorry for assuming the worst," Rosie murmured. "You must understand that this is...this is remarkable. You're telling me that I might not be completely ordinary?"

Kit looked at her hands as a smile crept across her lips.

"I fear you have no idea how truly extraordinary you are. I've known you for a few hours, and I seem to be the only one aware of how rare you are—or at least how rare you could be if you applied yourself."

Rosie fiddled with her nails.

"You've been bound by your own expectations of conventional," Kit continued, seemingly getting excited. "Once you break free of your chains and realise your true potential, you'll be able to leave behind those who want to limit you. There will always be people who try to...to judge you by their own definition of *enough*. But it's only your definition that matters. The only explanation you need to provide for your actions is the one to yourself."

Rosie looked up. *What could she possibly say to that?*

Had Kit practised the speech, or was she really that good?

"I don't mean to preach," she apologised, her eyes now locked on the flickering candle. "But I see so much unfettered potential in you. I've watched you in action, and it's painfully obvious to an outsider like me that you have been held down your entire life. It's in your posture, your language, and your expression. It's in every ounce of your being. You've been trodden on and devalued over and over again until you're a shadow of who you could truly be."

Rosie was unsure whether she should be offended or inspired. One thing that definitely irked her was Kit's assumption that she knew anything about Rosie. She might be a master of studying others and acting aloof, but it didn't mean that she knew the slightest thing about Rosie or where she came from. What she'd endured and how she'd survived.

"I've never been held in any esteem," Rosie tried to explain. "The only time anyone treated me as if I had value led to my betrayal and humiliation, so what do you expect from me? You think that I should be a ray of sunshine who oozes positivity? My life...my life isn't like yours. I've not grown up with privilege and prosperity and—and...*opportunity*. I can't throw money at my problems and know full well that they'll shrink back into the shadows." Rosie's hands began to shake as she felt rage rising inside her. "I have to deal with my demons head on. Every. Single. Day. I have to face them repeatedly, even when it causes me physical pain and distress because I have *no other choice*. So please don't patronise me by acting like I've allowed this to happen to myself."

She stood up and felt her chest heaving as she sucked in angry breaths.

Who did Kit think she was?

"You have no concept of what I've been through or...or how hard I've worked to just survive. When was the last time you got your hands dirty? Or were hungry? Or humiliated for someone else's sick pleasure? When was the last time you felt as if you were drowning?"

Kit didn't meet her steely gaze.

"You have no clue," Rosie continued, feeling invigorated for standing up for herself. "You couldn't begin to comprehend how difficult it is for me to just breathe some days. My *chains* can't be lifted by a change in attitude. My chains are living people who own my body and soul. You don't know Lawrence. You don't know the scope of his grasp. You don't know..."

She gestured wildly with her hands as she tried to gather the right words for how she was feeling.

"You don't know anything. This is a holiday for you, a trip to a dazzling city that you'll probably walk away from with yet more money and opportunity. But for me? *This is reality.* Once you've moved on to your next exotic location and forgotten about the four days you spent with the poor servant girl in Roguerest, I'll have to deal with the fallout. I'll...I'll have to return to my subpar existence and my claustrophobic cupboard in the depths of the basement as if none of this ever happened."

The fight in her lost steam as the reality of their situation sunk in.

"You have no clue," she whispered, her shoulders slumping and her confidence waning. "No clue at all."

Rosie's throat was raw as she held back tears. She allowed her eyes to fall closed and took in several calming breaths. Confronting her life was exhausting. Relinquishing to the fact that she had nothing waiting for her even after the decade of imprisonment, that she had no family or friends to go home to, was draining. She had absolutely nothing. Sad as it was, The

Ruby Talisman had become all that defined her. The Ruby was her life and purpose.

Silence blanketed the suite again.

Rosie instantly regretted her outburst. Kit had been letting her guard down and actually treating Rosie like a human being. They'd been having fun. Rosie had been enjoying the company of someone who didn't seem to see her as a servant, but as an equal.

But she'd gone and blown it.

"I'm sorry," she whispered, not looking at Kit.

"No, the fault is mine."

Rosie knew instantly that she wasn't talking to Kit anymore, but instead to Kitty Khalar.

"I crossed a line. I have no business making broad assumptions about your life. I don't know you. You don't know me. I apologise."

Rosie saw movement in the corner of her eye and looked up to see Kit standing, her back ramrod straight and her chin slightly elevated.

"I think it's best if we go back to bed."

"Kit, I—"

"I'll see you in the morning."

"I'm sorry, I shouldn't have—"

"*Goodnight,* Rosie."

She watched as Kit retreated back to her bedroom and closed the door quietly. She'd definitely blown it.

"Good job, Rosie," she scolded herself, collapsing onto the sofa with a huff.

"Don't be so hard on yourself."

She jumped up at the new voice, resting her hand on her pounding heart as she took in the sight of Jal leaning against the doorframe of the other bedroom.

She hadn't even realised someone else was present, which

only made it more embarrassing. Rosie cleared her throat and wrung her hands together in her lap.

"I'm guessing you heard that?"

Jal sniggered. "You got pretty heated there for a second, it was hard not to."

"Sorry," Rosie apologised on instinct. "I shouldn't have crossed that line with Kit. I can only imagine what she'll be telling my boss in the morning."

Jal sauntered away from her doorway and sat down on the sofa Kit had just vacated. She wore a simple white sleep shirt and nothing else but didn't seem bothered by her attire in the presence of a near stranger.

"She wouldn't do that to you," she placated. "You need to give her a bit of patience. She's...guarded."

Rosie scoffed. "Understatement of the year."

Luckily, Jal found her amusing.

"You're right on that one." She chuckled quietly. "But I mean it when I say that she likes you. She wouldn't have even given you the time of day if she didn't. She's been through a lot. Don't believe the Kitty Khalar character she portrays to the world because it's all a mask."

Rosie nodded. "I already guessed as much."

"Exactly. If she didn't like you, you'd have no clue that she was anything but Kitty Khalar, eccentric millionaire and *kaarmiach* champion."

Rosie took a second to absorb the information. She wanted to believe what Jal was saying, but she couldn't stop herself from wondering why Kit was spending time with her when she would be leaving after the tournament.

"My job isn't to be liked," she eventually huffed and tucked some stray hair behind her ear. "This weekend, my job is to provide you all with anything you need."

Jal broke into a warm smile, biting her lip.

"That's exactly the point. Have you thought that maybe Kit *needs* to like someone? *Needs* to make a friend? She likes to act invincible, but she's the opposite. Underneath that character she dons as armour, she's the most sensitive soul I know."

Rosie had no response to that.

CHAPTER 14
JUST A MAN

H*eat.*

Sweltering, sticky, suffocating heat.

Rosie's eyes flashed open to reveal Kit leaning over her with a pained and worried expression, her brown skin clammy and her eyebrows knitted together.

"You were having a nightmare. I think. Uh"—Kit coughed, her voice gruff—"I was trying to wake you, but you continued to toss and turn. I was beginning to worry about you."

Rosie blinked to give herself a moment's grace as she composed herself.

She had no recollection of any dreams or nightmares. She remembered closing her eyes for a second on the sofa and nothing else. She must have fallen asleep after Jal went back to bed.

Her gaze darted over Kit's strained expression and she paused as she studied the signs of stress in her clenched jaw, sweaty skin, and furrowed brow.

"You don't look so good yourself," Rosie croaked, clearing her throat as she sat up. "Are you all right?"

"I'm fine," Kit snapped, putting distance between them as

she stood from her crouched position beside the sofa. She was like a beast in a cage, pacing as she fanned her face. Her shoulders were rigid, her jaw clenched, and her eyes cold.

Rosie took a moment to recall the events of the night before. As much as she wished for the amicable moments they'd shared to continue into the morning, the show had to continue as planned. Kit clearly didn't want to acknowledge what had happened in the small hours.

"It's almost seven." Kit's voice had somehow returned to the drawling lilt that Rosie associated with the VIP. "You should get to work. Do whatever has to be done before we leave. I have breakfast with your manager at nine, so you should return from your other duties by then in order to serve us. Understood?"

Rosie's mouth gaped open because she couldn't find any words. This was certainly not Kit in front of her. It was all Kitty.

She found herself beginning to despise the caricature that Kit embodied.

"Certainly," Rosie mumbled, running a hand through her hair. "Do you need—"

"Good," Kit confirmed without waiting for a response. "See you then."

She breezed from the living room, slamming her bedroom door behind her and leaving the suite in a crisp morning quiet. Streaks of sunlight poured through the large windows, illuminating what had hours before been a middle ground between VIP and dogsbody employee. But now it had unceremoniously returned to the gaudy, overpriced reality of The Ruby.

"Home, sweet home," Rosie sighed.

As she'd made her way to Jakob's office, the weight on Rosie's shoulders had lessened slightly. Though the break of day had driven home the realities of where she stood with Kit, their twilight conversation had somehow eased the burden that Rosie carried with her every day. Talking to someone about her past had made a world of difference.

She felt physically lighter as she strode through the foyer and towards the office. Something about Kit's words had sunk deeply into her subconscious as she'd slept. She had an unshakeable feeling that she was going to be okay. She managed to smile at every guest and employee that she drifted past.

Though their interaction had ended in an unsavoury way, Kit's words from hours before had invigorated her.

"I fear you have no comprehension of how truly extraordinary you are... Once you break free of your chains and realise your true potential, you'll be able to leave behind those who want to limit you. There will always be people who try to judge you by their own definition of enough. But it's only your definition that matters."

Having slept on it and also spoken with Jal, she was seeing Kit in a new light. Perhaps they were both lonely and misunderstood young women. She found herself wanting to believe in Kit's words. Despite how idealistic and ignorant they might be in some respects, they also held a lot of weight. Rosie hadn't wanted to admit it to her before, but she found herself seeing the truth in the argument now.

Perhaps she had allowed herself to be held down—perhaps she'd held *herself* down. As she made her way towards her ultimate tormentor, all she knew was that she didn't feel as devastatingly scared as she had yesterday. The anxiety was still there, simmering in the centre of her chest, but it wasn't consuming her every thought and making her hands shake.

And it was all because Kit had made her realise something vital.

Lawrence only had power over her because she gave it to him in the first place. She was made to feel inferior on a daily basis because she *allowed* Lawrence's position of power to make her feel inferior, not because she was truly lesser than him. If anything, she was a cut above the slimy, toxic man—she had morals, after all.

She rapped on the door of Jakob's office and squared her shoulders, determined to face the monster inside with dignity. She could do this.

Be available, be—

No, she scolded herself, coming to a momentous conclusion and physically shaking her head.

She'd been putting herself down all along. She'd been reciting those words to ground herself, but in reality, she'd been fuelling the idea. She'd been convincing herself that she was a second-class citizen. She'd been telling herself to be subservient, to be *invisible.*

But she wasn't made to be invisible.

"You have no comprehension of how truly extraordinary you are."

Kit's words could be true if she gave herself the opportunity to prove it. Before she could physically be extraordinary, she had to believe it herself.

She needed to channel the energy of her past self. The girl who had confidence in spades. The girl who didn't let anyone tell her how to limit herself.

She needed to embody the old Rosie.

"Come in," came Lawrence's muffled voice.

Truly extraordinary, Rosie thought. *Be truly extraordinary.*

She walked into the office and refused to look away from Lawrence's penetrating stare as she approached the front of the desk. Her insides felt as if they were quaking and twisting into knots, but her chin remained slightly raised and her posture straight as she waited for him to speak.

Be truly extraordinary, she reminded herself, commanding

her hands not to shake. She gripped them in fists behind her back so he couldn't see his effect on her.

"Good morning, songbird." Lawrence's smooth timbre brought the hairs up on the back of her neck, but she refused to let the sensation overpower her.

"Good morning, sir."

"You're...different today." His eyes travelled up and down her body, leaving a clammy sensation everywhere he looked. He assessed her stature and her unyielding eye contact with apathy.

Of course, he would notice something as simple as her maintaining eye contact. He didn't miss a trick. He knew everything that happened in the hotel.

"Need I remind you of your *duties* for the weekend? I would hate to think that you'd formed unruly ideas in that little head of yours."

Rosie studied him for a moment. She scrutinised each detail of his expression and his stance in the chair before coming to an astounding realisation. His lips were drawn into a thin line. His brow was slightly damp. He had crows feet in the corners of his eyes. His gaze was...uneasy?

She almost laughed as she belatedly understood what she should've known all along—what no one else had figured out yet.

Lawrence Haart was just a man.

She'd never looked at him in the eye long enough to realise as much. He had various characters that he portrayed just like Kit, but underneath it all, he was just a man. He donned his tailored suit and combed his hair back every day, constructing the illusion of an untouchable paladin for justice and equality. He fooled those around him into the belief that he was formidable and immortal. But no matter how much money he threw around—how many people he cheated and intimidated and ruined—he would one day meet his maker just as everyone else would. His existence would come to a halt, and what would he be leaving behind?

He was destined to become dust and bones just like every person.

He was just a man.

He ate and slept and bathed and did everything that made humans...well, *human*. How had it taken her so long to realise?

"I'm quite all right, thank you." Rosie couldn't help the twitch of her lips. "Miss Khalar is very pleased with her accommodations and her stay so far. I just need your assistance with my *captipheus* curse so I can take her for a tour of the city today—assuming that it's still all right for me to go with her?"

Lawrence's eyes made a much slower journey across her, lingering on her chest and legs. Though she still felt the grip of anxiety seizing her airway and still feared what he could truly do to her, she knew in her bones that he had no power over her anymore. She had to keep telling herself that.

Be truly extraordinary.

Lawrence stood and rounded the desk. "What are you up to?"

She choked on a breath. "Excuse me, sir?"

"I said," he growled, taking her upper arm in a vice grip, "what are you up to? What's gotten into you, girl?"

She clenched her fists tighter to stop the shaking and lifted her eyes to meet his now that he stood so close to her.

She was not inferior. He was just a man.

She could do this.

"I'm just...I'm excited to get some fresh air, sir." Rosie watched the suspicion grow in Lawrence's stare.

"Whatever you're planning," he hissed, slapping his other hand onto her forehead, "I promise you that it won't work. *I own you.* Don't you dare forget that. You are a street child and a criminal. You are worthless without me. You are *nothing.*"

The stifling heat from his hand signalled that he was altering her curse. She found it easier to cope with this time.

She poured all of her focus into breathing evenly and forgetting that he had her in his nauseating grip again. She kept her eyes on his. She dared him to taunt her by maintaining eye contact.

He was just a man. She wanted to laugh at the thought of it. All the barbed words and hissed curses were just the weapons of an insecure man whose only worth was in the power he held over others.

"Your curse is watertight," he hissed, removing his hand from her forehead but retaining his grip on her arm. "If you try to escape or even leave Miss Khalar's side, you'll be paralysed. You'll be returned to me on a stretcher and won't be able to move for days. And I promise you this"—he lowered his voice and moved so close that his lips brushed the side of Rosie's mouth—"when you're paralysed and all alone, able to see and feel everything but unable to move or speak, *that's* when I'll come and pay you a visit. I pray that you defy me, Rosie. In fact, I look forward to it happening."

The roiling, burning acid from his words sunk into her skin like hooks, each one raising her anxiety a little more until she felt at risk of crumbling in front of the monster. Her knuckles paled as her hands cramped in their tight fists.

She needed to leave.

Her voice miraculously didn't shake when she asked, "Are we finished here, sir?"

He was just a man.

"Hmm." He sat back against the edge of the desk and looked her up and down. "Remember my promise. I'll see you soon. I really hope I will."

He was just a man. A disgusting man.

She didn't grace him with further conversation and strode from the room on jellied legs, barely managing to close the door behind her. Being courageous was exhausting.

By the time Rosie returned to her room in the basement, the rigidity of her shoulders had loosened and her hands had unclenched. The welcoming scent of laundry detergent combined with fried breakfast foods engulfed her as she leaned her head back against her door and huffed out a sigh. She allowed her anxieties to surface in the solemn quiet and slid down the door, ending up a pile of limbs and curses on the chipped tile flooring.

Tears spilled down her cheeks. She'd done it. She'd faced her greatest tormentor—her cruellest demon—and she'd retained her dignity.

She was overcome with a sense of accomplishment, as if now that she'd conquered this, everything else was mere child's play. She could face the day and the weekend with the knowledge that she would prevail. Lawrence's noose around her neck had loosened a little, and she could breathe freely again for the first time in over a year.

Despite the ostentatious prison that she remained in, she'd become free. It was scary and it had taken every ounce of her energy, but a shift in mindset had changed everything.

Pushing off the floor, she quickly changed into clothes fit for a day of exploring the city and combed her hair. It was as she turned to leave the room that she noticed another note pinned to her travel journal, waiting to be seen.

"I'm on board," she whispered to no one. "You don't need to keep taunting me."

She whisked the note up and greedily read it, this time finding warm encouragement in the words rather than the usual slinking unease in her gut.

Continue on as normal. Everything you need will come to you in time. Arouse no suspicion and don't question favours that fall your way. Everything is as it should be. All you need is a dash of bravery.

P.S. I'd recommend visiting Emerald Bay in Provocion. You'd like the crystal-clear waters and the rainbow jellyfish.

"A dash of bravery." She grinned. "Now *that* I can do."

She scrunched the paper up in her fist and tossed it beneath her bed, striding from her room with a renewed sense of purpose. She'd add Emerald Bay to her list of places to research at a later date, not minding that the author had read her travel journal.

She had no idea how she'd pull it off or any clue as to how she'd escape afterwards, but she was filled with the unshakeable belief that she didn't need to fret over the details of her *wine tasting*. It would all work out in the end if she believed in herself.

This would be the last wretched weekend she spent in The Ruby Talisman Hotel and Casino. She knew it.

And, apparently, someone else did too.

CHAPTER 15
THE ONE WITH THE GHASTLY SCHEME

"What are you wearing? Where's your uniform?"

Jakob's unsavoury greeting as Rosie entered Suite Rouge was to be expected, and yet she found herself flushing as she saw Kit watching the exchange from her seat at the dining room table.

"I thought that Miss Khalar would prefer to explore the city as authentically as possible. If she was followed by an employee of the hotel, it might attract more attention than she'd like."

Jakob wanted to reprimand her further—she could tell by the tightness around his mouth and the narrowing of his eyes.

She added, "I can go and change if you'd prefer, Miss Khalar?"

Kit waved her off. "No need. Your idea has merit. I would prefer to explore the city in disguise, so I'll be needing something more...*common* to wear. Jal"—she waved at her employee in an incredibly *Kitty* manner—"see to it that I have appropriate clothing. We might not have anything suitable in our luggage, but I'm sure you'll figure something out."

Jal minced out of the room to prepare an outfit, leaving the three of them in uncomfortable silence. Kit was in full Kitty mode in front of Jakob, and it made Rosie even more curious as to why she wanted to have a meeting this morning.

"Rosie, pour us some tea and then take your leave." Jakob gestured at the spread in front of them on the table. "The chef has already prepared and presented our breakfast, as you were noticeably absent from your duties despite prior warning."

Rosie checked the grandfather clock to see that it was five before nine. She was right on time, and they all knew it.

"Right away, Mr Haart." The words tumbled from her mouth without thought, and she immediately fell into the role of dutiful servant. She'd conquered an interaction with Lawrence, but standing up to a guy she used to love would take more work. She could feel the combined gaze of two formidable personalities on her whilst she poured the tea and tried to keep her hands from shaking. She focussed on the smell of the fresh pastries, the yeast and sugar and fruit.

She was more than curious about what business Kit and Jakob had with each other; to her knowledge, they'd never met before and hadn't shared any in-depth interactions.

What was Kit up to? More importantly, what was *Jakob* up to?

She knew that there was no way she could sit this meeting out. She needed more information, and she needed to know if this had anything to do with the *wine tasting*.

"Is there anything else I can get for you before I leave?" She placed the pot of tea back on its rest and stood back from the table with her hands clasped behind her back.

The two of them looked at her with matching withering stares.

"Nothing." Jakob waved her off impatiently. "This is a private meeting. Off you go."

"Of course, Mr Haart."

She rolled her eyes as she proceeded to the door, only to be halted by a familiar lazy drawl.

"I trust you'll be back within half an hour so we can begin our tour?"

Rosie cleared her throat but didn't turn back. "Of course, Miss Khalar."

She'd already decided as she left the suite that she was going to let her curiosity get the better of her. There was a time and a place for snooping, and this was the perfect example of both. (Not that Rosie ever needed a time or place to snoop.) The only way to discover what was going on behind the scenes and what Jakob was really planning was to eavesdrop.

Information was a potent currency.

She snuck into the discreet maid's cupboard in the penthouse corridor opposite the lifts and got to work climbing into the air vent. Hopefully, they would still be exchanging pleasantries by the time she was in earshot.

A handful of scuffles, scrapes, and winces later, she began crawling on her belly through the stuffy steel tunnel, careful to make her pursuit silent. She counted the third, fourth, then fifth ventilation grate before coming upon the one above the dining table in Suite Rouge.

The disjointed voices of Kit and Jakob drifted into the vent, but it wasn't until Rosie turned delicately onto her back in order to take pressure from her knees and wrists that she started listening to the conversation at hand.

"—not that I don't wholeheartedly appreciate the invitation."

"You've been a very busy young man, Mr Haart."

"Please, it's just Jakob." A *clink* of bone china. "Can you elaborate?"

Kit scoffed. "I'm not sure whether I should trust you; you

seem so very talented at deceiving those around you. Especially those closest to you."

Jakob paused, and Rosie inched closer to the grate so that her ear was almost hovering over it. It would be in plain sight if anyone were to look up.

"I'm not sure what you mean, Miss Khalar. Is everything okay with your accommodations? Is Rosie an adequate personal liaison?"

"Please don't pepper me with niceties." A crunch of pastry. "I'll cut to the chase. The person you've been secretly conversing with to gather information on your father is me."

Rosie caught the gasp in her throat before it escaped. Her eyes widened. Why had Jakob been gathering information on Lawrence? Why had Kit been helping him in secret?

Unable to satiate her curiosity on audio alone, she turned gingerly in the cramped vent tunnel and crept gradually over the grate so that she could see them.

"Wait—*what?*" Jakob stammered and spilled some tea on his tie.

Kit's laugh was hollow. "Don't act so astonished, I might become offended."

"But you're—you can't be—is this a trick?"

"Why is it that I can't be your informant? Because I'm a woman? Or because I'm just an affluent gambler with bull for brains?"

"I—I just—"

"Take your pick."

Rosie couldn't help the satisfaction she felt in Jakob's scrambling for an answer. Kit waited patiently, sipping her tea with the practised elegance that Rosie had seen come through in both of her characters. Kit and Kitty shared the same delicacy, which told Rosie that amongst all of the acting and fabrication, this was a trait that the real Kit couldn't shake.

"I apologise. I'm just surprised to finally find the informant. I wasn't expecting them to ever reveal themselves, let alone as one of the most famous faces in the Twelve Territories. Colour me shocked."

"Hmm."

Kit poured herself another cup of tea and picked at a flaky pastry on her plate.

"I must ask why you're so adamant on dethroning your father. Is it greed for what you're yet to inherit?"

The rug had been well and truly pulled from beneath Rosie's feet. Jakob had been trying to get rid of Lawrence all along, and yet he was still adamant on treating her so poorly.

What was his plan? Was this the proof she needed to link Jakob to the mysterious notes?

Jakob winced and clasped his hands together in his lap, his gaze trained on them. His answer was quiet enough that Rosie almost didn't hear it.

"Because of her."

The grandfather clock ticked ominously.

"Who?"

"Rosie. Your personal liaison."

A lead weight settled in Rosie's gut, and every muscle in her body went taut. The same shock was painted all over Kit's face, her elegant composure shattered for a moment or two. As Jakob looked up from his lap, she somehow schooled it back to boredom, any ounce of humanity or personality bleached once again from her expression.

"Why are you trying to help her? From what I've seen of your limited interactions, you treat her as if she were less than the muck beneath your shoes."

Jakob grimaced. "That's what I want you to see. That's what I need everyone else—*my father*—to see."

"Meaning?"

"Meaning everyone is the hero of their own story. I'm just trying to be the hero in mine."

"And how's that working out for you?"

"It's difficult, to say the least."

"Hmm." Kit considered the man before her. "Have you ever contemplated, Mr Haart, that every so often the hero is actually hindering more than they're helping?"

Seemingly stumped, Jakob's mouth opened and closed several times.

What in Aakla's name were they talking about?

Perhaps they somehow knew that Rosie was hiding in the vents and had switched to speaking in a code. Or perhaps they feared that someone else could be listening.

However, if the look on Jakob's face was anything to go by, he was just as confused as Rosie was. It seemed that Kit was hiding something or that she knew more about the goings-on of Roguerest than she let on.

"The way you treat her is incredibly damaging," Kit continued. "She's much worse off now than she was before she met you. What does that say about your heroism?"

Rosie didn't know whether to be more shocked that Jakob was secretly trying to free her by undermining his father—which meant he had much more backbone than she gave him credit for—or that Kit was hiding information and standing up for her. She'd been helping Jakob gather intel on his father from territories away.

Kit pressed, "Does she know that you've been trying to help her?"

"No." Jakob shrunk back in his chair. "She can't know about it either. I have everything set in motion for this weekend, and I fear that if she knew what I've been doing for this past year, she would never forgive me for treating her the way I have."

Kit shook her head. "And I suppose you think that when you

banish the evil demon in her life and take over the city, she'll come running back into your open arms with tears of jubilation?"

Jakob cleared his throat and scratched the back of his neck.

"I can dream, can't I?"

"I've known Rosie less than twenty-four hours, and yet I seem to know her much better than you do. If she were given freedom from this hotel, she would run as far as her legs would take her. She wouldn't glance back at you once."

The words were harsh and the pain they caused lashed across Jakob's face in a twisted frown and a slump of his shoulders. Rosie almost wanted to reach out and touch him, to apologise for the bitter truth, but she knew that he needed to hear the words.

Yes, she had loved him once, and perhaps she would always love him in some way, but the last year had changed everything. He was no longer her protector and partner-in-crime. He was the reason for her imprisonment. He was the assistant to her greatest demon.

She still couldn't grasp the fact that he'd been plotting to free her. This confirmed her theory. It had been him all along, trying to keep her motivated. She'd been receiving the notes the entire time she'd been trapped at The Ruby. It made sense that he'd been trying to help her in his own way. This weekend had been in his sights for much longer than Rosie could comprehend.

At least she could pursue her *wine tasting* and know who and what she was doing it for. She needed to do this for Jakob. For whatever reason, he needed her to *taste that wine* to help give her freedom again. At least she knew Jakob's motives were honest. Against every prior judgement and fear that she'd had about him, he still had feelings for her.

He'd wanted to free her from Lawrence all along.

"We've gotten off topic." Jakob steered the conversation away from her and back to what Rosie wanted to hear about. "Why have you chosen now to reveal yourself? You've given me everything that I need, and I've paid you handsomely for your priceless intel on Irredore. This weekend could've gone without a hitch and I'd have never known that it was you. Haven't you just incriminated yourself?"

Kit let out a humourless laugh and swiped a bite-sized cake from one of the platters, eating it in one mouthful without breaking the air of decorum that oozed from her—a feat that Rosie figured not many could pull off.

She held Jakob's question hostage as she finished chewing and sipped her tea, seemingly in no rush to relieve his curiosity. Each of her movements were leisurely and deliberate, down to picking a stray crumb from the lapel of her black velvet blazer.

"You have quite the sense of humour, Mr Haart. Has anyone ever told you that?"

He didn't respond.

"You see, I've done absolutely nothing to incriminate myself. I have shared my past with a new friend in polite conversation. If that helps a hidden agenda of his, who am I to blame? You're the one with the ghastly scheme to overthrow your father and leave him rotting in a jail cell—not me."

Jakob's eyes shifted all over the room.

He pressed, "Why did you call this meeting?"

"Because I want to be confident in the fact that this tournament will go on uninterrupted. I can't risk any distractions or disruptions. The tournament may just be a front for your daddy-issues finally coming to a head, but it's my livelihood. I want your assurance that the games will go on as planned and that come Monday morning, I'll be leaving here with my winnings and my reputation intact. No deviation to the schedule."

Jakob scoffed. "You're confident, I'll give you that."

"There's a reason why I'm the most revered member of the Kaarmiach Five. It's not just hearsay. I'm very good at what I do."

"Well, rest assured that the two games this weekend will go off without a hitch. The winner will receive their full winnings, and you will all move on with your lives as if nothing happened. What I have planned will not interfere with the games and will be kept as discreet as possible. I assume I can count on your discretion on this matter, Miss Khalar?"

"You have my word."

"I'm glad we're in agreement. How about we enjoy the remainder of this breakfast spread and then carry on as if none the wiser?"

Rosie took the cue to hot-step it back to the penthouse corridor, her thoughts somewhere else entirely. She'd received so much information in such a short period of time. She hadn't decided which intel shook her more, but one thing was for certain: she needed to play her part in Jakob's plan to overthrow Lawrence. He had to pay penance for his behaviour; she just hoped that his plan worked.

Her descent into the maid's cupboard was just as stealthy, though she felt heavier and more clumsy with the thoughts in her head weighing her down.

Tomorrow.

She had no method yet for this madness. The stakes were so much higher this time, but instead of intimidating her, it filled her body with a thrill that she'd not witnessed since the day she was sentenced. Tomorrow she was going to pull off a *wine tasting* to win back her freedom.

Freedom. The word alone had her giggling like a child and vibrating with excitement. She shook out her arms and allowed herself to start dancing on the spot.

She'd survived. She'd made it long enough to find a way out. Through every taunt and demeaning task, she'd persevered.

As she danced, her visions of a life outside The Ruby came screaming back to her. Master of one and captive of none.

Master of one and captive of *none*.

When Jakob exited Suite Rouge some time later, Rosie was standing sentinel beside the lifts as if blissfully unaware of the proceedings of the days to come. She barely managed to keep her excitement contained.

Kit waited in the doorway of the suite as Jakob approached, waiting for Rosie to call a car for him.

"Is there anything else you need from me before I leave with Miss Khalar?" She hoped that nothing in her stance or tone gave away her newfound knowledge.

"Nothing comes to mind. Please *behave*. If you dare to step out of line, you'll have to answer to me when you return. Understood?"

Rosie couldn't take his threat as anything but elaborate acting. She knew too much now. He was doing all of this for her. The old Jakob had been beneath the ugly veneer all along.

"Yes, Mr Haart." She strove to appear humbled by his threat.

"Provide Miss Khalar with whatever she desires and have it charged to the hotel. Please be back at the hotel before five; the VIP dinner this evening begins at six, and you're to help the kitchen staff serve. Though I'm sure Miss Khalar will need to be back before then in order to prepare herself for the evening's events."

"Yes, Mr Haart."

Jakob considered her for a moment, gazing into her as if he could see through to her very soul, stripping her bare for a brief instant. The stare sent her tumbling back to *before* and how he could look at her for hours with a goofy grin on his face. He could lay on the creaky little bed in her room at the inn and play with her hair whilst they looked up at the stained ceiling and pretended to see the stars, pointing out made-up constellations to each other and laughing at the bizarre names they came up with.

He might try to hide it, but now that Rosie knew what he was up to, it was written clear as day in the way he looked at her.

Could he tell that she knew something? Had he heard her in the vent?

Her mind raced once again. The stakes and deceptions of the upcoming weekend had increased exponentially in such a short period of time. She'd thought that fear would be a driving factor in all of the complicated plans for the weekend, but all she felt was the *thrill*. Jakob didn't grace her with anything else as he boarded the lift car and demanded the attendant take him to the ground floor. Rosie visibly slumped as the lift doors closed, momentarily forgetting that she had an audience.

"You shouldn't allow him to talk to you in such a manner."

Rosie's head shot up, her posture straightening.

"Sorry, Miss Khalar. I forgot you were there."

Kit frowned and crossed her arms as she leaned against the door frame to Suite Rouge.

"You don't have to call me that when he's not around. You can disrobe now."

Rosie choked on an inward breath and coughed, looking anywhere but at the figure in the doorway. Her cheeks flamed, and she scratched at her shoulder to give her hand something to do.

"Excuse me?"

Kit's laugh was soft and unexpected. "Apologies. I meant that you can shake off your submissive character. You don't need to play that part when it's just us two. In fact, my only request is that you are entirely yourself around me."

Rosie nodded with her eyes still fixed on the floor. It seemed that Kit was back to being playful and friendly instead of aloof and closed off.

"In that case," Rosie broached, looking up to meet her gaze, "can I ask a favour of you too?"

"Favours are dangerous."

"Are they?"

"In my world, almost certainly," Kit replied. "Though I find myself trusting you, so ask away."

Her emerald eyes were fixed on Rosie from the other side of the corridor, her features slack with amusement.

Rosie stepped closer to the suite. "If I'm to be completely myself, I want the same from you. I don't want Kitty, I want Kit —the real deal. Open and honest. We're going out into the city as two normal young women on an even playing field."

Her answering smirk told Rosie all she needed to know.

"It's a tall order for someone like me, but I suppose I can let go of control for a few hours." She gestured for Rosie to follow her. "Come on in, we've got our work cut out for us if I'm to look like a commoner."

CHAPTER 16
A VULGAR STAIN

Rosie knew Roguerest inch by inch, step by step, road by road, and wall to wall. She knew each crevice and every vantage point. She was certain that no one in the city knew it like she did.

But walking with Kit, the sun beating down as the scent of ale mixed with fried savoury delights assaulted them, Rosie realised that she didn't know Roguerest at all. Not even close.

To have a companion who simply wanted to explore the walled circus changed every aspect of it. Rosie knew that she'd never be able to see the city in the same light again. Jakob had never been interested in exploring for the joy of it and had always been afraid that one of his father's cronies would see them together.

But exploring with Kit was a different matter entirely. The lights reflected in her eyes and off her cheekbones, casting sharp shadows and highlighting her natural beauty. For the first time in twenty-four hours, Rosie saw Kit smiling like a child, completely lost in the sounds and sights of what she usually classed as mundane.

Rosie knew that this, right here, was the real Kit. Unfiltered and freed of her chains to Kitty Khalar. Though, truth be told, if Rosie hadn't witnessed her outrageous transformation, she wouldn't believe that the free spirit wandering by her side was the same person.

Her signature sharp, dark bob had been replaced with two honey-blonde braids that trailed down her back, adorned with ribbons and delicate flowers. Rosie had no clue as to how her eyes had changed colour, but they had, now a warm brown instead of the vibrant green she was known for. The most jolting detail of all, though, was her outfit. Gone were the luxurious fabrics and sprawling capes. There wasn't a feather or a pearl in sight. She wore a pair of light linen trousers, cinched in at the waist, with a loose, long-sleeved smock blouse. The clothes were even speckled with dirt and stains, making her look every bit the regular working-class citizen of Roguerest.

Everything about her had become entirely forgettable, yet Rosie knew that the image would be imprinted on her mind for a lifetime. Kit was remarkable in that she was wholly unaware of her natural grace. She flitted from market stall to market stall as a butterfly would between flowers, dainty and fleeting.

Rosie was slowly but surely falling under her spell. She found herself wanting to get to know her.

"What's that smell?"

Rosie cleared her throat and looked away, knowing that Kit had caught her staring. She mumbled, "I think it's the fried *moonbons*. Do you want to try one?"

Kit's face lit up. "I have no idea what they are, but if they taste as good as they smell, I absolutely do."

Rosie laughed quietly and led her to the jolly woman at the *moonbons* stall, her stature the same shape as the doughy balls of pastry that she sold.

"What can I do for ya lovely ladies today?"

"Just one bag of *moonbons*, please," Rosie responded.

Kit furrowed her brow. "Don't you want some?"

"I'll have some of yours." Rosie grinned. "The portion sizes are...more than adequate."

"You got that right." The woman chortled and handed Kit the paper cone filled with sweet treats. She passed over payment in return but didn't wait for change as she stuffed some of the pastry into her mouth with a throaty groan, wandering away without a care in the world.

"Keep the change." Rosie politely smiled at the woman and followed Kit as she meandered through the crowds, marvellously unrecognisable. She was predictably drawn in by the entertainers of the market and watched in awe at fire-breathers, jugglers, musicians, and magicians.

The market square was vast and lined on each side with tourist-focussed shops that hiked their prices every time the high season rolled around. The cobblestones were covered in hundreds of market stalls with technicolour covers that billowed in the sticky breeze. Marketeers shouted and sang, offering their wares at knockdown prices —or so the tourists thought. Both sweet and savoury smells travelled with the wind, changing every time the direction of the breeze did.

Each covered stall was slightly different, from food to clothing to furniture. The only thing that connected them all was the stall covers, providing much-needed shade from the blistering summer sun.

The market square was one of the busiest places in Roguerest at all times of the day. At night, it would transform into a festival of lights and pleasures that was even more enticing than in the daytime.

Watching Kit experience the world was a sport in itself—a fascinating, effortless sport. How long had she travelled the territories acting aloof to all the simple delights? How long had she wanted to wander around cities just to experience the tourist traps and local delicacies?

"Look at him!" Kit laughed between mouthfuls of pastry as a man on stilts effortlessly juggled three bottles of wine.

They wandered the market like that for half an hour or so, Kit pointing out the weird or wonderful and Rosie watching her intently. Experiencing her joy was a joy in itself. Kit was like a child again, marvelling at anything that flashed or made noise or smelled good.

How long had she been Kitty Khalar and not allowed to live a normal life? How long had she been so detached from the rest of the world?

She desperately wanted to ask, desperately wanted any scraps of information that Kit would give her, but she didn't want to break the spell of her glee. Rosie couldn't stand the thought of taking this freedom away from her, so she simply watched. She felt her chest tingle every time Kit smiled without abandon. She felt herself smile every time Kit laughed.

It was intoxicating to be around.

"What's your favourite place that you've visited on your travels?" Rosie asked as they ducked beneath a red market stall and were engulfed in wafts of spicy smoke coming from huge pans on wood fires.

"Good question." Kit led her away from the stall and past one covered in beads and threads of every colour and material. "I don't think I have a singular favourite, more a collection of fond places for various reasons."

Rosie rolled her eyes. "I'm not letting you avoid the question."

They both dodged a stumbling drunk in unison before stepping beside each other once again, laughing quietly at the woman's tone-deaf, intoxicated wailing.

"I'll admit, that was a very journalist-safe answer," Kit

owned up. "I can't seem to shake the habits I've built up when I'm asked personal questions. But I suppose I'd have to say Tridon. It's a city in the centre of Lunaron. Though many flock to Qathe because it's the capital, I actually prefer Tridon's culture and architecture."

Kit pointed out a street performer painted entirely gold and acting like a statue, and Rosie didn't look at the performer but instead at Kit's excitement. It was much more engrossing.

She eventually asked, "What's it like in Tridon?"

"Clean, for starters, something I don't think you're used to."

Rosie barked out a laugh. "Harsh! But you're right there."

"It's a complex system of streets, all connected by central junctions like points on a compass or clock. The buildings are all built using the same sand-coloured stone and they're all the same height, about five stories tall, so there aren't any eye-sore skyscrapers or feelings of superiority. The people are very friendly and welcoming to tourists despite the fact that their lives are made harder by the presence of strangers. And the musicians—there's one on every corner playing charming, romantic melodies."

They finished a large loop around the outside of the market square, having been down every avenue and seen every stall, then began back towards the *moonbons* stall. As they did, a group of street children ran past them as they played tag.

"Watch out for the little ones," Rosie warned. "They're the least suspecting when it comes to—"

She watched a child knock into Kit seemingly by accident and apologise profusely. Before she could get away, however, Rosie grabbed her by the scuff of her neck and dragged her onto her tiptoes.

"I didn't mean to run into you, miss!"

The girl's eyes began to well up on cue, and her bottom lip trembled.

"It's all right, Rosie." Kit looked at the child with sympathy. "It was an honest mistake, you can let her go."

"Oh, I will." Rosie shot the girl an unamused glance and held out her hand. "Just as soon as she gives back the money that she pilfered from your bag."

"Money?" The child's eyes welled with unshed tears. "I promise I didn't—"

"Enough with the act. It takes one to know one, kid."

They remained in a stand-off for a moment or two, but the girl didn't understand how stubborn Rosie was when she knew she was right.

"Money," she said through gritted teeth. "*Now.* I don't have time for your games."

"Rosie, I really don't think—"

"Fine," the girl whined, reaching into her pocket and bringing out the pouch. "Please don't tell the market guards. I'm just so hungry."

Rosie took the pouch from her and released her neck, handing the money back to Kit with an amused expression.

"Here." Kit fumbled in the pouch and pulled out a few gold coins. "Take it and get something to eat."

The girl beamed and snatched the coins without a word, dashing into the crowds to find her friends again—and to no doubt buy something with no real nutritional value, like *moonbons.*

"You've whittled your instincts to a tee," Kit mused, continuing on.

"I used to be her, that's why."

"Then surely, you should be more sympathetic?"

"I had to learn the hard way how to identify a safe mark. She should too if she's going to survive in this pit. Lazy recon is sure to land her somewhere undesirable."

They didn't speak further as they bought more *moonbons* and ambled aimlessly around the market.

"Show me where you grew up," Kit spoke up after a few minutes.

Rosie almost tripped over a cobblestone. "I...I didn't have a home. You know that."

Kit's brow furrowed a little, and she shook her head.

"No, I mean the streets and the places that you spent a lot of time in. Where are the houses you squatted in and the places you played? I want to see what it was like for you."

Unsure whether it was pity or curiosity that interested Kit, Rosie began leading the way towards The Estate, which was accessible from the market square by two main roads. The buildings closest to the Tourist Quarter were much nicer than those deeper in the maze of streets and alleys. The further from the front-facing buildings you trekked, the more layers of Roguerest's disguise were peeled away.

"I should warn you now, it's not a nice place in the depths of The Estate."

Kit walked slightly closer so that their hands brushed together every now and then.

"I've experienced many horrors in my lifetime." She spoke so softly that Rosie almost missed it. "There's nothing that scares me anymore."

Rosie stopped and met her gaze for a few moments, seeing numerous emotions crossing her face, from sorrow to anger to acceptance.

Perhaps she wouldn't mind the darkest parts of Roguerest after all.

They sauntered towards The Estate in companionable silence, tuning into the surroundings and each losing themselves in thought. Rosie deliberated on which of the many dreary locations she should take Kit to first. All equally bleak and dingy, she was in for some surefire embarrassment whichever direction she took.

Walking back towards her childhood home brought a slew of memories to the surface of her mind: running from police officers with a loaf of bread in each hand, playing chase with other kids through filthy puddles, practising pickpocketing tricks over and over and over again until she could lift a wallet as easily as she breathed.

She took a deep breath in.

Home.

As they began down Avera Street, a neatly paved road connected to the market square, Rosie scowled at the upscale, overpriced houses that left tourists in awe. Ignorantly assuming all of Roguerest's citizens lived as the one percent did, they didn't care to explore The Estate further.

"I'm assuming this is not where you grew up?"

"No," Rosie retorted. "Not even close."

They continued on until the tourists thinned out and all that remained were bustling locals, pacing from one place to another with jobs and responsibilities. The transition was slow at first—a building in need of painting or a pile of litter here and there. As they reached Scorpion Junction, one of two main crossroads in The Estate, Rosie spied more telltale signs of wear that would only grow worse as they ventured on.

The smell was the most obvious token of The Estate. The scent of smoke and decay became more pungent the deeper they journeyed. Babies cried and adults argued. Paint peeled and bricks crumbled. The previous paving degraded into dirt tracks that became swamp-like in the winter. Litter and raw sewage grew more common until it became a continuous feat to not stand in something foul.

Kit's voice was almost inaudible against the burgeoning

chaotic soundtrack that surrounded them. "Where are we going first?"

"I thought I'd take you to Orphan Pass."

Kit cleared her throat. "Is that what I think it is?"

"You'll find out momentarily."

The deeper they ventured into The Estate, the more her memories transitioned from happy tales of adventure to horrific instances of pure survival.

Though she kept her head held high, the dread in Rosie's gut pulsed and slithered enough to make her feverish. She hadn't realised how difficult it would be to revisit the place that had raised her, the place that was so vastly different to her current home. She'd almost forgotten the depths of sorrow that existed in these streets. The injustice and barbarity was rife on every corner, in every starving, bag-of-bones child and sickly woman slumped in the gutters.

She'd been desensitised to the savagery as a child, but after spending a year with a roof over her head, clean clothes, hot food, and a few friendly faces, she was struck with the reality of The Estate.

Kit didn't comment as they wandered past beggars and foul-mouthed drunkards, seemingly immune to the vulgarity that surrounded them. She didn't even flinch when a man hollered down to them from a window above, screaming profanities for no clear reason. Rosie steered her clear of a hunch-backed woman with a racking cough, not keen on the idea of returning her to The Ruby with a roster of diseases to her name.

Keeping her hand on Kit's wrist, she pulled her into a large shadowed alley lined with piles of rotting food and discarded belongings.

"Is this it?"

"Not quite."

About to push on, Rosie realised the wrist in her grip was quaking ever so slightly. She halted and looked directly into Kit's flitting eyes.

"We can turn back if you'd like; I wouldn't think any less of you. The Estate isn't a gentle place to venture even in the daytime."

"No," Kit insisted. "I'm all right; it just brings back some of my own undesirable memories to be in a place like this. I want to see it. *Please.*"

Rosie took a second to memorise Kit's defeated stature and expression, the childlike fear evident in her wide eyes. The *kaarmiach* champion had been robbed of her stoney-faced confidence and left an anxious young woman.

What undesirable memories did she have?

"How old are you?" Rosie's voice was almost lost on the breeze.

"Nineteen."

She smiled softly. "You've never appeared as young as you do right now."

The melancholy in Kit's expression cracked just a little as she said, "I'll take that as a compliment."

Rosie let her hand slip down from Kit's wrist and grasped her palm as she began to drag her deeper into the grimy alley. The walls on either side of them towered up so tall, with washing lines strung between them, that it looked as if there were no sky at all.

The turbulent noises from the main streets became almost entirely muted as they dared farther into the alley. The walls grew closer together until the two of them were almost shoulder-to-shoulder, the buildings above them leaning dangerously from age and poor construction.

"Here," Rosie muttered, as they came upon the opening to Orphan Pass. "This is...uh." She coughed quietly and tried again. "This is what's known as Orphan Pass. It's where the majority of street children call home and a dumping ground for parents—ones without either the means or motive to bring up a child safely. Babies are abandoned here, one every few weeks, and they're taken in by the older children, raised by youngsters who suffered the same fate."

Kit didn't speak as she gazed upon the alleyway, no wider than the two of them side-by-side and almost entirely dark. Daylight didn't touch these children unless they searched for it. This was possibly the most abhorrent of all the pits in Roguerest and was certainly the most ignored. Not even Jakob knew of Orphan Pass. It served as a vulgar stain on the clean, white reputation of the city's elite. Even the idea of such a place was repulsive to a large percentage of the population, including a good portion of those that resided in The Estate. No one wanted to acknowledge the horrors that existed in Orphan Pass.

Out of sight, out of mind.

"Is this where you...where you grew up?" Kit's meek question was a stark reminder of the life she lived and the privilege she had.

Rosie released a harrowing breath.

"Yes." She hesitated before adding, "This is the closest thing you'll ever find to purgatory—to Venaak's Abyss."

CHAPTER 17

ORPHAN PASS

"Venaak is your evil God."

Rosie wasn't surprised that Kit knew about the Cidaelean religion and its customs despite her homeland having an entirely different belief system.

"Yes," Rosie confirmed. "Her Abyss has always been depicted as an endless maze of alleyways like this, which makes me think that the artists were once inhabitants of Orphan Pass or something similar to it. No one could conjure an image this cruel—unless they were truly wicked, that is."

They both stared at the alley in front of them for a moment, unable to see much past a couple of sheets fluttering in the breeze, a makeshift door.

"Can we go in?"

Rosie turned to look at her once more, their hands still joined.

"Are you sure you want to?"

"Entirely," Kit answered without hesitation.

"Then welcome to The Abyss, I suppose."

Bringing someone else, someone *willing*, into the void that had been Rosie's childhood home was jarring. When she was just fourteen years old, she'd left the alley with a promise to never return unless the world as she knew it was coming to an end. The other children had laughed at her audacity. They'd taunted her for having the courage to dream of a reality better than the one they endured together.

But somehow, somewhere along the way, she'd managed to carve a new version of normal for herself. It wasn't what she wanted, wasn't what she'd dreamed of, but it was so much more than they'd ever expected of her. For a moment, that had been absolutely everything.

Holding Kit's hand tight enough to feel her erratic pulse, Rosie realised that perhaps she needed her hand held more than Kit did. Perhaps her promise to those street children years ago had been correct: she was only back because her world as she knew it was coming to an end. If everything went to plan, she'd be fleeing Roguerest come Monday's sunrise. She would never glance back, not even to see her own footprints in the sand.

This could be the perfect time to say goodbye to the place that raised her.

"I know that you've given me an out." Kit gave her hand a squeeze and pushed the sheets aside so they could walk through. "But if it's *you* that needs an out, we don't have to do this. I understand some of your pain, but there is an awful lot that you had to conquer as a child that I'll never be able to comprehend. I was graced with a loving family for nine beautiful years. I had a home and protection from the world, but I know you can't say the same for yourself. I'll never be able to empathise on that part."

Rosie swallowed a growing lump in her throat.

She desperately wanted to know more about the pain Kit had experienced, desperately wanted to peel back the layers and take a look inside her mind. As she'd always suspected, Kit was far much more than Kitty Khalar.

"But please know this," Kit continued, pulling them to a stop, "I would never judge you or treat you differently because of your upbringing. I am here to hold your hand should you need it and pay for the *moonbons* if you want them. We share a great deal of pain, no matter what the root cause is."

Kit looked down at their joined hands and released a deep sigh.

"Show me everything, Rosie. I want to see it all."

The dry heat of the summer day was nonexistent in the alleyway, replaced with the damp, frigid air that never shifted from this dark corner of the city. Rosie led Kit deeper, beneath the makeshift roof of stolen bed sheets attached to either side of the alley. There weren't as many children about in the daytime as there would be once night fell. That was when they stayed together for protection from the vilest of evils that lurked in the darkness.

There were old doorways every so many steps that served as individual territories for the older children. They were filled with blankets and personal belongings to identify them as claimed space. Rosie had claimed a doorway once after one of the older children left, and it had been the first place she'd ever truly felt home. The younger children would sleep against the steps of the doorway that housed their fondest *elder child*, hoping to claim ownership of it once their predecessor moved on into young adulthood and pursued bigger things.

The first child they came across was a boy, no older than seven, with a book in his grip. His hair was cut in chunky tufts that stuck up in every direction, clearly trimmed by one of the other children. He was so engulfed in his literature that he didn't notice Rosie and Kit approach.

"Hey there, kiddo," Rosie broached.

The boy's head shot up, and he scrambled away in fear,

tumbling into the first doorway he came across and hiding beneath the blankets.

"He forgot his book," Kit whispered.

"Wait here." Rosie picked up the book and crept to the doorway, taking a seat on the cold stone step and letting out a sigh.

She glanced over the novel and gently smiled at the title.

The Piracy and Gaiety of Peachlock Bay.

She'd read it as a child, perhaps even this very copy. Items like books and games were passed between children and through generations that occupied the Pass. She flicked open the cover and saw lists of names scrawled inside, immediately seeing her own amidst them. She smiled as she stroked her finger across it. Novels were the best form of escapism for kids like these.

"'Captain Strongheart had nothing left to give,'" she began to read aloud, picking up on the page the boy had been reading. It instantly transported her back to when she'd read the book for the first time. "'No strength nor swordsmanship could save him from the plundering depths of Peachlock in a winter storm. Though his blood sang with the warmth of rum, his skin froze beneath the treacherous waves of the place he'd once called home. He would drown. He would return to the sands that had made him and the Gods that had deigned him life. Would they welcome him with open arms? Or perhaps curse him for his crimes of piracy, larceny, and lust—to name a few?'"

The blankets behind her rustled quietly.

"'Grace would be waiting for him in town, perched upon the stone balcony he'd scaled so many times to profess his love. She would face the brunt of the storm as the seconds, minutes, and hours ticked by. Alas, she would be disappointed by his lack of timekeeping once again, though this time would be his final misdemeanour. His lungs burned as he floundered in the suffocating depths, knocked one way and another, tumbling and turning and plunging further from salvation.'"

Rosie felt the presence behind her come closer.

"Please keep going..." The boy's timid voice was close enough to feel his breath on the back of her neck. "You—you read better than me." She didn't turn to face him, not wanting to scare him away again, and continued on with the adventure that she knew so well.

"'If only he'd been granted the opportunity to tell her one final time that through all of his dalliances and affairs, she'd always been the one. It would only ever be her. His heart was made for Grace, and yet he'd frittered her love as if a drunkard and a gambler—a poor one at that. Would he see her in the afterlife? Would she tell him one more time that he was a fool and a heathen, but that she adored him anyway?'"

The boy sat next to her now, enraptured by her storytelling.

"'Strongheart swam and swam till his arms grew heavy as lead, but to no avail. The ocean would claim back what it was owed, once and for all. He found a strange sense of peace in relenting to the eventuality of death, as if he couldn't believe that he hadn't given in much sooner. But as his weighty body, still wrapped in his finest velvet doublet and his posh breeches, hit the sands of the ocean floor, he fixated on the clean, bright moon shining through the treacherous waters above him. Was Grace peering at the moon too?'"

In her peripheral vision, Rosie noticed Kit inching closer and sliding down the wall opposite them, sitting crossed-legged on the dirty cobbles as she listened. Rosie tried not to focus on the fact that she could feel Kit's gaze burning into her and instead kept her eyes on the page.

"'That was the moment he knew he had more in his bones to give. Even if just for one last glance at his love, he had to power on. It was so effortless to let go, to relinquish himself to the clutches of death and finally be at peace. But when had Strongheart ever chosen the burdenless road? Life may be laborious and taxing at the best of times, but wasn't life damned beautiful? Life had brought him adventure, love, thrills, and rum. He couldn't give all of that up merely because it was the road less travelled. He couldn't give up on Grace under the guise of fatigue. He'd conquered tyrants and led anarchists into the throes of freedom; he'd sailed the high seas from corner to corner and come face-to-face with the foulest of beasts. What was one more adventure?'"

Rosie paused and lifted her head slightly so that she could glance at Kit, who seemed just as engrossed in the story as the boy.

The boy questioned, "What 'appens? Does he live?"

Rosie finally looked at him. His gaze implored her to keep reading.

"Does he die?"

She smiled softly. "Have you never read this tale before?"

"I'm tryin', I swear. Freeda has been tryin' to teach me, but —but it's hard to say the big words. I can say the letters and I know how it's s'posed to sound, but I just...I can't get the words right."

"That's okay," Rosie cooed, feeling all kinds of protective over the boy who reminded her of herself. "You'll get it eventually; you just need to keep practising. I'm sure Freeda is doing a great job, so you have to keep listening to her and continue reading. Don't give up just because you're finding it difficult. Nothing that's worth it is ever easy. Like with Captain Strongheart."

"Okay, Red."

Rosie laughed. "Is that the most imaginative thing you can come up with?"

"Never seen hair like yours. Are you a mermaid?"

"A mermaid?" Rosie's gentle smile grew into a beaming grin. "Now that's a new one. No one has ever called me a mermaid before. What do you think, Kit? Am I worthy of the title mermaid?"

The boy tensed and looked over to where Kit sat. She'd been watching the interaction with quiet amusement.

"She's better than a mermaid." Her voice took on the playful tone that adults used when talking to young children. "Do you know why she's better than a mermaid?"

The boy shook his head.

"Because she's a siren. Mermaids aren't real, but sirens? They're as real as you and I, living and breathing beside you this very moment."

The boy looked back up at Rosie in wonderment. "What's a siren?"

"I'm not quite sure myself yet, but my friend Kit here believes I might be one. As soon as I know for certain, I'll come back and tell you all about it. Deal?"

He grinned with renewed fervour. "Deal."

Rosie handed him back the book and stood, stretching lightly as her joints protested from sitting on the cold stone step. Kit joined her and reached into her bag, bringing out two gold coins. She crouched down in front of the boy and pressed the coins into his palm, closing his fingers over them.

"These are just for you," she explained. "Go and fetch yourself something to eat. Something good and not bags of *moonbons*, though I know firsthand just how delicious they are."

He giggled in excitement, shooting up and tackling her into a tight embrace. "Thank you, miss! Thank you!"

Kit's answering laugh was unrestrained and joyous.

"You're most welcome. Run along before someone tries to shake you down for your newfound riches."

He helped her stand before darting down the alley and out of sight.

Kit brushed herself off and didn't try to hide the adoring smile stretched across her face and the new light in her eyes.

Rosie murmured, "You're a good person, Kit."

She sobered slightly in response but boldly took Rosie's hand once again, leading them deeper into Orphan Pass. Rosie assumed that she'd decided not to answer the comment, but as they came across two girls, maybe five or six years old, Kit belatedly spoke in a delicate whisper.

"My worth isn't measured by the amount of coins in my pocket, but in the way that I choose to spend them."

With that, Rosie couldn't argue.

Kit gave a couple of coins to the girls in front of them and watched them run away in a fit of excited giggles.

"I was born in a small village on the very edge of Irredore, called Heshalla."

Rosie tried not to tense up as Kit offered the information without prompt. She was opening up. She was revealing a part of the *real* Kit. Rosie didn't dare speak or breathe or move in case it scared the truth away.

"It was known across the territory for having the most beautiful blue flowers that were unlike anything else," Kit continued as they walked. "The smell was a cross between honey and spring rain. My parents were not important in the grand scheme of things, they were fruit farmers who lived crop to crop. I grew up being shielded from the financial struggles that they experienced, and life was beautiful for me in more ways than one. Like you, simplicity was a blessing."

They came across a boy of about nine or ten, holding a newborn baby in his arms as he sat in a doorway, a book propped up on his knees. Kit crouched down beside him and tucked two coins into the baby's swaddle blanket.

"Until the age of nine, I had never ventured further than the next village," she explained as she continued wandering beneath sheets and around crates. "I had no comprehension of the wider territories or of any other lifestyle. I concluded that everyone must live how we did—what other choice was there? It was a naïve and secluded life, but it was idyllic in that sense."

Rosie admitted to herself that she was surprised. She, like many others, had figured that Kit had come from wealth and privilege.

"I'd never experienced pain or war or suffering, not in the sense that inevitably came upon us."

"The civil war." Rosie filled in the gaps.

Kit grimaced and shook her head, her hands gripping into tight fists before releasing slowly.

"Is that what they call it here?"

Rosie blinked a couple of times and frowned.

"Isn't that what it was?"

"No." Kit let out a harsh, clipped laugh. "Not in the slightest."

CHAPTER 18
CASUALTY OF BARBAROUS BEHAVIOUR

Rosie wanted to dig for more information.

She wanted to know more about the civil war that... hadn't been. How could the newspapers have gotten the story wrong? But being around this unfiltered version of Kit felt like walking on eggshells. One word wrong, one push too far, and it would all disappear. She didn't want to risk it.

They ventured further through Orphan Pass, and Kit gave a couple of coins to every child she saw, making Rosie wonder how much money she'd brought for a simple wander around the city.

Had she been expecting to go shopping? Rosie cringed at the thought that she'd wanted to flit around boutiques and had instead been brought to the unspoken pit of the city.

But then she looked at Kit, not an ounce of disgust or frustration in her features, and remembered that Kitty might have wanted to spend the day being doted on in boutiques, but Kit was a different story.

The young woman beside her seemed quite at home in the grimy back alleys of the city.

"Knowing that it was branded as a civil war here makes it even more infuriating."

Her voice cut through the relative quiet of the seemingly never-ending alley. Had it always been this long?

Rosie whispered, "What was it? If not a civil war, then..."

"It was a systematic slaughter of almost an entire race of people. It was barbaric and needless violence, all for the sake of power and profit. The Irredorian people had nothing to do with it. They didn't provoke it. They weren't involved. They were mere victims of a power struggle."

Rosie was speechless. *Slaughter?*

"We were warned by other villages that something catastrophic was coming. Word travelled fast back then because all of the villages were interconnected by webs of families and friends. I've never met an Irredorian who wouldn't take me into their home at a moment's notice, no explanation or verification needed. We're a peaceful, trusting race who knew nothing of violence on the scale that was brought upon us."

Kit ran her fingers along the brick wall beside them as they walked, almost as if she needed something to ground her whilst she relived the horror of her childhood.

"It came to our village in the night," she pressed on. "I woke to the screams of those who I'd played and eaten with the day before. I was so little, two months from my tenth year, so I had to climb on my bed to peer out the window in the bedroom that I shared with my"—her voice cracked—"with my younger brother. Everything was burning. The smell was...I'll never forget the smell or the billowing heat from the flames. The crackling and hissing still haunts me in my dreams. My parents grabbed us, and we ran. I have no idea where they planned to go because, looking back, there was no escape. The soldiers were not Irredorian; they looked so strange and foreign to me as a child. I'd never seen anything like them, tall with *clanking* armour that had been tarnished with soot. They spoke with harsh accents as they shouted to each other, lighting everything ablaze."

Kit took Rosie's hand again without looking at her, her jaw slack and her mind clearly somewhere else entirely.

The horrors she must have seen... Rosie thought with a wince.

"They saw us before we could make it to the woods," she whispered. "Grabbed my mother by her hair, tackled my father to the ground, and then they plucked up...they just...they grabbed him as if he weighed nothing." Her voice quaked and fell to a barely audible level. "He was so little. I just wanted to protect him. I screamed, but they had me by the neck. They... they wanted a young girl for themselves. I watched as these hideous metal monsters brought up their swords and..."

Rosie took the opportunity to comfort her, gently squeezing her hand.

The formidable Kitty Khalar was anything but. She was concealing so much pain and suffering; it was no wonder that she donned an act in front of others. She couldn't risk the strain and torment of her past once again.

Becoming Kitty gave her the opportunity to be something so far from her roots that she didn't have the chance to think about it.

Kitty was thriving, but Kit was just an orphan in pain.

Like Rosie.

"I watched on as my family was butchered, their limp bodies tossed aside as if they hadn't been souls just moments before—people with lives and responsibilities and relationships. The monsters dragged me to their parade of horses and carts, throwing me into the back of one with my hands and feet bound. I laid there for hours—or perhaps it was days, I don't quite recall—until we arrived at a camp, where they strung me up against a tree in the centre to be spat on and taunted."

Rosie wanted to say something, anything, but what could she possibly say? *I'm sorry* was completely redundant.

"I cried until I lost my voice. But it wasn't long until I reached a turning point. I could either crumble or I could rise. My only worth if I crumbled would've been another nameless casualty of barbarous behaviour." She paused and huffed out a sigh. "But if I rose? Well, then could I rain down on the evil that took everything from me—not for myself, but for the innocents slain. I owed it to my people to suffer." She cleared her throat. "Because through suffering, I survived."

They came upon a small crossroads where another alleyway met the one they were on. Rosie knew that it came to a dead end on the right, butting up against the city wall, and was cut off to the left by fencing meant to keep the orphans in. She used their joined hands to gesture ahead of them, encouraging Kit to carry on straight. It was easy for someone who didn't know the maze to get completely lost.

"Anyway." Kit let out a humourless laugh. "That's enough doom and gloom for one morning."

Rosie wanted to ask for more, wanted to encourage her to share the full story, but she also didn't want to push too far. Maybe if she gave Kit the space she needed to process what she'd explained, then she'd share more before the weekend was up.

"You can always share these things with me," Rosie told her. "I know we've only known each other for a matter of a day but... there's something about you. I feel like you just *get* me."

Kit smiled but didn't look at Rosie as they walked, their joined hands swinging lightly between them.

She replied, "I fear...I fear that no one has ever understood your pain before now—or that no one has *tried* to understand. But I do. I understand what it means to have a childhood ripped away by unimaginable hardship."

Rosie cleared her throat as traitorous tears welled in her eyes. "I think that's what I'm afraid of."

Kit pulled them to a stop, and their eyes connected.

"That I understand you?"

Rosie shrugged. "That someone understands me for the first time and yet...I'm graced with only a weekend of your time."

Kit's smile was sad. "Then we'll have to make the most of the time we've got, won't we?"

They stood in the grimy alleyway, the demons of both their pasts circling them whilst they held on tightly to each other. Whether they wanted to admit it or not, they'd bonded through shared pain.

They were both only human.

"You're nothing like I expected," Rosie admitted.

"And you are so much more than I ever expected."

Rosie was in awe as they reached the other end of Orphan Pass. Kit had tenaciously powered through the dark, damp pit and given away the entire contents of her bag to the children they'd passed. Luckily, it was daytime, so the majority of children were traversing the city and not lingering in the alleyway, otherwise they'd have come up empty much earlier and may have had a riot on their hands.

When they entered the larger alley on the other side of the pass, daylight began to filter down towards them, and a gentle breeze tickled Rosie's cheeks.

"Are you all right?" she asked, watching Kit's unfocussed gaze move to fixate on her.

"More than all right." Her focus still seemed distant. "I might not have helped as much as I wish I could, but I like to think that I've staved off the hunger for a few of them. Even if it only serves to delay starvation for one more night, it's better than nothing at all."

They hadn't talked any more about the murder or the pain or the past. Rosie liked to think that it was a conversation tucked away for another time. The door had been left open a crack, not closed completely.

Rosie shared her feeling of helplessness when it came to the kids in the alley, though she knew firsthand how much a few coins from a kind stranger meant to the children of Orphan Pass.

She squeezed Kit's hand and regretfully said, "I hate to say it, but we should probably begin our journey back to The Ruby. Responsibility awaits for both of us."

Kit dropped her hand as if burned and immediately put some distance between the two of them. The reminder of her identity and occupation was clearly an unwelcome one. She wrapped her arms around herself and cleared her throat, sucking in a few deep breaths.

Shit. Rosie winced.

She'd done it. She'd pushed Kit back into the shadows and hauled Kitty out to perform for everyone.

"I didn't mean to—"

"It's fine," Kit lashed out and rolled her shoulders back, visibly transforming back into Kitty by posture and stance alone. Her chin was lifted, her eyes blank, and her smile vanished. "We should return to the hotel. I need to prepare for this evening's dinner and the first round of the tournament. Lead the way."

"Wait, Kit," Rosie floundered, grasping for the version of her that she so preferred. This couldn't be it. They still had time. "We don't have to go just yet, I can show you—"

"I said, *lead the way.*"

Defeated and regretful, Rosie lowered her head. She wanted

to kick herself for disrupting the day they'd had. She'd finally gotten a taste of the real Kit, and she'd blown it with a single sentence.

She supposed it was inevitable, though. As much as they were kindred spirits in the dark corners of the city where no one could see, reality was a different story.

She was a criminal working off a prison sentence.

Kitty was a territories-famous VIP with more wealth to her name than Rosie could imagine.

Their time together was finite.

"Of course, *Miss Khalar*. I'll take us back to The Ruby."

CHAPTER 19
FOULEST DEMONS

The return journey to The Ruby was spent in taunting silence, wildly different from the way they'd spent the first half of their adventure through the city. The Estate grew cleaner and friendlier with every step they took until they came upon the market square in the Tourist Quarter once again. Instead of leading Kit through the hundreds of billowing stalls, Rosie took a more direct route around the edge and straight up Havana Avenue, in front of the Temple surrounded by crowds waiting to enter and pay their respects to Aakla.

Rosie didn't bother to check whether Kit was following her, assuming that if too much distance were to come between them, her curse would kick in and she'd become a pile of bones on the cobbles, held together by skin and wrapped up in agony. She scolded herself as she marched back into the Casino District, embarrassed and angry for both her actions and Kit's.

They'd had a diverting morning, and Rosie had ignorantly assumed she'd cracked Kit's enigmatic shell to discover who she was beneath it. She'd thought now that they were on an even keel, Kit would stay...well, *Kit*.

Yet at the first mention of reality, she'd shrunk back beneath her guises of superiority and aloofness as if ashamed that she'd forgotten what her role was in the grand scheme of things. As if she couldn't be both Kit and Kitty.

Rosie weaved between meandering groups of tourists and snuck through alleys that provided little-known shortcuts until they arrived back on the street that housed The Ruby, the flashing lights of the entrance in the near distance.

Her anger built and built as they walked, eventually reaching a boiling point. *It was now or never.*

Rosie paused and felt a body stumble into her from behind, clearly not paying attention.

"Sorry," Kit mumbled.

"This is it," Rosie explained. "Once we step back in there, I'm no longer myself and you're no longer yourself either." She turned to fix her stare on an awkward Kit. "Are you sure you're finished here? Finished being your true self for once in your life?"

Rosie figured that this was her only chance to vent her frustration. She was getting tired of everyone treating her with back-and-forth personalities. She was tired of not knowing who to trust.

Kit stood beside her but kept a few inches between them as she spoke.

"We both have responsibilities for this weekend, and though it was nice to forget them for a short while, they're still here waiting for us. The show must go on, Rosie. Even when we'd much rather it didn't."

"So you return to being the privileged VIP and I return to waiting on you hand and foot? Sleeping on the floor of the butler's cupboard as if I'm some animal? *That's it?* After you and I both know that we're the same when it boils down to being human?"

Kit winced. "I have never treated you as an animal."

"It's too late," Rosie fumed. "I've seen you—*all of you*—and you can't take that away from me. I know who you really are beneath the personality that you don in front of the public and your employees. Even though we have to return to our respective roles, I'll never let you fool me into thinking you've got it all together again. I'll never let you trick me as you trick everyone else, acting as if you have no soul, no feelings, and no heart."

Kit's eyes welled up, and she blinked back tears.

"You're a bleeding heart through and through." Rosie's voice shook as she spoke. "Maybe you should try to remember that when you speak to me as if I'm an inconvenience and a peasant."

"Rosie, wait—"

She ignored Kit's request and powered on down the street, unfazed by the jeers and laughter of the drunkards and sightseers as she approached The Ruby.

How could she be so stupid? How could she trust someone again? No matter what form they took, what role they played in her life, everyone was only out to trample on her.

Jakob, Kit, Lawrence—even Khristann's game plan was up for debate.

She took the steps up to the entrance of the hotel two at a time, about to push through the revolving door when a hand grasped her arm and pulled her back.

"Rosie, please," Kit begged.

Hector was on door duty once again and wore the same surprised expression as the first time Rosie had left the hotel two days prior.

He glanced at Kit behind her without an ounce of recognition and then back to Rosie. "You all right?"

"Yes." She cleared her throat and turned to face Kit. "What can I help you with, Miss Khalar?"

Kit's tears took her by surprise, but she didn't show it. She allowed herself to be dragged to the alley on the left side of The Ruby so that they weren't visible to nosy onlookers.

"I'm sorry." Kit slid her hand from Rosie's arm to her palm and squeezed it lightly. "I'm truly sorry it has to be this way, but please know that it's all just an act. You're the only person I've ever admitted that to, the only soul I've come across who understands that sometimes parts of yourself have to be sacrificed in the name of achieving what you desire."

She angrily swiped at her tears with her spare hand. "I want...I want you to remember the version of me that you met today. That's the truest form of Kit that I've been since I was a farm girl in Heshalla. You allowed me to finally shrug off all the pretence, all the layers that I've built up to protect myself, and just *be*."

Rosie looked into her beautiful eyes and studied the details that remained the same even through the disguise. She could detect genuine sorrow and resentment, but it wasn't enough to justify the behaviour that would come once they entered The Ruby. It wasn't enough to make their class differences okay.

Rosie had to reinstate the walls around her heart before she risked losing everything for the sake of someone else's image and reputation.

She couldn't go through what happened with Jakob again. She couldn't allow herself to be kicked to the curb.

"I may have to sacrifice parts of myself on a daily basis in order to get what I want," Rosie rasped. "But please don't mistake me for being like you. I can still find myself beneath the walls I throw up, but you? I pity you."

Kit recoiled, shock flashing across her expression.

But Rosie pushed on, "Until today, you'd lived as a series of characters, none of which were truly you, to the point that you'd almost entirely lost yourself. You don't know which parts of you are genuine and which parts have been manufactured along the way to achieve some arbitrary goal or win another pile of gold coins. The only time you can be *you* is in the darkest alleys of a strange city with a girl you barely know."

Rosie could see each barb sinking into Kit but couldn't restrain herself any longer.

"When you leave on Monday, "she continued, tears filling her eyes, "you'll forget that I ever existed. You'll go on your merry way to whichever dazzling city calls your name next and whichever casino promises you the greatest earnings. You'll forget all about me, and I'll be left wondering where I should go, where I'll find someone who treats me like they understand my foulest demons. Someone who not only understands my demons, but has similar ones to show me in return, to make me feel as if I'm not so alone in this world. All my life, I've been alone, and then you show up and give me a taste of...of...*I don't know what.* Is this what family feels like? To be understood and unashamed of myself?"

Tears tumbled down her cheeks as the pain she felt blazing through her chest appeared on Kit's face. Kit lifted a shaking hand to wipe the tears away with her thumb.

"Yes." Kit's voice was thick with sorrow. "That's what family feels like."

"Why?" Rosie whimpered, all of the fight gone from her. "Why would you give me a taste of something only to tear it away?"

Kit's lips twitched with words that she appeared desperate to say.

She sighed and settled on, "Someday soon, you'll understand exactly why."

Both of them stood in the alleyway, completely torn open and vulnerable, and Rosie knew that this would be her only opportunity. She knew that once they stepped back into the light, the precious moment they were suspended in would never return.

If this ruined everything, then she didn't care. Everything would be ruined once they left the alleyway anyway. It was now or never.

She leaned forward and gently pressed her lips to Kit's, taking her hand again and giving it a soft squeeze. She closed her eyes and savoured the moment. If it never happened again, she could be happy in the fact that she'd taken her opportunity. She'd kissed the beautiful young woman who'd shown her what it was like to live outside of other people's expectations, what it was like to open herself up to hope again.

It wasn't until Kit's spare hand pushed against her chest that Rosie realised she hadn't kissed her back. She immediately stepped away and looked at her feet, shame flooding through her as their hands disconnected and she blew out a breath.

She may not regret it, but she certainly felt embarrassed that she'd kissed someone without considering for a second whether they wanted it too.

"I'm sorry," she rushed. "I shouldn't have done that without asking you first, but I knew after this moment we'd go back to being who we're supposed to be with other people watching. I didn't want to regret not taking the opportunity, but now I—"

"Rosie," Kit interrupted, placing a finger beneath her chin and lifting it until their eyes met once more. Surprisingly, she didn't look upset or mad. If anything, she looked...resigned.

"There's no need to apologise. I shouldn't have been so misleading with my actions. It's my fault that I gave you the wrong idea. I suppose I got so caught up in being understood and *seen* by someone that I didn't think about how that might translate through my actions."

Rosie flushed from cheek to cheek.

"The truth is," Kit continued, "I don't feel that way about

you—or anyone. It's nothing personal. I've never had a romantic attraction to anyone, and I highly doubt I ever will."

Her words settled on Rosie like a blanket, an understanding passing between the two of them. They stood like that for a minute longer, comfortable in the knowledge that they were finally on the same playing field. They knew things about each other that no one else did. Even if they never saw each other again after the tournament, this relationship would forever be burned into Rosie's brain.

"I'm sorry," she murmured. "I didn't know. I shouldn't have assumed."

Kit laughed quietly. "How could you have known? I'm very close with those I hold dear, and I should have considered that you might take that in a different way to what was intended. There's no need to apologise. If anything, I should be apologising."

And just like that, the moment was over.

Their amble back into The Ruby was sobering. To see Jakob awaiting them in the foyer, perched against the concierge desk as if he hadn't a thousand other things to do, was grounding further still. He fumbled to straighten his suit and tie before approaching them in a breeze of irritating confidence and elation.

"Miss Khalar, I trust that you enjoyed your tour around our beautiful city and that Rosie was the perfect guide?"

"I couldn't have asked for more." Her tone was entirely Kitty, all traces of Kit gone. "Rosie deserves a raise at the very least, Mr Haart. I trust you'll see to it that she's rewarded for her time and efforts. I won't be needing her to prepare for dinner."

He flashed a look at Rosie, and she could see the confusion beneath his surface-level smile.

"Of course, Miss Khalar. She'll be at the dinner serving you and your fellow competitors. Please don't hesitate to summon her back if you need anything before then. Would you like an escort back to Suite Rouge?"

Rosie felt about an inch tall as the two of them spoke over her and about her. The two of them were equally practised at becoming heinous on demand.

"That won't be necessary. I'll see you both at dinner."

Even dressed in her peasant's garments and unrecognisable to the untrained eye, Kit's natural, authoritative sway as she walked away was unmistakable. She turned the heads of those around her effortlessly and acted as if she didn't realise she'd attracted a single glance, let alone a room full of people.

"I trust"—Jakob said without looking away from Kit's retreating figure—"that you did The Ruby proud and there were no complications on your little excursion?"

"I didn't embarrass you, if that's what you're wondering."

A flash of trying to kiss Kit resurfaced, but she pushed it down. Oddly enough, she didn't feel ashamed of what had happened anymore. If anything, it had helped her understand Kit better than before. There may be a tangible distance between them for the remainder of the weekend, but she'd seen a side to the *kaarmiach* champion that no one else ever would.

Jakob tore his eyes from Kit and looked at Rosie with a bizarre expression, trapped somewhere between guilt and pity.

"You could never embarrass me, songbird. Though you know my father's expectations are impossibly high, especially when it comes to you. I'm just trying to protect you."

Rosie wanted to lean into him, to have a friendly conversation like they used to in the streets of the city. Seeing the truth behind Kitty Khalar had opened her mind to the possibility of a truth behind everyone. Underneath the character that people portrayed in public, what were they really like when there was no one to witness their actions?

Now that she knew Jakob's true intentions and that he

wasn't as much of a tyrant as he liked to make out, she felt guilty for the way she'd treated him. He was trying to help in the background, putting together a plan to overthrow Lawrence and free her.

Wait.

Why should she feel guilty for being mistreated? No matter the intentions or the secret plan, there was no excuse for the abuse that she'd endured throughout the year she'd been at The Ruby.

She scoffed. "We all have to dance to your father's tune, don't we?"

Jakob winced and looked down at his polished leather loafers. "I hope you'll forgive me someday when this is all over."

Rosie knew that he meant the weekend and the tournament, but had to continue feigning ignorance to his plans.

"Nine more years." She laughed, but it was hollow. "Nine more years of this, and you think I'll still be able to forgive you after that?"

"I hold onto a vain hope, yes."

She shook her head. "While you waste your time hoping for the impossible, I'll waste my time serving you and your peers. *Duty calls.*"

CHAPTER 20
LIVE LIFE IN THE FAST LANE

Rosie had been drifting off to sleep on her bed, the exhaustion of the past twenty-four hours taking its toll, when there was a knock at her door.

Though she'd had Khristann knock on her door more times than she could count, and once or twice had Jakob do it too, something about this particular knock was different.

Softer.

She sat up on her bed and ran a hand through her hair to try and tame it into some form of presentable. Straightening her outfit, she cleared her throat as she pulled open the door.

Of all the people she'd thought could be visiting her in the dank corridor of the hotel, Kit's apprentice, Hud, hadn't made the list.

"Hi." His young voice squeaked just a little.

"Hud?"

Rosie cocked her head slightly as she took him in, a frown marring her brow. How in Aakla's name had he found his way down here? How had he found her room?

"You look shocked to see me," he surmised as if his presence in the staff corridor wasn't anything unusual. He seemed confused at her confusion.

"How did you find your way down here? Are you all right?"

She stepped out of her room and tugged the door closed behind her, embarrassed for him to see her extremely humble abode.

"Standard hotel practice says the kitchens and other staff amenities are in the basement," he said, sounding more like Kitty than a ten-year-old boy. It almost made Rosie want to smile. "I've been in enough fancy hotels to know that the lowest corridor in the building is usually where you'll find the person you need. There was a very helpful chef in the kitchens who steered me in your direction."

Rosie's lips twitched.

"Was his name Khristann?"

Hud waved in a dismissive gesture. "I didn't bother to get his name."

Rosie all-out cackled.

"You sound just like Kit. Did you know that?"

He smirked in a wolfish, youthful way that only young boys could manage to get away with, and the spell of arrogance was broken.

"She's taught me a lot. Like how to change the way I'm speaking based on the company I'm keeping. More formal, articulated speech gives off a superior and detached aura. It gives people the impression that you don't need to ask for what you want. You can take it if you'd like, but you're giving them the courtesy of asking first."

Rosie's grin grew until her cheeks hurt.

Who was this audacious boy?

"And what do you want from me for you to be using your *superior and detached aura?* You can just ask if you need something. It's my job to help you out this weekend, no personality changes needed."

His posture relaxed a little, and he held his hands out by his sides, gesturing to the corridor around them.

"I'm bored," he whined, instantly becoming the child he truly was. "I have to wait for the welds to settle on my latest project, so I have nothing to do before this stupid dinner we have to go to."

Rosie had several questions, including how he had a welder in his hotel suite, but decided that it wasn't important.

"And you thought I would be the best person to ask for entertainment?"

"Of course." His smile came back. "It's your job, right?"

"Oh, I see how it is!"

They both laughed, and Rosie couldn't help the feeling that Hud might provide her with the break from reality that she so desperately needed. She never got the chance to be a kid; maybe he would give her that, if only for two days.

"Plus, Kit was getting annoyed with me pacing around the suite, so she sent me to find you."

Rosie stumbled over the words, thinking about how she'd left things with Kit and feeling a pang in her chest. But if she'd sent Hud to find her, she couldn't feel *that* awkward about their non-kiss. This was a good sign.

"So it wasn't even your idea to hang out with me?" Rosie gave him a dramatic eye roll. "I'm devastated."

"Enough devastation. Let's do something fun."

Though Rosie knew Hud had been around casinos for years and was no stranger to gambling, she still felt wrong taking him into the thriving casino. It was pulsing with excitement for the first game in the *kaarmiach* final that evening and would be rife with mischief.

Instead, she took him to Colour, an outrageously fun karaoke bar on the third floor where the staff dressed in neon flapper dresses with oversized feather boas. Men and women became indiscernible from each other underneath all the makeup and hair pieces.

Rosie asked, "Is this fun enough for you?"

"This is exactly what I had in mind." Hud grinned and wandered over to a table, whilst Rosie flagged down one of the waiting staff members beside the bar. Without thinking, she glanced around the darkened room and reminded herself of where all the doors were, which were staff-only and which were open to guests, then filed away which were viable exits if needed.

"Hi, sweet boy," the waiter greeted with a notepad in hand. "What's a kid like you doing in a place like this?"

"I was told on good authority that you like to have a good time in here."

The waiter let out a surprised chuckle and raised an eyebrow at Rosie before looking back to Hud.

"We certainly do. What can I get you to drink? I'm gonna have to keep alcohol off the menu for you, I'm afraid."

Hud waved off the statement as if he would usually have alcohol but wasn't bothered by not being served here. It only made Rosie like him more.

"I'll take a fresh orange juice and a black coffee, please."

Rosie's head snapped in his direction.

"You drink coffee?"

He shrugged. "I live life in the fast lane, what can I say?"

She laughed again, shaking her head and slowly but surely falling in love with the kid. She'd never met anyone like him, smart, eloquent, and naturally funny. He was privileged beyond measure but somehow still just a normal child.

"And for you, Rosie?"

She turned back to the waiter and wasn't surprised that they knew who she was without asking. Every staff member was warned about her even if she never crossed paths with them.

"Uh..." She flushed as she looked at her hands. She had no money. She couldn't afford a drink. "I'm all good, thank you."

"Nonsense," Hud interjected. "She'll have the same as me. And a plate of chips if you can, please. Charge it to Suite Rouge."

The waiter smiled knowingly at Rosie and she shrugged, surprised and grateful for Hud's ability to read a situation.

"Coming right up."

When they were alone again, Rosie turned to him with an inquisitive smile on her face.

"You're very good at reading people, aren't you?"

He shrugged again, something she was realising he did to play off his smarts and maturity as a casual thing.

"When you meet as many people as I do, see every kind of person that the world has to offer, you begin to see patterns in behaviour. And I listen. It sounds silly, but it's rare for people to fully *listen* to each other and absorb the information, to note the inflections in their voice and the pauses in speech. It all means something."

Rosie nodded, once again awed by the maturity of a ten-year-old. She supposed, like both her and Kitty, he was having to grow up very quickly in the environment he was in. He didn't have much of a choice.

"Everyone thinks I'm just a foolish child," he said in an amused voice, "which gives me the edge. I remember everything people say; I look at how they hold themselves and how their eyes move. You'd be surprised what people will say when they think no one with a working brain is listening."

"And I suppose Kit finds a use for that quality too?"

"Of course." He laughed. "Opponents don't see threat in a child. If I'm sitting at the next table fiddling with a dumb toy, they assume I'm of no consequence. Little do they know, I'm filing away everything they say and reporting it back to Kit."

Rosie sat back in her chair and folded her arms, nodding with respect.

"I'll never underestimate you, don't worry about that."

That's when she realised she saw a lot of herself in Hud. The independence, the maturity, the kind of smarts that wasn't taught in school but instead in life. He was a younger version of her, simply in a different world—and likely a whole lot smarter than her.

Only once they had their food and drinks did Hud pull something out of his pocket and place it on the table.

"Wanna play a game? I'm not very good at blackjack, but we can give it a go."

Rosie looked down at the worn-out set of cards in front of them and knew without a doubt that he was a pro at blackjack.

"Nice try." She laughed at his innocent expression. "You can't fool me; I wasn't born yesterday."

A sly grin crept across his lips, and he shrugged.

"All right, fine. Blackjack is my favourite."

"Why don't you teach me how to play *kaarmiach?* I feel like I should know the rules if I'm to be a cheerleader on Team Kitty tonight and tomorrow."

His eyes widened a little in surprise.

"You live in a casino and you don't know how to play *kaarmiach?*"

"It's diabolical, I know."

"Well, you're having drinks with the right person. I'll give you the only tutorial you need, and I won't get all finicky about it like Kit would."

"Lay it on me then, big shot."

He smirked and pushed their dishes away to give them some more room.

"How much do you know about *kaarmiach?*"

"Not much. I know that there are five players who are given five cards each, and that the dealer controls them with their divine ability. They have to be specially trained for the job, right?"

Hud nodded. "The dealer is always an Elemental with control over air. They're vital in switching the cards between players without anyone knowing who is chasing who. That's why Air Elementals are well paid if they can train up as a *kaarmiach* dealer."

Rosie nodded. "That's about all I know. I've only watched games from afar. I've never been that interested in playing."

Hud's lips turned up slightly. "So there are five players and five cards each. The aim of the game is to take down your *kaarmi*—that's one of the other players that you're assigned in secret at the beginning of the game."

"Is that where the magic comes in?"

"Yes. But you know it's not magic." He rolled his eyes. "It's divinity and logic."

"Po-tay-to, po-tah-to."

Rosie stuck her tongue out at him, and in an oddly immature show of behaviour, he returned the gesture, which only entertained her more.

He continued, "The dealer controls the cards, so controls the game. With each turn, the players choose a card from their hand to send to their kaarmi. They place it face down on the table, and the dealer uses their divine ability to shuffle the cards and then transfer them to the relevant player's hands. All without the player's being able to figure who is chasing them."

"So...how are you supposed to take down your kaarmi?"

"I was getting to that. Certain combinations of cards can eliminate a player. Some combinations require two or three cards, some four, but once a player has a combination in their hands—courtesy of the player chasing them—then they lose the hand. The dealer has to keep track of who has which cards in their hands so they know when a combination has been made. Hence why they're so well paid and well trained. It takes a lot of work to be a *kaarmiach* dealer."

Rosie tried to wrap her head around it. "I think I understand. You're sending cards to your kaarmi in the hopes that they'll retain a combination that trips them up. All whilst they're doing the same to someone else and someone else is doing the same to you. It sounds quite maddening."

"It's much easier to understand if you watch a game. You'll be able to figure out which suits make up combinations."

"And I suppose you can't really teach me because you're not an Elemental with an air affinity?"

Hud's lip curled up on one corner, and he had the audacity to wink at her.

"You have no idea what my divine ability is," he taunted, shuffling the cards between his hands in an intricate and skilful way that she knew had taken hours of practice.

"All right, Mr. Smooth. That's enough for one day."

They laughed as they stood from the table and waved at the waiters.

"Time to face the music." Hud sighed, pocketing his cards as he looked at his watch. "Is there any way this dinner won't be *completely* dull?"

Rosie's cheeks ached from all the smiling, and she gave him a playful shove towards the exit.

"I'll be there. It's going to be a riot."

CHAPTER 21
THE RANCOROUS UPRISING

The kitchens were a bustling mess of bodies, steam, and clanging pots. But upon further inspection, it was clear that Khristann was orchestrating the masses in perfect harmony, without having to get his own hands dirty.

Rosie appeared silently behind him, dressed in the uniform she'd been given for the night: a maroon trouser suit with a gold silk blouse. In other words, a tasteless, itchy concoction that she couldn't wait to change out of.

"Delegation at its finest," she commented.

"*Gods,*" Khristann swore, turning to face her with a look of fright. "You scared me, songbird."

"I try my hardest."

He smirked. "Your timing is impeccable. The guests will begin arriving within the next half an hour. The canapés have been taken upstairs already, but I need your assistance taking these trays up through the back corridor that runs alongside the gallery."

He gestured to three gold trays topped with domes on a trolley.

Rosie's brow furrowed. "The dinner is taking place in the gallery?"

"Yes..." Khristann drew out the word, not understanding her confusion.

"I thought it was in the scarlet event suite. I'm not allowed in the gallery."

"You are this evening. It was moved this morning, much to the dismay of the hospitality team." He dismissed her concerns with a wave of his hand. "If you ask me, Lawrence is trying to taunt you, knowing that you'll be working around that painting for the next couple of hours to keep reminding you of his power over you. I'm sorry that you have to do it, but I'm only taking orders."

"It's, uh—it's all right, don't worry about it."

Rosie cleared her throat and scratched the back of her neck as she expelled a deep breath. As if she wasn't already dreading being around Lawrence in a public arena, the thought that he was actively taunting her without trying made it that much more embarrassing.

"I could always keep you down here and allow you to conduct this orchestra instead?"

Rosie looked out at the chaos again, then let out a laugh and shook her head. "This is a whole different kind of circus."

"That's what I thought." He flashed her a dazzling grin and pointed towards the trays in need of transporting. "This will only take a minute."

He took a tray in each hand and left the remaining one for Rosie, leading her over to one of the many large store rooms.

"What are we doing in here?"

"Going to the gallery."

Rosie narrowed her eyes but followed his lead anyway, past metal shelving units filled with every kind of ingredient until they came across a metal door at the far end.

"What's this?"

Dumbfounded that she knew the hotel from top to bottom but had never come across this door, Rosie inwardly scolded herself for lacklustre reconnaissance.

What else was there in the hotel that she didn't know about?

"This is the discreet entrance up to the gallery and adjoining event spaces, so that staff don't have to transport food and beverages through the main hotel thoroughfares."

Rosie ran through every plan of the hotel that she'd mapped out over the past year and tried to place the concrete stairwell that they walked into. She couldn't have missed this stairwell, especially as it was one that led to the gallery.

They began to climb as she asked, "Is this new?"

"It was a disused lift shaft originally, but in preparation for the tournament this weekend, it was converted into a haphazard stairwell for employees."

Rosie was floored. Little happened in The Ruby without her knowing about it. She made it her business to know the comings, goings, maintenance, and renovations of the hotel. She recalled coming across several closed-off doors. She'd snuck in some time with plans of the hotel on one of her evening excursions into Jakob's office, but she'd realised that the doors all led to the same abandoned lift shaft.

How had she missed this?

"The work must have been done discreetly," she thought aloud.

"You're shocked to not know all of the goings on in this place," Khristann deduced, stepping on a particularly creaky metal step that seemed unsafe to stand on.

"Slightly." Rosie laughed at the subsequent look he gave her. "Okay, *entirely.* My surveillance skills must be getting rusty."

"Not as rusty as this forsaken stairwell. You'd have thought it'd been here for decades. Nothing like a bit of hospitality for the staff, is there?"

They climbed the remaining steps cautiously, and Rosie pushed open the door at the top to allow them both through, bringing them into a short, dirty corridor with several doors. She'd been in this corridor once or twice before, but as she'd been banned from entering the gallery, she'd had no use for the space over the past year and hadn't deemed it of any importance to her.

How wrong she'd been.

If she was going to orchestrate a *wine tasting* the following evening, this entrance into the gallery was priceless. It could be the key to the entire thing. She could discreetly access the kitchens from her room in the basement, traverse the stairwell without being noticed in the main hotel, and enter the gallery without the guards even knowing.

Jakob had to have planned this. He'd promised in his notes that everything would be taken care of and all she had to do was...*taste the wine.* This was surefire evidence that he was, indeed, the author. He'd even built a staircase so that she could access the gallery unseen, knowing that after their failed heist, Lawrence had shut off and sealed all of the air vents above the gallery.

The thought abolished any remaining doubts she had about the following evening. She was going to do this. She was going to st—

"Where'd you go, songbird? I need you to open this door."

Rosie was brought back to the present by an impatient Khristann waiting by a door marked *Gallery.*

"Sorry," she mumbled, pulling open the door for them and walking straight into the vast, white-walled space that was the hotel's gallery. She hadn't entered the room in a year, and she tried not to glance around at the works of art adorning the walls. She couldn't have anyone thinking that she was planning something.

"Over here," Khristann instructed, leading them to a table covered in a pristine white cloth and filled with tall, thin glasses and bottles of sparkling wine. He placed his two trays at one end and gestured for Rosie to do the same.

"It must be strange for you to come back in here," he commented.

"Strange is one word." Rosie didn't restrain her wandering eyes this time, finally settling on the large framed painting that hung on a wall by itself—the golden goose of the entire room and her previous mark.

"*The Rancorous Uprising,*" Khristann said, naming the painting they were both now staring at. "A truly remarkable piece."

"You don't have to tell me twice," Rosie whispered, once again in awe of the large swathes of dark paint detailing a village that had been destroyed but was in the process of being rebuilt. It was sinister in its brutal depiction of sorrow, but oddly hopeful at the same time. Rosie had fallen in love the first time Jakob had shown her, telling her of his plans to steal it from his father and how she could assist him.

Khristann tore his gaze from the painting to look at Rosie. "It brings out a sensation of determination...don't you think?"

She met his stare and flashed a quick study over his features, so focussed and uncharacteristically serious.

What was he thinking?

"I couldn't agree more," she replied.

They looked at it for a beat longer.

"Come along," Khristann coerced. "I need to speak with some of the event staff up here, but you should get back downstairs to help with ferrying things back and forth."

Rosie passed multiple waitstaff on the return journey back

to the kitchens, only narrowly missing each other on the treacherous spiral steps, but she found herself breezing past them all
with her head in the clouds.

Her plan for the *wine tasting* formed as a picture book in her
head, the new knowledge of the secret access to the gallery
changing absolutely everything. It was finally beginning to look
like a possibility. She had multiple other hurdles to jump before
her plan appeared anything close to ship-shape, but she had to
put faith in Jakob. She had to believe that, like the staircase, the
other details would rectify themselves too.

She thought about the last note that she'd received from
Jakob and allowed a small smirk to grace her features.

*Continue on as normal. Everything you need will come to you in
time. Arouse no suspicion, and don't question favours that fall your
way. Everything is as it should be. All you need is a dash of bravery.*

She was beginning to believe that everything really would be
exactly as it was supposed to be. She had her tools, her access
route, and a dash of bravery at the ready, now all she had to do
was wait.

CHAPTER 22
ALL A BIT FRIVOLOUS

Rosie held a gold tray of sparkling wine in one hand and a platter of slimy seafood nibbles in the other. The gallery was teeming with meandering, ritzy guests dressed in their finest regalia and making vague comments on the surrounding art, acting as if they knew a damn thing about the priceless pieces.

The chorus of over-exaggerated laughter and slow, drawling voices grated on Rosie unlike anything else. She continued her rounds, allowing the guests to take what they wished from her trays and look down their noses at her, all whilst keeping a polite smile plastered on her face that made her cheeks cramp.

To calm her nerves and keep her mind occupied, she counted the exits in the room and remembered how the system of ventilation tunnels in the ceiling worked. She identified the few guests in the room who could potentially help her out in a sticky situation. She also identified those that she wouldn't touch with a barge pole.

Amongst the guests in attendance were four of the Kaarmiach Five and their entourages. The first to arrive had been Han Selks, a short, tanned man in his thirties from Forge

Valley. His groupies were made up entirely of men his age, dressed in matching suits, with the same slicked-back haircut and predatory glints in their eyes. Rosie had avoided them at all costs after seeing them make lewd comments at some of the other men and women on the waitstaff.

Second to join the dinner party had been Allie Archais, a wisp of a girl with shocking white hair the same colour as her luminescent skin. The serene calm that surrounded her and her guests was characteristic of people from Lunaron, one of the neighbouring territories to Cindervale.

Dominich Patronne of Etetalle and Phoenix Mikelle of Blue Reach had arrived together and were clearly friends outside of the *kaarmiach* tables if their jovial buffoonery upon entering the gallery was anything to go by. The two appeared as polar opposites on the surface—in skin colour, hair style, clothing choice, and stature—but their differences had clearly bonded them for the better. They swallowed up an entire section of the gallery with their posses, making an uproar and causing the most trouble for the waitstaff.

The room was almost at capacity. Lawrence and Jakob were mingling through the crowds whilst keeping their eyes trained on Rosie whenever possible. She'd pretended not to notice their lingering gazes but took every opportunity to slip away from their sights, to give them a moment of doubt for her own amusement. It was the only thing keeping the bubbling anxiety in her chest at bay.

She'd been patiently waiting for the arrival of Kit, knowing that the entire gallery would stop to witness the event that was Kitty Khalar. Despite it being half an hour past the beginning of the festivities, the elusive champion hadn't shown up yet. Rosie was about to discreetly ask Jakob if she could go and check that everything was okay in Suite Rouge when a ripple of murmurs spread through the room.

The laughter stopped, and the clowning died down.

Kitty Khalar had arrived.

Rosie found herself nimbly skirting around the edge of the open space, dodging limbs and excusing herself behind guests as she tried to reach a vantage point where she could see Kit through the crowd. Not finding any luck, she sagged against one wall and cursed as the gallery's previous soundtrack began to grow in pitch.

"Take this." A woman draped in technicolour silks and a ceremonial headpiece shoved a wine glass into her hand and strode away without a second glance.

"Right away," Rosie muttered, making her way towards the serving tables at the back of the room. She evaded voices calling on her for refreshments and kept her head lowered until she returned to the tables, desperate to get the evening over with.

An arm slinked around her waist from behind and a mouth sidled up beside her left ear, warm breath tickling her jaw.

"Fetch me a finger of *shenakk.*"

Rosie's body went rigid, and she cleared her throat, closing her eyes and willing herself to stay calm.

Breathe. Breathe. Breathe.

"I'll need you to remove your hand from me if I'm to do that. *Sir.*"

Lawrence's answering chuckle was low and sinister.

"I suggest you watch your tone with me." His grip became painfully tight. "We may be in mixed company, but when the party is over, you and I will be left to nurse the fallout. You can be sure that I'll be waiting to collect on all of your misdemeanours come Monday morning, including your poor attitude. I'm keeping a list, my songbird."

He was just a man. He was just a man. He was just a man.

"I'll get your *shenakk,* sir."

She fought to tug free of his grip and didn't turn to look at him as she pushed through the door into the side corridor. Collapsing against the wall, she sucked in a few full breaths and tried to ignore her trembling hands.

He was just a man.

She shook her hands out as she paced up and down for a moment. Servers came and went, manoeuvring the haphazard steps down to the kitchen with ease whilst Rosie took the time to reorientate herself.

She couldn't allow Lawrence to keep shaking her like this. She was better than that. Better than him. She thought back to her conversation with Kit from the early hours of the morning and rolled her shoulders back.

"Be truly extraordinary," she recited. "He's just a man."

She jumped up and down on the spot in an effort to spur herself on.

"He's just a man," she repeated, spinning to make her way down to the kitchens but skidding to a stop and choking on a breath.

"Indeed, he is just a man."

Kitty Khalar was a vision. *Scratch that.* She was *the* vision.

Rosie gaped at the woman standing in front of her, a queen in the wrong kingdom. There was so much to take in, so much to ogle over, that she hadn't a clue where to start.

Kit was wrapped in a floor-length black gown made from tumbling layers of material that formed a billowing train behind her. Her hair was slicked back to flaunt natural beauty and sharp features, unfettered by dark streaks of makeup and instead highlighted by subtle, neutral tones. Her skin glowed in the low lighting of the back corridor, her high cheekbones shining as if carved by the Gods.

Rosie's thoughts flashed back to their awkward not-kiss earlier that afternoon, but she pushed it back, determined to move forward in the same breezy fashion she knew Kit would.

"Kit, you're—what are you doing back here?"

"I came to check that you're all right."

"Haven't you got—aren't there people you should be talking to out there? Important people?"

Kit scoffed. "If they can't wait a few moments for a conversation, they aren't worth my attention."

"And here I was thinking that this kind of people were your kind of people."

She laughed, and it played out through the back corridor like a song.

"You couldn't be more wrong if you tried. I despise these dinners, but the other four seem to thrive when they're allowed to revel in their riches. In my opinion, it's all a bit frivolous. It only serves to stroke the egos of the *Kaarmiach Five*." She shuddered at the title.

"I see." Rosie shifted her weight from foot to foot. Kit was in a strange no-man's land between her two characters, looking every bit Kitty but sounding every bit Kit. Rosie didn't know how to take it or how to act.

"Well, I'm fine," she eventually confirmed. "As you can see. I was fetching some *shenakk* for Lawrence. Do you want some? I know it's your drink of choice."

Kit's eyes trailed up and down Rosie's uniform with disdain.

"What are you wearing to the game later this evening?"

Rosie blinked several times. It was definitely not the direction she thought the conversation would go.

She asked, "What am I *wearing?*"

Kit apparently didn't feel the need to further explain herself.

"I suppose I'll wear this uniform," Rosie mumbled, straightening it and looking down at her shoes. "I'll have to serve you in the casino. I don't want to cause any trouble with my...*employers*. I don't want to embarrass you or anyone else."

Kit waved off her answer.

"Jal has a suit that she's tailored to your measurements. Go to Suite Rouge with her before the game starts and change, then come and find me in the casino."

Rosie wasn't sure what part of the sentence to question first.

The first thing she came up with was, "Jal has my measurements?"

"She doesn't need to take measurements in order to know them." Kit smirked. "She's very talented, hence why I keep her around."

"I'll try to escape and change, but I can't promise that Jakob or Lawrence will let me leave. Lawrence is watching me like a hawk tonight."

"Then you'll remind them of your duties to me and threaten ungodly consequences if you're not wearing what I've prepared for you when you enter the casino." Kit actually *winked* at her. "What the VIP wants, the VIP gets."

Rosie processed what she'd said much slower than usual. How did Kit manage to keep surprising her? Every time she thought she'd pinned the young woman down, another pivot would send her reeling again.

Rosie bit her lip to stop a smile. "You'd bring down ungodly consequences on them over a mere suit?"

Kit unleashed a devastating grin. "I've done much more to men over much less."

She turned in a flurry of dark material and sweet perfume, striding over to the door back into the gallery. She took one last look at Rosie as she pulled it open.

"I'll take some *shenakk* too. You're the only one I trust in this place to ensure my drink isn't tampered with."

Rosie nodded. "Right away."

Kit moved to walk away but stopped again, meeting Rosie's gaze one final time as she held the door ajar.

"*Thank you.*" She annunciated each syllable as if it were her last and floated back into the gallery as quietly as she'd appeared. A flustered waiter came through the door from the stairwell, glancing after Kit in complete awe.

He gasped. "You spoke to Kitty Khalar? Actually *spoke* to her?"

Rosie groaned and pushed past him without responding, venturing back into the bowels of the hotel in search of Irredorian liquor.

By the time Rosie made it back upstairs, the guests had taken their seats at the large, round tables in the second half of the gallery. She immediately sought out Kit, finding her seated at the table closest to *The Rancorous Uprising*, along with Lawrence, Jakob, and the rest of the Kaarmiach Five. She found Florelle, Jal, Mae, and Hud seated at their own table slightly further back and vowed to visit them as soon as possible to check if they needed anything.

She swiped two small tumbler glasses from one of the long tables and stored one of the bottles of *shenakk* beneath it, donning her emotional armour as she made her way over to the head table.

The Rancorous Uprising taunted her as she approached, still as beautiful as it had always been. Lawrence had done this on purpose, she was sure of it. She plastered on her hospitality smile as she came upon the table, unobtrusively placing the two glasses between Kit and Lawrence and stepping back to open the bottle.

"It's almost entirely unbelievable, isn't it?" Lawrence chortled along with Han Selks. "You can't imagine someone being stupid enough as to assume that they can meander over and begin talking!"

"That's exactly what I said." Han's cheeks were flushed.

"Apologies, miss. I don't have time in my busy schedule to entertain the whims of peasants. Can I sign an autograph instead?"

The two of them broke out into laughter, and Rosie briefly imagined herself slinging the bottle of *shenakk* over her head and bringing it down onto Lawrence's thick skull.

He's just a man.

"Ah, it took you long enough, girl." Lawrence's attention became fixed on her as she poured him some *shenakk*. She fought to hide her shudder and hoped to Aakla that not a hair was out of place on her head.

"Apologies, sir."

"This is Rosie," he explained to Han. "She's The Ruby's resident songbird. Well, that, and a proficient maid. We have to allow them to diversify, you see. The help these days have to be widely experienced in order to find more work."

Rosie wanted to scream and cry and run. Her entire body was tense, and heat flushed up her spine. Kit said nothing beside her as she poured *shenakk* into the second glass.

"Would you like me to leave the bottle, sir?"

Lawrence looked positively shocked as he looked at Kit this time. "These waiters have no idea, do they?" He took his time glancing up at Rosie as if she were a dog that had forgotten its training. "I know that you're still learning, but you must try to remember what we've taught you, especially in mixed company. More than a finger or two of *shenakk* will have any patron on their back, which is quite clearly not the kind of behaviour tolerated at this dinner. So tell me why we would need to keep the bottle if that were the case? One serving is more than enough. Quality over quantity. It's uncouth to leave the bottle."

Rosie coughed and tried to come up with a semi-intelligent answer, completely humiliated and demoralised by Lawrence's blatant desire to belittle her. It was bad enough to experience it in private with Jakob, but in a room full of people, some of whom she respected?

Much worse.

She could see Kit in her peripheral vision, also waiting for an answer. How could she sit by and watch such behaviour? Where was the Kit that had given away all of her money to street children just hours before? The one who had checked if she was all right in the service corridor?

Then she remembered: this wasn't Kit, it was Kitty.

"Apologies, sir," Rosie mumbled, her face damp with perspiration and her cheeks flaming. She shrunk back to step away when Kit held up a single hand, effectively halting her.

"Actually, Mr Haart," she drawled. "I find myself quite immune to the effects of *shenakk.*"

"Well"—Lawrence cleared his throat—"you are a native of Irredore, after all. Though you didn't grow up there, is that right? You didn't have to witness the horrors of the civil war."

Rosie froze at the mention of the one thing that she knew would infuriate Kit and that affected her more than anything else. But Kit merely raised a single eyebrow and gave him a withering look.

"You're correct." She took a sip of *shenakk.* "My family moved out of Irredore when I was a baby. As a result, the only war I ever had to witness was whether my mother should buy a red hat or a blue one."

She lied as easily as she breathed.

Lawrence and Han cackled, and Rosie stood awkwardly with the bottle in her hands. A small, warm hand encircled her right wrist, and she looked down to see Kit gazing up at her with an almost-smile twitching at her lips.

"Please leave the bottle," she asked, sounding less conceited than either of the men but still one hundred percent Kitty. "And I'd appreciate it if you could attend to my employees."

"Right away, Miss Khalar."

Kit gave her the slightest squeeze, a tender and discreet gesture before letting Rosie walk towards the table in question.

"Rosie!" Hud beamed as she approached, looking older than his years in a tailored suit with a wonky bow tie.

"Hello, Hud," she greeted with a warm smile, hoping that perhaps her treatment at this table would be kinder than the previous.

"It's nice to see you again." Florelle gave her a matching smile and struggled to maintain eye contact. Her braids were arranged in an elegant, swirling stack, the beads now silver to match the shimmer of her dress. "Will you be watching the *kaarmiach* later?"

Rosie nodded. "Kit requested it, so I don't have a choice in the matter."

"You've got that right." Mae laughed softly. "You can sit with us if you'd like. We're quite the entertainers when it comes to narrating Kit's games."

"I'm the funniest!" Hud interjected. "Remember that time in Mannash when we were kicked out of the casino for laughing too loud? That was all me."

"And you never let us forget it." Mae ruffled his unruly hair.

"Can I get you anything to drink or eat?" Rosie asked, trying to steer the conversation back to being somewhat professional. "I know the food in here is quite pompous and the portion sizes are for a sparrow. If there's anything else I can get you instead, just let me know and I'll do what I can."

"My word, you're a God-send," Jal groaned. "Can I trouble you for some bread and butter? Nothing fancy, just simple thick-sliced white and some soft butter. I'm absolutely starving, and they've served us what I can only describe as edible art. There must be a sum total of a tablespoon of food on this plate. Someone should be fired for subjecting us to this."

Rosie glanced at their plates and sniggered quietly.

"That's not a problem. Anything else?"

"Have you got any fried *strix?*" Hud's eyes widened in excitement. "I've not had any since we were last in Lunaron, but—"

"Hud, she's not a magician. Let's keep it simple," Jal scolded, flicking her long, brown hair over one shoulder. The headscarf wrapped around her was adorned with crystals that twinkled each time she moved, casting shimmers of light on random surfaces around them.

"It's no problem," Rosie soothed as she saw Hud's downtrodden expression. "I'll speak to our head chef and see what he can whip up for you. If he can't make some fried *strix,* I'm sure he'll have a close replacement."

In truth, Rosie hadn't the faintest idea what fried *strix* was, but she hoped that Khristann might have a clue.

"I'll go and speak to the chef now and sort that for you. If there's anything else that I can get you, please don't hesitate to—"

"Rosie," Jal interrupted, taking her hand. "You don't need to keep up the formalities with us. I know you have to act in a certain fashion around your bosses and around Kit when we're in public, but we're just people. You can relax around us, all right?"

Rosie felt a calm warmth in her chest. She wasn't sure why it happened, but a sense of deep belonging enveloped her without warning. She glanced over the four people sitting at the table, dressed in their finery and eating pretentious food, but saw four regular folk who were as out of place in the situation as she was. They were related in that respect.

Muddling through in a world that wasn't their own.

Unable to find words as a lump of emotion swelled in her throat, she nodded and ducked away, swiftly making her way back downstairs.

"I swear to Aakla, I'm going to have you strung up if you don't get that berry reduction served up two minutes ago, Fina!"

Khristann's booming tenor welcomed Rosie as she entered the kitchens.

Was now the best time to ask him about fried *strix*? Probably not.

"Khristann!" She laughed as she dodged flying ingredients and swerved around chefs in crisis, making her way to the centre again.

"If this isn't life or death, songbird, I'm going to have to ask you to leave before I have a meltdown."

Rosie held in her sniggers. "If it's any consolation, upstairs is going off without a hitch."

"That's because down here is a madhouse." He took a moment to actually look at her and grinned when he saw her smile. "What do you need?"

"I've had a special request from one of Miss Khalar's employees for fried *strix*. Do you know what it is and do we have it?"

He paused for a second and shook his head. "Of course they request something like that."

"It's the young boy that travels with them. He mentioned something about having it in Lunaron, but I can tell him that we don't have any in the hotel if it's any trouble—"

"It's all right." Khristann was smiling now. "I'd be happy to make him some myself. I can find the time." He summoned a chef and instructed her to take over command for the time being as he led Rosie to one of the pantries.

"Are you sure this is all right?" she questioned, thoroughly confused as to how he'd miraculously found time and patience to cook a bizarre dish from another territory.

"Of course it is. Fried *strix* brings back happy memories from when I first trained as a chef. I'd actually like to make it again so I can eat it too."

"Can I try some?"

"You certainly can. Fetch some flour and eggs whilst I track down the rest of the ingredients, then I can show you how it's done."

CHAPTER 23
BLOOM

"There she is," Jal sang, brushing off Rosie's shoulders and straightening her lapels.

The suit that she'd tailored was garish at first glance, but upon further inspection, it was expertly designed and of the highest quality. The ensemble fit as if moulded to Rosie's body, stitch by delicate stitch.

The blazer and trousers were made of a luxurious emerald material with a velvet paisley print. Rosie hadn't been given a blouse to wear, and though it felt slightly uncomfortable at first, it began to feel less of an issue the more that Jal talked her up.

"This is the Rosie I've been waiting to meet," she chattered as she pulled pieces of lint off the suit and circled Rosie with a knowing grin.

"Look at you," she continued. "No one will be able to take their eyes off you. The green suit with the red hair was a brilliant decision on my part. Striking but not overstated. You weren't meant to wear off the rack. You're born to wear custom designs."

Rosie flushed at the praise and kept looking at herself in the large mirror in Suite Rouge. The double-breasted jacket was buttoned closed, but it gave a glimpse of her pale chest in the slim V of the tailoring. The heels she wore were simple and elegant, black and shiny, but pulled the entire outfit together.

She somehow felt the most *her* she had in...well, *ever*.

How had she not known the power of an outfit? No wonder Kit acted untouchable when she was dressed up. Just wearing something like this, something that was made to make her feel good, changed her very outlook.

Rosie was so much more than a maid tonight. She was more than a thief and a prisoner.

"You look like one of us," Jal said, somehow reading her thoughts. "Welcome to the crew."

Rosie decided then that even if it was just for one night, she was one of them. She was with the VIPs, and they were treating her as an equal. She might never again get to be amongst the rich and famous in the most talked-about event in the entirety of the Twelve Territories.

Tonight she would be the old Rosie, the one who had confidence in spades and didn't fear anything. The one who took what she wanted and didn't look back.

She met her own gaze in her reflection and smiled.

Scratch that. She wouldn't become the old Rosie. She was the *new* Rosie, the one who'd been through hardship and imprisonment and humiliation but was still standing on the other side, as tall as ever. *This* was the Rosie she wanted to be. No more looking back.

"That's the look," Jal said, a smirk gracing her features.

"The look?"

"The look of someone who finally knows their worth."

· · ·

Between the vivid green of the suit and the brilliant red of her hair, Rosie turned every head that she passed as she powered towards the casino. In this suit, she was an entirely new person. She was her own person, no longer a servant to The Ruby. The person she'd envisaged two days ago in a borrowed pair of stilettos was becoming a reality.

For the first time since her imprisonment, Rosie sashayed into the casino as if she belonged there amongst the high-rollers. She gained a small taste of what Kit must experience on a daily basis, catching the attention of passersby and witnessing unmistakeable double-takes. Even some of the casino staff who Rosie knew relatively well had to glance at her twice to see that she wasn't one of the VIP guests.

The suit was armour, the heels a weapon.

Rosie was ready to combat her greatest demon.

Be truly extraordinary.

She approached the wide steps up to the VIP game room in the casino, where the biggest games were played and spectated by a lucky few, and saw Jakob waiting behind the red velvet ropes. His eyes flicked over her without recognition as he appeared to be searching for someone amongst the masses, many trying to bargain their way into the biggest *kaarmiach* tournament of the year. It was only when she stepped immediately in front of him that his jaw slackened and his eyes became saucers beneath his perfectly shaped eyebrows.

He stammered, "R-Rosie?"

"I should probably be offended that you didn't recognise me."

"You look...I mean that you—what you're wearing, you look..."

Rosie revelled in letting him squirm for a little longer.

"You've never looked so...I can't explain it. You look fantastic. I feel as if I'm—it's almost like I'm meeting you for the first time."

The deep satisfaction from his words flowed over her like a wave.

Be truly extraordinary.

She channelled everything she'd learned in the last two days. Every encouragement, every rousing speech, every push towards owning her existence instead of shrinking behind the expectations of others.

Rosie blew out a quiet breath and said the words she wished she'd said a long time ago.

"Would you like to hear what I've learned over the past two days?"

Jakob licked his lips and continued to stumble over his words. "Uh, yes. Okay."

She stepped close enough to see the sweat beading on his upper lip, almost level with him in the shoes that she was wearing.

"If you nurture a flower instead of hiding it in the dark— just a little water and sunlight does the trick—then it will bloom in the most beautiful ways."

Jakob's jaw slackened, and he stared at her in complete awe. She realised as she pulled the velvet rope aside that Kit had given her the greatest gift of all. The suit was not just an outfit that inspired confidence, it was a symbol that Rosie was worth something to someone. She may have been a street child, an orphan and a criminal, but somebody cared about her enough to clothe her in finery, and that spoke volumes above any taunt or ridicule that Lawrence could throw at her.

She was worthy.

How was it possible for one group of people to change her life so irrevocably in less than forty-eight hours?

Striding on, Rosie noted that the room was a microcosm of

upper-class Roguerest. Everything oozed opulence, from the splashy decor to the bright lights to the fully-stocked and over-staffed bar. It was filled with the city's wealthiest citizens schmoozing each other to forge connections.

She took a quick look at the doors in and out of the room, reminding herself where each one led and which were viable escape routes. The ventilation shafts in the ceiling were also a great option if need be, as there were plenty supplying cool air to the casino. There were so many people in the room that it would take no effort to slip away amongst all the distractions. Rosie thrived in packed out spaces.

She sought out Kit and the gang, finding them gathered to one side near the *kaarmiach* table, which was located in a sunken pit in the centre of the room to provide all-round viewing of the game. She breezed past overzealous stares and descended the three steps into the pit, approaching the group and catching their attention without a word.

"My, my." Mae's dark cat-like eyes flitted up and down her body in delight. "You look like one of us. Confidence suits you."

Rosie flushed, and a shy smile crossed her features.

"I think I've outdone myself," Jal declared with a grin and smoothed her azure silk slip dress. "Tomorrow evening's outfit will have to be quite something to surpass this one. I'll get to work first thing in the morning."

"Wow." Hud couldn't stop staring at her. "You look really pretty. Like, *really* pretty." Mae elbowed him. "I meant to say, you look strong," he stammered. "You look fierce, as if you've got everything together. And you also look really pretty."

Rosie chuckled and gave him a warm smile. "Thank you, Hud. I appreciate that."

"Are you going to sit with us?" Florelle's voice grabbed her attention. "We'll be on that table, just there." She pointed to a bar table with stools next to the railing above them, with a perfect view of the *kaarmiach* table.

"That's my plan," she replied, anxious but excited for the game to begin.

A deep, echoing sound from a large gong rang throughout the room, announcing that it was time for the Kaarmiach Five to take their seats.

After brief words of encouragement, Mae, Florelle, Jal, and Hud left to take their seats at their table, leaving Rosie and Kit facing each other while everyone bustled around them to ensure preparations were complete.

"I'm not sure whether I should wish you good luck or whether that would be an insult," Rosie said with a grin. "You seem quite adamant that the tournament is already in the bag for you."

Kit's lips tilted up on one side.

"You don't need to worry about me. This is my arena. Much like your comfort in a bustling market with deep-pocketed tourists, I'm at peace when I'm sitting at that table."

"I see." Rosie brushed her hands over the soft material of her jacket. "Thank you for the suit. It's so much more than just an outfit to me; I hope you understand that."

Kit's eyes lit up as she visibly restrained a full-blown smile.

"It cost me nothing, and yet it's clearly worth value beyond words if your newfound persona is anything to go by. It's a pleasure to finally meet you, Rosie Wren. I hope you enjoy your evening. You deserve it."

They shook hands delicately like acquaintances at a business function, but the discreet stroke of Kit's thumb on the back of Rosie's hands spoke a thousand words.

"I suppose I'll be seeing you after the game?"

"You will," Kit replied, letting go of her hand. "If for some reason you get called away by your bosses, please come back to

Suite Rouge tonight. It would be nice for you to join the celebrations of my winning the first round."

Rosie broke out in an unapologetic smile at Kit's audacity. It wasn't the sort of arrogance that slithered around her and made her recoil, but rather the kind that warmed her with a feeling of certainty.

She realised she reluctantly trusted Kit. Despite the back-and-forth, the awkward kiss, and the multiple personalities, Kit was the first person to ever give her worth, to ever treat her like she deserved *more*. She seemed like she wanted to give Rosie the tools to help herself, to help her grow.

"I'll be there."

CHAPTER 24
WITH EVERYTHING I HAVE

K it ducked away to take her seat at the round table in the centre of the pit, whilst Rosie stepped back up to the main floor of the room and found a space to lean against the railing. Though she would sit with the others at their table a bit later, she wanted to first spectate without the humorous commentating that had been promised by Hud.

The noise in the room gradually fell to a muted murmur as the Kaarmiach Five each took their seats, their game faces firmly in place. Rosie still wasn't entirely sure how *kaarmiach* worked, despite her meagre crash course earlier in the day.

A presence settled beside her against the gold railing, but she decided not to peer at them in case it was Lawrence leering or Jakob gaping. She let her gaze cross the room to take stock of who was in attendance and saw Lawrence with Jakob and a couple of other suits in a booth with a direct view of the *kaarmiach* table. The four men were not looking upon the table, however, but all staring straight at her with menace. It was as if they couldn't decide what she was doing in the room with them, looking like she belonged.

As she carefully met Lawrence's stare, she recognised his

sneer and put the pieces together. She was going to pay for this at some point in the evening. If she was lucky, it would wait until Monday morning, when Lawrence would be embroiled in Jakob's anarchic plan. She was laying all her cards down tomorrow night, and if for some reason Jakob's scheme failed, she would pay the ultimate price. She'd be cursed to an eternity trapped in The Ruby at the hands of a contemptible demon. There was no way Lawrence would let her go again if she failed another heist in his hotel.

She had to remind herself as she looked back at Kit that sometimes risks had to be taken. This was an opportunity that she couldn't afford to give up, the chance to have revenge on Lawrence and gain her freedom in the process. She had to believe that Jakob had everything figured out and that once she'd stolen the painting, he'd be able to remove her *supresis* and *captipheus* curses.

Rosie's breath hitched.

Her chest tightened.

She took in several quiet, deep puffs of air.

She had to be imagining it—*surely?*

She'd thought about stealing the painting and hadn't triggered her *supresis* curse. She'd thought about the heist—called it a *heist*—and hadn't collapsed in a fit of writhing agony.

I'm going to steal The Rancorous Uprising, she thought with purpose.

She breathed.

In. Out. In. Out.

Nothing.

To ensure her suspicions were correct, she envisaged her plan thus far for the heist. She saw herself entering the gallery after taking the perilous steps from the kitchen. She would creep through the room, mercifully empty by some grace of Aakla, then approach the painting and haul the frame from the wall. She'd crack open the gold wood with her hammer and chisel, unpin the painting from the canvas frame, and roll it up silently. After checking the coast was clear, she'd leave the crime scene to be found by an appalled Lawrence and hot-foot it back into the kitchens and beyond.

She waited.

The *kaarmiach* began.

And nothing.

No pain, no stabbing sensation in her skull or loss of feeling in her legs. No sweating or crying or screaming.

Nothing.

What had Jakob done?

"Have you ever watched the Five play before?"

The deep, quiet baritone of the figure next to her distracted her from the startling revelation that she'd come to.

"No, this is my—I've never seen them play." She stumbled over her words, trying to orientate herself back in the game room. Thoughts of stealing *The Rancorous Uprising* would have to wait for now.

But she could *think* about it. That's what mattered.

"You're in for a treat," the man murmured. "I've seen them play a few times myself, and I've never found a thrill quite like it."

Rosie looked at him and was shocked to see that it was Khristann's friend from the hotel's garage, Rupee.

She got a much better look at him now that he was closer. He was no older than thirty with a neatly trimmed dark beard. Everything about his appearance was impeccably groomed, from his swept-back hair to his navy suit, and he stood close enough to Rosie that she could see how striking the gold of his eyes was.

"I don't really understand *kaarmiach*," Rosie admitted,

looking away from him so that she didn't further embarrass herself by gaping at his beauty. "Do you play?"

The man snickered under his breath. "I have a history with gambling. I choose not to partake in it anymore for my own good."

"But you still enjoy watching?"

"Call it a second-hand thrill."

They both looked on as the first round of cards was dealt out, but Rosie couldn't concentrate with the stranger standing so close.

"I'm Rosie," she offered, not taking her gaze from the table.

"Rupee," he replied. "It's a pleasure to meet you."

"Likewise."

She waited a beat before asking, "What do you do, Rupee? What brings you to Roguerest?"

"Isn't it always business that brings one to these places?"

"Either that or pleasure."

"Unfortunately, I'm not in the market for any of that these days. More important things are taking priority—"

"*Rosie.*"

Rosie and Rupee turned to see Jakob standing behind them, his pallor that of a ghost and his frantic eyes flicking between the two of them.

"Mr Haart." Rupee held out a hand for him to shake.

Jakob ignored his hand and instead took Rosie by the wrist and dragged her away. She spared a glance to Florelle, Jal, Mae, and Hud as she passed, finding them shocked at the interaction but choosing not to cause a fuss in the quiet room.

It wasn't until Jakob had escorted her out of the room and back into the main casino that Rosie yanked her wrist from his grip, refusing to be dragged around as if a petulant child.

"In here," Jakob instructed, leading her through a discreet staff door which opened into a break room. Only two employees occupied the space, but they scarpered as soon as they saw Jakob enter.

"What was all that about?" Rosie didn't hesitate before unleashing her frustration. "You just caused a scene in there for absolutely *no* reason."

Jakob turned away from her and tugged at his hair, ruining the perfectly styled quaff as he paced.

"I'm so close, you can't possibly imagine," he muttered, still not looking at her.

"What are you talking about?"

He was talking about the heist. Overthrowing Lawrence. Giving her back her freedom.

Freedom. Freedom. Freedom. It called to Rosie like nothing else.

"I'm talking about you," he snapped, whirling around to face her and throwing his hands out in frustration. "I'm trying so hard here and you're just...you're waltzing in there and drawing everyone's attention, and my father is looking at you like you're a piece of meat, and then you...and...you're just *there*, talking to *him*, and I—"

Rosie couldn't decide if he was overcome with jealousy or if he was having some sort of panic attack.

"Jakob, just breathe," she said, frustrated but trying to be the calm one in the room. It clearly wasn't going to be him.

He looked her dead in the eyes and took several deep breaths.

"Now, tell me what's going on."

He scoffed and rubbed a hand over his eyes.

"I can't," he whispered. "I just need you to stop drawing attention to yourself for one more day."

When she didn't reply, he looked at her again.

"Please," he added softly.

She was torn. She wanted to do as he said—she knew that

he was working to free her as much as she was working to steal *The Rancorous Uprising* for him—but she also couldn't deny that what he thought of as her drawing attention to herself was simply her no longer letting everyone walk over her.

He saw it as an issue, but she saw it as an asset.

"I don't think I can do that," she replied. "For the first time in a year, I feel like myself again. I'm being given an opportunity to enjoy myself with new people. After everything you've put me through, I need this. I have to have this. Even if just for another day."

He frowned, clearly not expecting her answer.

"For the first time in a year," she added, "I'm being selfish. I'm not thinking about you or Lawrence or cleaning up after strangers who don't give a damn about me. I'm thinking about myself." She let out an incredulous laugh. "I think I'm allowed that. Don't you?"

His expression turned guilty and downtrodden. He knew she was right. But then his eyes softened, and he smiled gently.

"Do you remember that night at the Basin?"

Rosie took a step back at the turn in conversation.

That night at the Basin? Why was he bringing up a memory from *before?*

"Of course I do," she replied, narrowing her eyes and crossing her arms over her chest.

It had been two weeks before the failed heist. Jakob had meant to meet her for a late dinner at the inn but never showed, leaving her fuming and pacing the darkened streets of the city. It wasn't until the early hours of the morning, when she'd been sitting on the grass banks of the Basin, that Jakob had found her looking out at the huge lake.

"Hi," he'd rasped, collapsing beside her, still in a ridiculously expensive suit and shoes that were speckled with mud.

Rosie hadn't replied and hadn't looked at him.

"It's not an excuse, but my father had me join him at a meeting and I couldn't...he wouldn't let me leave. I tried several times, but he needed me."

Again, Rosie hadn't said anything.

"I'm sorry," he'd added. "I know it doesn't make it better, but it's true. I tried to get out of there, but you know what he's like..."

She hadn't. She'd never met the elusive Lawrence Haart, the people's King of Roguerest. The way that Jakob talked about him had made her feel like she didn't want to. Despite all of the charity work he did and the way that locals sang his praises, Jakob had made it sound like there was another side to his father.

She'd finally turned her head to look at him, her arms resting on her bent knees, and was taken aback by his beauty. Looking at him never got old. She'd had moments throughout the day where she'd remember that he'd chosen her. That somehow, this wealthy, attractive, wholesome guy had chosen her, and she'd never quite known what to do with the information.

"It's not okay, but I'll forgive you," she'd whispered, resting her head sideways on her arms so she could still look at him.

A relieved smile had spread across his lips, and he'd reached a hand out to stroke her hair.

"Soon," he'd whispered. "Soon we'll be out of this place, and it'll be just you and me."

Rosie had felt herself smiling too. "You promise?"

"With everything I have."

He'd taken both her hands and managed to pull her into his lap. Their lips had been only inches apart.

"I have something for you," he'd murmured, using one hand to fish something out of his pocket. When he'd held something up between them, Rosie had frowned.

She'd questioned, "A notebook?"

She'd taken it from his hands and flicked through the blank pages of the dark green leather-bound book, no bigger than her hand.

"I thought you could use it as a travel journal," he'd explained. "Wherever we go, you can collect stamps and drawings and maps, then document everything so we never forget where we've been. It'll be like reading a story. *Our story.*"

Her heart had practically burst in her chest at the gesture. She'd been so in love with him that it hurt to think about sometimes.

"I...thank you," she'd managed, holding the notebook close to her. She had pressed a light kiss to his lips. "Thank you for taking care of me. Thank you for wanting...*more.*"

"How could I not?"

In a moment of adoration, she'd reached inside her shirt and pulled out the necklace that she'd worn ever since she'd left Orphan Alley. It was a long silver chain with a small key pendant. She'd found it in the market square on her first night on her own when she was fourteen, determined to make something of herself in a world that told her it was impossible.

She'd lifted it over her head and gently placed it over Jakob's, tucking the pendant beneath the open collar of his shirt so it was no longer visible. She'd patted the pendant through the shirt and felt his chest rising and falling beneath.

It likely had no worth, and perhaps Jakob would think it was a foolish gesture, something he'd throw away as soon as he got home, but she'd done it anyway.

"That's yours," he'd whispered, using a finger to lift her chin so that she'd looked at him again. "Why are you giving it to me?"

"It's a piece of me," she'd replied with a half smile. "And now it's a piece of you."

He'd smiled. "You promise?"

She'd looked straight through him then, through every emotion on his face and every hope he had for the two of them. She'd seen it all.

"With everything I have."

"Do you remember," present Jakob asked, "what I promised you?"

Rosie looked around the staff break room, unable to meet his gaze. She couldn't do this right now.

"Jakob, I—"

"I promised you everything I have."

Rosie turned away and scoffed. "And then you strung me out to dry. You betrayed me, not the other way around."

When she turned back to him, she realised he'd stepped close enough to reach out and touch her cheek.

"I don't care what happens this weekend," he whispered. "I need you to know that I still hold that promise dear. I still love you. I still want *more.*"

She darted her gaze across his face and studied each of his features with a scrutiny she knew he felt deep in his bones. She knew why he was saying these things. She knew he was going to let her go on Monday morning. She knew that he wanted to say goodbye.

But he didn't know that she knew these things. He thought she was still clueless to his plans, his work, his mission.

And for whatever reason, he didn't think he could tell her.

"It's too late," she whispered back, her eyes traitorously welling up.

Why was he doing this now? Why was he bringing up the past and causing her pain at the most inconvenient time? Why couldn't he let her enjoy the evening for what it was and think about the fallout later?

"I know," he said just as softly, their faces so close now that his breath tickled her nose. "Which is why I need to give you this."

He used his spare hand to reach inside his shirt and pull out the necklace. He lifted it over his head slowly and then gently placed it around Rosie's neck again, careful not to muss up her hair. He tucked the key pendant beneath her suit jacket. The key, still warm from his chest, seemed to burn her skin.

Something caught between a sob and a laugh escaped her.

Why was he doing this? *Why?*

"It's a piece of me," he murmured.

"Don't say it."

"And now it's a piece of you."

"Jakob—"

"I promise you, with everything I have, that I will make things better. I just need you to hold on a little longer. It's despicable of me to ask, but I need you to trust me. One last time."

Rosie's throat closed up. She couldn't say anything even if she had the words.

"And I need you to keep the necklace."

She swallowed the lump in her throat.

"You're asking an awful lot," she said, managing a sad laugh.

"I'm nothing if not predictable."

She looked into his eyes again, memorising every detail and feeling for just a moment like they were themselves again. Just kids in love.

"I guess I can—"

The door to the break room swung open, and the two of them leapt apart, the moment shattered in an instant.

CHAPTER 25
UNTOLD POTENTIAL

Luckily, it wasn't Lawrence who opened the door, but Rupee.

"Rupee," Jakob grunted. "You shouldn't be here."

"Nonsense," he said, holding the door open. "I believe Rosie has places to be. You know, after being dragged from the game like a petulant child."

Jakob huffed out a sigh. "I don't have time for your shit right now."

So Jakob and Rupee definitely knew each other well.

And Rupee knew Khristann well.

"Off you go, Rosie."

Rupee's nonchalant attitude was as charming as it was infuriating, but she couldn't miss the opportunity to get out of there and away from the emotions Jakob had dragged to the surface.

She scarpered from the break room without looking back at the man whose key now jostled against her chest. The key that had been her symbol of freedom had been returned to her.

Upon reentering the main floor of the casino, Rosie knew she needed to take stock of her new circumstances and the information that she'd garnered in the previous day. The last twenty-four hours had changed everything.

Firstly and most importantly, her *supresis* curse had miraculously been lifted—or so she suspected. Taking the opportunity to test out this theory was at the top of her to-do list, a thought that she revelled in as she prowled the tables of the casino, greedily eyeing every potential mark.

She swept glances across the vast room as she paced, clocking each security guard or employee and giving them familiar smiles as if she was working the main floor too.

After several nonchalant rounds, she felt confident in the spots where she'd garner the least concern and the patrons she'd gather the most spoils from. She had to restrain the grin that threatened to spread across her face at the ease with which she fell into old habits. Rosie had always been a firm believer that Aakla, despite being the God of virtue and peace, had deigned her worthy of nimble fingers and unparalleled instincts.

She was born to pilfer and plot. It was in her blood.

Approaching a *kaarmiach* table surrounded by spectators, she easily made her way to the centre under the air of wealth that her outfit provided. She revelled in the fact that power was a mindset. She'd always been capable but never deemed herself worthy of such clout. She settled beside a middle-aged gentleman who appeared to be the most in-pocket player at the table.

The lift was the easiest part; it was the waiting that took skill. The perfect opportunity was worth the patience. Her most ludicrous and lavish thefts in the past had been the ones she'd waited the longest for. Stealth was about more than silence and delicacy; it was about waiting longer than anyone else when the prize was worth it and walking away unscathed.

So she waited.

And *waited.*

Two rounds later, the opportune moment revealed itself. A lean forward, a faux stumble, and a giggling apology littered with batting eyelashes later, Rosie had the roll of cash that the man kept in his right pocket in her hand. A blink later, the roll was in her own pocket and she was striding away as if nothing had happened—as if she hadn't just proved what she'd suspected: her *supresis* curse had been lifted. She had no clue how or when it had happened.

Perhaps it was an accident or a test.

Had Jakob been hiding his divine ability all his life because it matched Lawrence's?

The weight of the cash in her pocket was damning, and she knew she'd be unable to hide it because of its size. Following a brief scan, she spied a woman with her head in her hands perched at a game table. Though she'd have previously taken advantage of her gaping bag and swiped any valuable contents, Rosie did the exact opposite, managing to drop the roll of cash into her bag inconspicuously.

"Rosie!"

She jerked away from the woman and spied Hud wrestling through the crowds, followed by one of the security staff. His russet brown hair fell in strands to his shoulders, bouncing as he ran towards Rosie with visible panic.

"Are you all right? What's going on?"

He grabbed the sleeve of her jacket like a lifeline. "Mae told me to find you and make sure you're all right, but this man tried to make me leave. He won't listen to me, no matter how hard I enunciate."

Rosie instinctually pushed Hud behind her as the security guard caught up, out of breath and flushed in his uniform—an impractical three-piece suit blazoned with the hotel's initials on the breast pocket. Rosie recognised him from her reconnaissance of the casino but had never spoken to him before.

He frowned as he took in Hud and Rosie. "It's Rosie, right?"

"Yes. I work for Jakob and I'm the personal liaison to Kitty Khalar for the tournament weekend. Is there a problem here?"

"Of course. I thought it was you." His tense brow softened a little. "Well, you should know that he's far too young to be on the casino floor. I could be fired if I don't remove him."

Rosie felt pity for the man, knowing the tight spot that he found himself in and that he was only doing his job.

"You're quite diligent, and I'll be sure to pass that knowledge on to Jakob, but this is Hud. He's part of Miss Khalar's group of personal guests. He's allowed to go wherever he'd like in the hotel and casino. That's non-negotiable, I'm afraid."

The man's eyes widened slightly, and he shifted his gaze, nodding but not making further eye contact.

"Apologies. I'll alert the other security personnel on duty tonight. Enjoy the rest of your evening."

He shuffled away with his tail between his legs, scrubbing a hand over his head and ducking out of sight within seconds.

"That was a close one, Ro."

She laughed and turned to face the child behind her. "Ro?"

"Everyone in the group needs a nickname."

"I'm honoured that you consider me part of your group. I don't think I've ever been part of something before, even for a fleeting weekend."

He smiled, but it didn't quite meet his eyes.

"Why don't we go back?" He tugged her towards the VIP game room without further discussion.

Rosie stumbled every other step in her heels but remained upright as they breezed past the doorman to the game room without the need for verification. She risked a glance towards

Lawrence's table in the corner as they entered to see that Jakob and Rupee hadn't yet returned.

"How's she doing?" Hud queried as they took the remaining two stools at the group's bar table.

"It's hard to tell." Jal's eyes were fixed on the game as she spoke. "I'm not sure what play she's going for this time. She's in last place at the moment, which could mean one of many things."

Rosie hid her shock at the revelation.

"She'll be fine then," Hud surmised. "She did this when we were in Windelle."

"That's what we thought." Mae kept her voice low. "But if she were using that play, she'd have begun to move up by now."

"What round is it?"

"Four."

"Oh." Hud looked thoroughly confused. "I suppose there's nothing left to do but wait and see."

Rosie frowned at their absolute belief in Kit's ability to win despite her standing in the game.

She hazarded a question. "Does she always win?"

Florelle let out an uncharacteristic snigger. "No." She dragged her eyes from the game and gave Rosie a flash of her shy smile. "She likes to think that she's the best player of the Five, and perhaps she is, but that doesn't mean she always wins. Though I'm sure she'd like you to think that."

"She likes to pretend she's invincible," Jal added.

"Sometimes I almost believe she is," Mae agreed. "Then we get a glimpse of the vulnerable human beneath and it restores our faith in her."

Interesting, Rosie thought.

The small talk continued throughout the remainder of the first half. To the surprise of everyone in the room, including the rest of the Kaarmiach Five, Kit's last place standing was unchanged by the time the interlude rolled around.

The dealer called the halfway break, and the chatter from before the game ramped up again, the tension in the room melting away.

"Do you think she's distracted?" Florelle asked, a crease appearing between her dark brows.

"Possibly." Mae blew out a breath and stood. "I suppose we best see if there's anything we can do to help. Hud, stay here."

"Fine," he drawled and kicked his dangling legs impatiently.

Rosie followed the three young women as they descended into the pit and approached Kit, the only player still seated at the table. Her head rested heavy in her hands and her shoulders were slumped forward.

"Hey, Kit," Florelle said with her signature softness. "How's it—"

"Where is she? Where's Rosie?"

The three women turned to look at her and parted without preamble, not daring to further poke the beast.

"I'm..." Rosie closed the small gap between them, crouching slightly beside the infamous Kitty Khalar. "I'm here," she murmured. "Can I get you anything?"

Kit moved just enough so that Rosie could see her mouth below her hands, revealing a menacing grin.

"*Shenakk.*" She licked her lips. "Bring the bottle. I've got work to do."

Was she...*bluffing?*

"Are you—"

"Play the part, Rosie. Help a *despairing, defeated gambler,* would you?" Her grin spoke volumes before she hid it beneath her hands again, this time allowing her head to rest on the mahogany wood of the game table.

"Oh." Rosie coughed awkwardly and stood, straightening

her suit. "Right away, Miss Khalar," she said, raising her voice so that the lingering crowds could hear.

"What is it?" Jal queried, the four of them returning to the table where Hud waited for them.

"What's going on?" he pressed. "She's never done this before."

"She requested a bottle of *shenakk*." Rosie didn't know whether Kit wanted the rest of the group to know about the charade. "I'll be back shortly."

Rosie left them wondering.

"Your *shenakk*, Miss Khalar."

Rosie poured her a finger in the bottom of the crystal tumbler she'd brought and settled the bottle next to it. Kit hadn't moved from her slumped position on the *kaarmiach* table, though Rosie was no longer worried.

"You're a gem," Kit mumbled. "Come here."

It felt as if the entire room was watching as Rosie crouched beside Kit, moving close enough to hear the hushed words meant for her and her alone.

"Did Jakob cause some trouble for you earlier?"

Rosie blanched but shrugged off her shock. "Not particularly."

"What was so important that he needed to drag you from my game?"

"You saw that?"

"It wasn't exactly discreet."

Rosie shifted, her legs aching in the crouch.

"He was concerned I was drawing too much attention to myself by talking to a man named Rupee."

"Hmm." Kit tapped her foot lightly. "Where are they now?"

"I'm not sure."

"Will you be staying for the remainder of the game?"

"Of course. Can I get you anything else? Should I tell the others that...that you're all right?"

Kit risked a quiet laugh. "If they don't know by now that I've got the other four eating from the palm of my hand, then they don't know me at all. Let them squirm. This time, it's about the long-con. I know what I'm doing, and I trust that you believe me when I say that."

"I do." Rosie was unequivocal in her response. "Don't ask me why because I couldn't give you the darnedest reason, but I believe that you're exactly where you want to be."

Kit's foot ceased its incessant tapping. "I knew there was a reason I liked you."

"I think it's perhaps more because I endure your many characters, Miss Khalar—warts and all."

"That too, I suppose."

As the second half of the game began, Kit's *despairing and defeated* persona was shed, round by round, to the dismay of the other four players as well as the entire room. Everyone was unanimously in favour of Kit being knocked down a few pegs.

By the time the seventh round of ten began, Kit had clawed her way to third place, and Hud had stopped paying attention, instead focussing on a bizarre contraption made from springs and pieces of sharp metal that he'd produced from one of the inside pockets of his jacket.

Rosie leaned over and whispered, "Are you bored already?"

"I know the play she's going for now," he explained, tightening a bolt. "She'll continue to pull big-hitter combinations to climb the ranks quickly and effectively. The other four are rankled and nervous now, which only makes them play worse. As usual, she's got them all on strings. I don't need to pay attention to know how she's going to play, so I might as well do something worthwhile."

"Which is?"

"Build a spring-loaded security system for my trunk."

His matter-of-fact nature about the contraption made Rosie smile.

"Have you been experiencing problems with theft?"

"Regularly. People assume that our belongings are ripe for the picking because travelling with Kit must make us rich. Though it's a partially correct observation, it doesn't give theft a moral high ground. It's my stuff, not theirs."

Guilt settled in Rosie's stomach at the statement. She recalled how many times she'd stolen from the rich without a second thought. How many of her victims had been just like Hud?

"How does it work?"

He flicked his eyes up to her for the first time since their conversation began.

"You're interested?"

"Would I ask if I wasn't?"

They spent the next fifteen minutes exchanging hushed ideas on how to improve the device, which apparently pleased Hud to no end.

"No one normally wants to know about my inventions, so I can't bounce my ideas off anyone, but you've helped me massively. Thank you."

His beaming grin gave Rosie more joy than she knew what to do with. He was an incredibly intelligent boy in a very strange circumstance. It would be so easy for him to develop into a spoiled, clueless teenager, but his passion for mechanics and inventing seemed to be keeping him on the straight and narrow. Rosie selfishly wished that she'd be able to see him grow up into a compassionate adult. She knew he would, but unfortunately, she wouldn't be granted the opportunity to see it.

"Hud?"

He looked up from his contraption again. "Yes?"

"When this weekend is over and you have to leave, do you think we'll ever see each other again?"

His mouth pinched, and his eyes shifted for a split second before he regained composure. "I suppose, statistically, it's not likely."

Rosie slumped a little.

"But that's only if we don't try," he continued.

Hope blossomed in Rosie's chest. "And you'd try?"

"I think you have a lot of untold potential. My kind of crowd. We'd be fools if we didn't try, right?"

She smiled when the lump in her throat prevented her from answering.

The room broke into polite applause as the round in play came to a close.

"She's shedding her skin." Jal chuckled. "Two rounds to go, and she's in second place. My prediction is that she remains in second tonight and when the game continues tomorrow, she'll push up into first and take the title."

"I don't think she'll play it that predictably," Mae countered. "She'll bounce around second and third place before snatching up the top spot on the last round tomorrow. She's a fan of the drama."

"*Kitty Khalar Snatches Last-Minute Victory* is a much better headline than *Khalar Is Victorious Once Again,*" Florelle agreed. "She's well-versed in keeping the competition guessing and the press talking."

As the following round began, Jakob reentered the room and joined his father in their corner booth. Rosie tried to quell her growing anxiety at the thought of Lawrence's leering and plotting. Surprisingly, in her present company she found it easy to forget that he existed, let alone the fact that he made it his personal responsibility to taunt her at every opportunity.

Upon the closing of the final round for the evening, Kit was firmly in second place behind Phoenix Mikelle and ahead of Allie Archais, followed by Dominich Patronne, with Han Selks coming in last place. No one seemed overly bothered by the results; the points would be carried into the following evening for the final game of the tournament.

It was all still to play for.

CHAPTER 26
HERE'S TO MONDAY

After the game, the Kaarmiach Five had press duties and adoring fans to tend to. From what Rosie had gathered, thousands had saturated the city streets in celebration of the tournament, partaking in every degree of debauchery and festivity. Though the Five would likely be staying inside The Ruby to ensure their safety, they were greeting the masses that had been allowed entrance to the hotel and signing autographs as if their lives depended on it—which, she supposed, they did.

The sheer amount of noise in the hotel foyer was enough to cause a persistent ringing in Rosie's ears as she rode the lift to the penthouse suites. She'd been tasked with ensuring Suite Rouge was in ship-shape by the time Kit and the others returned.

In all honesty, she was glad for the reprieve from the never-ending carousel of screams, cheers, and laughter that followed the Five around like a persistent smell. She much preferred the serenity that came with staking out a mark or creeping through an occupied house in search of riches. She could control everything in the silence; she only had to worry about herself. But out there in the hysteria of the Twelve Territories' Kaarmiach Tournament?

She had no control. It left her more embittered than she'd like to admit.

Entering the stillness of Suite Rouge was like a cool drink on a stifling day. Rosie paused as the door clicked shut, closing her eyes and breathing in the calm as if she could save a slice of the sensation and take it with her.

The grandfather clock chimed twelve bells just as Khristann appeared from around the corner in the kitchen.

"Songbird." He smiled. "I thought I heard the door. I've finished preparing and setting out all the food our VIP requested earlier. I can't promise that it'll still be warm by the time they get here, but I've left anything temperature dependent under gold covers."

Rosie took in the sight of her only friend in the hotel and was overcome with dread at the idea of leaving him. Khristann was the closest she'd ever had to family; no matter what his connection to Rupee or Jakob or anyone else was, Khristann had been there for her when she'd needed it. Fed her. Loved her. Given her a sense of home.

"What's going on in that head of yours?"

She exhaled deeply and approached him. "Can I have a hug?"

"You don't even need to ask." He chuckled quietly and pulled her into his arms, resting his chin on her head and running his hands up and down her back.

"It's all a little bit overwhelming," she mumbled into his hard chest.

"You don't need to tell me twice. I'm glad my job entails hiding in the basement and pretending I don't exist. I can hear the chants and singing coming from the streets outside down in the bowels of the building. It's absolutely bizarre to think that all of these people have descended upon the city just because five people are present. It's hysteria out there. I've no clue how I'll get home this evening. It might take me until the breakfast shift just to battle my way to my flat."

"To be honest, I think I'd rather go with you than endure more of this. It really takes it out of you when you're accustomed to quiet work. I don't like the noise very much."

Khristann released a deep sigh that rumbled in his chest beneath Rosie's ear as he held her tight.

"If it helps, you won't be doing this for much longer," he placated her. "It'll all be over on Monday."

He didn't know how much his words resonated with her. It would be over soon because come Monday morning, she'd be gone. Not that he had a clue how deeply his words cut into her conscience.

Or did he? Perhaps she could tell him of her plans. Perhaps he already knew. Perhaps he would leave with her and travel the territories.

"Khristann." She pulled away enough to look up at him. "If you could leave here tomorrow and travel the territories, do you think you would?"

A warmth and ease blanketed his features.

"I have far too much to do around here tomorrow." He laughed. "But when Monday rolls around, ask me again. The weekend may have drained me of any loyalty I have to this place."

"I'll hold you to that."

"And you? Would you leave and travel the territories if you had the chance? Visit every place in your journal?"

"In a heartbeat. There's no question about it."

"Here's to Monday, then." He let go of her and reached for two of the filled wine glasses on the kitchen island, handing her one. "Here's to what Monday brings us."

"Cheers to that."

They toasted their glasses with a *clink,* and Rosie sipped the sweet liquid, but Khristann refrained, citing his responsibilities that required sobriety.

"I just want you to know," Rosie broached, hoping she wasn't giving the game away at the eleventh hour, "that you're the only person I've ever considered family. You're the only person who's truly taken the time to understand me. I don't think I'll ever be able to repay you for that."

Khristann's forehead wrinkled, and he considered her for a moment.

"Is everything all right, songbird? Are you in trouble?"

"No!" She flushed crimson and laughed off her suspicious behaviour, taking a sip of her wine. He couldn't know that she knew. If he was in on Jakob's plan, he couldn't find out that she knew what was happening.

"I just don't think that I articulate my feelings often enough," she continued, hoping to throw him off the scent. "I'm so grateful for everything you've done for me over the past year, from feeding me every day to listening to my complaints. You've been my everything, and I suppose...I suppose I have this overwhelming inkling that Monday is going to be a very different landscape in The Ruby—for everyone. The tournament will have changed us and the way that this place works. I just hope that we make it out the other side in one piece; Lawrence is chomping at the bit to punish me for all sorts of things that I'm pretty sure I don't deserve."

Khristann's posture became rigid and he put his glass down, taking her by the shoulders and pulling her closer.

"If he *ever* touches you again, I won't hesitate to crush him like the bug that he is." His tone dropped to a deadly timbre, his expression shuttered. "Do you understand me? If he touches you, I want you to come straight to me."

Rosie blinked several times, shocked at his outburst.

"*Do you understand me, Rosie?*"

"Yes...yes, I understand."

His gaze bore into her for a few seconds more, ensuring she was sincere before he released her and embodied his familiar casual confidence.

"How about some music to get the celebrations started?"

He approached the gramophone with the solid gold horn perched on the sideboard and began flicking through the sizeable collection of records beside it.

He asked, "What mood do you think they'll be in? Did she win?"

What had overcome him a moment before?

His one-eighty in demeanour wasn't so much frightening as it was reassuring. Rosie had someone who wanted to protect her. She had family.

Khristann had to be in on Jakob's plan. They were working together, no doubt about it.

"She placed second." Rosie leant against the sideboard next to him. "Though I'm told it's a tactical move and that she has everything under control. Puppets on strings that only she can see."

He snorted. "Why doesn't that surprise me?"

"Have you seen her play before?"

"I've heard stories about her and her tactics. Some believe that she shouldn't be playing in the tournament because she could win every game if she wished. When she loses, apparently, it's quite deliberate."

Rosie considered his answer before countering, "Are you part of the *some* who think she shouldn't play?"

"No." He slid a record from its sleeve. "I think she's worked very hard to become the person she is. If she's better than the rest, she shouldn't lower herself to their standards to make them comfortable. The others should improve to be in her league."

The record crackled as it began playing, a soft and jolly melody filling the suite. It was tropical and light as if it belonged in the beachy confines of the Grande Palms Casino down the street with a gaggle of dancers in grass skirts.

"How about a quick dance before—"

The door swinging open interrupted Khristann and revealed a multitude of stumbling, merry guests. First to enter was Mae, hand-in-hand with Jal, shortly followed by a giggling Florelle who was accompanied by two men that Rosie recognised from the entourage of Allie Archais. Several other strangers with familiar faces entered, the suite filling with perhaps twenty party-goers before Kit meandered in last of all, something off-kilter about the lilt to her step.

"Rosie." She beamed and sauntered over to stroke Rosie's hair with a childish grin on her face. "Thank you for organis-ing...things."

"It was all Khristann." She gestured to her friend. "This is Khristann, The Ruby's head chef. Khristann, this is Kitty Khalar."

"It's a pleasure to meet you," he greeted, his eyes twinkling. "I hope that everything I've prepared is up to your standards, Miss Khalar. The bar has been refreshed and is fully stocked with a variety of local specialties as well as those from further afield, such as your beloved *shenakk.*"

"My, my...you're quite competent, aren't you?"

"I try my hardest, especially for our most distinguished guests."

Kit's dopey grin remained as her head lolled back in Rosie's direction.

"You'll stay, won't you?"

Rosie opened and closed her mouth a couple of times,

looking around at the crowded room and inwardly cringing at how rowdy it would likely get in no time.

"Of course I'll stay," she replied.

"Good. Good. Good." Kit nodded to herself.

Rosie looked up at Khristann with raised eyebrows.

"Drunk," he mouthed with a wink.

She couldn't help but think back to their kiss again, grateful that Kit seemed to have forgotten about it entirely.

"I'll keep you company." Rosie glanced back at the slothful celebrity in front of her with a knowing smile.

"Khristann, it was lovely to...to meet you, yes." Kit glanced towards the kitchen where the food was laid out, already being ploughed through by the multitude of guests spread across the living space.

"I'll leave you to it, Miss Khalar," Khristann said, folding his hands behind his back. "Just one question: may I ask where your youngest employee is? I wanted to get his feedback on the fried *strix* I prepared him earlier. I haven't made it in some time."

"Other suite," she mumbled in reply as she began to stumble towards the kitchen. "Inventing something again!"

Rosie and Khristann stood beside each other in awe of the situation unfolding in front of them.

"I think I should check that Hud is all right," Rosie decided.

"The young boy?" Khristann waved her off. "Don't worry, I'm on it."

"He doesn't know you; it might be a bit bizarre to have a random man go into his suite when he's all alone."

"I'm sure we'll bond quickly over our shared love affair with fried treats. Don't worry about him, I'll make sure he's all right before I leave. Focus on trying to keep this party in relative check. I foresee a long night ahead of you, songbird." His amusement shone in his cheeky grin and the crinkled corners of his eyes.

"I guess I'll see you in the morning."

"That you will. Bring it in."

He embraced her tightly and kissed the top of her head.

After he'd passed through the adjoining door to the partner suite, Rosie took stock of her situation and the state of the guests. She spotted two of the Five, Allie and Phoenix, as well as their companions, but it seemed that Han and Dominich were partying elsewhere for the evening.

"Rosie, come on over!"

Mae was waving her over to the kitchen enthusiastically, her sleek black hair shimmering in the low lighting as it fell to her waist. She'd changed outfits somewhere between the casino and reaching the suite, now decked out in a slim-fitting mustard suit that perfectly accompanied her olive skin.

Rosie ambled over, her heels beginning to rub sores on her toes and proving to be more uncomfortable as time went on.

"Take your shoes off; you look like a bumbling child in those things. This is the part of the evening where you can shed all pretence and formality. Take the jacket off too. Get comfortable!"

Mae was slurring every other word, her arm slung around Jal's shoulders.

"I'll make you something pretty," Florelle mumbled into her glass of wine, taking a sip and placing it on the kitchen surface next to her. "A crown, you should have a...a crown."

Unsure of what she was implying, Rosie watched in awe as Florelle cupped her palms and stared into them for a few moments. Just as Rosie wrote off her mumbling as drunken thoughts, something green began to grow in Florelle's hands. What appeared to be a vine spiralled and extended until it formed a circle, perched on Florelle's palms and sprouting bright red flowers.

Rosie's mouth hung open as she saw a flower crown appear from nothing, a delicate and miraculous accessory fashioned from thin air.

Florelle was an Elemental. Furthermore, she was a botanist.

"For you." Her shy gaze shifted from Rosie to the crown multiple times before she plucked up the courage to place it on Rosie's head, a satisfied but wonky smirk settling on her lips. Her dark skin had taken on a sheen that Rosie suspected was alcohol induced, but it only served to highlight her natural glow.

"I'm speechless." Rosie tentatively touched the crown. "Thank you. I can't believe you can create such beautiful things from nothing. You're very gifted."

She hiccuped and closed her eyes. "It has its uses. Not as clever as singing people to sleep, though. That's got to have some fun involved."

Rosie furrowed her brow and glanced between the three inebriated women, wondering how much Kit had told them. Apparently, she'd clued them into her suspicions about Rosie's divine ability. Strangely enough, between the tournament, Kit, Jakob, and finding out that her *supresis* had been lifted, she hadn't had much time to think about her siren ability.

But now that Florelle mentioned it...it could certainly come in handy when pulling off something like a heist.

"Yes." Rosie treaded lightly. "I'm still getting to grips with my ability, though. It's not much use to me at the moment. It's going to take some practice."

Kit appeared next to them, and Jal broke awake from Mae, grabbing onto her boss's hand instead.

"We're going to change," she explained, haphazardly gesturing at Kit's dress that trailed behind her, trampled on by guests as they passed. "My hard work is being violated by stumbling morons. We won't be a minute."

True to her word, they miraculously emerged from the spare bedroom not thirty seconds later, both dressed down in casual attire.

"How did they do that?" Rosie floundered, remembering how many layers had made up Kit's previous outfit.

"Jal is our Artist," Mae explained as they approached. "You're our fashion-designer-slash-hairdresser-slash-everything, aren't you?"

"Indeed." Jal twirled, and her outfit transformed into a leather skirt with a silk shirt right before Rosie's eyes.

"Wow," tumbled from her mouth. "I've never met anyone like you; it's fascinating to me."

"Honey, you haven't seen anything yet." Jal laughed just as another large group of people entered the suite with hollers and applause.

"Time for shots!" someone shouted, much to the delight of everyone in the room.

"This is...rowdy," Rosie mumbled, her gaze darting all over the room and her discomfort growing. She could barely hear herself think. She needed to go somewhere quiet. She needed time to think. So much had happened in a single day.

Kit must have noticed her discomfort, even in her drunken state.

"You don't have to stay," she mumbled, fiddling with a piece of Rosie's cropped hair again. "I know I said...I said I wanted you to, right? But I know this isn't your scene. You should go somewhere quiet. You should go...go and practice being a siren. Yes. Sing your heart out."

Rosie's eyes flared, and she placed a silencing hand over Kit's mouth. There were so many people close by that could've overheard.

"Let's keep that between us for now, okay?"

In an adorable show of inebriation, Kit nodded enthusiastically. Rosie couldn't help but smile.

"Are you sure it's all right if I leave?"

Kit nodded again.

"I'll come back to check on you in a bit, in case you need anything."

"Go on, songbird," she said dopily around Rosie's hand before removing it from her mouth and starting to whistle like a bird. "I want to hear all about your ability tomorrow. I don't want to see you again until...until you've tried it out. Fly away now, songbird."

Kit turned with a flourish and left her standing there, relieved at the fact that she didn't have to hang around the raucous party any longer.

Quiet. She needed quiet.

She left the suite without another glance back.

CHAPTER 27
SING

R osie should've known that her need for quiet wouldn't lead her to her room or the library. The hotel was never quiet, especially on a weekend like this, so neither of those places would actually afford her any sense of peace. The only place she knew that would be relatively calm was Jakob's office. The soundproofing in his door and walls meant that even with the hysteria in the foyer, it would still be peaceful there.

Plus, with everything going on in the main casino and the rest of the hotel, there was no way Jakob would be locked away in his office. He had business partners to sweet talk on behalf of Lawrence.

If Rosie had a quiet place with some paper and a pen, she could plan out her heist. Combined with the fact that Jakob kept up-to-date plans of the hotel in his office, it was the only logical place to go.

Which was how she found herself in the sticky ventilation tunnels that ran alongside the foyer, quietly crawling towards the grates in Jakob's ceiling. She'd taken the route so many times that she didn't even think about it. One of her favourite midnight activities was sneaking into Jakob's office to read or explore or simply sit in his chair and feel smug about the whole thing.

When she took the final bend in the tunnel before his office, she slowed her pace down and took each crawling movement with the utmost care. Sound travelled far in these tunnels, and she couldn't risk anyone in there hearing her.

She came upon the vent grate in the office ceiling and slowly peered over, the low lighting from inside shining up at her. A quick glance and a couple of minutes listening for any sounds confirmed that the room was empty, much to her delight. She pulled the grate up and slid it over, sticking her head through and double-checking for anyone before lowering herself down with controlled motions and dropping to silent crouch on the plush carpet.

The almost-silence was deafening. She puffed out a relieved sigh and closed her eyes for a second, appreciating the peace.

This was where she thrived—in the background, crawling through small spaces and infiltrating rooms she wasn't supposed to be in. She didn't belong in the limelight at parties.

She looked down at her gorgeous suit, now unfortunately marred by streaks of dust and Gods-know what else. She'd had the forethought to stash her heels in one of the many storage closets in the staff corridors, but she hadn't wanted to return to her room before going to Jakob's office; it risked seeing more people and getting distracted.

Once she'd brushed herself off as much as she could, she took in the space she knew so well and marvelled at the hundreds of books surrounding her. She dragged her fingers along several leather spines and felt an easy smile spread across her lips.

She was destined to be around books. Nothing calmed her quite like a book, a comfy chair, and room without distractions.

She wondered briefly if Jakob had a copy of *The Piracy and Gaiety of Peachlock Bay*.

Before she could get distracted by looking for it, she approached the large chest of drawers in the back right corner of the office and opened the top one, where the most recent drawings and proposals for the hotel were kept. She rifled through the huge sheets of paper before finding the ones she was looking for: the gallery, the basement with the kitchens, and the casino.

Once she'd gotten herself settled in Jakob's chair with a pen and paper and the floorplans spread out on the desk, she began to plot her route for the following evening, starting at the gallery and making her way backwards. As the ventilation tunnels to the gallery were shut off, she knew she'd have to enter through the new secret staircase from the kitchens. From the kitchens, she worked her way back down the staff corridor to find viable routes from the casino.

Within twenty minutes, she'd planned and memorised three possible routes from the casino to the gallery using a mixture of ventilation tunnels, staircases, and corridors, but avoiding being in public view at all costs.

She sat back in the chair with a grin on her face and folded her hands behind her head.

She could do this. She *would* do this.

There was so much she didn't know, so much that the people around her were keeping secret, but she had to trust that Jakob knew what he was doing. Otherwise, he wouldn't be asking her to do this for him. She placed her hand against her chest where the key pendant touched her skin and reminded herself that he'd asked for her trust. He was doing this for her, even if he didn't realise that she was onto him.

He still cared about her. He still loved her.

She might not be able to bring herself to ever love him

again, but one thing was for certain: she would never forget what he'd done for her or what he'd done *to* her. It was a double-edged sword.

Once bitten, twice—

The sound of a key in the door had her head shooting up and her heart leaping into her throat. There was no hiding the plans. There was no escaping.

No. No. No. No. No.

All she could do was stand up as the door swung inwards to reveal a chuckling Jakob and an equally amused Rupee in the throes of conversation. The sounds of hysteria in the foyer poured in and made Rosie wince. They both halted in the doorway as they took in the sight of her, the plans, and the open ventilation grate.

Jakob's expression immediately sobered, and he ushered Rupee in without a word, closing the door behind them and locking it.

Rosie wasn't as scared as she would've been two days ago or even yesterday. The feeling of the key against her chest reminded her that Jakob was on her side. He loved her. He wanted to protect her.

She didn't know who Rupee was or how he fit into the weekend, but she had to trust that if he was a threat, Jakob would help her out.

Wouldn't he?

"Rosie," he sighed. "Do I even want to know what you're doing in here?"

"I was..." She looked at the plans and pursed her lips. "Uh..."

"It's a pleasure to see you again," Rupee interrupted her.

His tone wasn't mocking or superior, but more amused. He helped himself to one of the plush chairs in front of Jakob's desk and crossed his legs in a manner that spoke of practised confidence.

"Who are you?" The question slipped from her lips before Rosie could stop it, much to Rupee's amusement.

"He's none of your concern," Jakob interjected, his tone back to the cutting and cold version of himself that Rosie hated. "What are you doing with plans of the hotel? What are you doing in my office? What are you doing sneaking around in the ventilation tunnels when you should be making sure Kitty has everything she needs for the night?"

Definitely back to the version of himself that she hated.

Brilliant.

"Kitty dismissed me," she replied. "Something about not wanting the help to hang around at her party and put off the guests."

The lie slipped from her so easily that she wondered if Kit was rubbing off on her already.

"So you figured you'd trespass in my office instead?"

He crossed his arms and walked slowly to his desk. She didn't know how to get herself out of this one. She didn't know how to explain away what she was doing in front of Rupee, who likely wasn't in on the plan and could well be working with Lawrence.

"*What*"—Jakob gritted his teeth as he spoke—"are you doing in my office?"

Rosie opened and closed her mouth a couple of times, unsure what to say. Surely, by looking at the plans, he knew what she was doing. She was planning the heist that he wanted her to perform. She was doing exactly as he'd asked her to.

What did he want her to say?

She looked between the two young men in front of her, and panic began to bubble up in her chest for the first time in what felt like forever.

Had she blown it for Jakob? Had she ruined his plan?

Her breathing sped up, and she felt the signs of a full-blown panic coming on. But then she remembered something vital. Kitty hadn't sent her away for nothing. She'd sent her away to practice her siren ability.

Her *siren* ability.

Figuring there was no time like the present and she had nothing left to lose, Rosie did the only thing she could do in that moment: she started to sing.

It began as a hum from the back of her throat, a lullaby with no words and no sheet music. Jakob and Rupee frowned to start with, but as she allowed the song to burst from a hum into a full-blown melody from the depths of her chest, she watched as they became glassy-eyed.

It was *working*. How could she not have noticed this before?

She didn't know the song she was singing—had never heard it before—but it flowed from her like the most natural thing in the world, note after note strung together without a thought. When she was absolutely sure she had them entranced, she began to think about how to go about the next stage of her plan.

What had Kit said about her ability?

"You were hypnotising them. You could've instructed them to fight to the death, to tear limb from limb until only one remained standing, and they'd have done it."

All she had to do was instruct the two of them to do as she wished. She hoped it was as easy as it sounded. She desperately needed an easy win right now.

Unsure whether it would work if she spoke as opposed to singing the instructions—or if it would even work at all—she began to lyricise her desires and watched on as Rupee and Jakob stared at her with blank expressions.

She wanted them to forget that they'd seen her. They'd forget she had been in the office tonight. The last time they saw her was during the *kaarmiach* game. They'd come to Jakob's office and it had been empty; as soon as Rosie left, they would carry on as they'd planned. They wouldn't remember ever seeing her there. As far as they knew, she was tending to Kitty and her guests.

She continued to sing the commands to them as she climbed onto Jakob's desk to reach the open ventilation grate, sliding it shut with a clang. They miraculously remained under her spell as she collected up the hotel floor plans and slid them back into the correct drawer.

Gods, she hoped it worked.

After straightening her outfit once more, she wandered over to the office door and turned the lock, looking back at the two young men one final time and praying to Aakla, Midina, and Venaak that this worked. She would take help from any of the Gods at this point. She let the song slowly die as she opened the door and left without another glance at them, softly closing the door behind her and sending up several prayers.

This had to work. She had no clue what she'd do if it didn't.

She waited outside of the office for a couple of minutes, the circus of a foyer reaching deafening levels as she waited for the door to be pulled open and a fuming Jakob to come out.

But it never did. The shouting and singing and dancing continued around her. The staff members behind the reception desk flitted about at double speed. The guests partied like tomorrow wouldn't come.

It worked. It must have worked.

Rosie covered her mouth as an incredulous laugh escaped. She'd done it. She'd hypnotised not one but *two* people at the same time and made them forget about her. She'd taken a dead-end situation and flipped it on its head.

She'd been the one in *control.*

The thought was dizzying as she walked behind the long reception desk to the door into the staff corridor. She was much more than just a songbird with a voice that captured the attention of anyone she targeted. She was a siren with the ability to control the actions of others using a melody that only she could truly hear. Did that make her...*an Imperial?*

The mere thought of being one of the elite when she'd always been told that she was a commoner meant to serve was entirely too much to process in a public setting. She swatted the thought away with a dark promise to revisit it soon, most likely when the weekend was over—when she was a free woman. That was also a concept she found herself struggling with.

Focus, she chastised herself. *One step at a time.*

She pushed through the door into the back corridor and blew out a cleansing breath as the noise level came down slightly.

She had a method of subduing any danger that came her way from now on. She had a way to protect herself from the vilest evils.

From Lawrence.

The thought made her all-out giggle. It was like coming up for air after being held beneath water for so long, like her lungs could finally expand to their full capacity.

This was the beginning of her freedom.

CHAPTER 28

NICKNAMES

R osie had never been out on the rooftop of the hotel, though she knew exactly which service staircase to use for access. She'd always assumed that her *captipheus* curse would be activated if she stepped out onto the wide, flat space, so she'd never tried. Instead, she'd opened the door many times in the last year and sat just inside the threshold for some much-needed fresh air—as fresh as she could get in Roguerest, anyway.

It had been the first place she'd thought about going to after discovering the depths of her ability. Or perhaps she'd only just scratched the surface. But what she hadn't expected was to find Kit, Jal, Mae, and Florelle already laid out on the rooftop, drunkenly pointing out stars that Rosie knew for a fact weren't visible. Rosie watched from inside the door frame, both envious and amused at their antics.

Behind them, a large steel frame propped up a towering red sign that read *The Ruby Talisman;* she knew it could be seen all over the city. She'd often found herself gazing at it whilst she was growing up on the streets of the city, climbing to the rooftops and watching the revelry from far above. She used to wonder what it was like to join in the fun and gamble in the casinos, to drink until her vision swam, and laugh with friends until her chest hurt.

The reality of being in The Ruby was far darker. She wanted to go back and take her younger self by the shoulders, to shake her and tell her to flee the city before it was too late. But dwelling on regrets was a fool's game.

"Rosie?"

She looked up from her feet and saw Kit struggling to get into a seated position.

"Come join us," she added. "It's so nice"—she burped—"oops. It's so nice out here; we're looking at the stars."

Rosie couldn't help but smile at the young women who were living lives that she so desperately wished she had; surrounded by friends who were considered family and travelling the territories without a care in the world.

"I can't," she explained, her voice sounding smaller than it had in a while. She dropped her gaze to her feet as a blush spread across her cheeks and down her neck.

It was so demeaning to watch this group of young women thriving whilst she had to watch from the dark sidelines and wish for the dignity of being in control of her own body.

Two hands held onto her own, making her glance back up to see Kit in front of her, swaying heavily. The others stayed where they were, chattering animatedly.

Kit asked, "Have you ever come out here?"

She shook her head.

"Does your curse...does it stop you?"

"I..." Rosie chewed her bottom lip. "I haven't tried because I assume it will trigger the curse. I don't want to risk the agony unnecessarily."

Kit blew out a heavy breath that made cheeks puff out, and Rosie adored how much of a teenager it made her look.

"I think you might be selling yourself small." She articulated every word with a little too much effort. "I mean *short*. You're not technically leaving the hotel grounds by coming out here, you're just on the top floor. Right? You're on the sun deck. You're not goin' nowhere."

Rosie's head shot back up as she thought about it, looking into Kit's glazed-over eyes. She actually had a point.

"I know I've got no clue what it's like to"—she gestured heavily at Rosie's body—"trigger your curses. I would never ask you to do something that would cause you...lots of pain. But I think you're missing out on the fun. I mean, look at us."

She swung around a little too enthusiastically and threw her hands out in the general direction of the others.

"We're a riot," she continued. "You deserve to enjoy yourself with friends."

Rosie laughed quietly. "Friends?"

"That's *all* you took from that?"

"I've not got many friends; I don't know if you can tell."

They both snorted, and Kit gave her a dopey smile.

"If you don't want to, then I understand. But I think...I think life is too short to miss a good time."

Rosie thought about it for a second. She glanced over at the giggling women on the floor not too far away, drinking wine and eating from a platter of meat and cheese. She wanted so badly to be part of their circle. To be part of something bigger than herself, if only for the night.

The Rosie from two days ago wouldn't have dared to try and venture outside. She wouldn't have stood up to Jakob or faced Lawrence with her head held high. She wouldn't have strode into the *kaarmiach* game tonight like she owned the place.

But she was no longer that Rosie. She'd grown wings since then; grown confidence and a backbone and reclaimed her sense of self.

She could do this.

Barefoot and dressed in the most expensive outfit she'd ever worn, she stepped out onto the concrete before she could second-guess herself, knowing that whatever happened, she was taking the step, and that was what made the difference. True failure was never taking a chance to begin with.

Kit frowned as they became inches apart, and she darted her gaze all over Rosie's face as if checking for signs of pain.

But nothing happened. No agony. No sweating or screaming. No poison in her veins or crushing sensation in her chest. Everything was...normal.

"Shit," Rosie whispered, lifting a hand to her mouth as she gasped. She'd done it. "It worked. It actually worked."

She began to laugh, and Kit pulled her into a hug. The others cheered from the other side of the rooftop.

"I know that we're leaving on Monday and your life will return to how it was," Kit murmured, sounding strangely more sober as she held on tight, only stumbling over her words a little. "But I want you to remember this moment. I want you to remember how—how fearless and bright and strong you are, no matter what anyone says or does to you. Rosie Wren is a force to be reckoned with, and you should never forget that."

Rosie squeezed her tight and breathed in her sweet perfume. No matter what happened on Monday morning, she had changed her life.

Kit held her at arm's length. "What do you say to having a drink and getting the party started?"

"I say let me try that *shenakk.*" Rosie laughed and allowed herself to be dragged out onto the rooftop.

Watching Kit become progressively more intoxicated with every sip of liquor was a joy in itself. It had been perhaps half an hour of Kit's rambling stream of consciousness tumbling from her mouth—as if a dam had broken and freed every thought she'd never expressed.

"—was only the once but I just thought...well, I—uh, I just thought..."

She'd become less elegant enigma and more fumbling teenager.

"What was I...saying?"

Rosie hid her snigger behind her hand. "I couldn't tell you if I tried. You started out explaining the best combination in *kaarmiach,* but it transitioned to a recollection of a particularly rowdy night in a far-out city in Blue Reach. Then we swiftly cut that topic of conversation and fell slap-bang into something about a hallucinogenic strain of ivy that Florelle created from her bare hands."

"It was great," Florelle agreed, her usual shy demeanour replaced with a dopey, giggly one. "I only noticed I was seeing things when Mae walked in with two heads."

Kit was no longer listening but instead humming a low tune to herself and gazing wide-eyed at the starless sky above them.

She mumbled, "Have you ever seen the stars, Ro?"

Rosie turned her head to look at her. "Hud told you about his nickname for me?"

"Sure did." Kit hiccuped. "You're part of the group when you have one."

Rosie felt a tingling sensation in her stomach, and she didn't try to hide her grin. Kit thought she was part of the group.

"No, I haven't seen the stars," she admitted.

"They're beautiful in Irredore, so bright and crisp, and...and there's just so many of them to see."

Rosie took the opportunity to ask a question she'd been thinking about on and off all day.

"How did you get out of that camp? When they destroyed your home, when they took you away...how did you escape?"

For a moment, she thought she'd completely blown the moment and that Kit wouldn't speak to her for the rest of the night. The silence between them stretched on for longer than usual before Kit's voice finally came out in a timid whisper.

"The soldiers there were foolish."

Rosie noticed the other three quiet their conversation as Kit began to speak, perhaps wanting to hear the story too.

"They talked about their plans and their superiors in front of me as if...as if I'd never be able to do anything with the information. They thought I'd end up in a ditch somewhere once they'd had their fill of tormenting and abusing me. How wrong they were." She laughed, but it was humourless. "Within days, I knew who was in charge, I knew the name of the man who'd given the order to invade Irredore without mercy...I knew the government officials who'd taken bribes for their silence."

She paused—to gather her words or her emotions, Rosie couldn't tell.

"I also knew the name of the man who'd provided soldiers and weapons. I knew that he lived in an...an ivory tower"—she gestured to the air above them in a wide arc—"in a territory that I'd never heard of with riches that I couldn't comprehend. He'd never seen war or suffering or hunger or abuse or, or, or..." She trailed off but found her pace again after a few moments. "He'd never seen war, but he'd financed it. He'd financed a genocide in return for political favour and social standing and foreign riches. So I knew. I knew from then on, from being tied to that tree with no dignity...or family...that my only goal in life would be to make him suffer. Even if it was only a fraction of what I'd gone through. I wanted to take everything from him."

Rosie waited to make sure that she'd finished before asking, "How did you end up here, then?"

Kit's expression transformed into ease and arrogance, seamlessly becoming Kitty even in her drunken state. She changed characters as naturally as she breathed.

"It began as a means to an end. Escaping was easy because the monsters were lazy and drunk on power. But moving on from my life and becoming a rogue was...much harder."

She held her hands up in the air above them, waving them slightly from side to side in a gesture that Rosie didn't pretend to understand.

"I crossed into the next territory, Acrothas, on foot and found refuge in the first city I came across. Lumgate was like... like being doused in iced water. I had no concept of life like that, thousands of people living on top of each other." She laughed quietly. *"Minimal space and maximum experience,* they used to say. I wandered the streets for days, taking in every sight and smell. The debauchery lived in every dark corner, and the wealth adorned every billboard.

"The *one* lesson"—she held a finger up close to Rosie's face—"that I learned in those first few days is that if you wait long enough...trouble will always find you. Affliction is drawn to the vulnerable. I fell in with a band of street kids. That's where I first learned to play *kaarmiach*. I was *surprisingly* good at it."

Rosie found herself beginning to smile, the tension that had blanketed them moments before beginning to ease away.

She surmised, "That's when you discovered your divine ability was in card play?"

Kit's lips twitched.

"It was only a matter of time until I became this," she continued, haphazardly gesturing to herself. "Until Kitty Khalar became my life and...and *Kitrella Mazgerald-Haast* became a ghost."

Rosie tried to hide her shock at learning Kit's name, though she wasn't entirely sure if she was successful. Kitrella Mazgerald-Haast was so...*normal.*

Kit laughed. "My peasant name is highly classified information, all right?"

"Of course, I—no problem."

Only the sounds of the city below them permeated the air.

"I have one last question," Rosie announced.

"Is this an interview or a party?"

Rosie laughed. "Weirdly, I think it's somewhere between the two."

"Then go ahead. Ask away."

"Do you...do you have any regrets?"

Kit looked as if she was about to check out of the conversation with her head rolled to one side, but then perked up unexpectedly. "I've never particularly believed in regrets. Not really. I just...it's almost like I figure that regret is a pretty pointless emotion." She hiccuped. "It's not helping anyone, especially not me. Why waste time, energy and seconds and—and energy regretting something you can't change. Why? After everything I've been through, it would be a shame to spend the rest of my second chance wishing for a different past. My past brought me here, didn't it?"

"That's very true."

Kit snorted and took hold of Rosie's hand.

"Anyway. I'm waiting for Hud to invent a time machine."

Rosie frowned. "If he did, would you use it?"

Kit stared into her eyes for so long that Rosie figured she'd forgotten the question.

The soundtrack of the city faded in and out.

Laughter, music, cheers.

Clinking glasses.

Off-key sea shanties.

The other three giggling.

"No," Kit croaked, suddenly as broken as ever. "I don't believe I would."

And that was the crux of Kitty Khalar.

Flayed, shattered, and vulnerable for all to prey on. Damaged beyond measure but still standing—metaphorically, anyway. Kit knew she'd suffered and knew she'd bore the brunt of more pain than the average person, but she was determined to make something of it rather than drown in the regret of a time gone by. The two of them were so alike in that respect.

Rosie knew that they all needed to go to bed, but she didn't want the night to end. She knew that when they all woke in the morning, the magic of the evening would be gone. She'd have to fall back into her role of personal liaison, and Kit would resume her role as Kitty.

If she could bottle up a moment in time and hold onto it forever, it would be this one. The smell of fried food on the humid breeze. The sounds of the street parties below. The feel of the rough concrete beneath her hands. The taste of *shenakk*. The sight of Kit, hair ruffled and gaze unfocused with bare feet and a distracted grin.

This moment. This was quite possibly the happiest Rosie had ever been.

Kit broke into her thoughts. "What's on the agenda tomorrow?"

Rosie blinked a couple of times to focus and sorted through her thoughts.

"You've got that luncheon with VIP guests of the hotel."

"Ugh." Kit groaned and rolled her eyes. "Promise me you'll be there? I need someone to save me from the *very important people*. What even makes a person very important? Money? Gender? I don't think I'm very important. I'm a card player. I gamble for a living. Is that important?"

Rosie smiled at her rambling and shook her head.

"I'll be there, I promise."

The truth was, she didn't have a choice in the matter, but the relief on Kit's face was worth not clarifying that fact aloud.

"You're my friend, aren't you, Rosie?"

She paused briefly, thinking of their one-sided kiss. She smiled.

"We're definitely friends."

"Good. I don't have many, but I know I need you."

They fell into a comfortable silence, the revelry far below them becoming like another presence in their conversation. Horns blared and people screamed. Groups cheered and bottles smashed.

Roguerest was on top form for the weekend. Rosie realised as she lay with the four other women that she wouldn't want to be anywhere else in the city at that moment, freedom or not.

This was exactly where she was meant to be.

CHAPTER 29

THE HELPLESS GUIDING THE CLUELESS

As Rosie re-entered the war zone that was Suite Rouge the following morning, she was hunched as if she had weights on her shoulders, exhaustion and a faint melancholy dragging her down.

It was the last day of the tournament.

The suite was a boneyard of characters from the night before strewn out like clothes to dry in varying positions of disrepute. The numb silence only added to the eeriness. Rosie stood in the doorway, admiring the scene like a prized painting in a gallery, each minuscule detail building up a picture too atrocious to not stare at. From the spilt beverages to the broken dishes, leftover food, and strung-out bodies on every available piece of furniture or floor space.

"If any of those bodies are dead," Rosie muttered with a growing smile, "I swear to Aakla, I'm out of here."

"You and me both."

Her head shot up to see Kit standing in the kitchen, nursing a mug of something as she assessed the scene in front of them. She'd changed since Rosie last saw her, now wearing some loose-fitting trousers that cinched in at the waist and a cropped dress shirt that left her midriff exposed.

"You left at the right time," she added. "Coming back here was a mistake. I haven't slept yet."

Rosie winced. "I'm exhausted from the few hours of sleep I managed, so I can't imagine how you're feeling."

Kit snorted. "I'll teach you how to tactically doze. For now, we need to coordinate a clean-up so I can order breakfast. I'm a different character when I'm famished."

Rosie scoffed. "You have even more characters in your catalogue?"

"For that comment, you can wake these ghouls up. *Good luck.*"

It had taken blood, sweat, and tears, but an hour later, the suite was empty of bodies and almost entirely back to its previous state of overzealous grandeur.

Florelle had been rescued from a huge plant pot with a palm tree in it, whereas Jal and Mae had been tangled in each other on top of a pile of coats. Rosie had escorted the three of them to the adjoining suite to join Hud, letting them rest until breakfast arrived. They'd been anything but pleased to be moved, all either in the beginnings of prime hangover territory or still outrageously drunk.

Just before the grandfather clock in the living room struck nine, Rosie pulled the suite door open to reveal Khristann with a trolley of food.

"Have I ever mentioned that you're my favourite person?" Rosie praised, holding the door as he wheeled in the large breakfast spread.

"Many times, but I wouldn't mind hearing it again."

It was as they laid out the multitude of dishes on the

kitchen island that Kit emerged from her bedroom, nose turned up and outfit immaculately pressed. She'd chosen a pristine white blazer dress with double-breasted tailoring and a pair of pointed stiletto heels that matched her skin tone as if made for her—Rosie assumed Jal had made them..

"Good morning, Miss Khalar," Khristann greeted, pulling the china plates from one of the cabinets.

"What an honour to have the head chef hand-deliver breakfast for me," she said with faux-sincerity. Kitty was back. "You must have a thousand other important jobs to indulge in."

Rosie fetched the cutlery from a drawer as Khristann placed the crockery down, a grin trying to escape across his features.

"I can always make time for an important guest such as yourself. If there's anything you need, please don't hesitate to contact me directly."

Kit's eyes twinkled with amusement. "I hope my guests and I haven't been too much work for you and your staff."

"Not at all; it's an honour. I'll leave you to your breakfast now. There's both coffee and tea in the pots, and fresh juice here. There's also iced water if you need it."

He left without thanks from Kit, and the suite became serenely calm for the first time all morning. It was quiet once again.

"I don't know about you"—Kit reached for a plate—"but I'm a damn sight too hungry to wait for the others to wake up. Please eat something. You must be as ravenous as I am, if not more."

It was true that Rosie's dinner the night before had consisted of leftovers that she'd scrounged from the plates of guests at the VIP dinner as she bussed them back down to the kitchens.

She followed Kit around the buffet spread of pastries, cold meats, and fruit, filling her plate so that it formed a small mound. They sat side-by-side at the dining table, and Rosie poured them both some juice and coffee.

"So tell me," Kit began between mouthfuls of tropical fruit, "have you had a chance to try out your divine ability yet?"

Rosie inhaled some flaky pastry and choked, coughing violently until she could breathe properly again. She sipped her water and avoided Kit's gaze.

"I'll take that as a yes," her companion mused with a knowing smile.

"Last night, I—" Rosie was unsure how to explain what had happened without incriminating herself. "I tried it out. It worked."

Kit pushed a piece of sliced meat around her plate.

"Is that all you're giving me? I'm not worthy of further detail?"

"I don't want to put you in an awkward position."

"At least reassure me that you had fun. A divine ability like yours is something to be enjoyed."

Enjoyed? Was that how it felt to be an...*Imperial?*

Rosie stabbed a piece of fruit with her fork and chewed it before she made eye contact with Kit again, nodding but not explaining herself.

"That's all I need to know." Kit continued on with her own breakfast, sipping her coffee and letting them fall into comfortable silence.

The calm remained until the adjoining door opened and Hud slumped through, his hair falling around his face in a greasy mess as he piled a plate with food. Collapsing into a chair, he began stuffing his face.

He was a noisy eater, like a piglet in a trough.

"Hud," Kit sighed.

He continued as if he hadn't heard her, crumbs catching in his locks as he used his hands instead of a knife and fork.

"*Hud,*" she tried again with more force, this time catching his attention.

"Hmm?" His mouth was so full that his cheeks puffed out.

"Where are your manners?"

He chewed his mouthful as quickly as he could and swallowed, washing it down with a glug of orange juice.

"Good morning," he rectified, looking between Rosie and Kit.

"And what of your table manners? Were you raised in a barn or were you raised in five-star hotels?"

"Sorry, Kit," he mumbled, wiping colourful streaks onto a pristine white napkin. He tucked it into the collar of his white shirt and carried on, this time using the gold utensils laid out for him.

"So, Hud." Rosie tried to lighten the mood. "How long have you been Kit's apprentice? And what is she teaching you?"

"I've been travelling with her for three years. She picked me up in Malesh. It's a slimy city in Forge Valley."

"I've heard it mentioned in books."

"That's all you want to hear of it. I wouldn't wish that place on anyone. Kit found me after she'd won her first Twelve Territories' Kaarmiach Tournament. Everyone was up in arms because she was so young. I was far too busy attaching a hidden compartment to the underneath of her carriage to notice. She hadn't got a fancy motorcar at that point."

Kit sniggered and poured herself some more coffee.

"The little scoundrel thought that I wouldn't notice a stowaway in a box beneath the carriage," she carried on the story. "I waited until we'd been travelling a day to pull the carriage over and drag him out. If only he'd asked for a lift, I would've let him sit in the carriage with me all along."

Rosie smiled at the audacity of the boy, realising that it

wasn't a trait he'd learned from Kit but instead something he'd possessed all along.

She asked, "Where were you hoping to go?"

"Anywhere but Malesh."

Rosie sensed that he didn't want to speak more on the subject of his past, which she understood all too well. She mentally crossed Malesh off her travel go-to list.

"He impressed me with his mechanical know-how, and the rest is history," Kit provided, finishing off her plate. "If we have anything malfunctioning or something in need of a quick fix, he's the only person we need."

"But you call him your apprentice. Doesn't that imply that you're teaching him something?"

Kit laughed. "If anything, he's teaching me. It's easier for others to see him as my apprentice so that red flags aren't raised about how young he is and where his parents are."

Hud scoffed and grumbled, "None of their business."

"All right, folks," a raspy voice groaned from the adjoining door. "Time to resuscitate this party."

Mae traipsed in, dark-lensed glasses perched on the end of her nose, still in the clothes from the night before with her long black hair piled on top of her head. Florelle followed in a similar state of dress, dragging an almost-comatose Jal behind her.

"I'll pour the coffee." Hud sighed and got up from the table.

"Shh," Jal mumbled, her eyes closed.

Kit chuckled. "It's the helpless guiding the clueless."

"Hush, you pesky Irredorian," Jal cursed as she was dragged into the spare bedroom with Mae and Florelle to get changed.

"That looks like a place I don't want to be." Rosie laughed quietly as she finished her breakfast.

"*That* is exactly why I know my limits," Kit said with a smug grin.

"Is that what last night was?" Rosie asked with a laugh. "I thought you were just as inebriated as the others."

Her only response was a wink.

Hud brought over three plates filled with assortments of treats and poured three cups of coffee.

Kit explained, "They'll be right as rain in a moment. Florelle has lots of remedies for a hangover; she'll just need to mix them up from her collection of herbs and plants in her trunk. Jal will have them all dressed to impress in no time, and it'll look like they've been at the spa all morning. Just you wait."

Mae was the first to reemerge.

True to Kit's word, she looked immaculate. She wore a black and white striped suit with the jacket draped over her shoulders, revealing the cropped white shirt she had on beneath. Her hair was slicked back in an effortless, casual look.

"I feel like a new woman." She slurped her coffee and moaned as she bit into a sweet pastry.

"Exhibit A." Hud sighed and rolled his eyes.

Florelle and Jal joined them simultaneously, both dressed in sharp trouser suits in bold prints, the picture of coordinated sophistication.

"Exhibit B and C," Hud commented.

Jal held out a coat hanger to Rosie with a grin on her face.

"Fresh from the press," she explained. Rosie took the hanger and looked at the taupe mini-dress and blazer, a blush rising to her cheeks. She'd dressed in her cheap work dress just before she'd come back to the suite, but she felt embarrassed by it now.

"I'll be back in a moment." She tried to hide her excitement as she ducked into the butler's cupboard.

She didn't know why she'd expected anything less, but the garment fit her to the stitch, made of a lavish, clingy material that felt luxurious against her skin. It was worlds apart from her itchy work smock.

She adjusted her hair and took a deep breath, about to re-enter the living room when she spotted a slip of paper on top of her blankets in the corner.

Her heart sank inside her chest.

Of course. She couldn't forget her duties for the evening ahead.

She plucked the note up and had to prepare herself for its contents.

You'll be provided with a replica later in the day, in your basement room. You must seamlessly replace the original. Your window of opportunity in the game tonight will be slim, but you'll be able to slip out during the interlude.

It was happening.

"Shit," Rosie whispered to herself and crumpled the note in her hand. There was no backing out of this now. She had to trust that Jakob had laid sufficient groundwork to pull this off. She had to trust in herself and her ability to do this. She made a mental checklist of everything she'd gained in order to pull off the heist.

A route to the gallery from the casino—*check.*

Two back-up routes—*check.*

An unguarded entrance to the gallery—*check.*

A method of distracting guards, staff, and patrons—*check.*

A replica of *The Rancorous Uprising* on the way—*check.*

A window of time to escape unnoticed—*check.*

She could do this.

All that remained was further detail on where she'd take the painting and who she'd take it to. Rosie had no clue how Jakob was going to release her from her *captipheus* curse, but he'd managed to lift her *supresis,* so she had to trust him and whatever his divine ability was.

He'd kept it close to his chest his entire life for a reason—perhaps tonight was that reason.

"Rosie?" Jal knocked on the door. "Does it fit?"

She shoved the crumpled paper into her blazer pocket and pasted a smile onto her face as she pulled the door open.

"Of course it does," she teased. "I wouldn't expect anything less now that I know your divine ability. You've spoiled me rotten. I'll always hold my expectations of clothing up to your standards from now on."

"That's what I like to hear." Jal held out a pair of flat pumps for her to take. "Come on, we've all got worlds to conquer today, and you can't do it in those ugly work loafers."

CHAPTER 30
SONGBIRD'S CHOICE

Before reporting to the kitchens for the VIP luncheon, Rosie stopped by her basement room to check whether she'd received any mysterious deliveries from Jakob. There was a comfort to the scents and sounds of the corridor that left her with a bizarre sense of homesickness despite not having left The Ruby yet.

Whether she liked it or not, this corridor had been her home for a year, and she would miss the stuffy warmth that she'd been so grateful for after years of living on the streets.

She ducked her head into her room and was disappointed to see it undisturbed since she'd left earlier in the morning. When she noticed her waitressing uniform hung up on the wall above her bed, she realised with a groan that she'd have to change out of the gorgeous outfit handmade for her by Jal. She coerced herself into changing by reassuring herself that it was only for the luncheon. She would be dressed in finery again later on.

Her morning had been much calmer than she'd expected, and she liked to think that Kit had made it that way on purpose. As her friends all had responsibilities to attend to in and out of the hotel, Rosie had been more than happy to keep

Hud company in the suites. Whilst he'd been tinkering with yet another bizarre contraption, Rosie had taken the opportunity to pick her way through the bookcases for a couple of hours, flicking through the non-fiction titles that provided her with glimpses into the territories she didn't know much about.

Though she tried to keep the page-tearing to a minimum, sometimes she couldn't help but want to keep things for her travel journal. She ended up with a neat little pile of pages, some with annotated text and some with illustrations or photographs.

Though Hud hadn't spoken much as he'd toiled over his invention, it hadn't been an awkward silence at all. She'd left the suite with the sense that they'd grown more comfortable in each other's presence. He'd begun to feel like a younger brother to her.

She straightened her uniform as she entered the kitchens, the usual chaos carefully orchestrated by Khristann on a pedestal in the centre.

"You have a secret admirer, songbird," he greeted her without looking, tasting something held up to him on a spoon.

Rosie's brow furrowed as she approached, a large purple flower arrangement in a tall vase displayed on the kitchen surface.

"What's this?"

"It's for you, apparently." He pointed to a chef farther back and made a series of hand gestures that clearly conveyed a specific message. "One of the receptionists brought them down for you. They were delivered to the front desk from a local florist, but you weren't in your room, so they brought them here."

"Is there a note?"

"There sure is. I'd love you to indulge my curiosity and tell me what it says. I've guarded them for the past couple of hours whilst you've been galavanting off with the celebrities."

Rosie laughed. "You sound bitter."

"Only because I don't think I've ever sweated this much in my entire life." He wiped his brow on his sleeve. "I'm about ready to hang up my chef's hat after this weekend; it's been a killer."

"I'll second that notion," Rosie mumbled and plucked the small envelope from the bouquet, tearing open the seal and pulling out a handwritten note.

A little thank you ahead of this evening. Stay sharp.
   See you there.

"So?" Khristann pressed. "Is it a declaration of undying love, as I suspected?"

"No." Rosie folded the note away again and swiped the vase up. "It's much better, but unfortunately, you'll never know why."

"Wait—"

She walked away with the arrangement barely fitting in her arms and proceeded to hide it away in her room, removing the note just in case and placing it beneath her bed where she kept the others.

Jakob had bought her flowers.

She tried to forget all of the horrendous things he'd said to her over the past year, all of the things he'd done and the ways he'd treated her. She tried so hard to think about the Jakob that bought her flowers and sought out ways to free her from her curses. She thought about the Jakob who professed his love to her last night, who kept the cheap necklace she'd given him and returned it to her as a gesture of freedom. She kept the Jakob she knew from *before* in her mind as she returned to the kitchens and prepared for the onslaught of the VIP luncheon.

A torrent of abuse from Lawrence was imminent, but she had to persist.

Freedom was calling.

Following dessert service, Rosie was commanded by Lawrence to fetch some *shenakk* for Kit.

She poured a measure and placed the bottle on the table.

"Thank you." Kit's demure gratitude made a refreshing change from the leers and put-downs that Rosie had been dealt throughout the luncheon.

Lawrence, Jakob, and the Five were again seated at a head table in the gallery, making self-indulgent chit-chat. Rosie took a step back with a practised bow of her head only to be stopped by Lawrence's inevitable need to humiliate her.

"Rosie, why don't you sing us all a song?"

He didn't deem her worthy of a single glance as he took a sip of his wine.

"I wouldn't want to interrupt your luncheon," she tried.

He looked at her with venom and curses.

"*Sir,*" she added without a thought before scolding herself for playing into his narrative that placed her at the bottom of the pecking order.

Appeased, he laughed and waved his hand. "Nonsense, girl. I doubt any of our distinguished guests have had the pleasure of hearing some of the best talent that The Ruby has to offer."

Stunned by the compliment, Rosie wasn't given an opportunity to practice faux gratitude before Lawrence added, "What she lacks in intelligence, she makes up for in her singing voice, you see."

The men of the table chuckled in unison as an automatic response, as if the belittling of women was a common, jovial hobby they all took part in. Kit and Allie, however, remained stoic.

What bothered Rosie more than anything else was Jakob's compliance with his father's behaviour. He laughed along with them and watched on without a beat of hesitation.

How could he sit by as she was publicly humiliated? A seed of doubt in relation to Jakob's intentions took root, but Rosie shoved it away as she focussed on the task at hand. If she kept trying to figure Jakob out, she'd run herself ragged.

The back and forth was exhausting.

"What would you like me to sing?"

When Lawrence glared at her for the lack of *Sir* affixed to her question, she chose to swallow down her budding panic and hold her ground.

He was just a man. She was worthy.

"Songbird's choice." His tone was velvety, but his gaze was barbed.

Rosie floundered for a second as all eyes landed on her expectantly. She reverted to looking at Kit, and instead of the cold demeanour she expected from Kitty Khalar, she found the familiar warmth of Kit staring back at her. She broke their eye contact to turn to her table of guests and motion for them to leave.

As Hud was being dragged from the room, Rosie let the beginnings of a melody bubble up and form itself into a song— one that she'd never heard before but somehow knew—and she realised that this was the perfect opportunity to test her siren ability again.

How far could she push it?

How much could she do?

One by one, each head in the room turned to look at her as her voice grew louder and more seductive. Before long, both guests and staff were watching her reverently, mesmerised by each word that left her lips. She could see now that what she'd thought was admiration for her talents was an uncontrollable draw to her siren tendencies. No one in the room could resist her whilst she sang.

Apart from Kit, of course.

Though, as Rosie looked at her for confirmation, she saw sweat trickling down Kit's temples and a frown marring her forehead. She was concentrating and pushing with everything she had to resist the pull of the song.

Rosie knew it was now or never. She let her eyes fall closed as she focussed on controlling the entire room of people. She imagined them all standing from their seats and breaking into enthusiastic dance, moving to a beat that didn't exist in reality but thrummed in their bodies like a pulse.

She swayed her hips to the same beat, feeling it flow through her as she hoped it would them. It was a sultry, rhythmic feeling that made her grin, and she let her head fall back as she danced along with it.

Her eyes shot open at the sounds of multiple chairs scraping on the hardwood floors as the hundred or so guests and staff began to dance, some with each other and some alone. They swayed and dipped, jived and twirled, all slightly different but all in unison. It was a sight to behold. The hypnosis had hooked them all in an effortless exercise of power, one that left Rosie devastated by her own ability.

It was a religious experience, feeling the submission of so many to her whims, the malleability of their minds under her influence. For a moment or two, she revelled in being the powerful one for once. She danced to the same beat and sang harder, louder, meaner, until it became a frantic competition between her victims as to who was more passionate.

Rosie watched in awe as previously pious and rigid individuals lost themselves in the thrill of it, sweating and writhing as they moved without pretence. Lawrence had his eyes closed as he rolled his hips and lifted his hands as if to praise Aakla for the experience. Rosie growled into the melody and pushed harder with him in her crosshairs, seeing the immediate effect as he collapsed against the wall behind him and began to rub against it.

He had no control. *She had all of it.*

Jakob was arm-in-arm with Han Selks, the two of them appearing in pain from the bliss of it all.

It could have been minutes or hours that the room remained in the bubble of her domination. VIPs collided with staff. Inhibitions were long forgotten. Rosie revelled in it. She fed off their energy and used it to sing louder and with more passion than the moment before. She could've remained suspended in the seat of power for much longer, but it appeared that Kit had other plans.

"Rose...Rosie," she gasped, white-knuckling the back of her chair and sweating profusely. Her hips moved almost imperceptibly to the hypnotising beat. "*Rosie,*" she hissed. "*Please.*"

Her pleas were like a bucket of cold water poured over Rosie.

She'd lost control. She'd pushed it too far. She was no better than the Imperials she hated so much, intoxicated by her own ability.

Flummoxed and embarrassed, she wondered how to fix the mess of weaving bodies without incriminating herself.

"Make them...*forget.*" Kit groaned as she continued to fight the pull of the song. Rosie hesitated still. "*Now!*"

Shocked into action, she changed the way she imagined the room, this time closing her eyes and seeing the guests falling back into their chairs, the staff returning to their posts. They would not remember what they'd done. They would remember her singing a beautiful song for them all. They would agree on how warm the room had become and how sweaty it was making them all. They would applaud her for her performance. But they would not remember anything else.

They would not remember.

She hesitantly opened her eyes to see her thoughts becoming reality, slowly but surely. After a few fumbling moments, the room returned to how it had once been, a clear divide between demure guests and submissive waitstaff. A beautiful silence settled upon the room like a warm blanket, allowing Rosie to finally cease her singing, to let go of her hold on them all and return to who she once was—the powerless help.

She sucked in a ragged breath and lowered her head as she finished, a boiling, acidic dread rising from her chest. Panic gripped her throat and left her motionless.

Did Lawrence know? Did they all know?

The first slow clap began in one of the far corners of the gallery, gradually followed by others until the entire room was applauding her.

They had no idea. They were entirely unaware of what she'd done to them and how she'd controlled them.

She'd lost control.

"It's mighty warm in here," Rosie heard someone comment over the wavering applause.

"Thank you." Lawrence had a false gleam in his eyes, one that Rosie knew she'd put there with her control. His gratitude was manufactured.

For a short, glorious time, she'd had complete control of her oppressor. That knowledge was dizzying and dangerously addictive.

"Rosie." Kit summoned her and spoke close to her ear. "Go to your room in the basement and sleep. Not only are you exhausted from last night, but that show will have taken it out of you completely. Go now before you crash. I don't want to see you until the game later."

Rosie straightened and risked a wary glance around the room of people, now back to their own behaviours. *Was it all a dream?*

"Go, Rosie." Kit spoke louder and with more authority so that everyone on the table could bear witness. "You're no longer needed here. Make yourself useful somewhere else."

Without looking back at Jakob or Lawrence, she scarpered into the back corridor and took the rickety steps down to the kitchens one at a time.

What had she unleashed?

CHAPTER 31
THE SHOW MUST GO ON

Rosie had managed to sleep for an hour or so before the need to do *something* took over.

She was getting amped up about the heist and knew that lying in her bed wasn't going to help matters. So she considered what was left to do before the final *kaarmiach* game started. She walked through the heist in her head.

She had several routes out of the casino. She'd been told she could leave during the interlude. She had a hidden way up to the gallery which also passed by her room, so she could collect her tools.

She reached under her bed and pulled out the hammer and chisel she'd acquired from Mr Jack. They weren't particularly delicate, but she didn't have much of an option. All she needed to do was find something like a pair of pliers to remove tacks and nails more delicately.

She ran through every potential place in the hotel to find a pair of pliers and knew that the most likely place was in the maintenance office, just off the garage.

Feeling pleased with herself that she'd found something productive to do, she hopped up from her bed and reached for her uniform. She paused, her eye catching on the taupe dress and blazer she'd worn that morning. She knew instantly which she'd prefer to wear.

Dressed in comfortable finery once more, Rosie arrived at the door to the garage in no time, quietly pulling it open and listening for any movement. Satisfied with the silence, she was able to cross to the maintenance office without a sound thanks to the comfortable flat shoes Jal had given to her.

She knocked once before opening the door marked *Mainte-nance* and walked in, finding one man sitting behind a desk. The other chairs and tables were empty.

"If this is 'bout one more clogged toilet, I swear to Venaak I'm outta here," the gruff man pronounced, not even looking up at her.

She hadn't thought about the fact that the antics from last night had probably spawned an infinite list of repair jobs for the maintenance team.

"No clogged toilets." Rosie's words came out with a laugh. He looked up, and his features widened a little in shock as he sat up straighter and tried to discreetly brush his hair with his fingers.

"Sorry," he mumbled, clearing his throat. "You all right? Can I help you with somethin'?"

Though her first thought was to use her ability to take what she wanted without any risk of being found out, her second thought was that she wasn't that kind of person. She couldn't allow her ability to give her a sense of superiority. She might be an Imperial by proxy, but she refused to act like one. She refused to ever become like Lawrence.

"Actually, I think you can." She played up to the image of a young woman in need of assistance, smiling shyly and looking around the room littered with tools.

"I'm working for Kitty Khalar this weekend, and she's been

absolutely dreadful. She keeps sending me out to fetch random things, and half the time I just have no clue where to get them."

The man stood and rounded his desk, coming to lean against the front of it. He was perhaps fifty or so, with tanned, leathery skin and greying, wiry hair. There was kindness in his eyes, in the way they crinkled despite the fact he wasn't smiling.

"I'm sorry 'bout that, little lady. If there's anythin' I can help with, I'll do my best. What do ya need?"

Fifteen minutes later, she left the office with three pairs of pliers in various sizes, a small pouch of frame tacks and glaziers points, and half of Alan's sandwich. He had four children under the age of ten, and his wife, Henrietta, was currently expecting their fifth.

Rosie felt good as she left. She was satisfied with the fact that she hadn't needed to use her ability to get what she wanted. Sometimes people were good and that was all there was to it.

She promised herself then that she would never use her ability unless it was absolutely necessary. She'd grown up on the streets having to work for what she wanted and using her wits to get herself out of tricky situations. She wasn't about to leave that all behind now that she had a secret weapon.

She walked with a pep in her step through the garage, casting a glance across the carriages and motorcars with an ease that she hadn't felt in a long time. It was as if everything was working out exactly as it should.

She had what she needed for the heist, she had a chance at freedom in the morning, and she had people who were fighting for her. For the first time in a year, Rosie felt an unrelenting sense of hope. There was light at the end of the tunnel—and it wasn't just Lawrence holding a candle to trick her, it was real, honest *daylight*.

As if the thought alone had summoned him, Rosie stumbled to a stop as she saw movement inside one of the motorcars. She ducked down next to a carriage on instinct and peeked around to see that Lawrence was sitting inside the car, having a conversation with someone, clearly not meant to be overheard and not wanting to be seen together.

Though Rosie knew she couldn't get close enough to hear the conversation without being seen, she was close enough to see who else was in the car with him.

Her heart sank in her chest as she took in the sight.

Rupee.

"No," she whispered. "No, this can't be happening."

She had no clue what the man did or how he was linked to the heist, but she knew some things about him for sure.

He was an old friend of Khristann's. He was a friend or employee of Jakob's. He was having secret meetings with Lawrence.

Which side was he on? Who did he work for? What were his motives?

All Rosie knew was that she couldn't trust him. She wasn't sure Jakob could either, especially if Rupee was somehow relaying information back to Lawrence.

What if he knew about the heist? What if Lawrence knew about it too? What if Jakob was being set up?

More and more questions mounted as Rosie scarpered, wanting to get out of there as quickly as possible.

Only once she was back in her room, slightly breathless and sweaty, did she drop the tools on her bed and blow out a nervous breath. She could be in the midst of a setup. She could be playing right into Lawrence's hands. She could be giving him a reason to keep her imprisoned forever.

She was about to go into a full panic but jolted to a stop when she saw multiple items on the floor that had certainly not been there when she'd left. From the dim light of her bedside lamp, she could only make out something white and fluffy.

"Damn you, Jakob," she muttered, sliding to the floor in front of the mysterious gifts and reaching a hand out to pull the white fluff towards her.

It was a coat. A long fur coat that would easily reach the floor if Rosie wore it, possibly even drag behind her as she walked.

Why had Jakob given her a fur coat in the midst of the summer? Granted, The Ruby was kept at a comfortable, ambient temperature throughout all seasons, but she would likely be far too warm if she wore this.

Pushing it to one side, she explored the other items left for her. A red sequinned mini dress, a pair of red stilettos, and something far more ominous—a copper tube with a diameter perhaps the size of her palm.

Her brow creased as she reached for it, spying a note tacked to the end where it appeared to open up.

It's finally time. We've come so far together, don't you think? The coat has large inside pockets so you can use them to conceal your tools and the copper case during the second half of the tournament. Do not leave the painting unattended.

I trust that you've planned everything else to overcome any obstacles. Once you have the painting, replace it seamlessly with the forgery inside the copper tube. If someone knows the painting is missing, you'll never escape.

Return to the tournament before the end of the interlude with the painting on your person and wait out the remainder of the game.

Everything is as it is supposed to be.

P.S. I'm glad you liked my flowers.

Rosie huffed out a breath.

He hadn't bothered to instruct her on what she had to do after the game when she would be burdened with a priceless painting inside her coat and clear evidence of her theft, yet he'd taken the time to notice the flowers perched on her nightstand.

Typical Jakob, keeping her on her toes.

She tentatively opened the tube that was only the length of her elbow to her fingertips and pulled out a rolled-up canvas. Turning to her bed, she unrolled it and gasped at the beauty of *The Rancorous Uprising*. The resemblance was breathtaking, and she severely doubted for a second whether it was a forgery. Glancing to the bottom right corner, she began to laugh to herself as she realised that the original artist's signature had been replaced with, of all things, a smiling face.

Who had managed to create such an impeccable replica?

Voices in the corridor shook her from the momentary amusement and reminded her of reality. Of the impending task.

What if she failed?

This could be the last time she set foot in her room. If she was caught and arrested, she might never see the inside of The Ruby again. Lawrence could give up on taunting someone who caused him so much hassle and throw her to the city jail she'd originally been destined for.

She would be stripped of every semblance of freedom she'd developed despite being held prisoner in the wealth and splendour of The Ruby Talisman. She would be beaten and made to endure awful, laborious tasks for the enjoyment of the prison officers. She'd heard the stories of what happened in the jail, and it was nothing to look forward to.

And if she somehow wasn't sent to jail, she would surely be punished with the doubling of her sentence at the very least. Lawrence wouldn't hesitate to prolong her suffering. Perhaps he'd even decide to keep her for the rest of his life, a servant to his whims at the cost of her youth. She'd only be free of him in death—his or hers, whichever came first.

And that was all assuming Lawrence didn't already know about the heist because of Rupee or any other uncontrollable factors.

The question that kept playing on Rosie's mind was: *how much is freedom worth?*

And without a second's pause, as she rolled up the replica painting and slid it back home in the tube. She knew her answer.

Everything.

Because yes, if she failed, the consequences would be dire. But what if she succeeded? What if Jakob was able to lift her *captipheus* as he had her *supresis* and she could wander the Twelve Territories as she'd always dreamed? What if she was free of Lawrence's torturous tendencies?

What if?

Needing no more convincing, she excitedly donned her outfit for the evening. It was a much more garish combination than she would choose for herself, but she supposed she should enjoy it one last time.

As she shrugged on the coat and filled the inner pockets with her tools for the evening, she couldn't help the nervous giggle that escaped her. She peered into the dirty sliver of a mirror she'd hung on the wall and managed to tame her sleek bob into a purposely ruffled look. The heels would prove to be uncomfortable as the night went on, but she couldn't find it in herself to be worried.

The giddiness only grew as she shook her hands out and gave herself a moment to go over her plan.

Attend the tournament.

Slip out during the interlude.

Access the gallery via the kitchen entrance.

Use her new-found ability to deal with any hiccups.

Replace the original painting with the replica.

Return to the tournament before the end of the interlude.

Await further instruction.

It all seemed almost...*too easy.* Roiling dread replaced the giddiness, gripping her like a vice. She had to have faith in Jakob. As much as his actions from the previous year told her that it was probably a disastrous idea, she had nothing left to lose.

This was the final push for freedom.

She pulled open her door and looked at her room one last time—a combination of reverence and nostalgia setting in—before striding down the corridor towards the lifts, her fur coat billowing behind her.

After all, the show must go on.

CHAPTER 32

A BOND STRONGER THAN BLOOD

The atmosphere of the VIP game room was arguably more vibrant and eager than the night before.

Rosie felt the weight of a combined gaze on her as she entered the room, anxiously searching out familiar faces. Her nerves subsided considerably when she spotted Hud's beaming face and his over-exaggerated waves from the booth in the furthest corner, where Kit's gang had set up camp for the evening.

As she strode towards them, Rosie made sure to glance over the room casually, seeking out Lawrence and Jakob. The two of them were in the same booth they'd occupied the night before, on the opposite side of the pit to Kit's booth.

She'd have his gaze on her all evening.

"Ro!" Hud jumped out of the booth and embraced her in a hug, stunning her for a moment before she wrapped her arms around his shoulders.

"Hey there, Hud." She laughed. "Excited much?"

"Of course, it's the final. We've just ordered some platters for the table, so hopefully we can dig in before the game starts. Come and sit. Come on."

He took her hand and dragged her to the circular booth, sliding in before gesturing for her to sit beside him on the end. At least she'd be able to make a quick getaway.

"Rosie, we missed you this afternoon," Mae greeted, positively glowing in a delicate dress that wrapped high around her neck and appeared to be made from thousands of pearls, beads, and tassels. Rosie couldn't tell what colour it was because every time she moved, it changed from pink to silver to gold and beyond.

Rosie asked, "What did you get up to?"

"We explored the Tourist Quarter and indulged in the overpriced boutiques. Jal bought some garments for Kit and stocked up on clothes for Hud."

Jal scoffed. "Yes, when the rascal goes through clothes the way he does, it becomes exhausting and frustrating to create them for him. I've resorted to buying him off-the-rack instead. Much less stress."

"Hey!" Hud whined. "I can't help that I'm the next best inventor in the Twelve Territories. In a few years, *I'll* be the one buying *you* clothes."

Rosie laughed politely as the three continued the teasing chit-chat. Her gaze landed on Florelle at the other end of the booth, seemingly lost in thought. Her face had been speckled with glitter to highlight her cheekbones and the bridge of her nose, her appearance entirely ethereal.

Rosie broached conversation softly so as not to startle her. "Did you go out with them, Florelle? Explore the city?"

She blinked furiously, and her previously unfocused eyes zeroed in on Rosie.

"Uh, no," she mumbled and tucked a couple of her braids behind her ear. Rosie could make out the top half of a silk dress —the same mossy colour as her hair—over the table.

"Did you stay in the hotel?"

"Yes." She averted her gaze before trying again, looking up. "Yes, I stayed in the hotel. I spent some time in the library so I could recharge. I didn't fancy the hustle and bustle that I've seen from the windows. I'm not one for large crowds or places I don't know."

Rosie tried her best to give her an understanding smile.

"How do you manage on the road all the time? Surely, you must visit plenty of places that aren't familiar to you."

Florelle peered at the other three, still ensconced in their own bickering, and fiddled with the gold coaster that her drink rested on.

"It's hard. I have a past with travelling, but back then...I had no control." She paused and met Rosie's gaze again before clearly feeling comfortable enough to continue. "I grew up following the rules, doing what I was told, and never having a solid home. We travelled for as long as I can remember, so my childhood was a series of unfamiliar places, never settling in one place for more than a week or so. I think...I think when Kit offered me this opportunity a couple of years ago, I just saw it as a way to have more control. I don't have to go out—if I don't want to, I mean—because Kit's never made me go out and face anything. She doesn't force me to do anything I don't want to do. I'm in control of my own life."

A clearer picture of the shy botanist was beginning to form in Rosie's mind. She was a complex young woman, who at times appeared as young as eighteen and others took on the stress behaviours of a thirty-year-old. Rosie couldn't pinpoint her age if she tried.

"Are you still in contact with anyone from...before?"

Florelle shook her head furiously. "My family was unconventional. Any life outside of..." She sucked in a deep breath and tensed her jaw. Appearing to make a decision, she looked back up to Rosie and nodded.

"Any life outside of the circus was not an option to them and apparently not to me. When Kit offered me this freedom, I couldn't turn it down. I had no roots, no home to return to, so a life on the road seemed to be my destiny. But that didn't mean that I had to remain a performing monkey for the rest of my life. Kit's embraced me as she would a blood relative. These people are my family now; they're my home."

Rosie wanted to reply—she honestly did. She wanted to smile politely and nod along as if she understood the sensation of true family, of a bond stronger than blood. *But she didn't.*

And worse still, she feared she never would.

She'd been given a taste of it from Kit and her unconventional family, but when they moved on in the morning, she'd be left in the same place she'd been all along. Alone.

She grew clammy, and her heart beat furiously in her chest as the panic of reality settled in. She'd be alone again. She'd have gained and lost everything in a single weekend, so easily granted and yet so easily snatched away.

Could she brave leaving The Ruby? Could she leave the only city she'd ever known and brave the outside world on her own?

"Finally!" Jal's cheery voice skimmed over her spiralling anxiety, sounding far away. "It took her long enough; she's barely made it in time for her own tournament."

White noise rang in Rosie's ears.

She managed to raise her gaze from her clenched fists to see Kit floating through the crowds, a long plum dress trailing behind her, diamonds glittering amidst its silk layers.

Predictably, all eyes were on her stoic expression as she wandered towards the booth where Rosie and the others sat. But Rosie's attention couldn't remain on her for long as the growing panic that threatened to suffocate her raged on.

She'd never see any of these people again.

She'd never hear Hud's jokes or his wild ideas.

She'd have no roof over her head, no money or stability.

The world grew exponentially smaller around her. Every muscle in her body felt taut and hot. She could feel the sweat beading on her forehead and trickling down her temples.

A hot, tight sensation bloomed in her chest. A tingling spread across her tongue and the roof of her mouth.

She'd be all alone.

Again.

All she could hear was her heartbeat, a bird thrashing inside a cage. She couldn't see anything around her, couldn't feel anything besides her nails digging into her palms. She was sweating.

She'd be all alone.

Again.

What if she got in trouble? If something happened to her, no one would know or care. She wouldn't be missed. She could disappear from the world around them and not a soul would bat an eyelid.

How long would she wander? How long would she be alone?

Her only worth lay in The Ruby Talisman. Her only purpose was in The Ruby Talisman.

Her chest tightened as she struggled to get air into her lungs. She wouldn't be safe out there. The Ruby was the only place she'd felt some semblance of security. She couldn't leave. She'd never leave. Trapped as she was, The Ruby was safe. She couldn't leave.

She'd be all alone.

Again.

"Rosie!"

She became vaguely aware of a blurry face in front of her. Her cheeks were wet with tears, her lungs throbbed, and she was soaked with perspiration.

"Rosie, can you hear me?"

A familiar voice called out like a beacon amongst the deafening ringing in her ears. But she couldn't breathe. She couldn't leave. She couldn't be alone again.

"Give me your hand. Here, put it on my chest and feel me breathe. Breathe with me, Rosie. *Just breathe in with me.* Feel that? Do you feel my chest rising and falling?"

She could. She could feel the deep, steady rise of skin and bone against her palm.

The Ruby was safe. She'd be safe if she stayed here. She wouldn't face fear or hunger or poverty or uncertainty. The Ruby was safe. The Ruby was safe. *The Ruby was—*

"Rosie, I need you to focus. Focus on me. Look into my eyes. Show me those beautiful eyes."

She met a familiar emerald gaze. Safety and warmth. She could focus on nothing but those eyes, panicked as they were.

"That's it, look at me. Breathe with me. You're all right. Breathe with me."

The first racking inhale was by far the hardest, painful but also glorious. One breath. Two breaths. Three. Four.

The tingling on her tongue faded away. The warmth in her chest cooled.

Each breath became easier than the last until she could hear something other than her own heart and the piercing white noise inside her skull. She could hear distant chatter and tinkling glasses.

"There she is." Kit beamed with relief as she stood in front of her.

One of her hands held Rosie's against her chest and the other was tentatively resting on Rosie's shoulder. Her eyes flitted all over Rosie's face, sheer panic beginning to subside.

"You're all right; just take a moment to calm yourself down. I'm not going anywhere."

A hot flash of embarrassment seared Rosie as she caught her breath, taking a slightly out-of-focus look around to see they were in a side room that was attached to the VIP room. It was just the two of them, some spare stools, tables, and an old piano.

She was safe here. With Kit.

"You can't..." Rosie's voice was gritty and raw.

"Don't try to talk just yet." Kit had various emotions crossing her features, a spinning carousel of worry, relief, and anger. Rosie was vaguely shocked that Kit had broken character long enough to drag her somewhere quiet, but she had to remain focussed on her breathing in order to stave off the fizzling anxiety in her chest.

Fresh tears tumbled down her cheeks as she blinked and fixed a stare on Kit, hoping she'd truly listen when she said, "You can't leave me here."

A small crease appeared between Kit's brows. Shortly after, her features slackened with understanding.

"I can't...I can't bear the thought of being alone again. I'm trapped here if you leave. I'm trapped forever in this ruby prison, and I can't face that any longer. I can't. You can't. *Please.* Don't leave me here."

"It's all right," Kit soothed, curling their hands closer together and letting them fall against her rapidly beating heart. "You'll never be alone, even if you're not with me."

"You're still going to leave. I'm still going to be alone and—"

"We'll talk about this later. After the game has ended, we'll return to Suite Rouge and we'll have a serious talk. I need you to hang on for me until then, okay? I have to go back out there. *We* have to go back out there."

Rosie bowed her head in defeat. "I might not have a later."

She felt Kit stiffen. "What do you mean by that?"

"Nothing," she mumbled and pulled away so that no part of

them was touching any longer, beginning to pace in the cramped room. She needed to push her away. She needed to sever the friendship they'd developed to save herself from the crushing loneliness coming tomorrow.

"You need to go back out there and win this game. I'll be all right. Go on. You have a reputation to uphold. I'm sure they're whispering and gossiping already. Your social standing is at stake if you're seen comforting a servant girl in a back room when you should be peacocking out there and putting off the competition with your withering gaze and your—"

"My reputation is meaningless if I can't protect the ones I care about."

Rosie stumbled over a wrinkle in the carpet. After righting herself, she turned back to Kit with her eyes narrowed and her brow furrowed.

"What do you mean—"

"We need to get out there. Please just...just come to Suite Rouge after the game. *Promise me.*"

Rosie thought about the heist and the fact that she was supposed to wait for further instruction from Jakob. As she looked over Kit's pleading gaze, her heart on her sleeve, she couldn't say no. Jakob would have to wait.

"I promise."

"Thank you." Kit sighed. "We're leaving very early in the morning, so if I don't see you later tonight, I fear I won't see you at all before we go. I don't want to leave without a goodbye."

"I'll be there. I'll meet you after the game. *I promise.*"

CHAPTER 33
JUST A MAN

O nce seated back in the booth, Rosie realised that not all eyes were on her as she'd feared, but on Kit descending into the pit and taking her seat at the *kaarmiach* table.

Mae, Jal, Florelle, and Hud sat in suspended silence, no one daring to broach the elephant in the room. Rosie had just about decided it would be better to leave when Hud grabbed one of the side plates in the centre of the table, beginning to pick and choose various items from the platters that had been delivered sometime between Rosie's panic and her return to the table. Once he'd constructed a small mountain of savoury goods, he turned to Rosie with a hopeful gaze.

"You must be hungry." He spoke so softly that she almost didn't hear. As he held the plate out for her, Rosie felt her heart crack in two.

Who was she to deserve someone as sweet as Hud taking care of her?

Blinking back tears, she croaked, "Thank you."

She took the plate and placed it in front of her, seeing Mae pick up one of the many drinks on the table and holding it out also.

"You should drink something," she explained. "It's not alcoholic, but it has plenty of sugar in it. You need sugar and fluids."

Rosie gratefully accepted the drink and glimpsed the four of them watching her not with pity but with understanding. With a desire to ensure that she was all right.

They *cared*.

She began to delicately eat the finger food on her plate as the *kaarmiach* started, but she found herself completely uninterested in the game. She had to regain her strength and her wits if she was going to leave during the interlude and perform a heist.

There were more important issues than a card game.

She focussed all of her attention and energy on eating the food in front of her and savouring it, continuing to pick more from the large platters until she'd eaten her fill of Khristann's delicacies. This could very well be the last luxurious meal she ate, at least for a very long time, so she'd be damned if she didn't relax and enjoy it.

By the time she leaned back in the booth and closed her eyes momentarily to adjust to her full stomach, a couple of rounds had already passed by. The other four were fixated on the game, and she didn't dare break the palpable tension by asking what place Kit was or how the game was progressing.

She acted as if she were paying attention to the *kaarmiach* for a short while longer before a waitress approached the table, a teenage girl that Rosie had spoken to several times in passing.

Shana? Sabba?

"Good evening." She greeted everyone at the table quietly so as not to attract attention in the quiet room.

Sahra. Her name was Sahra.

"Hello, Sahra," Rosie replied with a polite smile.

"Apologies for the intrusion, but Mr Haart has requested your presence at his table," she spoke directly to Rosie.

Her heart sank in her chest.

Not now. Not tonight.

Rosie swallowed the rising acid in her throat. "Which Mr Haart?"

"*Senior.*" Sahra emphasised the word with a pointed stare as if Rosie had no option but to follow her. No doubt Lawrence had been firm and rude in his request.

Rosie risked a glance over at Lawrence's table on the other side of the room and saw the predatory glint in his eyes as he smiled at her like the cat that got the cream.

He couldn't allow her a night or two of freedom from his grasp. He had to consistently remind her of her place in his world whether she liked it or not. She hoped that Jakob could pull off his plan and that Lawrence would pay for his actions sooner rather than later.

"Do you have to go?" Florelle's soothing voice dragged Rosie's fixed attention from her tormentor to the kind eyes of someone she hoped was a friend. Someone who *cared* about her.

"I have to if he's summoned me." Rosie's cheeks were inflamed, and she looked down at the table. "Although I work for Kit this weekend, whilst she's preoccupied, I have to listen to Lawrence. He's my...my boss, after all."

Her tone spoke volumes. It was clear to everyone bearing witness to the conversation that he was much more than a boss, but the four of them sat with remorse, knowing that they couldn't control this particular outcome.

"I'll be back later, I'm sure." Rosie tried to placate them. "Thank you for the wonderful food and the lovely company. I'll see you later."

She stood to leave, the bottom of her fur coat falling to the floor and pooling around her, but a small hand grasped her own and dragged her attention back to the table.

"You'll come back, won't you?" Hud's eyes were pleading. "We'll see you before we leave?"

Rosie's heart clenched in her chest. She'd grown very fond of the audacious apprentice. She'd miss him a lot.

"Of course I'll come back. I'll see you in Suite Rouge later if not before."

His eyes flitted between both of hers.

"Okay." He relented and let go of her hand. "Come back as soon as you can."

"I will, Hud. I promise." She ruffled his lengthy hair, and he grinned, slapping her hand away as he tried to tame it back to something less wild.

With trepidation, Rosie began to follow Sahra around the circular pit that held everybody's focus. As they walked, she tried to formulate a plan in her head as to how she would step out of the room during the interlude. She could offer to fetch drinks for the table. Or perhaps use an excuse involving Kit, claiming that she had an errand to run during the break that couldn't be ignored.

Yes. She'd play the Kitty Khalar card. Lawrence couldn't say no to that.

She steeled the resolve she had left as they approached the booth where Lawrence and two other men leered at her as if she were meat in the city market. Jakob watched her too, though his posture was slumped and his fingers drummed on the table. No doubt he had several plates spinning at once in his head with the tournament, the heist, and the takedown of his father all occurring at once.

How would he go about toppling Lawrence from his ruby throne?

Rosie briefly panicked that Jakob's plan would fail;

Lawrence controlled the majority of the city's officials, if not all of them, so Jakob was tying his own noose by trying to defy his father. She panicked that Lawrence knew everything because of Rupee. That Jakob was digging his own grave right beside hers.

They arrived at the booth before she could further explore the flaws in Jakob's plan, and a crawling, slimy sensation slithered across her skin as all of Lawrence's attention lay solely on her.

"My beautiful little songbird." He flashed a wolfish grin. "Please, sit. We've been admiring your finery from across the room and decided that we'd much rather see it up close instead. It's not often that we see you in anything that makes you attractive."

Rosie clenched her jaw and knew better than to rise to the comment, taking a seat on the end of the circular seat beside Jakob. Lawrence sat in the centre, directly facing the pit.

The two gentlemen that joined them were Lawrence's age, though not nearly as well put together as he was. Their protruding guts and round, reddened faces were a far cry from Lawrence's slim, roguish appearance. Rosie didn't care to spare them more than a fleeting glance as they continued to stare at her.

"Your outfit is lovely." Jakob spoke quietly and with restraint. "You look beautiful this evening."

"Thank you," she replied without meeting his gaze.

Of course he would like it. He chose it for her.

"I was indulging my friends here in stories of your charming voice." Lawrence gestured lazily with his hands as he spoke. "Perhaps when the game is over, you'll join us for a private concert."

Rosie didn't dare to meet the evil eyes she felt fixated on her. She couldn't let him see her fear; she'd come too far now too regress to her former self.

He was just a man.

"Unfortunately, I'm unavailable later on, occupied with Miss Khalar and her guests," she said easily, feeling Jakob tense beside her. "The private concert will have to wait for another night." She pasted a false smile on and looked up to match Lawrence's stare. "*Sir,*" she added with malice.

His nostrils flared, and his expression flattened. She knew that if Jakob's plan this evening fell through, she was in for a world of pain courtesy of the demon at the table. But she couldn't sit back and allow him to torture her any longer. Even if it was for an evening, she was determined to let him know that he would never own her, not completely.

She would rise from this weekend a different person, one who knew her true potential and was absolutely sure of her worth.

Looking at the empty man in front of her fuelled her fire. He was just a man. She would ensure that everyone knew it, no matter how long the feat took. She wouldn't lie powerless as he trod over her any longer.

"When this next round has finished and we have a short interlude, I'd like to speak to you outside." Lawrence was all smiles as he spoke, leaning back and widening his stance to appear bigger and more intimidating.

Too bad he didn't fool her anymore.

"I have a couple of errands to run for Miss Khalar during the interlude." Rosie kept her tone cool and polite. "Though I'd be happy to speak with you once my duties to Miss Khalar are fulfilled. I don't want her to feel neglected."

He narrowed his eyes and sat up, leaning towards her over the table.

"Miss Khalar can wait. I'm your boss. I house you and feed you. *I own you.* So I'll be damned if you disobey me under some false guise of superiority."

"Father." Jakob held up a pacifying hand. "We can't afford to upset any of our VIP guests, not least the most popular of them all. A bad review or snide comment about the hotel from her would cripple us."

Lawrence looked between the two of them, visibly suspicious as he reclined back in his seat and smiled at his two guests.

"Apologies for the outburst, gentleman," he said. "I just can't get competent staff these days. Why don't we order another round of drinks?"

Rosie remained stiff as a board as the next round of *kaarmiach* began, her back ramrod straight and her fists clenched in her lap.

It was almost time.

She tried her best to concentrate on the game, on Kit's expressions and the movements of the cards. In all honesty, she had no clue who was ahead or whether Kit was on her way to becoming the champion again. She didn't particularly care either.

She ran over her plan in her head. She had the tools and the knowhow, she just needed the opportunity to present itself and she'd be on her way.

She focussed on her breathing, on the waitstaff circling the room and the concoctions they carried to individuals. Noticing that Kit hadn't opted for a drink at the table this evening, she secretly hoped that it was because Rosie hadn't been available to fetch it for her.

Rosie watched Phoenix throw his cards down on the table. A mixture of groans and cheers rang throughout the large room, signalling a change in circumstance for some of the players at Phoenix's expense.

Her heart beat ferociously in her chest when the dealer

announced that it was time for the interlude and that play would resume in half an hour.

It was time.

She stood with purpose, straightening her coat and turning to face the men at the table.

"If you'll excuse me, gentlemen, I have some errands to attend to."

"Nonsense," Lawrence fought her. "I will speak with Miss Khalar myself and make sure she knows you are needed here this evening. No affairs of hers can be so important in the midst of the game. You will stay here and that's final."

Rosie froze.

What would she do now?

Trying not to express her alarm, she managed a meagre smile. Jakob would step in, surely? She looked over at him, but he remained emotionless.

Why wasn't he helping her?

"I—" Rosie clammed up as she fumbled for an excuse or retort.

She began to heat up, her breathing shallow.

Think. Think. Think.

"If that's the case," she attempted, "then perhaps I should fetch you gentlemen another drink and something to eat." She lifted her gaze to the two suits who continued to shamelessly drag their greedy eyes up and down her form. "I'm sure you two are famished from all of the evening's activities so far. What might I get for you? Our head chef is quite talented, and the menu for the evening is as eclectic as it is delicious."

The words fell from her mouth on autopilot, her hospitality smile coming out as she recalled the spiel used by all the employees.

"You're right." One of them chortled, dabbing his damp forehead with a silk handkerchief. "I'm *starving.*"

Rosie's skin crawled as his eyes fixated on her legs.

"A few platters for the table, then?"

Jakob chose to answer for them, his jaw locked. "Thank you, Rosie. And another round of our drinks, if you would."

"If you aren't back in five minutes"—Lawrence pinned her with a vicious stare—"then I'll make sure you can't leave my side ever again. Mark my words, songbird."

Rosie didn't hang around to respond to his threat, instead pacing towards the bar with dread swirling in her gut.

What would she do?

She couldn't leave the room, much less use the entire interlude to steal a prized painting. She'd failed before she'd even been given the opportunity to try. She'd failed *again*.

She hopelessly repeated the food and drink order to the young woman behind the bar, who scribbled the instructions down furiously and sent the order to the kitchens before starting on the drink preparation.

The room had grown much louder now that the break had commenced, and the mayhem could continue for half an hour. Rosie blocked out the droning noise and instead looked at her shaking hands. Jakob had been relying on her to do this for him, yet he hadn't helped her when she'd needed it most.

What sort of game was he playing?

Momentarily tearing her eyes from her hands, she gave a sweeping look across the patrons around her as the first of four drinks was slid across to her on a tray.

Wait.

She peered beyond the bar and saw something...flashing?

A flickering light came from inside one of the storerooms through a narrow crack in the door. As she furrowed her brow and tried to figure out what it was, it stopped.

How bizarre.

As she was about to turn away, the flashing began again, a

pinprick of light at shoulder height in the small opening. Feeling her heart begin to race again, she glanced at the bartender, seeing her preparing the second drink. She had time.

"I'll be right back," she told the woman and hazarded a glimpse at Lawrence's table to check that he wasn't watching her. Thankfully, Jakob seemed to have them enthralled in a story that he was embellishing with wild hand gestures. Perhaps he really was trying to help her.

She snuck in between raucous guests and stumbling VIPs to make her way over to the storeroom, the light having stopped as soon as she'd stood up. She warily pushed the door open to reveal darkness but slipped inside anyway, fumbling for the light switch beside the door.

Once she'd located it and flicked it on, she swung her head around to see who or what was making the light flash.

What she encountered took her breath away. Her throat clamped shut and her jaw slackened as pure, unadulterated shock took over her.

It couldn't be.

It wasn't possible.

And yet there she stood, witnessing it with her very own eyes. Standing across from her, amongst piles of chairs and tables, was herself.

CHAPTER 34
THE THRILL OF THE STEAL

Rosie blinked several times.

She looked away and then back, trying to decide whether she'd truly lost the plot this time. However, the person in front of her—the person who looked just like her—wasn't moving, only grinning. She held a burnt-out match in one hand and a shiny coin in the other; her tools for causing the flashing light.

"Hello," her doppelgänger said. "I know this must be quite the shock, but I don't have time to explain."

Even her outfit was the same. It was like she was looking into a mirror.

Rosie stammered, "How—who—what is this?"

"There's no time. You need to listen to me very carefully. I'm going out into the bar to act as you whilst you climb into *that* vent"—she pointed at the ventilation grate in the ceiling—"and do what you need to do within the next twenty-five minutes. If you haven't returned within that time, we'll run into trouble."

"Who are you? What's happening? Did Jakob hire you —*make* you? "

Rosie had no clue what Jakob's divine ability was; for all she knew, he could conjure visions or create clones. The thought made her shiver.

"Enough questions; I have to go and so do you. Good luck."

The doppelgänger rolled her shoulders back and straightened her hair before opening the door and breezing out.

Was she dreaming? Was any of this real?

"I have...a twin? Or a clone? Or a..."

Rosie floundered with her racing thoughts.

"Enough," she scolded herself and shook out her hands. She had a job to do and a very limited amount of time to do it. Luckily, the ventilation tunnels above the game room had been one of her back-up exit routes, so she didn't have to panic about a change in plan.

The show must go on.

She dragged a stack of chairs beneath the grate in the ceiling and climbed them with only one or two fumbles until she could reach the grate. She pushed up on the metal and felt it give beneath her hands, sliding up and across into the shaft.

"Here goes nothing," she muttered, grasping the edges of the hole in the ceiling and hoisting herself up.

She hadn't realised how much the weight of her coat would hinder her until she was gasping inside the metal shaft, sweat running into her eyes.

This was it. She was doing this.

She allowed her on-the-job mindset to settle in and pushed any emotions or unnecessary thoughts away. Locking them in a box as she pulled off jobs was the only way to stay focussed and impartial.

Her adrenaline was pumping as she began crawling through the vent shaft, keeping a mental copy of the layout to the ventilation system in her mind as she went.

She counted grates and navigated twists in the shaft until

she looked down through the holes in a grate to see the flooring of a service corridor that ran alongside the casino and the foyer.

"Thank Aakla," she gasped, feeling penned in because of her large coat. She pulled the grate up and slid it over, halting and listening for any movement.

Thankfully, with the tournament, it was all hands on deck for the staff. They would all either be front of house for the evening or attending to press and crowds outside of the building, which left the corridor mercifully quiet and empty.

Rosie lowered her head gently until she could see into the corridor to confirm her suspicions. She swung her legs into the opening and used her hands to lower herself down with lacklustre finesse. She hung for a second or two before allowing herself to drop into a crouch on the floor.

Without further pretence, she took her shoes into her hand and sprinted towards a stairwell, taking them two at a time until she arrived in the basement. Straightening her coat, she strode out into the corridor and paced towards the chaos seeping from the kitchens.

Be truly extraordinary, she recited to herself.

She stopped by her room to grab her tools and the replica painting, stashing everything in the pockets on the inside of the coat. She took all of a second to glance over the room in case this was the last time she saw it. At the last second, she picked up her travel journal and slipped it into her coat as well, then took off back to the kitchens.

The further she was from Lawrence's gaze, the more she believed in her ability to carry out what needed to be done. This was her passion. Before Lawrence and Jakob and The Ruby, she'd been a thief who'd survived sixteen years without any outside help. She'd be damned if Lawrence made her feel as if she couldn't do this after a year under his influence.

She sauntered into the kitchens as if she was supposed to be there, a wall of heat and noise slamming into her. Chefs were running ragged, pots were clanging, and voices were shouting. It was somehow worse than the circus from the evening before.

Thankfully, amidst the bustling confusion of the room, no one batted an eyelid at her presence or her outfit. They barely managed to dodge her as they moved in synchronised motions. She tried to catch a glance at Khristann and briefly saw a glimpse of him beside a pan, trying whatever was cooking.

It was probably best that he didn't see her and question her presence.

Slipping into the kitchen store unnoticed was almost too easy, but Rosie didn't have time to contemplate it. Her sights had zeroed in on the prize; *The Rancorous Uprising* was waiting.

She pulled open the metal door to the steps that led to the gallery and began a steady climbing pace, feeling her chest burn and her legs cramp. She was decidedly out of practice since staying in the hotel, that much was clear.

As she reached the top of the rickety stairs and bent over to catch her breath, she checked her pockets for her tools.

Hammer? *Check.*

Chisel? *Check.*

Tacks and glaziers points? *Check.*

Pliers? *Check.*

Copper tube? *Check.*

"Showtime," she muttered and straightened, waltzing into the staff corridor beside the gallery. She sincerely hoped the gallery would be deserted amidst the excitement of the tournament but prepared for the worse. She was a siren. She could handle anything or anyone that stood between her and the painting.

She could do this.

Be truly extraordinary.

Leaving her worries and her stilettos behind her, she pulled the door to the gallery open and advanced into the open space. She was beyond relieved to find it dimly lit and empty, presumably closed off to the public during the tournament.

"Perfect." Rosie couldn't help the grin that broke out. She soundlessly crossed the room, out of view from the front entrance due to half walls placed at intervals to display art. Once she'd arrived at the large open space towards the back where *The Rancorous Uprising* was displayed, she shrugged off the coat.

"Mercy," she muttered, cool air surrounding her and giving her a break from the stifling garment. She dropped the coat on the bench in the centre of the room and turned to face her prize.

There was nothing quite like the painting in front of her. Priceless, forbidden, and entirely hers for a short while.

She rubbed her hands together in excitement and got to work. She feared the time she'd already spent in making it to the gallery; each second was precious and potentially deadly.

She removed the tube and her tools from the coat and placed them on the floor beside the painting. Risking a glance behind her to check for guards one final time, she figured that it was now or never.

Tentatively, she grasped the weighty frame—only a hand or two shorter than the span of her arms—and lifted it from its hooks on the wall.

"Slowly does it," she whispered, feeling as it freed from the wall attachments and rested entirely in her arms.

"Beautiful." She laughed quietly to herself and lowered it to the floor, fumbling for the hammer and chisel.

Prying the frame apart was harder than she'd thought and further hindered by the noise involved in knocking a chisel into a splinter-sized gap with a hammer. She winced at the loud clinks and paused as she thought she heard movement behind her.

"Shit," she muttered, scrambling to grab her fur coat and skidding back to the floor. She covered the end of the chisel with a layer of fur and continued knocking it with the hammer, pleased by the muted sound. Able to hit the chisel harder, the frame mercifully came apart in one corner.

"Come on, come on."

Her frustration bred strength as she pried apart the other three corners in a much shorter time. She lay each side of the frame to one side and fixed her attention on the nails pinning the painting to the thinner canvas frame. Grabbing a pair of pliers, she began to prize the rusted nails from their home, catching each one before it rattled on the floor.

Ten nails to go. She was so close she could almost taste it.

Nine. The painting was hers.

Eight. Would Jakob let her keep it?

Seven. Why did he want her to steal it in the first place?

Six. Not important.

Five. Her hand was beginning to cramp.

Four. Almost there.

Three. How long would it take someone to notice the forgery?

Two. Hopefully long enough for her to get away.

One.

The gallery lights flicked on, blinding her momentarily as multiple voices came from the direction of the entrance.

"No, no, no," Rosie whispered. She looked back and forth between the painting and the visitors several times before deciding that she'd have the best advantage if she was out of sight.

Shooting up, she crossed the space where *The Rancorous Uprising* was kept and pressed her back against one of the half walls used to display artwork.

"Come on!" someone bellowed. "It's in here!"

Several drunken cheers followed, and Rosie cursed whoever it was for disrupting her. She didn't have time for this.

As the voices got closer and travelled to her right, she silently switched sides of the half wall just as the visitors passed by, keeping out of sight. With them now on the other side, about to come across the frame in pieces on the floor, she was able to peek around the wall and see who they were.

Four young men and two women were in varying states of disrepute.

"We shouldn't be in here," one of the women tried to whisper, but it came out much louder.

"I know the guard," one of the men boasted. "He won't tell anyone we're in here."

Rosie hated to admit it, but she was going to need her ability.

She had no other option when every second was precious.

Just as they were about to turn to see where *The Rancorous Uprising* should've been displayed, another voice joined the fray.

"Excuse me, ladies and gentleman. Unfortunately, the gallery is off-limits tonight, and I'm going to have to ask you to leave."

Why did Rosie know that voice?

"Come on, man." One of the men stumbled. "We just wanted to have a peek."

"If you don't leave immediately, I'll be calling security and you'll be banned from the premises and any other casino in the Haart group."

"Let's just go," one of the women said, tugging the hands of two men. "I want to get another drink anyway."

"We were just having some fun, there's no harm," another of the men placated. The six drunken strangers stumbled away, leaving the painting miraculously undiscovered on the floor.

Perhaps the mystery man wouldn't see it either.

Rosie held her breath.

One beat. Two. Three. Four.

The footsteps retreated without any fuss, and Rosie sucked in some much-needed air. Who was that? The voice had belonged to a man, but the face to match it slipped from her grasp.

Surely, it couldn't have been that easy?

She slowly poked her head back around the wall and found the gallery space empty. A second later, the lights overhead shut off again, leaving her in the dim room that she'd started in.

Unbelievable.

Not one to kick a gift horse in the mouth, she sprinted back across the room and skidded to her knees, picking up where she'd left off and pulling the wooden frame off the canvas. She fumbled for the copper tube and unfastened the end, sliding the replica out. As delicately as she could manage, she began to roll up the real *The Rancorous Uprising,* checking that none of the paint cracked or flaked. Just because she didn't know its final destination didn't mean that she could throw it around without care.

She slid it home in the tube and screwed the lid back on, a sigh of relief whooshing out. She soldiered on, placing the frame on top of the unrolled forgery and ensuring it was straight before nailing the top side of the canvas to the frame. She turned it over and pulled the canvas as taut as she could manage whilst holding the hammer in one hand and a nail between her teeth. Once satisfied that the painting was in place enough to not arouse suspicion, she began nailing in the bottom side of the painting.

The rhythmic tapping of the hammer beat in time with her pulse, steady and calming as she did what she loved. Before long, she'd finished attaching the painting to the frame and held it out in front of her, checking for any creases or uneven layers in the canvas.

"Perfect." She grinned, placing it on the floor as she collected the four parts of the larger frame.

She had no idea how much time had passed or if she'd failed already because Lawrence had seen through her doppelgänger and called the authorities. Or maybe Rupee had told him about the heist and he already knew everything that was going on.

He could be on his way to the gallery. He could be releasing the hounds to find her. He could *know*.

She shook her doubts away and reminded herself that she'd made it this far, against all the odds and the doubts she'd had on Thursday when she'd received the note to tell her what her job was over the tournament weekend.

Back then, it had seemed impossible. She'd had the weight of a *supresis* curse to contend with amongst many other obstacles; and yet somehow, she'd made it to this point, fixing the frame around the replica painting and lifting it up.

"You beauty," she whispered. "You're going to do great."

Scrambling up, she approached the wall, having to try multiple times before the hooks on the canvas slid home on the nails protruding from the wall. She let it go with extreme caution, praying that it was attached and wouldn't come crashing down.

As she took a couple of steps back and admired her handiwork, she couldn't believe what she was seeing.

A perfect forgery of *The Rancorous Uprising* hanging in the gallery—by her hands, no less. She'd done it.

Knowing that time was slipping through her fingers and that she could be found out at any moment, she swept up her tools and the case holding the painting, shrugging on her coat and filling the inner pockets.

The suffocating heat from the coat engulfed her, but she

pushed through it as she strode back towards the staff corridor beside the gallery.

She was so close to success. She couldn't afford to stumble now. It was as if her entire life so far had been leading to this momentous job. Her adrenaline pumped, and her smile remained unfaltering.

She was destined to do this. Nothing came close to the thrill of the steal. She managed to cross the gallery without encountering anyone else, slipping back through the door into the service corridor and hooking her shoes onto her fingers.

She flew through the door into the staircase and bounded down, uncaring for the sounds she made as the soundtrack of the kitchens was sure to drown out any noise.

She stumbled to a halt at the bottom and hurried to slip her shoes back on, wincing as she felt the spots where they'd begun to rub.

Not important, she reminded herself as she entered the kitchen store. She encountered a kitchen porter fetching ingredients and flashed him a show-stopping smile which he feebly returned, not daring to question what she might be doing dressed the way she was in the storeroom.

She fixed her game face as she strode in the kitchens and narrowly dodged a bumbling chef carrying trays, her coat sweeping out behind her as she twisted and regained pace towards the corridor. She'd reached the threshold when movement up ahead made her pause.

She squinted to see down the very long corridor, watching three of the hotel's security guards pacing in her direction. As soon as they realised that she was standing there, they broke out into a run.

"She's there!" one of them shouted.

"Oh shit," Rosie whispered. "No, no, no, no."

She took a step back and stumbled into someone. Spinning around so quickly that her neck hurt, she found Khristann.

"You okay, songbird?"

His eyes flicked over her head to see the guards coming and then looked back down at her.

Without hesitation, he pulled her behind him and into the kitchen, dragging her towards the storeroom she'd just left.

"Oh shit," she breathed. "This can't be happening, I—"

Khristann shut the storeroom door behind them and turned to her with a panicked look in his eyes.

"What do you need?" he asked without pause.

"I—I—"

Rosie's mind went blank.

Lawrence knew. He had to know. How did he know? What had gone wrong? What about her doppelgänger? Had Jakob told him? Had Rupee told him? Was it all a set-up all along?

"Rosie!" Khristann took her by the shoulders. "Tell me what you need."

Her eyes welled up as she reached into her coat and fumbled to get the copper tube out.

"I need you to hide this." Her voice cracked. "I need you to hide this somewhere, and only when the time is right can you give it to Jakob. I think...I think it belongs to him, but I don't even know by this point. I don't know who I've been working for, I don't know who that is supposed to go to, I d-don't know anything anymore and I—"

Khristann grabbed the tube from her hand and rolled it underneath a shelving unit without an explanation, then leapt back up and pulled her into his arms.

"Go up to the gallery and escape through there," he instructed, kissing her head for the briefest of moments. "I'll distract the guards. *Go.*"

"B-But there's nowhere I can go," she cried, her hands

shaking and her heart pounding. "I can't escape him in this place. There's nowhere I can go that he won't find me. I can't escape him. I can't—"

"*Go!*"

Khristann pushed her through the door to the staircase, and she nodded, her lips trembling and tears spilling down her cheeks.

"Can you tell Jakob that I'm sorry? Can you tell Kit thank you?"

He shook his head and began walking back towards the kitchen without looking at her. "I won't tell you again, songbird. Get out of here. Hide until I come to find you."

He re-entered the kitchen and left her standing there on her own, petrified, betrayed, and hopeless. How had it gone so wrong so quickly?

Everything had gone perfectly. *Too perfectly.*

Instead of wasting time trying to figure out what part of the plan had fallen through, she kicked her heels off again and began to sprint back up the stairs, taking them as quickly as she could without tripping over the stupid coat she wore.

Where would she go? She couldn't leave the hotel. She couldn't trust anyone inside.

No, she corrected. She could trust Kit. She could trust Hud. She could trust her friends. But how would she get to them without crossing more guards or even Lawrence himself? There was no way.

Her next thought was that the ventilation tunnels would be a good place. Lawrence might not know that she used them to traverse the hotel. And there were so many places she could be hiding that it would definitely take a while for her to be found.

Her adrenaline sang viciously through her blood as she reached the top of the stairs and threw the door open, not stopping for a breath. She flew across the corridor and pulled the door to the gallery open.

Go, go, go, she told herself. She had to run faster. She had to act smarter. She couldn't let Lawrence trap her again.

Crossing the gallery was easy, but what lay in wait for her at the entrance was not so simple. She skidded to a stop.

Guards. Lots of them. Waiting for her.

"Think, think," she whispered.

Her voice. Her song. She could control them all with a thought and a melody.

She took a deep breath in to begin singing with abandon when a hand slapped over her mouth from behind. Someone pulled her into their hard chest.

"Not so fast," a man's voice said as two guards appeared on either side of her. The man holding her let go of her mouth to better restrain her arms whilst another shoved some sort of rag between her lips, making her gag. She shook her head violently, but the men simply laughed as they wrapped a tie around her face and across her lips to keep the cloth in place, quickly and effectively gagging her.

"Play time's over," one of them grunted.

Without further pretence, she was picked up and thrown over a shoulder.

She'd blown it.

CHAPTER 35
UNFINISHED BUSINESS

No matter how much Rosie squirmed and kicked and screamed into her gag, she couldn't get the man holding her to put her down. As they walked, the group of three guards grew to five, then to seven. By the time they got to the service lift, there were ten guards filling the car and heading up to somewhere Rosie wasn't privy to.

She tried to speak against her gag again to no avail, finally relenting to the situation and falling still.

"Finally," the guard carrying her muttered just as the lift doors opened on the penthouse service corridor.

She was carried to the stairwell in a few paces, and they began the climb up to the roof.

As soon as the door was opened, the sounds of hysteria on the streets below them permeated the air and left Rosie feeling truly hopeless. Everyone was down there having the time of their lives, and no one would ever know that she was suffering.

What would Lawrence do to her? Had he finally grown tired of her antics and decided to throw her off the roof? He could so easily call it an accident, and everyone would believe him. No one would care about a nobody maid in a city of sin. She was just another lost soul amongst the masses.

Her world was suddenly turned back upright, sending a wave of nausea over her as she was pushed against the metal structure that held up the towering and flashing *The Ruby Talisman* sign above them.

In no time, she'd been secured to the railings with bindings tight enough to cut off the circulation to her hands. The balmy city air whipped around her, leaving her pleased that she'd kept her coat on.

"Don't move," one of the guards joked, blowing her a kiss as the others jeered.

They all left her there, tied up and gagged on the rooftop, completely on her own with only the soundtrack of the city to keep her company.

What had gone wrong? How was she the only person in the shit right now? Where was Jakob? Where was Khristann?

The second half of the *kaarmiach* must have started by now, but it felt a world away. Would anyone be worried about her disappearance? Would anyone have noticed? What happened to her doppelgänger?

The warm breeze brought with it the foul smell of the Industrial Sector, and Rosie tried her hardest not to gag with the cloth shoved in her mouth.

How had she ended up here?

The sound of the rooftop door opening caught her attention, but she didn't dare look up from her feet, already knowing who it was that had come for her. He'd always promised that he would make her suffer, but she'd always believed she was better.

So stupid, she cursed. There was no escape from Lawrence Haart. She'd been a fool to ever believe she could outsmart him.

"Well, well, well. What do we have here?"

His voice haunted her. It was the first thing he'd said to her when she'd tried to steal the painting the first time. It was the first thing he'd *ever* said to her.

"A little bird trying to escape her cage," he drawled as his shiny leather shoes came into view in front of her.

His hand grabbed onto her chin and lurched her head upwards so that she had to look into his villainous eyes. How she hated those eyes. Hated the way they looked down on her. Hated the way they saw right through her. Hated the way they—

"Oh, don't be so sad," he taunted, those eyes lighting up with sick pleasure. "We're connected, you and I. There's no escaping me, no matter how hard you flap those little wings." He leaned close enough to make her want to be sick. "There's so much unfinished business between us, I could never let you go."

He let go of her chin as the rooftop door opened again and three men stepped through: the two guests that had been sitting at Lawrence's table in the casino and...*Rupee.*

She should've known. She should've trusted her instincts.

The writing had been on the wall down in the garage.

But the question still remained: did Jakob know? Did he set her up?

The feeling of her necklace and the pendant against her chest said otherwise. The conversation she'd had with him the night before said otherwise.

"You thought you could outwit me." Lawrence's tone was slick with amusement. "But I know everything that goes on in this hotel. I know everything about every employee I allow through the doors, and I especially know everything about the thieving little bird I keep imprisoned here. Like how she has a habit of borrowing tools from my friend Mr Jack and the maintenance department. Tools that are perfect for prying open a frame and putting it back together again."

He smirked at the men gathered close by, then looked back at her.

"And the fact that she's not a poor little Artist." He sidled up next to her again. "Not even close, are you, siren? Perhaps you shouldn't have spoken so loudly with Miss Khalar about your ability at the party last night. Lots of curious ears were in there. It only takes a little bit of cash to persuade someone to keep an eye out for anything unusual."

She didn't look at him, instead staring straight ahead and fixating on Rupee. She would stare him down. She would make sure he knew what he'd done to her by her burning gaze alone.

"I figured the best time for you to steal the painting was during the tournament when you assumed everyone would be preoccupied. How right was I? You're stupidly predictable—or perhaps just stupid. But the best part for me was your twin." Lawrence began to chuckle, pacing in front of her. "You really thought I wouldn't realise that she was someone else? As soon as I touched her, I knew."

He stepped close again and brushed his hand against her cheek, making her flinch involuntarily away from him.

"You flinch so beautifully when I touch you," he whispered. "But she didn't react at all. Plus, she had more backbone in her stare alone than you'll ever have in your entire body. But I applaud your efforts."

He stepped back again, signalling for his friends and Rupee to come over.

"The only question now is: how should I punish you for your little scene? Not only have you disrupted the most important event the hotel has ever hosted, but you've managed to royally *piss me off* too."

Friend One and Friend Two rubbed their hands together as

they approached, their eyes still feasting on her like they had in the casino. Rupee, however, kept his eyes on Rosie's and his expression blank.

"Luckily, I have three friends with very interesting divine abilities that they just love to use on people whenever they get the opportunity. So I thought I'd let them have their fun with you first. Once they've sufficiently broken you down, I'll put some much more interesting curses on you. That's when our fun will really begin, little songbird."

Lawrence stroked Rosie's cheek again, brushing away the tears that had begun to fall uncontrollably from her eyes.

Why hadn't Jakob come? Why hadn't he protected her from the demon? He'd promised. He'd *promised*. He should be here.

The wind whipped some of her hair into her face, and Lawrence stepped back as Friend One approached, a sick grin on his face. He didn't touch her but lifted a single hand, making an exaggerated *come hither* gesture in her direction. The wind around them suddenly changed direction, and Rosie physically felt the air being sucked from her lungs and through the gag.

She began to cough uncontrollably, but try as she might, she couldn't suck any air in. The gag only exasperated the problem, leaving her lungs burning and her chest feeling like it was about to collapse in on itself. Her eyes bulged and she thrashed against her bindings, but within ten seconds, her vision began to swim and her head felt heavy.

It was like her lungs had hollowed out and shrivelled up. Like her chest would give in from the pressure.

Just as she thought she'd suffocate, Friend One released his hand, and the wind settled again, allowing her to suck some semblance of air in through her gag. It wasn't enough. She heaved and gagged as she tried to get enough oxygen, her heart pounding in her chest and her head and her throat.

She couldn't breathe.

She gasped in as much air as she could, feeling like the veins in her head were about to explode from the pressure of her trying to suck air through her gag.

The men in front of her simply laughed.

Only when she'd regained some form of a breathing pattern did Friend One lift his hand again with that same twisted grin. She shook her head, tears streaming down her face as she pleaded with him through her gag.

Please, no, she tried to say. *Not again.*

His hand moved almost imperceptibly, but the effect was exactly the same. Her lungs burned. Her chest heaved. Her legs gave in.

Shecouldn'tbreathe. Shecouldn'tbreathe. Shecouldn'tbreathe.

She thrashed until her energy waned and she was left slumped on the floor, her head resting back against the metal structure she was bound to. Black spots danced in her vision. White noise rang in her ears.

Was this what death felt like?

The hold on her lungs was released, and she heaved out a sob as she was granted oxygen again. She wanted to put on a brave face and show Lawrence that she was unaffected by his torture, but there was no way she could manage it. She greedily sucked in air through the gag and began to cry uncontrollably. Her coughing and wheezing was the only sound on the rooftop as Friend One walked away.

Why was this happening to her? Why had she been so close to freedom only to have it snatched away? Why? Why? *Why?*

When her vision began to clear, she watched as Friend Two approached her and crouched down to meet her tear-filled gaze.

"Don't cry," he whispered. "We're only just getting started."

That was the moment she knew there was no escape from

this. For whatever reason, Lawrence had taken a sick interest in her, and he wouldn't stop torturing her until she was dead. Whether that was tonight or months from now, he wouldn't let her rest. He wouldn't leave her alone.

Why couldn't she have just settled with her ten-year sentence and behaved? Why had she foolishly decided to risk it all?

Rosie flinched away from Friend Two's touch, but he persevered, pressing his palm against her forehead. The effect was instantaneous.

She hadn't even recovered from the suffocation when she felt as if someone had physically gripped her heart in their hand —then *squeezed.*

She gasped through the gag, her eyes bulging as she jolted and began to convulse, trying anything to get this man's hand off her. But it was no use. The hand was *inside* her. Her heart pounded faster, faster, faster. The hand gripped tighter, tighter, tighter. Her whole body heated in an instant. Her pulse pounded in her chest, her ears, her wrists, her head. Her heart was being crushed.

She hadn't realised that she was screaming into the gag until he pulled his hand away, a triumphant smirk on his face.

She sobbed and sobbed and sobbed. She couldn't manage a glance up at them; she couldn't bear to see the pleasure in Lawrence's eyes at the sight of her suffering.

Her whole body was pulsing with agony. She couldn't breathe, couldn't move, couldn't speak.

Where was Jakob?

She felt the heat of the pendant against her chest but wanted to scoff at it. What use had his promises turned out to be? He couldn't love her if this was what he was subjecting her to.

She was so lost in her own thoughts that she didn't realise Friend Two had placed his hand back on her forehead until her heart began to thrash in her chest again.

"Like a little hummingbird," the man said with a laugh.

She all-out screamed into her gag. Her chest was caving in. Her heart was about to explode. Her eyes were bulging from her skull.

Despite the grip being on her heart, the pain pulsed through her body with every heartbeat. It throbbed in her fingertips and her toes, in every sinew of muscle and each joint. It was all encompassing.

So this is how she'd die, she thought.

It was a little less guns-blazing and explosions roaring than she'd like, but at least she'd die doing what she loved: pissing off Lawrence Haart.

"Leave her with a little bit of life," Rupee's voice broke through her agony. "I want to have my turn."

And in that very moment, between her heart pounding and Friend Two's grip releasing, she realised something miraculous.

The voice in the gallery—the one that coerced the drunken strangers out during her heist—had been Rupee's. He'd been there. He'd gotten the guests to leave. But had it been to help her, or had it been to make sure she was caught red-handed for Lawrence?

Her thoughts dipped in and out of focus along with her vision as the torture began to take its toll on her body. A figure crouched down in front of her, but she couldn't bring herself to focus on them. All she could focus on was breathing. Trying to get her heartbeat under control. Trying not to give Lawrence the satisfaction of her sobs.

The pain was everywhere. The burning and pulsing and—

"Hey," Rupee whispered, taking her face into his hands.

She couldn't bear it. Whatever his divine ability was, she

knew she wouldn't survive it. She couldn't hold on much longer. She just wanted it to be over. At least then Lawrence wouldn't get his hands on her.

Take it too far, she tried to beg through her gag. *Just end it.*

"Look at me," Rupee whispered again, wiping away her tears.

She trembled as she used every ounce of her energy to lift her head and her eyes, finally looking up into his familiar golden gaze. He looked...enraged or guilty. Rosie couldn't tell.

"I'm getting you out of here," he said so softly that the breeze almost took his words away. "Hold on just a little longer for me, okay?"

She must have been imagining it. The toll on her body had become so great that she was hallucinating. Rupee stood up again without causing her pain, but then he held his hand out, and she braced for the impact. She could hear Lawrence's deep chuckle amongst those of his friends.

Everything hurt. She just wanted it to be over.

Then, without her permission or any effort on her part, her body began to lift up. She slowly stood up, every creaking joint throbbing and her muscles screaming.

How was Rupee doing this?

She realised as she stood back to her full height and collapsed against the metal that he hadn't caused her any pain. Sure, she'd been in pain already because of what the others had done to her, but Rupee hadn't actually made her feel more pain.

He'd simply lifted her up so that she stood again, able to look into his eyes once more as he smiled and winked.

"My divine ability," he said with a showman's voice, presumably for the entertainment of the others, "is an affinity for bone. I can control it, I can move it...I can *break* it."

A spike of adrenaline shot through Rosie as she braced for

agony, but to her utmost surprise, it never came. In one fluid motion, Rupee spun around on the spot and swept his arm out.

Rosie would never forget the resounding cracks that filled the air or the gut-wrenching screams from the three men on the rooftop as they crumpled to the concrete.

That was when all Abyss broke loose.

CHAPTER 36
ALWAYS

Rosie watched as the door to the rooftop flew open and Jakob ran through, followed by guards—who were followed by police officers. There were too many of them to count.

Jakob took all of a second to assess the scene in front of him before he gestured to the three men on the floor and the police officers converged, leaving Rosie unable to see them anymore.

"Rosie," Jakob said her name like prayer, pushing Rupee out of the way and finally reaching her. He looked over her face and her body several times with horror, leaving her wondering what physical toll the torture had taken on her body.

"Gods," he whispered, tears in his eyes as he took her face in his hands and leant his forehead against hers. "You're okay. You're okay."

She couldn't tell if he was trying to reassure her or himself, but either way, she felt relief covering her like a soft blanket.

She was all right. Jakob came for her. Rupee...Rupee wasn't the enemy after all. She'd survived. Despite feeling like she was at death's door, she'd made it through the other side. *Again.*

"I think she might appreciate being unrestrained, Jakob."

Rupee's voice was light despite the circumstances, encouraging a laugh of disbelief from both Jakob and Rosie.

As the two young men worked on her gag and restraints, she sagged against the metal frame, not sure how to process everything that had happened. It had all happened so quickly. The elation of pulling off the heist. The devastation of realising she'd been caught. The agony of realising that her life as she knew it was over. And then the bone-crushing relief of not being alone again—of having people truly care about her.

She'd survived.

She thought about the tournament down in the casino and how it all seemed so stupid now, so surface-level and irrelevant. She'd gotten her freedom back.

She didn't want to wait to leave. She needed to get out of the greedy hands of The Ruby Talisman as soon as possible, otherwise she'd somehow fall back into its trap.

Her arms were mercifully released from their restraints, and Rosie felt herself collapsing forward, the pressure of the evening overcoming her and her relief making her dizzy. Both Jakob and Rupee caught her before she could hit the concrete, slowly lowering her to the floor.

"It's all right," Jakob recited like a hymn. "We've got you. You're all right. Everything's going to be okay now."

He sat on the floor next to her and pulled her into his arms, holding her so tight that she could feel him trembling. Rupee left them to approach the other three men, now in cursed handcuffs that stopped their divine abilities from being accessible and still writhing in pain from whatever bones had been broken.

"I suppose you'll be easier to deal with if you're not squealing like pigs," Rupee mused, lifting his hand and making several small gestures which caused Lawrence and his cronies to scream in agony.

"Now, now," Rupee said through a chuckle. "There's no need for all that. I've fixed what I broke."

Rosie turned to look up at Jakob as he held her so tight.

She whispered, "Who is he?"

"My lawyer," Jakob replied just as quietly. "He's been helping me to collect information on Lawrence—testimonies, evidence, photographs—all to prove him guilty of war crimes. The civil war in Irredore, it wasn't—"

"I know," Rosie interrupted. "It was genocide."

Jakob frowned down at her but didn't question how she knew that information.

All of the pieces to the puzzle began to slot together. The information Kit had been feeding to Jakob was evidence to help put Lawrence away for good. The demon in her story had also been the demon in Rosie's story. She blew out a deep breath as she realised they shared a lot more than she'd ever thought.

The three men panted and cursed on the floor, but Rosie wasn't listening to what they were saying. She watched Lawrence reduced to a pile on the floor, just like she had been so many times at his hands.

"I need to get up," she told Jakob. "I need to stand. I need to—"

"I've got you."

Jakob stood effortlessly with her in his arms, gently letting her feet touch the floor and holding her as she found her footing, every muscle in her body still throbbing. She held in her wince as she sucked in a few deep breaths, a burning sensation racking through her lungs.

She could do this.

"You don't have to speak to him," Jakob said. "You don't even have to look at him."

"I need this," she whispered, pushing away from his hold

and ambling to Rupee's side where he stood looking down on the three men.

"You think you've won?" Lawrence hissed at Rupee. "You have no idea what you've just unleashed. There isn't a single person in this city that isn't in my pocket or in my debt. I'm going to make sure you wish you were never born."

He then turned to Jakob.

"And *you*," he growled. "Good luck getting any of my assets. No one in this city will deal with you after what you've done. No one will break their loyalty to me out of fear. I'll be back here in the morning after I've spoken to my friend Judge Waltham, and I'll ruin you. After everything I've done for you, after everything I've given you... How *dare* you embarrass me like this? The girl was caught stealing in my hotel. I'm allowed to punish her as I see fit; that's not a crime." He turned his head to some of the police officers. "Do you hear that? I've not committed any crime here!"

"That's the best part," Rupee said as he crouched down to be at Lawrence's height. "You're not under arrest for grievous bodily harm. You're under arrest for war crimes in Irredore, specifically blackmailing government officials and funding a genocide."

All the colour in Lawrence's face drained away. His jaw slackened, and he looked between Jakob, Rupee, and Rosie several times.

"Songbird got your tongue?" Rupee mocked. "You're being extradited to Irredore to undergo trial there, in front of a jury full of people whose families you murdered. Enjoy."

Rupee stood up again with a chuckle.

"You have no evidence to—"

"It's my turn," Rosie interrupted and hobbled forward so that she towered over him, just a man sprawled out on the concrete with no dignity left.

Just a man.

"And what do you think you can—"

"I said"—Rosie began to hum an enticing song—"it's my turn, so *shut your mouth.*"

Lawrence's mouth snapped shut, and try as he might, he couldn't get anything to come out, sounding gagged like Rosie had been just minutes before.

"Nothing to see here, officers!" Rupee called out. "Turn around and look at that beautiful Roguerest skyline!"

Every officer on the roof happily turned away, and Rupee joined them, walking to the edge of the roof and striking up a conversation about the delights of a back-alley restaurant he'd found in the Industrial Sector.

Lawrence tried to scream and shout, but his lips physically wouldn't open. Rosie told herself that this was the only time she would abuse her ability. This was the only time she'd use it for her own gain. For a small slice of revenge on her biggest oppressor.

"It's time you let me do the talking," she said softly, refusing to crouch to his height. "I don't know what happens from here. I don't know if you'll suffer for what you did to all of those innocent people. I don't know if you'll be found guilty. But I do know *this.*"

She let a melody bubble from her chest, embracing the sways and dips of it until she saw Lawrence's jaw slacken and his eyes go soft.

"You'll regain your ability to speak when I'm finished," she began. "But every time you think of me, until the day you die, you'll be overcome with the same agony that you gave me through my curses. You'll crumple to the floor and writhe as the agony takes over your body."

Unsure how her ability worked, she sang another melody to ensure she kept his attention—but it looked like she didn't need to worry if the besotted look in his eyes had anything to do with it.

"And if you think you can just *stop* thinking about me?" She chuckled and shook her head, lasering her focus onto him and pushing her ability with all her might. "I'll be the first thing you think about when you wake up and the last thing you think about when you go to sleep."

He swayed a little under her spell.

"*Always,*" she finished, stepping back and allowing her siren ability to retreat.

How the tables had turned.

"It's over, Lawrence," Jakob said.

The shock of not being called "father" showed on Lawrence's face as he came back to his senses after Rosie's hypnosis.

"Get me my lawyer," he hissed to the police officers who were making their way back over. He was lifted to a standing position by two officers, as were his friends. "I'm not saying another word without my lawyer!"

"I can fix that," Jakob replied, stepping forward and reaching a hand out to place it on his father's shoulder.

Lawrence looked at the hand and the anger vanished from his face. "Don't do this, son. There's no going back if you do this to me."

Rosie held her breath. Was she about to see what Jakob's divine ability was?

He gripped Lawrence tighter. Lawrence's face reddened as his jaw clenched; his eyes widened and lips trembled.

"Tell the lovely officers what you did to the Irredorian people. Tell everyone what monstrous things you did to millions of people."

Jakob pressed his hand harder against his father's shoulder.

Lawrence fought whatever force was impressed on him

valiantly, sweat beading on his forehead as he tried to shake off the multiple grips on him. His shoulders shook, and his eyes narrowed. He began to stammer.

"I—I—"

"*Tell them,*" Jakob hissed, "*what you did.*"

"I... It's..."

Lawrence's gaze flicked between Rosie and Jakob rapidly, fear taking over his features and tightening the corners of his mouth. Whatever Jakob was doing to him, he couldn't resist it much longer.

Rosie saw the moment that Lawrence gave up fighting. His features slackened, and he released a long sigh, his eyes glazing over. Visibly entranced, he began to speak. He revealed every sordid detail, incriminating himself over and over again. Minutes later, he'd detailed each official he'd bribed, the military he'd armed, and the cities they'd razed—all in the pursuit of profit. He spoke of stealing priceless artworks, collecting Irredorian gold, and selling centuries-old artefacts to the highest bidders.

He was calm as he explained, unaware of the damage that he was doing to himself. He'd funded a genocide in tandem with several governments and then he'd confessed to these indescribable evils in front of the city's police.

There was no going back from this.

Rosie was overcome with the deep knowledge that they'd won. It settled into her bones and made her slouch with relief. They'd conquered the demon king who reigned from a corrupt throne and brought him into the scorching light. The relief was dizzying.

The rooftop fell silent as Lawrence finished implicating himself in a rap sheet of inexcusable crimes, everyone frozen in time as they digested the volume of information they'd received.

How had Jakob made him confess?

She noted his hand still firmly against his father's shoulder and came to a clear understanding. He could draw the truth from someone by touching them. He'd been saving the nature of his ability for an important moment.

"Lawrence Haart." Rupee stepped forward. "After mounting evidence and your own confession, you are under arrest on suspicion of war crimes against Irredore, bribing government officials, funding genocide, and so many other atrocities that I'll let someone else bore you with. You should know them well already."

The police officers advanced, and Jakob stood back as one of the officers read off his rights. It was awful to witness but impossible to look away from.

"This is ludicrous!" Lawrence roared as they tried to walk him away. "Let go of me! Call my counsel immediately and have them put a stop to this nonsense. *Jakob!* What have you done?"

He struggled as three officers dragged him towards the door followed by his two cronies, who were much more placid and clearly in shock.

"You vile boy!" Lawrence hollered. "I'll never forgive you for this!"

His shouting continued as he was taken from the roof. He would likely cause more of a scene as they paraded him through the main foyer and out into the heaving streets.

Good, Rosie thought.

Lawrence's reign had come to a screeching, grinding halt. Jakob blew out a long, sagging breath. Rupee began to laugh quietly to himself. Rosie let her head fall back as she began to cry deep, racking sobs.

It was over.

It was finally over.

CHAPTER 37
WON'T GO FREE

It wasn't until the three of them were in the lift, heading back to the casino to see out the end of the tournament, that Jakob finally asked,

"What did Lawrence mean by you being caught stealing in the hotel?"

Rosie frowned and let out a laugh.

"You know what he meant."

When she looked over at him, his face was the picture of confusion, his eyes narrowed and his brow furrowed. She looked past him to Rupee, who was staring straight ahead as if he wasn't paying attention.

"I have no idea what he meant," Jakob said slowly. He turned to face her completely, blocking out Rupee and making it feel like it was just the two of them in the lift.

"What's going on?"

Rosie began to feel a weight growing in her gut. Something was wrong.

"The...painting..." she said slowly. "*The Rancorous Uprising.*"

He raised an eyebrow and gestured for her to carry on explaining.

"You wanted me to...steal it? Again. You told me to steal it."

His eyes widened, and he sucked in a breath, taking a step back and almost bumping into Rupee.

"What are you talking about?"

Oh no.

"Are you telling me that you...you *stole* the painting?" He lowered his voice. "Is that what you were doing when you disappeared from the tournament? Is that why Lawrence started losing it in the VIP game room when he realised it wasn't you sitting at the table? You were gallivanting around stealing a painting whilst I was trying so hard to—"

He cut himself off and ran a hand through his hair, looking away from her.

She fumbled, "I thought you asked me to—I've been receiving instructions from you on how to do it. You removed my *supresis* curse. You built the staircase from the kitchens. You —you—"

His expression only grew more bewildered as she explained and realised with horror that it hadn't been him at all. If Jakob hadn't been leaving her notes and instructing her on how to steal the painting, then who had?

The service lift doors opened on the ground floor, where the screams and hysteria from the foyer could be heard even in the back corridor.

"The tournament must have ended," Rupee commented. "I wonder who won in the end."

The three of them approached the door into the foyer with caution, Jakob taking one last bewildered look at Rosie before pushing through first, allowing the bubble of chaos from in the main entrance to burst.

Rosie had never seen anything like it. There were hundreds of people crammed into the room, shouting, cheering, singing, dancing, drinking. Luckily, they were protected by the long reception desk because there was no room to move in the rest of the foyer, the crowds spilling up the huge staircases, into the bars, restaurants, and casino. There wasn't any room to breathe.

Jakob shouted to one of the receptionists over the noise.

"Who won the tournament?!"

Though Rosie couldn't hear her response, she could definitely read her lips.

Kitty Khalar.

Of course she'd won. Hud hadn't expected any differently. And Rosie supposed that she hadn't either. There was a bizarre thrill in believing in the invincible Kitty persona with reckless abandon. She made it feel like anything was possible.

Jakob sidled up to her and bent close to her ear.

"We need to talk privately," he said, taking her hand. As much as she wanted to find Kit and the others like she'd promised, as well as race down to the kitchen store room to get the painting back, she also knew that she owed Jakob an explanation. And perhaps he owed her one too.

"I'll see you later!" Rupee shouted over the chaos, signalling to the back corridor again. Jakob nodded and led Rosie along the wall to his office, pulling them in and closing the door as quickly as possible.

The quiet was almost deafening. Rosie had never been so grateful for soundproofing. Though the noise was definitely still audible from out in the foyer, it had a beautifully distant quality that gave the two of them a moment to pause and think.

To digest.

What in the Gods' names had happened over the weekend?

"You have an awful lot to explain to me." Jakob removed his dinner jacket and sat on one of the guest chairs in front of his desk, expelling a sigh.

"I could say the same to you," Rosie grumbled, sitting in the seat beside him.

"Point taken. You go first, considering you may or may not have stolen a priceless painting from my hotel this evening."

Rosie blew out a breath and shook her head, gazing at the bookcases around her as she tried to decide where she'd start.

"Do you promise you won't have me arrested?"

He frowned. "I wouldn't dream of it. I've had enough with arrests for the night."

"Then I suppose this all started not long after I got here."

She began recalling every meaningful event to him. She explained each note and where it had been left for her to find, the teasing and taunting. She explained the start of the tournament weekend and her time with Kit, then detailed the heist and how it had come to fruition.

Throughout it all, he remained stoic and calm, appearing more bewildered towards the end than angry or embarrassed. At times, he almost looked proud.

"And I guess I'm waiting for further instruction on what to do now," she concluded, huffing out a sigh and relaxing in the chair. "I thought it was you all along, so I assumed you'd tell me what you wanted with the painting."

She turned to look at him in the warm lighting of the office and was reminded of how incredibly beautiful he was. The shadows cast by his cheekbones and jaw were particularly devastating.

"That's a lot of information to digest," he murmured. "But there's merit in your assumption that it was me, especially after you spied on my breakfast with Kitty. But if you're waiting for further instructions, I can't help you. I have no idea how your *supresis* curse was lifted or if your *captipheus* will still be effective."

"So...all I can do is wait." She groaned. "It's your turn now. Explain your takedown of Lawrence. How did you manage it? Will it really work?"

He chuckled at her enthusiasm but shook his head.

"Firstly, I need to apologise."

If he expected her to cluelessly ask what he should apologise for, he'd be waiting a while.

"The list of things you should never forgive me for is endless, starting with the hot and cold nature of my behaviour over the past year. My failure in our original heist is also inexcusable; I wasn't prepared and, quite frankly, I was frightened of Lawrence. When things started to go pear-shaped, instead of sticking it out with you as any loyal partner should, I bailed and hoped that coming clean with my father would save my own hide. I was a coward. I loved the idea of running away with you. I loved the thrill of doing something so wrong for the right reasons. I wanted forever with you—I still do—but I wasn't willing to sacrifice everything for it."

Rosie nodded as he paused and waited for a response. She made him wait a little longer than was comfortable before replying.

"That's probably the most treacherous thing anyone has done to me," she said honestly. "And I grew up on the streets where loyalty was nothing but a passing commodity to be dropped at any moment when something better came along."

Jakob shook his head. "My behaviour a year ago was shameful, and I don't expect your forgiveness for it. There was no excuse for my cowardice. But not long after you were imprisoned here, I came to my senses. I began desperately wanting to free you in whatever way possible. The feeling only grew stronger as I watched you be demeaned and embarrassed and starved. It seemed like fate when I was approached by an anonymous source claiming that they'd found evidence of my father's horrifying behaviour in Irredore.

"At first I brushed it off, convinced that it was Lawrence trying to test my loyalty after our escapade. However, days later, after I hadn't responded to the letter, a document arrived for me. It was some correspondence between an Irredorian general and my father, speaking of plans to clear hundreds of miles of land and pilfer treasures to sell to the elite. A map was also included with the letter that showed potential areas for destruction. As before, I was sceptical. I left the hotel and found myself in a bar in the Tourist Quarter. After a couple of drinks, I began talking to a man who was visiting for work. He was a lawyer and I—perhaps recklessly—confided in him. Maybe it was the alcohol or my overwhelming stress, but he said he could help me explore the matter further."

"Rupee?" Rosie whispered, seeing the puzzle pieces begin to come together.

"Yes, Rupee. I gave him the documents in question, and he promised that he would look into it on his travels. He said he would return in a month or two once he had wrapped up his current cases."

"What did you do in the meantime?"

"The evidence against my father continued to mount up—horrifying letters and receipts, drawings and paintings, confessions from soldiers and survivors. It continued to arrive in the post. In the back of my mind, I stayed suspicious that it could have been a setup, but the evidence was compelling. When Rupee returned two months later, he brought with him numerous witnesses to the horrors of the Irredorian invasion. I would meet with him in secret several times a week and began paying him to compile a case against my father, deciding that I had nothing left to lose."

Rosie snorted. "I know the feeling."

"I suppose you do. When I was growing up, it was obvious to me that my father was not a good man. I saw the ugly side of him, whereas the rest of the city saw what he wanted them to see. It wasn't until you came along that I felt less alone in my opinion of him. The way he treated you only strengthened my resolve to make him pay for the horrors he'd caused, not only in Irredore but here in Roguerest too. He had tricked, taunted, and controlled for too long. Enough was enough."

His voice broke, and he cleared his throat, looking at his hands.

"If that's the case, why were you so cruel to me?"

It took him a few moments to come up with an answer.

"I was so afraid," he croaked, suddenly sounding like an entirely broken young man. "I was looking over my shoulder every day, convinced that my father had found me out. The only way I knew he wouldn't suspect anything was if I conformed to the image of a perfect son in his eyes. I wore cruelty like a mask in front of you and him, but sometimes I found myself forgetting that it was only a mask. For the times I was needlessly cruel and rude, I apologise profusely. When in front of other staff, I had to maintain my act in case Lawrence had people spying on me. But in private, there was no excuse. I suppose I lost myself in it all sometimes, forgetting who I really was and what I stood for. There were times that I would lie in bed at night and realise I was inching closer to becoming my father. It petrified me, but I had to persist. For you and for the murdered Irredorians."

Rosie considered leaving him hanging and taunting him for a little longer, but then she would be no better than every other demon out there. His treatment of her had been inexcusable, but she knew that holding on to the resentment would only hurt her in the long run.

"I forgive you." She forced the words out, feeling lighter for speaking them. "You were wrong in the way you treated me, and we'll never have the relationship we had before this, but I forgive you for it. Your intentions were good even if your tactics were not. And just to be clear, I'm forgiving you for my sake, not yours."

He met her gaze with tears in his eyes, releasing a deep sigh as the tension left his body. He had been carrying a large weight for the past year, as had she, and it was proving cathartic for the two of them to finally speak openly.

"Thank you." He blinked away his tears and tentatively took her hand. "You should know that there are thousands of Irredorians still gunning for justice. Though much of the land was sold off to surrounding territories as facilitated by my father, Irredore still remains, and they haven't forgotten the atrocities that he brought on them. So many were bribed or beaten into silence, but there are members of the remaining government who have been instrumental in this process. They're keen to bring him to justice for his crimes. He won't go free from this."

"Aren't you afraid?" Rosie imagined the worst. "They could execute him for his actions."

Jakob shrugged. "I suppose...I suppose when you see the depths that evil runs in a person, when you can safely say that they're irredeemable, they no longer deserve your emotional energy. Lawrence is evil incarnate, I'm sure of it. I grew up with a monster who stole every ounce of innocence and hope from me. So why would I worry about a man that has never loved me? I've lived my life as a tool and a weapon that he's exploited time and time again. He's the one who made me keep my divine ability hidden from a young age so that he could unleash me as a secret weapon on those who tried to defy him. For as long as I can remember, I've attended covert meetings and drawn the truth from powerful people in order to provide my father with leverage.

"A child can only be used for so long before their walls become impenetrable. I have no memories of ever loving Lawrence. He's been my father in title only, which is why my hesitation in bringing him to justice was only brief. But my feelings for you? They remain the same."

Rosie was overcome with pity for him, knowing that despite his riches and seemingly perfect life, Jakob was as troubled as everyone else. He'd been used and abused by Lawrence Haart. Not even being a direct relation had saved him from the turmoil.

It turned out that money couldn't solve all problems.

"I built a case against my father and Rupee made sure everything was perfectly legal," Jakob continued. "He also facilitated contact between myself and Irredorian officials, joining me on a trip over there."

"I remember." Rosie gasped. "You were gone for a month."

"It took so long to travel there and back that we needed a month, and even that wasn't nearly enough. Lawrence was under the impression that I was touring through Lunaron, Forge Valley, and Etetalle, meeting with potential business partners and closing property deals. Once I'd seen the devastation in Irredore for myself, there was no turning back. I was resolute. The evidence continued to trickle in from my anonymous source, which we both know was Kitty, and I decided that I wanted to make his fall from grace as spectacular as I could. I'd hoped that I'd be able to have him arrested in front of the VIPs this evening, but when he called security to ransack the hotel and find you, I knew my plan had to change."

"How did you know where to find me?"

Rosie's mind turned to the torture on the roof, but she shoved it aside, refusing to give it any more thought.

"I had the police officers on standby. When Lawrence left the game room with his cronies and told me to stay put, I knew I had to call them in. I'd managed to get them in through the service entrance when I came across some security guards in the back corridor. I used...I used my ability on one of them to get the truth out. Then it was just a matter of getting to you as quickly as I could."

Rosie absorbed the information with a nod of her head, resting it back against the plush armchair and sighing.

There was so much to think about, so much to absorb.

"What about the reputation of the hotel?" she asked. "What about all the hotels Lawrence operates? When the truth is revealed to the public, surely you stand to lose a horrendous amount of money?"

"Perhaps I will." Jakob shrugged. "I'm not concerned; I'm living proof that money isn't important, as are you."

Rosie scoffed and gave him an unamused stare. "Coming from someone who has it. Money certainly makes things easier though, doesn't it?"

"That it does." Jakob grinned, and she couldn't stay mad at him if she tried. "Even if all of our hotels and casinos in the city were to close, there are lots of other income streams that Lawrence set up and the majority of them are in my name—in case he ever got caught, I suppose. Too bad he didn't foresee being brought to justice by his own son. He thought I'd always be his perfect little apprentice."

Rosie took a second to absorb the information and found her lips tilting up slightly. This was the real Jakob. The one unburdened by his father's expectations. The one allowed to think and act for himself. This was the Jakob that she'd loved and admired.

She used to think the sun rose and set with him. That he held the keys to the city in his hands.

"Lawrence never imagined you'd risk it all for the sake of doing the right thing," Rosie said. "It wouldn't have crossed his mind that you weren't like him. You're braver and better than I've ever given you credit for...so I guess I should apologise to you too."

Jakob huffed out a quiet laugh. "You don't need to apologise to me for anything. You had no reason to suspect anything else about my behaviour after my actions, and I certainly haven't made things easy for you over the last year. There's nothing to apologise for."

A comfortable quiet settled between them, distantly accented by the chaos in the foyer. For the first time in over a year, they were just Rosie and Jakob again, two teenagers trying to find their way in the world without the fear of a tyrant over them.

"Where do we go from here?" Rosie queried. "Lawrence is gone and so is one of my curses, but unless we can figure a way to lift my *captipheus,* I'll have to stay here in The Ruby. Plus there's the whole heist situation to figure out."

"I will find a way to free you." Jakob was all business, taking her hand and squeezing it in a silent promise. "I don't care what I have to do, I'll make sure you leave here and can explore the territories. I'll also provide you with any financial support you need because I know you haven't been paid for your work here. We'll call it a back-payment on wages."

Of all the things he could've said, Rosie wasn't expecting that.

"Thank you," she murmured, squeezing his hand back.

Suddenly remembering something, she reached into one of the pockets of her now dirty coat and pulled out her travel journal. She held it up for Jakob to see and then let him take it from her hand.

"I used it," she explained. "It's one of the only things that kept me sane this year; planning out where I'm going to go and how I'll get there."

His face slackened with surprise as he began to flick through the thick pages, covered with pictures and maps and annotations. He let out a quiet laugh as he stroked some of the pages.

"I can't believe you kept it," he whispered.

"I can't believe you kept my necklace," she replied.

He delicately turned each of the pages, studying her ideas in silence and smiling at her scrawling notes. He closed it a minute or two later and held it close to his chest for a second before looking at Rosie again.

"I want you to promise me that you'll stay safe when you go," he said, his smile turning sad. "I don't expect you to ever come back to Roguerest, but I hope you'll think of me from time to time...perhaps even send a letter to reassure me you're all right."

Rosie realised with astounding clarity that Jakob, despite his faults, did want the best for her—wherever that might take her.

"I'll come back to Roguerest," she promised. "As awful as some of my memories here have been, it's still my home. I'll come back one day."

His smile reached his eyes again, and he looked away.

Rosie took the opportunity to settle into the first comfortable silence she'd felt all year. No fear, no thoughts of where she should be or what she should be doing. It was dizzyingly peaceful.

But as much as the protective bubble they'd formed in the office was perfect in the face of the anarchy outside, she knew they still had a mystery to solve.

Who'd been writing the notes?

And who had she stolen the painting for?

"What are we going to do about the painting?" Her trepidation came through in her tone. "We don't know who I stole it for or what I'm supposed to do with it."

Jakob sighed and shrugged. "In all honesty, I have no attachment to the painting. In fact, I think it was created by an Irredorian painter, so there's a high chance that my father stole it during the invasion. Whoever asked you to steal it can keep it for all I care. It stands as a reminder to me of everything my father has done to you, so I likely would've sold it anyway." He lifted his eyes to meet hers once again. "I still can't believe you managed to steal it from under our noses."

"I'm good at what I do." She let her lips turn up. "I've been doing it my entire life. Besides, I had lots of help—but I have no idea who it was from."

"I should've known." Jakob laughed. "It was inevitable that you'd find a way to best me."

As they shared a friendly smile, Rosie remembered the promise she'd made to both Kit and Hud. She needed to go to Suite Rouge and say goodbye to them. The mystery of the painting could wait until she'd seen them.

"I have somewhere to be," she admitted, standing up. "I promised Kit and the others that I'd see them tonight and say goodbye because they're leaving so early in the morning. I suppose I should congratulate Kit on her victory too."

"That sounds like a great idea." Jakob stood from his chair too. "Do you mind if I join you? As the manager of the hotel, I should probably offer my congratulations as well."

Rosie hesitated but figured there'd be no harm in it.

"Okay," she agreed. "But I need to go down to the kitchen store room to pick something up."

CHAPTER 38

REFRAIN FROM THREATENING ARREST

"We have a problem," Rosie said as she stood up from the floor in the kitchen store room.

Jakob frowned at her empty hands.

"It's not there," she explained, panic starting to rise in her chest.

The copper tube wasn't beneath the shelving unit, which could only mean that Khristann had moved it somewhere else. Or so she hoped.

"Well, where else could it be?" Jakob began to pace. "Who could've taken it?"

"I'm not going to panic just yet. It's most likely that Khristann came back for it. I told him to give it to you when I...when I thought it was you who wanted me to steal it."

"So Khristann is the only person who knew where it was?"

"Yes."

Jakob sighed. "We'll go and ask him where it is, then."

However, when they reached the kitchens, the bedlam wasn't being orchestrated by a familiar tall figure with a shaved head, but rather a short, plump lady called Fillipa.

"Fillipa," Jakob called out, catching her attention and striking a look of fear into her features.

"Is everything all right, Mr Haart?"

Her face was covered in a layer of sweat, and her hands trembled slightly—from exhaustion, no doubt.

"Where's Khristann?"

"He wanted to deliver the celebratory dishes to Suite Rouge himself, sir."

Jakob frowned and gave Rosie a glance before looking back at Fillipa.

"On the busiest night in the hotel's history...he's on delivery service?"

She opened and closed her mouth a couple of times before shrugging.

"I-I don't know, sir. He just asked me to take over for him, so I did."

There were several shouts for orders and assistance, so Jakob waved her off to return to her work before holding an arm out for Rosie to take.

"Up to Suite Rouge, then?"

Rosie laughed, playfully pushing his arm away and leading the way back to the service lift. When they reached it, she pressed the call button, and it opened up immediately.

"After you." Jakob mocked a bow and spoke like a true gentleman.

"Thank you, good sir." Rosie laughed, and for a moment, it felt as if the past year had never happened. She would never forget the pain he'd put her through, but she could put it aside for the evening.

They didn't speak as they rode up to the penthouse, but Rosie found the silence to be comforting rather than awkward. They were entirely content in each other's company.

As they arrived at the door to Suite Rouge and knocked,

Rosie noted the quiet and calm atmosphere of the floor. No stumbling drunks or celebrating guests, no music or singing. It was silent. Wasn't there an after-party?

"Maybe they're still in the casino," she hazarded a guess. "But they definitely told me to meet them here after the game. And Khristann should be here too."

Her questions were answered as the door swept open to reveal Jal, who pulled Rosie into a tight hug without a beat and held her close.

"I'm so glad you're okay," she said into her hair. "We were so worried in the casino. Hud was chomping at the bit to find out what happened to you." She pulled away and inspected Rosie from head to toe. "Are you all right?"

"I'm fine, I promise."

Her genuine care wrapped around Rosie like a soft blanket. Though her entire body ached and probably would for a few days, her euphoria about Lawrence distracted her from the pain.

"Hello, Jakob," Jal greeted him, and he blinked in surprise.

"Uh, hello," he replied. "I wanted to come and congratulate Miss Khalar in person. If that's all right, of course."

Jal smirked. "There's no need for niceties anymore. They're redundant by this point, don't you think?"

Rosie frowned but kept quiet.

"I suppose...you're right," Jakob replied, just as confused.

"Come on in," she sang, leading them into the suite.

The living space was empty save for Kit, Mae, Florelle, and Hud, who were all deposited on the sofas in the living room, casually chatting. There was no after-party in sight.

Jal led them into the kitchen.

"Would you both like a drink?" Khristann said, appearing as they rounded the corner into the kitchen. He was lazily preparing food and smiling at them.

"Khristann, what are you doing here?" Jakob questioned. "The kitchens are chaos without you. You need to get back down there now. I can have someone else come up here to serve food."

He smirked and continued chopping tropical fruits without giving any sort of indication that he feared reprimand from his boss.

"Unfortunately, I'm giving you my verbal resignation," he replied with a laidback smile. "Effective immediately."

Rosie blinked.

Jakob opened and closed his mouth several times.

Khristann laughed.

"Your faces are a picture." He chortled, sweeping the fruit on his chopping board into a large serving bowl and starting on some kiwis.

"Is this the one you were talking about? I've never seen a fruit this shape before." Rupee emerged from the pantry with a large, red fruit in his hand, halting as he saw Rosie and Jakob standing there.

"Ah." He laughed, placing the fruit down on the kitchen counter. "It's that time already?"

"Indeed," Khristann confirmed.

"What are you doing here, Rupee?" Jakob was as confused as Rosie—or at least he sounded it. "Do you know these people?"

"Sorry to interrupt," a familiar drawl came from the living room behind them. They all turned to face Kit, who lounged as if she owned the place, still in her regal getup from the tournament. "I believe there are some explanations needed, and it'd be much easier if we were all comfortable. I wasn't expecting you here, Jakob, but if you can promise that you won't have me arrested, I don't mind you listening in."

"That's the second time tonight I've been asked to refrain

from threatening arrest. I promise it's far from my priorities right now."

Kit studied him and nodded, making a sweeping gesture to the spare seats in a way that only she could pull off. It always amazed Rosie how she commanded a room with her presence alone.

But it was her next words that left Rosie decidedly breathless.

"Wouldn't you like to know why I had you steal that painting for me?"

CHAPTER 39
RESCUE MISSION

The nine of them had settled around the coffee table. Hud and Florelle had been relegated to the floor to give everyone else seats on the sofas. Khristann had provided food and drinks on the table, but no one had touched them yet.

Kit revelled in the loaded silence, fully aware that the onus was on her to clarify the situation but waiting anyway with a sly grin.

"Can I eat something now?" Hud whined.

The tension in the room eased as several of them chuckled.

"Go ahead, kid," Khristann encouraged. "It's there to be eaten. But don't think I'm unaware of how much you've already gorged this evening. I can bet that your diet hasn't been balanced since I've been away, has it? No more fried *strix* for a while."

Hud ignored him, instead piling a plate with food and beginning to shovel it into his mouth.

"Blame Jal." Mae laughed. "I tried to keep up with your meal plan, but Jal continued to bring in the fried food. I'm only one woman. I didn't stand a chance against the two of them."

"It's the thought that counts." Jal patted her head dismissively and winked at her. "Don't act like you weren't all too happy to eat what I brought home."

There was a collective chuckle between the seven of them, leaving Rosie and Jakob entirely flummoxed.

What was going on?

"All right, I suppose we should get started whilst the night is still young," Kit began and held out her hand to Khristann. "Have you got it?"

He walked over to the sideboard and picked up the copper tube resting against it, making Rosie sigh with relief. She'd known deep down that he would have it but still worried it had somehow gotten into the wrong hands. She felt strangely possessive of it, as if she didn't want to see it go just yet. She'd been hankering over the painting for so long, and now she had to give it away.

"Thank you." Kit sighed in relief and palmed it off to Rupee, who opened it up and checked the contents, giving her a nod in confirmation. She turned back to Rosie.

"I'll admit I was afraid for a good while that you wouldn't go through with it."

"If you knew how close I was to giving up, you probably wouldn't have trusted me in the first place," Rosie admitted.

"I had faith." Kit gave her a warm smile. "First off, are you feeling okay? After your panic attack before the game and then disappearing from the casino, you must be a little off-kilter. What happened whilst you were gone?"

"Panic attack?" Jakob turned to her. "What panic attack?"

"It was nothing." Rosie flushed and shook her head. "I'm all right. I'll be sore for a few days, but it's nothing I can't handle. Especially now that Lawrence has been dealt what he's deserved all along." She looked back at Kit and had to push back the memories of the rooftop again. "What happened during the tournament isn't important right now. I need to know what's going on and how you're involved with the painting."

Kit took a sip of what Rosie presumed was *shenakk.* "Where should I start?"

"At the beginning," Jakob proposed. "That would probably be best."

"Get comfortable," Hud said around a mouthful.

Florelle swatted him with a newspaper from beside her, earning collective laughter from everyone present.

"The painting is an Irredorian treasure. My father told us stories about it when my brother and I were young. He'd only seen it once but could detail every colour and item within the landscape. During my time as a prisoner after my village was destroyed, I saw it for the first time. Though I'd never been given a visual reference, I could recognise it from my father's lengthy descriptions. The soldiers had destroyed the museum that housed it and taken the most priceless pieces to be sold off. *The Rancorous Uprising* had been specifically requested by one Lawrence Haart for his private collection.

"Though *kaarmiach* has become my greatest talent and I will undoubtedly continue to play, it was only a vehicle to gain the resources I needed. Along the way, I found family and friends alike, but it was never about the cards or the money. When it was announced that the next *kaarmiach* tournament would end in Roguerest, I knew the opportunity had finally presented itself. Combine that with the evidence I'd been compiling for several years against Lawrence, it all came together quite nicely."

"How did you know about me?" Rosie floundered. "I was receiving notes long before you came here. We'd never met before this weekend. In fact, I didn't know any of you except for Jakob and—"

She shot a glance at Khristann, who was grinning from ear to ear.

"It was you?"

"I've been here for you all along, songbird," he confirmed.

Rosie looked back at Kit. "How did you know about me?"

"*You.*" She let her head fall back as she laughed softly. "You were the most lovely miracle for all of us. Imagine my surprise when shortly before I begin setting the groundwork for the fall of Lawrence Haart and the return of a priceless painting, some unknown street thief has the audacity to try and steal it for herself. We were travelling through Acrothias when it hit the papers all over the Twelve Territories. I saw that front page with the image of your snarling face after you were arrested, and I knew instantly that you needed to be part of the plan. It was fated."

"I was already on my way here when I found out the news," Khristann added. "I'd planned to work in one of the other hotels owned by Lawrence and lay in wait for the tournament weekend, feeding information to Kit until I was needed. But after we heard about you, we decided that I should get much closer. Kit paid off the previous chef and I got the job with minimal effort. Apparently, having a head chef with a food divine ability was high on Lawrence's to-do list."

"But what about you, Rupee?" Jakob turned to him, eyes wide with betrayal. "I bumped into you by accident. I went to that bar on a whim. I thought we were friends."

"Do you really think our meeting was an accident?" Rupee smiled. "I apologise if you feel misled or betrayed, but in my defence, you never asked about where I'd come from or who I'd previously worked for. I was only doing my job in helping you build a case. And we are friends; despite the shit you put Rosie through, you're a decent guy. Your methods are just a little bit misguided."

Jakob didn't pause. "Are you a genuine lawyer, or was it all an act?"

"I'm a lawyer," Rupee said with a quiet laugh. "Who do you think makes sure that Kit stays in line and doesn't get duped by the vultures that surround her? Plus, Jal has had a few too many close calls with the law to risk not having me around."

One by one, the pieces of the puzzle clicked into place.

They'd all known about Rosie long before she'd met any of them. She looked away as embarrassment crept to the surface.

Kit must have known her trail of thought when she said, "We never wanted to deceive or hurt you, Rosie. But for your own good, it was better to keep you in the dark. We needed your talents as a thief for this and...and I knew that we'd need them long after, too."

Rosie's head snapped back up. "What do you mean?"

Kit gestured to all of her family. "Each person here has a specific talent or knowledge that makes them irreplaceable to me and to each other. Florelle's botanist ability ensures we all remain healthy on our travels. Jal keeps us dressed, presentable, and provides stunning pieces of illegitimate artwork when the opportunity calls for it."

Rosie gasped and looked at Jal's smug expression.

"You can fawn over my forgery skills later." She smirked. "But yes, I'm the Artist of the group. Clothes and makeup, but sometimes paintings too. If something needs creating, I'm your girl."

"Hud is our resident mechanic," Kit continued, though the boy in question didn't respond, still ploughing his way through the spread of food. "Khristann is our chef, Rupee our legal counsel, and Mae—"

She paused, looking over at the young woman in question.

"I'm the chameleon in the family," she explained casually

around a mouthful of cured meat and cheese. "I'm the reason you were able to leave the casino during the interlude."

Rosie's jaw popped open. "Wait—"

Before she could ask further questions, Mae's appearance began to morph, bones shifting and skin paling. Her waist-length dark hair gave way to bright red and her warm skin paled. In seconds, the room contained not one but *two* Rosies.

"Well, I never," Jakob muttered.

"My thoughts exactly." Rosie couldn't stop staring at Mae's likeness to her. "What happened when Lawrence realised you weren't me? How did you get out of there?"

Mae waved off the question.

"Once his security guards came back with news that they'd found you, he forgot about me entirely. I suppose he was so caught up in the fact that his hunch was right that he wasn't bothered by me anymore."

Rosie mulled over the information. She couldn't believe that it had been Mae but was also relieved to hear that nothing had happened to her doppelgänger at the hand of Lawrence.

"So you're an Imperial," Rosie commented.

"I hate that word." She tutted, effortlessly transforming back to herself. "But unfortunately, you're right. Though you're forgetting that you're an Imperial too."

Jakob's head whipped from Rosie to Mae and back again.

"What is she talking about, Rosie?"

She tried to placate him with a guilty smile.

"I only discovered it on Friday. It was Kit who noticed it, not me."

"That was another joyous surprise," Kit continued on. "When I heard that you were a singer, I was most certainly intrigued. To find that you're a siren was definitely lucrative. Not only are you a talented thief, but you also have the ability to hypnotise others. So you see, the plan morphed from an act of revenge on a truly evil man into a rescue mission for a talented but trapped individual."

Rosie peered at every member of the bizarre family, each of them providing her with encouraging smiles.

They'd known all along. Whilst she'd be miserable and hopeless, lost in her own grief for a life that'd been stolen from her, a group of people were plotting and planning, putting steps into place to rescue her. People she hadn't even even known until three days ago.

She'd never been alone.

For as long as Khristann had been in the hotel, she'd been in all of their thoughts. She'd been part of their story even if they hadn't yet become part of hers.

Tears tumbled down her cheeks as the realisation came to a head.

She whispered, "I'm not alone?"

"You were never alone." Kit's eyes welled up. "When you cried earlier, so broken and defeated, asking me to not leave you here..." She averted her gaze and wiped at her eyes. "I can't describe how hard it was for me to hold my tongue. I wanted to tell you that you weren't on your own, that we'd been there for you for a year and you just needed to hold on. We're not leaving you here, Rosie. You're family now."

The determination in her voice gave Rosie shivers as she smeared her own tears across her face.

"If you'd like—and please know that we'd really like you to —would you come with us?" Rupee had taken over as Kit tried to manage her emotions. "One thing we're missing in our gang is someone with seamless sleight of hand. Plus, the siren ability would really help us out too."

"And you're really nice," Hud said, rubbing his full belly. "We like you a lot. You treat us like normal people and not a travelling circus."

Florelle swatted him again with the newspaper.

"That's a bit close to the bone, Hud." Her words were stern but her expression was jovial.

"Sorry," he whined, reaching for some more food despite rubbing his distended stomach.

"What do you say?" Jal asked. "Will you come with us?"

Rosie was completely overwhelmed. This family wanted her to be part of them, to join them on their travels across the territories and experience the life she'd always dreamed of. *How could she say no to that?*

"I would love nothing more," she announced, sniffling.

There was a triumphant cheer from everyone involved apart from Jakob, who turned to her with pale-faced doubt.

"What about your *captipheus?* You can't leave without removing it."

Of course.

"How did you do that?" She looked back to Kit, who had composed herself. "How did you remove my *supresis* curse so I could steal the painting?"

"Ah." Kit chuckled, wiggling her fingers. "Jakob, I have to ask that this secret remains in the room. After the journey we've been through, I feel like we can trust each other. Don't you think?"

"You have my word," he replied.

"Well." Kit blew out a heavy breath. "My divine ability is not in card play. I'm not an Artist."

"We hate to admit it, but she's just naturally talented at the game," Khristann teased with a grin.

"We *really* hate to admit it," Florelle mumbled.

"I'm also an Imperial," Kit clarified. "My divine ability lies in altering the effects of Imperials on others. Any sort of curse or control an Imperial has over someone else can be transferred by my hand to someone else. I can also resist the abilities of other

Imperials to a certain extent. The only thing I can't do is destroy an ability's consequences completely. Divine energy has to be transferred to something; it can't just cease to exist. My ability became very useful when we discovered your predicament and punishment for your failed theft."

She addressed Rosie, "Yesterday morning, when you woke on the sofa with me, I'd absorbed your *supresis,* which is why you were overheating and uncomfortable. It wasn't particularly pleasant, and I foolishly tried out the limitations of the curse when I was alone—something that I had to warn Khristann about when I transferred the curse to him."

Rosie blanched. "You what?"

"We weren't sure of how the curse worked in relation to gambling, and to have me crippled at an inconvenient time when in mixed company wasn't a risk we could take. Khristann volunteered to take the curse until we could figure out who we would leave it with."

Hud piped up, "I voted that we should give it to Lawrence, but apparently that wasn't a valid idea."

"We'll find someone suitable to give the curse to," Kit pacified him. "In the meantime, we need to remove your *captipheus* and find someone to take it on."

"I don't know what to say," Rosie croaked in disbelief, holding back tears again. "You've given me so much and now you're offering to free me of my curses too? Why would you do so much for someone you barely know?"

Kit leaned back in her chair. "We know you much better than you think. But more importantly, lost souls are always better together. We call out to each other in a way that no one else can possibly understand. You belong with us. That much was clear from the first time we met."

"Thank you," Rosie whispered, holding her head in her

hands and taking several deep breaths. "Thank you. Thank you. *Thank you.*"

There was a beat of silence.

She lifted her head to further thank them all for what they'd done when Jakob spoke up and changed everything.

"You should give it to me," he tentatively said. Looking at Kit with determination, he clarified, "You should give both of the curses to me."

Nobody moved.

Nobody spoke.

Hud ceased chewing.

"What?" Rosie mumbled. "Why would you suggest that? You'd be trapped here for...forever. Unless you could find someone to destroy the curse, you'd have to stay in the hotel, and I can promise you from experience that it's not fun. And the stealing? It's not just the physical act. If you even think about the possibility of stealing something, you become crippled with indescribable agony. Full-body, writhing, searing pain. You can't take that on. I won't let you."

"You don't have much choice in the matter." He gave her a sad smile. "You can't leave Roguerest with your *captipheus,* and poor Khristann doesn't deserve to remain saddled with the *supresis.* I've not been good to you for a long time, no matter what my intentions were. Please let me do this for you. Let me bear some of the weight and pain that you've had to navigate. All I want for you is to discover the territories like you've always wanted to. I'll find a way to deal with the curses, but in the meantime, you don't belong here anymore. You belong with these people, wherever they go next."

Rosie sat perfectly still, stunned by his offer. Jakob was twice the man she'd deemed him to be, if not more. This was an indescribable gift.

"I can't..." Rosie's throat tightened. "You would do that for me?"

"A thousand times over, *with everything I have,*" he whispered. "It's time you discovered yourself out there. You outgrew this city a long time ago. I'll always be here to run the hotels and casinos either way, so I'm not getting out, but you? You're meant to do so much more with your life."

"Thank you," she cried, wrapping her arms around him and holding him as tight as she could. "You don't know what this means. You don't understand how much this changes everything."

He laughed quietly into her hair. "I do, songbird. That's exactly why I've got to do it."

When they pulled apart, all eyes in the room were on them and more than a few tears had been shed.

"With everything I have," she whispered.

"With everything I have," he replied.

Someone cleared their throat.

"There's not much left to do," Kit announced, a mischievous grin on her face as she rubbed her hands together. "Who's up for some fun with a couple of pesky curses?"

CHAPTER 40
LITTLE BIRD

A glorious sunrise decorated the skies above Roguerest.
Swathes of speckled clouds were strewn across the purple and blue. They grew brighter, from deepest red through orange and peach, all the way to fluffy white. Roguerest had fallen almost entirely silent following the events of the night before, its residents and guests either passed out in a gutter or sleeping off a hangover.

Rosie found herself glancing up at the sky and breathing in the filthy city air. She was perched on the steps outside the service entrance to The Ruby, hidden away from public eyes where local vendors would bring food and supplies for the hotel.

That particular morning it was mercifully empty save for the two ostentatious black motorcars. The two drivers, dressed in fine black coats with shiny gold buttons, had disappeared in search of breakfast.

She'd never travelled in a motorcar before.

Having collected the few belongings she wanted to take with her and placed them in a small leather briefcase provided by Jakob, Rosie had said her few goodbyes to the place that had become her home. Though she still couldn't believe that any of it was happening—that she was outside the hotel, waiting to leave on the adventure of a lifetime with a family she never thought she'd have—there was a resounding sadness cloaking her at the thought of leaving behind the only home she'd ever known.

Roguerest was a cruel city, filled with crime and monsters that went bump in the night. It was a playground and a prison. It was dirty and suffocating and rife with inequality.

But it would always be home to her. It wasn't until the reality of leaving had settled in that she realised she would miss the familiarity of the city. She would miss knowing every twist and turn, every rooftop and escape route.

But there was so much more to see, she promised herself.

"Look at the early bird!"

Laughter came from behind her as she saw Khristann and Jal exiting the hotel, baggage in their arms. Kit had requested a covert exit from the hotel, no crowds or porters with gold luggage carts. In fact, everything about their departure was a world away from their flamboyant entrance. It was charmingly normal.

"She couldn't wait to see the back of this place." Jal flashed her a grin as they passed her and placed their luggage beside the vehicles.

"Are you excited to get on the road?" Khristann asked, somehow more relaxed and youthful than before. Her only friend was coming with her on this adventure. He was home now, she supposed.

"Words can't describe my excitement." She wandered over to join them. "After we settled down last night, I couldn't sleep. I think I might have caught a few winks between two and three, but that was all. I've been vibrating all morning."

She shook out her hands with nervous laughter.

"Hud, I'm not going to tell you again." Mae's voice came from behind them. "Stop dragging your feet and whining like a child, otherwise we'll be forced to treat you like one."

"But I'm *ti-ired*," he grumbled, the two of them descending the steps.

"I told you to go to sleep, but *no,* you just had to finish that bizarre pile of nuts and bolts. It's your own silly fault. Come on."

The child in question followed behind her, dragging his feet on the floor and refusing to lift his gaze from the ground.

"Morning all," Mae said, flashing everybody a keen smile. "Prepared for the long journey?"

"After staying in one place for a year, I'm more than ready," Khristann groaned and laughed.

"How do you think I feel?" Rosie spluttered, unable to hold back the grin on her own face.

"Ooh, she's right," Jal teased. "Put your self-pity away, Chef."

"I'm the one who has to begin catering to all of your bizarre culinary requests again," Khristann argued. "Kit's are the craziest and, quite frankly, disgusting at times."

"Like what?" Rosie gasped.

"You honestly don't want to know," he shuddered as he replied. "Some things just shouldn't go with cheese. As time goes on, you'll see for yourself. Behind the curtain, Kitty Khalar isn't poised and formidable, she's a pint of kook in a half-pint tankard."

Rosie already had a good idea of the Kit behind Kitty but didn't comment on it. Several hotel employees emerged from the service entrance, carrying trunks and other bags and closely followed by Rupee, Florelle, and Kit. Surprisingly, Kit was not dressed in one of her many overwhelming Kitty Khalar outfits, but had instead chosen to wear white trousers and a matching blouse.

She was all Kit.

The drivers arrived in time to handle the distribution of luggage across the two vehicles with the help of the porters, leaving the eight passengers to join in excited chatter.

"We did it," Kit triumphantly announced, coercing an eruption of cheers from everyone. "None of this would've been possible without each of you doing your part, and I couldn't be more thankful for your help. Though we have a long journey ahead of us to Irredore, I'm so grateful that I get to share some of my homeland with you all. And after that, who knows? We'll see where the cards take us."

Everyone scrambled aboard the two motorcars, and Rosie watched with anticipation and fear.

This was it.

"It's scary, isn't it?" Kit was the only person still outside with her.

"Very," she whispered.

"I promise you, when we pass through those city gates and you can look out of the back window at the place that held you for seventeen years, you'll feel the greatest release of pressure. As if you're lighter than a feather."

"I'm hoping with everything in me that you're right."

"Before we go"—Kit touched her arm gently—"I believe there's someone just inside who wants to say goodbye."

Rosie turned to look at the service entrance. The door was propped open and Jakob stood before the threshold, a distraught look on his face.

"I'll only be a minute," Rosie said.

"Take your time; we're not going anywhere without you."

She waited a beat before jogging back to the service

entrance, up the steps until she was directly in front of Jakob, though this time it was he who couldn't step outside.

How her world had changed in just four days.

"I just"—he clenched his jaw—"I wanted to say goodbye one last time. I know that you're excited to leave and I don't want to hold you back, but—"

Rosie didn't let him ramble any more as she leapt forward into his arms with such force that he stumbled back several steps. He laughed quietly and wrapped his arms around her, squeezing her so tightly that she briefly wondered if he'd let go.

"You are the most incredible girl I've ever had the pleasure of meeting," he said as if reciting a prayer. "I won't sleep a night without dreaming of you or spend a day without thinking of you. You've changed my life, and I hope you know how extraordinary you are."

He let her slip to the floor but kept his arms around her as he looked into her eyes.

"Thank you, Jakob." She welled up but couldn't stop smiling. "Thank you for the gift you've given me."

"No thanks needed. I want you to go out there and conquer the world. You need to take your pain and turn it into power. Will you do that for me?"

He delicately kissed her forehead and scrunched his eyes closed as if in pain. Tears tracked down his cheeks as he pulled away, his eyes flitting all over her face, memorising every detail.

"You have my word. *With everything I have.*" She wiped his tears with her thumbs. "And who knows? I might even send you a postcard."

They parted with laughter and smiles, happy tears and exuberant waves, with Rosie looking back at him several times as she skipped to the vehicle that contained a vivacious Hud gesturing for her to join him.

She climbed up, finding Khristann and Hud on one side with Kit and an empty space on the other.

"Welcome aboard!" Hud sang as she sat down on the luxurious black-stitched leather. The driver closed the door gently behind her and climbed into the front.

"Can I count on your excitement for the entire ten-day journey?" Rosie asked Hud with a raised eyebrow.

"Oh, you can count on it," Kit groaned. "You won't be so enthusiastic when day five or six rolls around, I promise you that."

They lurched into motion out of the closed square behind the hotel. Rosie looked out of the window just in time to see Jakob waving sadly but still managing a smile. She returned his wave until he was out of sight and faced the others, a resounding sigh deflating her chest.

"This is it," she murmured.

"No turning back," Khristann teased. "Even when Hud drives you crazy and Jal has her mood swings and I'm forcing you to eat vegetables. You're part of our family now, and there's no way out."

He grinned at her so that she knew he was joking, but she didn't mind in the slightest. This dysfunctional family was the best thing that had ever happened to her. She finally had people who cared about her enough to make sure she ate properly.

As she watched the city pass by out of the window, a deep sense of peace settled into her bones.

She wasn't alone. She hadn't been alone for a long time.

And her fears of disappearing one day without anyone to look for her? They were long gone. She'd gained not one, not two or three, but seven people who had been looking out for her all along. When she'd felt the most alone, trapped in her stuffy basement room after run-ins with Lawrence and abuse from guests, they'd been plotting and scheming to free her. They'd been there when she'd needed them the most, even if she hadn't known it.

"Ro?"

She looked back over at Hud, who held something metallic in his palms.

"I spent last night working on something for you. Once you'd agreed to come with us, I knew that you'd really like it."

Rosie spied the object, seeing pieces of metal sticking up in various directions to form what looked like a bird. Hud turned a lever the size of his thumb nail several times to wind it up before letting it stand in his palms, wings moving up and down.

"It's a wind-up bird," he explained. "It reminds me of you. You're free to fly wherever you want to go now, just like a little bird."

The metal animal moved magically in his hands, each dainty detail making it the most beautiful gift she'd ever received. He'd made it just for her.

When he tore his eyes away from the bird and looked into hers, she wiped away yet more tears and carefully took the contraption from his hands.

"Thank you, Hud." She cleared her throat and further inspected the device when it stopped moving. It was incredible, painted red and orange, with bold stripes across its wings. It even had bright blue bolts for eyes, just like her own.

She held the bird close to her chest, a talisman of her former life as she returned her gaze to the outside world, seeing the city gate fast approaching. The motorcar rattled across the cobblestones leading to the towering gate, echoing the rapidly beating heart inside Rosie's chest.

Five.

Four.

Three.

Two.

One.

They passed through the gate, and for a second, she didn't dare breathe. She didn't blink or move. Didn't say a word.

This was it.

Like the tiny mechanical bird in her hands, she was free to fly from her cage and beat her wings, to go wherever in the world she wanted to go.

Fly, little bird, she thought, *fly away.*

COMING SOON

The next book in the Twelve Territories series...

ACKNOWLEDGMENTS

For as long as I've known I wanted to be a writer, I've been imagining who I would thank in the acknowledgments. But now the moment has finally come to do it for real, I'm at a loss for words. If I've forgotten you, just know that I owe you a glass of wine (or a bottle).

I'll start where it all began. To Andrew, Louise, Alexandra, and Henry: this book wouldn't exist without long walks in the evergreens. Thank you for so kindly accepting me into your beautiful home for a year. It's a time I'm so grateful for and I'll never forget.

I'd like to thank everyone online who encouraged me to bring this story into the light. Joining the bookstagram community was a way for me to pass the time during COVID lockdown. It brought me to so many incredible people that I couldn't possibly mention every name, but if you've ever commented, messaged me, or supported my book buying habit, then thank you.

To my incredible beta readers who changed this book for the better in ways I never could've imagined. Thank you to RaeAnne, my editor, who made this book read as a book should and for highlighting just how useless I am with commas. To Handy Paul, for the incredible artwork of my characters.

Rae, thank you for inspiring me to take the leap and publish this. Ben, thank you for being my manuscript buddy and for listening to my incessant book-rambling. Sue, I could write an essay of thank you's and it still wouldn't be enough. Thank you for making me believe that being an author didn't have to just be a dream.

Chaos Club, where do I begin? Thank you for the endless entertainment and ridiculous debates. Thank you for supporting me from near and far, right from the beginning, and for sticking by me when I turned into a hermit several times to write this book.

Grandma and Grandad, there's far too many things to thank you for but the thing I'm most grateful for is your unwavering belief in me, to do whatever I want and to succeed at it. You've given me more than I can ever repay you for.

To the rest of my (huge!) family, thank you for always asking about my book, for the endless laughter at family gatherings, and for supporting me in every way you can.

To my parents. You've taught me that I can be rich beyond my wildest dreams in more ways than one, and that sometimes you've just gotta roll with the punches. I can't put into words how grateful I am for everything you do so I'll just say this: Mama, I love you a million purple parrots. Pops, guess how much I love you? Right up to the moon... *and back.*

Bub. For every car ride sing-along, FaceTime call, scar, wine-drunk hangout, and big bear hug. Thank you for always being my biggest fan. I did my thing, now go do yours. You got this.

Watson, you're a dog and you won't read this but I love you anyway.

And finally to David: my partner-in-crime, graphic designer, therapist, shoulder-to-cry-on, ridiculously funny and talented, dog-napping best friend. (*Did I remember everything?*) This book certainly wouldn't exist without you. Thank you for being the most generous, sarcastic, and thoughtful human that I know.

And to you, Reader, for picking this up and making it to the end (or did you skip to the acknowledgments like I do?).

About the Author

China Andie is an emerging author of YA fantasy.

She'd like to say that she was raised in the rolling hills of the Underworld but it was actually the rolling flats of Lincolnshire, England. Much more tame.

Often found with a coffee in one hand and a book in the other, it was inevitable that she'd turn to writing sarcastic but loveable characters who have no business burrowing into her heart the way they do.

For more updates:

www.chinaandie.com